Blue Dreams

Blue Dreams

or The End of Romance and
the Continued Pursuit of Happiness

BY WILLIAM HANLEY

DELACORTE PRESS / NEW YORK, N. Y.

to Andy Hardy and Junior Miss

R. I. P.

His soul is ailing. As you know,
he is at an age when struggles
with sex begin.

Hesse

—And you thought you could
live a life that was what it
seemed! Not that what it seems
is not enough. Cannot you be
content with it?

—Content to live on the surface,
with all this simmering under-
neath?

—Why not be thankful that that
is where it is?

Compton Burnett

1.
The Amorous Arts

Something old . . .

1 Walter slowed and stopped and permitted himself a temporary delay at a section marked SPECIAL FICTION. Perusing
the titles, he speculated on the nature of the market for
this sort of thing. He pictured pale young boys and elderly
florid-faced men, a book clutched sweatily in one hand, vigor-
ously worshiping Onan with the other. *The Romance of Lust* and
White Thighs seemed to be fairly representative titles.

How far we've come, he thought, since the first puritanical
noise over the alleged obscenity of Mrs. Chatterley and her
gamekeeper's John Thomas. Far! And rightly so! And moving
ahead all the time. And rightly so, too! Too long had we lived
with the repression of country matters! *Do you think I meant
country matters?* Had sly old Will been punning there? Cuntry
matters? The card of Avon.

He moved to the category marked PSYCHOLOGY. There were
so many to choose from! Perhaps too many. But unquestionably
he would find exactly what he was after here, he knew. Respecta-
bility. Authority. Systematically he proceeded to scan tables of
contents, sampling a little of the text of each book, thoroughly
checking authors' credentials detailed on the back covers.

It took him the best part of an hour. Finally he narrowed the
field of possibles to three, any one of which he felt would be

ideal for his purpose, so that his final choice was almost an arbitrary one. Feeling a faint restirring of his earlier apprehension, he carried the book to the cashier's counter.

There were several salesclerks behind the counter, all of them young hippie types, all of them busy. The place was doing good business. *This Christmas Give Books.* Affecting an extravagant ease, he handed the book to an overweight young girl with long, stringy hair, wearing a very short, sacklike dress, careful to look her directly in the eye as he did so: She was not to be given any opportunity to suspect him of being one of those shifty-eyed, middle-aged types (over thirty and therefore not to be trusted) who lived alone in dim rooms and bought this sort of thing for ulterior motives obscenely related to solitary practices. He tensed himself for her reaction: Would there be the slightest flicker of an eye when she saw the title, the faintest hint of a dirty smirk? She looked like the type. Then he realized that his grip on the book was so tight that the girl was being forced to tug on it slightly in order to free it. Disconcerted, he relinquished the book and smiled. "Would you gift wrap it, please?"

He realized that it was somewhat of an imposition to ask that an inexpensive paperback be gift wrapped, and he regretted the rejection of his original intention to buy at least one other book, something on medieval religious history, perhaps, in hard cover and expensive. But in that plan there *had* been an ulterior motive. And he had dismissed that idea even before entering the book shop. Because there was nothing to be nervous or embarrassed about! He was obviously a respectable individual, purchasing a perfectly respectable book authored by a respectable medical man obviously (the laudatory critical comments of his professional compeers were there on the back cover) highly thought of in his profession! But the girl merely glanced at the cover to determine the price, apparently without the slightest interest in either the book or the motives of its buyer.

He gave his eyes their freedom again. They fell immediately upon a low stack of New Year's greeting cards on the counter. *Happy New Year!* it said. A little early, he thought—we haven't gotten through Christmas yet. Idly, he opened the top card on the pile. *Have a Wonderful 69!* it said on the inside. He closed the card, smiling, tempted to buy a few, but unable immediately to think of anyone to whom he might appropriately send such a holiday greeting. His gaze drifted upward to study the huge picture posters that lined the walls of the store near the ceiling. The usual psychedelia, of course; motion picture stars, past and present, were heavily represented; and a good many sinister-looking young men, individually and in groups, with guitars and motorcycles, few of whom he was able to identify. The poster directly over the cashier's counter, he suddenly realized, was of George Brady, full-length, in the gangster picture he had made a few years ago. He had been terrible in it. But only because it was impossible to believe George Brady as a gangster, even a basically decent, antihero gangster of the James Cagney, Depression, Warner Brothers social consciousness school who dies in the end doing something Foolhardy and Good. (*The Roaring Twenties*, Cagney, Bogart, Priscilla Lane, 1939, Gladys George cradling the just-expired Cagney on the church steps. *His name was Eddie Bartlett. He used to be a Big Shot.*)

He wondered if that column item Miriam claimed was about Brady and Faith was true. It was hard to imagine Faith having an affair with George Brady. Perfectly possible, he supposed, but hard to imagine nevertheless. Probably because he still tended to think of Faith as what she had been, not what she had so recently and suddenly become. Then too, Brady would be a little old for her. He would have to be in his late forties now at least. And Faith, how old was Faith now? Twenty-four, twenty-five? But age aside, it could be a messy situation considering Brady's position now. Assuming there was anything to it. It was a blind item, of course, no names, but Miriam was certain it was Brady who was meant. And Faith. It was one of Mimi's most annoying habits to spend days puzzling over one of those blind items in a gossip column until she had established to her satisfaction the identity of the nameless subjects of the libelous rumor. She was very often right, too, he would discover sooner or later, since most of the private gossip—with names attached—eventually slithered through the office grapevine. Or gapevine, as he was inclined to refer to it, not without a sense of humor since he too hung upon it, as shamelessly interested as the next man in the private doings of the celebrated, so many of whom he had come to know personally, if casually, during his years with the network. Jack Finley could usually be counted on to know who was putting it to who in whose hay. (*Are you ready? Guess who's fucking who blind?*)

It was hard to believe that there could be any truth in this particular one of Miriam's guesses, however. Brady would have to be out of his mind to be playing around like that now. His ice was already thin enough. Surely he was the only member of the United States Congress ever to have been elected to office in spite of his record of four marriages and three divorces, a record that had been made so much of, understandably, by his opponents during the campaign. To no avail, since last month enough of the voters of southern California had exercised their curious attraction for the eccentric and Brady went in in a walk. The recent spate of his old movies on television was to be expected, of course.

"Sir?"

"Oh. I'm sorry." The plump girl was pointing the package at him like a loaded gun. "How much did you say?"

"One dollar."

Smiling, he exchanged a dollar bill for the small, gaily wrapped package. She had done a nice job on it. He thanked her and wished her a Merry Christmas.

She smiled vaguely and nodded, turning toward the cash register with the dollar bill. "Enjoy it," she said.

He tried to detect some subtle note of irony in her tone, but could find none: Surely she said that to every customer, a perfunctory hope for the reading pleasure of others? On the other hand, these kids today were so goddam hip you could never really be sure *what* they were thinking.

It had begun to snow again. He turned up Third Avenue, the bright package tight in his cooling fist.

This might be it, he thought. He knew now where he had been making his mistake: He had allowed her to assume (indeed, probably *hope*—yes it was exactly what she would *want* to believe) that the dreams were his alone, the private hallucinations of an exotic malady peculiar only to him, her weird husband. But she would not be able to question the written evidence of authority! Fully documented, with intimate case histories, clinically detailed.

Now he could show her the truth! Some part of it, at least, the beginning of it.

This is only the beginning, baby!

He wondered why he hadn't thought of this before.

2 "Mim?" He waited, listening to the scrabbling scratch of her fine-nibbed, antiquated fountain pen.

"Hm?" she murmured finally, absently.

"Which one of us would you rather died first?"

"*What?*"

He turned from the plate glass door beyond which the snow was deepening on the dark terrace and looked to where she sat behind the writing desk on the far side of the living room, her licking tongue paused on the flap of an envelope.

"Would you rather you died first or I died first?"

She frowned, puzzled, as she lowered the Christmas card envelope to the desk and distractedly sealed it with the heel of her hand. "*When?*"

"Whenever," he shrugged, and moved casually to the bar. "When it comes time."

Miriam laughed indulgently. "What kind of a question is that?"

"Think about it for a minute," he suggested reasonably, as though to imply that independent thought on her part would make his purpose clear without further explanation.

"Why?" she asked, perplexed. She shrugged. "I mean, *I* don't know."

"No, but listen, Mimi, this is a very interesting thought."

"Darling, I'm thirty-two years old, who wants to think about dying?"

She rose with her empty cup and moved toward the silver teapot on the coffee table. He regarded the shape and movement of her wonderful hips, the unconsciously sensual glide of her perfect legs, and was forced to concede once again that, whatever dissatisfactions there might be, he could not fault her there, she had never abandoned the physical disciplines of her earlier youth and, if anything, childbirth's and time's fullnesses had left only the most desirable thickenings. Desirable. And desired. Aye, there was the rub! Looked upon objectively, a less desirable wife would be the desired thing, would serve to smother the fire of his needs. Or, at the very least, redirect its heat (the sexual malcontent's usual alternative) toward a more inflammable object.

But Miriam Hartman, the *physical* Miriam, was a standing invitation; unfortunately, she did not share his view of the party's style. *Alice was throwing this tea party, the Mad Hatter would please to behave himself.*

"Want some tea?" she asked, sugaring her own.

He shook his head, sipped from his glass. "You don't understand," he said as she straightened, stirring.

"What don't I understand?"

"Well . . ."

"Well, what?" she urged helpfully, evidently prepared, if cautiously so, to know what it was she did not understand.

"Well, it was just a hypothetical question, you see, it's an interesting thought. But you don't even want to think about it. I mean, you dismiss it out of hand. That's the trouble, you see?"

"What's the trouble?"

"It's a matter of growing."

She shook her head as though to clear it. "What do you mean, growing?"

"Expanding." He moved, waving the hand with the glass in it. "Emotionally, intellectually. You resist it."

"You're spilling that. How do I resist it?"

"Well, take sex, for example." He was startled by the baldness, the unbelievable clumsiness of the transition. He had planned and hoped for and assumed far more subtly than this! Stealthy ambush from cover, not frontal assault. Context was the fault, of course, this time. *Context was important.* Not all, but important. Going down in an elevator was one thing; in the back seat of a car . . . Always in the past he had pursued invention's possibilities with subtle carnality in their natural milieu—the bedroom dimmed, clothes falling, sheets being voluptuously drawn down. But here they were in the living room, brightly lit, fully clothed: It might have been a miscalculation after all.

Very quietly, she said, "You aren't going to start that again, are you?" and moved back toward the writing table.

With a smile and an air of lightness that he hoped might somewhat repair the bad start, he said, "We never finished it."

Sitting, uncapping her pen, her eyes averted (a deliberate evasion, he knew), she said, "What brought *that* up? I mean, is there some connection?" she asked, her hands overly busy with Season's Greetings.

"Connection where?" he asked, trying to connect.

"Dying," she said. "What's all this about *dying*, for God's sake?"

He opened his mouth to explain; then closed it. Then said, "Excuse me a minute, I need some ice," and retreated quickly toward the kitchen.

There *was* a connection. But he had to admit that it might be too impossibly complicated to expound. It began with the scene on the Late Show the other night, Barbara Stanwyck to James Mason, *I hope I die before you,* thereby declaring the unbearableness of life without her true and only love. Touching, very touching. At first glance. But, look again! Suppose, just suppose, that his love is as strong as hers. And suppose her hope is realized and she makes her wished-for prior departure on schedule —*where does that leave her true and only love?* The truth then, the real truth, not the evident one, was that it was a *goddam selfish wish.* So, if one *really* loved so much the one she claimed to love so much and so well, she would hope that *he* would be the first to cash in the old chips. And if that wasn't a goddam interesting thought he didn't know what was!

A little complicated, maybe, but goddam interesting.

His inquiring, probing mind had extended his investigation (in what he felt to be a perfectly natural progression) to the old saw about living each day as though it was your last, a tenet reputed by some to be the key to the full life.

Wrong again!

There was only one true way to the full life. It was absurdly obvious. You lived every day of your life not as though it was *your* last, but the last of the one you loved!

So, there it was, then: *Miriam, if you knew I was going to die tomorrow, what would you do for me tonight?*

He returned to the living room knowing that it was all too impossibly complicated, knowing that the context was indeed probably all wrong, but committed now to his course and with no option other than to go forward.

"Who are Paula and Harold White?" Miriam asked, holding a card in her hand.

"Business," he said distractedly.

"Should I send them a card?"

"Mm." He sat in an armchair and crossed his legs casually, calculating a picture of ease. "Do you ever have fantasies, Mim?"

The scratching pen nib stilled. She took up her teacup. "What kind of fantasies?" she asked carefully.

He shrugged. "Romantic ones," he answered, choosing the more discreet word for the moment.

She gazed at him for a moment. "You mean about sex," she said bluntly, dismissing the need for discretion.

"There's a definite correlation," he grinned, "in case you hadn't heard." He was pleased that she seemed so willing to come directly to the point. Any little shortcuts would help.

"What exactly *is* romance, Walter? By your definition."

"Discovery," he said without hesitation.

"Of what?"

"Of something new, of course." He smiled again. "I should think that would have been obvious by now."

"I'm married to the Christopher Columbus of the bedroom." She smiled, but too late.

"Well, shit, Mimi, there has to be more," he said, his voice rising, "than lying in bed watching *Weekend in Havana* on the Late Show with a quick bash during a commercial." (*Tropical magic, moon of temptation, strange fascination, adios to my heart,* sang Alice Faye in the hay of an un-Communized Cuban countryside, surrendering her heart but nothing else to John Payne.)

As though composure might hopefully be communicable, she said, quietly but firmly, "Fairy-tale romances happen in fairy tales, darling, not on East Sixty-ninth Street. And *you're* the one who likes to watch movies on television. And besides, you loved it and you know it."

"Well, I always love fucking you," he granted, deliberately indelicate, hoping to jolt her out of her complacency with a small, explosive charge of vulgarity. "But, there's fucking and fucking," he persisted. Jolt, jolt.

"I didn't mean that," she said levelly, averting her face. "I meant *Weekend in Havana.*"

He grinned. "Of its kind, it wasn't a bad picture."

She moved to the bar. "And you exaggerate, too. Why do you always exaggerate, Walter?"

"About what?"

"A quick bash during a commercial, to use your words. I mean, there's a little more than that, isn't there," she declared, daring him to deny it.

He couldn't. She tried. She played the games. But she was a reluctant player, recruited against her will and her giggles were of embarrassment, not delight. *If only she didn't giggle like that all the goddam time it might be all right!*

Of course, he might very well be up against the insurmountable barrier: the true absence of fleshly curiosity. There had been indications. (*Didn't you ever wonder what it would be like to make love in the bathtub before we did it? Frankly, Walter, no.*) But they were, as yet, only indications, no hard proof. And hard proof was dreaded and would be sought no further. For the time being.

But this was getting him nowhere! *The point, Walter, get to the point!* Should he just come right out with it, now, right between the eyes, as it were? *Listen, Miriam, there is going to be delivered here to this very apartment within a very few days now* . . . Or should he adhere to his original plan, approach it more subtly through the Apthekers, his own inspiration that might serve as well for Miriam's. Perhaps he should have begun with the book, then worked his way from that to . . .

"I think if you had your way," Miriam said, "we'd probably be like the people upstairs," and jerked her head at the ceiling.

Walter smiled broadly. "That's what I would call a very successful marriage."

"I don't doubt it," she said loftily. "They've probably been married about three months."

"They've been married for eight years," he told her with barely disguised triumph, feeling like George Sanders trapping Anne Baxter in *All About Eve—There is no Shubert Theatre in San Francisco, my dear* . . .

It got the expected response. "Eight years! And *that's* still going on?"

It was in the bedroom two months before that they were first aware of the new tenants in the apartment directly over theirs. Until then the only sound from above had been the violin of the musician who lived in the apartment, who practiced for hours each day and was fortunately a talented professional. In bed late one night, watching the Great, Great Show, they heard for the first time bedroom sounds above their heads. Momentarily surprised, they managed to ignore the murmuring voices at first. But when the low, long laughter of the woman came down upon them they both looked at the ceiling, then at each other. Walter suggested that their fiddler was entertaining a guest, a little fiddle diddle. Miriam told him, no, the musician had moved out the week before. These must be new tenants, she concluded. Evidently so, Walter agreed, the apartment certainly did seem to be occupied at the moment. Miriam commented regretfully on the flimsy construction of new buildings and they managed to turn their attention again to the television screen and tried to pick up the missed threads of the plot.

But pretense at indifference soon became impossible when the activity above moved sharply into a new key (the key of F, thought Walter, with a crazy grin), with the woman's alternating moans and guttural grunts in response to her now unheard companion—who apparently was no longer inclined to give voice to his emotions. Shouldn't they turn the sound up or something, Miriam suggested desperately. Walter didn't think that would do much good and, besides, from the sound of it, things were coming along nicely up there and would probably be over very soon now.

It was then that the woman began to scream repeatedly, the classic, blunt, two-word plea for her partner to do what he was all too obviously already doing, with fervor to judge by the sound of what could only be the headboard of their bed thumping rhythmically against the wall. Then there was a sustained, piercing shriek as though, in some murderously Dionysian ritual, the man had perhaps cut her throat at the supreme moment.

Then she wept for a little while what could only have been tears of gratitude.

Then there was silence.

"Good God Almighty," Miriam breathed, stunned.

Walter leered. "There's nothing quite like a woman who enjoys it a lot," he observed.

Either not hearing or not sharing his sentiment, Miriam whispered desperately, "What are we going to do?"

"What do you mean, do?" Walter asked, perplexed.

"Well, good God, suppose that goes on all the time?"

It did. But not always only in the bedroom and (more interestingly to Walter) not always at night. A few days later what he began to refer to as the Festivities in 11B appeared to be relocated in their new upstairs neighbor's living room and thereafter were conducted with verve on a good many afternoons between, roughly, the hours of one and two o'clock.

Miriam's first suggestion was soundproofing. Walter dismissed it as useless: Any soundproofing, to be effective at all, would have to be upstairs in that apartment, not down here in this one. She next wondered if it might be possible to talk to them, somehow let them know that they were being heard. Walter, comically dubious, assured her that he, for one, would not know quite how to go about doing that. Would she? She wouldn't, no.

After the first few weeks, by which time the regularity of the afternoon activity had been firmly established, it was Cassie whom Miriam worried most about. Suppose, she pointed out to Walter, suppose their daughter was in the house some day when *that* started? But Walter observed that, so far, there seemed to be daylight, living-room action only on the days between Monday and Friday, never on the weekends. And, since Cassie was at school during the zero hour each weekday, he reminded her, they had little or nothing to concern themselves about on that score as yet. *We'll cross that hump when we get to it*, he suggested.

Now, Miriam asked, curiously, "How do you happen to know they've been married for eight years, may I ask?"

"Well, I've gotten to know the guy," he shrugged. "Slightly. Just to talk to in the elevator."

"How?"

"How, what?"

"I mean," she said, a note of suspicion easing almost imperceptibly into her voice, "how did you get to know him to talk to in the elevator?"

He turned away carefully, shrugged, and waved his hand casually toward the door as though setting the scene for her. "This man got into the elevator one night and he pressed the button for the eleventh floor and I'd never seen him before so I asked him if he was the new tenant and he said yes, in 11B, and I introduced myself and more or less welcomed him to the building and *he* introduced *him*self and I've bumped into him two or three times since then, that's all." He inhaled deeply and rushed his glass to his mouth. He waited a moment before chancing a look in her direction and found her staring at him with the enigmatic look that often indicated intense, if not always ordered, thought. She nodded, vaguely.

"But how do you happen to know how long they've been married, I mean?"

"What do you mean, how do I happen to know," he said, too loudly, with an irascibility born of apprehension. "How do *I* know? It just happened to come up in the course of a conversation!"

Was it as absurd a suggestion as he feared? Was such a piece of information likely to be imparted in the course of a few brief, cursory conversations between strangers in ascending and descending elevators? But how could he tell her the truth? How tell her that he had purposefully sought out the knowledge? Because, once told, she would of course want to know *why* he had sought it out. And he would not be able to say with any certainty. The only certainty was that his curiosity was vaguely disturbing, even to him.

"Have you met his wife, too?" Miriam asked casually.

He almost laughed with relief. The more complex implications had escaped her entirely, she had jumped to the obvious, wrong conclusion: *She thought he was interested in the wife!* "No, I haven't ever met her," he said, truthfully, then went into a crouch, flicking an imaginary cigar and, with bouncing eyebrows and a Groucho Marx leer, added, "But I'd recognize her voice anywhere."

She forced a distracted smile. "Do you find that attractive?"

"What," he said, mildly disconcerted that his lightheartedness was going unshared.

"All that noise."

"What noise?"

"The noise she makes," she said, precisely, impatient, ill at ease. "Enjoying it at the top of her voice."

He was touched. She was still worried about his possible attraction for the woman upstairs. "Screaming has its points," he smiled, "but I wouldn't say it was mandatory."

Ah, but how he did wish she *would* scream. Just sometimes. Just a little. But Miriam was not a screamer. Definitely. An occasional gasp, perhaps, involuntary, a sometime hiss of air through her teeth, but no shriek of ecstasy had ever in twelve years forced those perfect teeth apart. *Would* ever? Maybe not. Unless he found the key, *where was the goddam key?* . . . To Miriam's box. *The Sex Scream: Its History and Application,* by Walter A. Hartman.

"Walter?"

He returned to her with some effort.

"The man upstairs . . ." She was gazing into the middle distance, trying to see something there. Then she turned to him. "Does he work nights or something?"

"Nights?" he asked, perplexed. "No, he doesn't work nights. Why should he work nights? He's in advertising."

"Then what is he doing home so many afternoons?"

"We already know what he does home so many afternoons, Miriam."

"Seriously. Why is he there, I mean?"

"Maybe he comes home for lunch and one thing leads to another," he grinned, persisting.

"Or maybe he doesn't."

"Doesn't what?"

"Come home for lunch," she said, oozing cool innuendo. "Ever." She looked at him in challenging silence, forcing him to share with her the obvious and inescapable conclusion that would have to be drawn if her suggestion had any validity. "It seems very unusual for a man in business to come home for lunch," she suggested, forcing him steadily to the wall. "Let alone so often."

Her suspicion, with its implied alternative, was completely unacceptable to him. He did not want the situation upstairs to be that. He wanted it to be what he had always assumed it was, he wanted to know that it was possible for a man to be married to a woman for eight long years and for both still to want him to come home and tear off a quick piece now and again on his lunch hour. And to act on their wanting. (As to wanting, he knew well enough: How often at the office, after all, had the noon whistle blown in his own loins? Often enough. Never had he acted, however.)

"It would explain a lot of things, Walter, let's face it. For one thing, it would certainly explain the weekend moratorium up there, wouldn't it. I mean, as far as the afternoons go. Because on the weekends her husband *would* be . . ."

"As far as I'm concerned, her husband comes home for lunch, Miriam," he declared. *If I'm wrong, don't tell me!*

She smiled and sighed. "You're an incurable romantic, darling, I think."

"Can we stick to the point, Mimi?" *Whatever the hell it was!* For a moment, confused, disconcerted, he lost track of his mind's original pursuit.

"It seems very much to the point to me, darling," she said with dangerous condescension. "You're the one talking about romance. So, is that her husband up there all these afternoons? Or isn't it? And is it romance?"

"I don't care what's romance up there, Miriam, it's what's romance down here that I care about at the moment!"

After a moment, she asked quietly, "Why are you shouting?"

He breathed deeply. "I think we should talk about it, Mim," he almost whispered.

"About what?"

"Well," he said, reasonably, "that a real woman gives some thought to her husband's, well, contentment. To his needs. A real woman gives some thought to that."

"I'm as much of a woman as anyone you care to mention, Walter," she claimed.

"Joan Aptheker."

It was out! Not well, perhaps, but finally given the perfect, irresistible opportunity, the name had dislodged itself from the tip of his tongue where it had been clinging all evening. And certainly that absence of any required thought was hurtful, both to Miriam and his cause: It wasn't his intention to undermine her self-esteem; he might at least have feigned some difficulty in naming a woman more woman than she.

"You're getting crueler by the minute," Miriam said, quietly, deadly, as expected, as he deserved.

"Just for example," he went on quickly, feigning the only thing left to feign: unawareness of offense, "just for example, whose idea do you think that mirror is they have, she and Tom?" He paused long enough to permit her silence to acknowledge the obvious. "Right," he said, "Joan's."

"And how do you happen to know that, may I ask?"

"Tom told me, that's how I know." And that's not all he told me! You should only know what he's told me!

"It doesn't surprise me," Miriam said, "Look at her."

"What about her?"

"Well, she's just one enormous erogenous zone, Walter!"

"Well, what's wrong with that?" It was very likely—almost certainly—true about Joan, and he found it remarkable that Miriam had realized it and put it so well. If only she knew how easily he could find out for himself, firsthand! Tom's incredible offer was there! Rejected, but standing!

"As for that mirror," Miriam said, "it's obscene, if you want my opinion."

"What's obscene about it?" he wanted to know, probing casually. "It's just hanging there on the wall."

"At the head of their bed, Walter," she pointed out precisely. "At a very cunning angle."

"But what's obscene about it?"

"If it was on the ceiling it couldn't be more obscene, as far as I'm concerned, darling."

He wondered how long she had been aware of the Apthekers' mirror. Certainly she, no more than he, had not given any indication until tonight that she knew of its existence, much less that she was aware of its purpose. His own knowledge of it dated to a night many months ago, in early spring when, at a party at the Apthekers' new house in Sneden's Landing, he had gone into their bedroom in urgent search of an unoccupied bathroom. The room was dimly lit and he was immediately startled by what appeared to be some sort of optical illusion: There appeared, in the half light, to be two beds in the room, back to back, both of them piled high with coats. Then he realized that one of the beds was only a reflection in the mirror on the wall. It was enormous, nearly as wide as the king-size bed and some three feet high. It looked quite handsome, he thought, but it seemed an odd place for a mirror, even such a big one, because it was not possible, of course, to be any closer to it than the foot of the bed and, standing there, he saw, one could see oneself only from the waist down because of the angle at which the mirror appeared to be canted from the wall. Then, concentrating less on what he could see of himself in the mirror, and more on what was visible, it was clear that what was fully reflected was the entire surface of the coat-covered bed. And, instantly, there could be no mistaking it: Anyone actually *on* the bed would be able to see themselves completely, Tom and Joan *on* the bed would be able to see themselves . . .

"It's what's happening, Mim."

"*What's* what's happening?"

"Let me put it to you this way. . . . Times are changing, Mim. And a lot of people are beginning to do something about their secret dreams and . . ."

"What secret dreams?"

"Everyone has secret dreams. And . . ."

"Speak for yourself, Walter."

"And in everyone's secret dreams there's an enormous mirror hanging at the head of the bed." He grinned. "At a very cunning angle."

His smile slipped on the ice of her eyes and almost fell.

"Not in *mine* there isn't, Walter!"

Startled at her quiet vehemence, he watched her stride abruptly from the room.

Fleeing secret possibilities? he wondered.

3 *Will you, won't you, will you, won't you, will you join the dance?* asked the placard over the checkroom cubicle, one of hundreds of such that dotted the exposed-brick walls of the Mod Hatter together with more hundreds of small mirrors in brightly enameled frames in a variety of shapes and sizes. Walter handed his coat across the counter to the sweet-faced girl with the blue-ribboned straight blond hair and the frilly Alice-in-wonderland gown modified to end near the tops of her shapely thighs. He greeted the girl familiarly, took the small brass coat check from her, and glanced over the counter at the backs of her thighs as she turned away.

The Hatter's was unusually busy for this time on a Thursday night, he thought. Seasonal revels, he supposed.

He walked to the bar, one hand dapper in the pocket of his sports jacket, George Raft. He found an unoccupied stool and nodded heavily when the bartender asked (by name—he knew the regulars) how he was tonight. "Fine," he lied and ordering a double bourbon on the rocks, found his tongue annoyingly clumsy, and tried to remember the exact count of drinks he had already had that evening. He thought it had been three. At least.

The negroid voice singing "Sunny" on the low bandstand in the corner belonged to a pale, blond young man who accompanied himself (badly, Walter thought) on the guitar. He was a new booking; Walter had not seen him here before. To see him, it was necessary to look across the profile of the girl seated on the next stool who gazed directly forward, as though she might be studying her own reflection in the mirror behind the bar. Walter glanced down, reflexively. Her skirt was tight and high across the tops of her smooth pink thighs. As he watched, the thighs moved, crossing. He imagined their inside surfaces, planes pressing against planes in sweet, warm resistance.

Somewhere behind him, at a table, unseen, a girl laughed, an enchanting tinkle, like small bells. Walter fell in love with her as he lifted his glass from the cocktail napkin and sipped, reading on the napkin, *But I don't want to go among mad people. Oh, you can't help that: we're all mad here. I'm mad. You're mad.* He wondered idly (speaking of mad people) if the Apthekers were having one of what Tom called their special little get-togethers tonight. He wondered how often they occurred. Tom's expression had been "every so often." How often was every so often?

Not in mine there isn't! she claims.

Doth the lady protest too much? How he wished that might be the case.

But she probably dothn't, he thought, despondent at the memory of the occasions of recent months when he had attempted to inject some revitalizing newness into the too well worn and all too familiar patterns of their sexuality and her unfailingly neophobic response to those attempts. Beginning with that very night of his discovery in the Apthekers' bedroom when everything began to get so openly complicated. Driving back to the city from Sneden's Landing he had gotten lost, found himself on a dark, narrow country road, stopped the car on a sudden lustful impulse—or was it really so very sudden?—and, after a few brief preliminaries, suggested they get into the back seat. She resisted, of course, but playfully enough, and only briefly. Still, she had been so nervous that someone might happen by and discover them that she nearly didn't come: Danger, it seemed, was not for her the added aphrodisiac it was for him. Afterward she told him that he would have to admit that "there was something pretty damn weird about your husband wanting to have sex in the back seat of a car after you'd been married for ten years." He told her he admitted no such thing; there was nothing at all in the slightest weird about it.

No more, in his opinion, than there was about the occasion several weeks later when he put on his old clothes and played a janitor come to fix a leak in the bathroom and she in her negligee and they finished in the half-filled bathtub. She said she'd nearly drowned, a comment not at all in the spirit of the thing.

No more than there was anything weird about the call-girl game. She was hardly the call-girl type, she claimed. He tried to point out to her that some of the most beautiful, straightest-looking women around were getting a hundred clams a shot and worth every nickel, that she was precisely the call-girl type, that that was precisely the point. If she could have seen that, she might have been able to see what he was getting at. But she couldn't see it and demanded to know how a woman was supposed to pretend she was a call girl if she wasn't and hadn't the slightest idea what a call girl did? *Everything*, he told her, leering, Groucho Marx. But, even though she finally acquiesced, she giggled constantly. And she certainly didn't do everything. . . .

But of course it was not as though it was always a matter of playing the games of altered identities; he wasn't some kind of fetishist, for Christ's sake. He would be the first to admit that the desired thing was to be who they *are* and have fun.

It was merely a matter of finding the key! There might well be certain techniques of carnal persuasion as yet unknown to him, to be discovered, mastered, judiciously employed. *Because the end of romance is the death of marriage, Walter!* he told his mirror image behind the bar, sandy-haired, flecked with gray, neatly trimmed. Should he let his hair grow a little, he wondered, more in the current fashion?

His image answered: That could be a very unrealistic position to hold, Walter; it might even be an immature one.

Who says so?

Well, a lot of people, Walter, just about everyone, as a matter of fact.

Not me!

Romance is the vermiform appendix in the evolution of marriage, Walter.

Fuck off!

His argumentative reflection dismissed, he saw not it, but mirror, and remembered Miriam's reaction to the Apthekers'. It was not good, not at all good. Not even promising. But, there was time yet. Delivery wasn't due for another week or so. He would work it out somehow between now and then. Somehow . . .

Now is the winter of our discontent, glorious summer might yet come . . .

The girl beside him appeared to be alone. Guardedly, he studied her reflection in the bar mirror. She was beginning to look familiar. An actress? Model? There was something odd about her, the nature of which he was unable to pinpoint at first. Then, after further, necessarily less guarded scrutiny, he realized what it was: She didn't appear to blink her eyes. It was weird.

The singer finished "Sunny" to enthusiastic applause. Walter clapped, a reflexive courtesy only.

"Isn't he terrible?"

He turned, the girl's face so close to him that he was able to distinguish from all the other odors and scents around him the sweet airy perfume of her. She too was applauding, but her face was somber; as with him there was no reflection on it of her hands' enthusiasm.

"I beg your pardon?" he asked, smiling stiffly, trying to recover from the abruptness of her presence in his life.

"I said, isn't he terrible!" she repeated loudly, over the sound of the applause that included her own.

"Really awful," Walter agreed, applauding.

Was she a hooker?

The instinctive, uncontrollable suspicion shamed and irritated him. *Why should she be?* True, he could not remember ever in his life having been spoken to first by a woman in a bar who had not proved ultimately to be a hooker. But that had been in another world, not in this one, this was a new world now, things were changing, changed, everything.

The girl certainly wasn't pursuing her opening. She had returned to her reflection in the mirror, he saw out of the corner of his careful eye, poking her swizzle stick into the ice of her almost empty glass. She reached down with a distracted hand and gently scratched the inside of her left thigh with one fingernail, lifting her glass to her lips with her other hand. Her scratching hand rose again to the bar top and lifted the cocktail napkin. After a moment he was aware that she was reading it; then she turned her head toward him and extended the napkin. He turned, looked at her, to find her staring at him, eyelids locked open (*Don't her eyeballs get incredibly dry?*), and realized that she wanted him to read her napkin with its fragment of Lewis Carroll. He smiled nervously and read: *Rule Forty-two: All persons more than a mile high to leave the court.*

"I should leave," she said.

His smile assumed more certainty. "Are you high?"

"As a kite," she said somberly. "Are you alone?"

"Yes I am," he said.

"So am I," she said. "Everyone is alone, you know."

A warning bell clanged faintly in his brain. Against his better judgment he ignored it. "Can I buy you a drink?" he offered, smiling, hoping that she would not be offended at his evasion of her depressing philosophy of life.

She gazed at him for another moment, inscrutable. "May you," she said finally.

"I beg your pardon?" Was she really very stoned and transposing words unintentionally?

"May you," she said again, with precisely the same inflection, confusing him further. "You said *can* you buy me a drink. Well, of course, you *can*. That is, you have the *ability*. What you want is permission. So, it's *may* you—buy me a drink."

"Oh. Oh, yes," he said, grinning, nodding wildly. "Yes, I see what you mean. Yes. *May* I. Of course." She spoke sweetly, soft, and seemed to do so without opening her teeth appreciably, if at all; it reminded him of the imitations Joan Aptheker did of Katharine Hepburn, the Massachusetts malocclusion, but more natural. "Well, then, *may* I?"

"You may." She turned away and emptied her glass.

He signaled the bartender and tick-tocked one pendulous

finger over the two drained glasses, wondering why. He hadn't bought a drink for a strange girl in a bar in years. Years! And this one probably a hooker!

What was he doing?

"I'm a schoolteacher," the girl said, more challenging, it seemed, than informative.

"Oh? Are you really?" Nodding, smiling, interested.

"In case you think I'm trying to pick you up or anything like that," she warned charmingly.

"Don't be silly," Walter said, chiding her gravely. "What do you teach?"

"English."

"I might have known," he grinned again.

"Why?"

Had she forgotten the recent grammar lesson already? She might be even more smashed than she had already admitted to being. He wanted to let it pass, but she appeared to be waiting for an answer. "Can I, may I," he explained.

"Can you, may you what?"

The bartender delivered salvation in both hands. Walter seized his glass and wished her cheers; she wished him Merry Christmas with an unseasonally mournful smile.

"What do you do?" she asked.

He hesitated. "Well, I'm in television, as a matter of fact," he said reluctantly. "Ordinarily."

"Really? What do you do in television, you're an actor?"

"Oh no, no, I'm in the executive end," he said. "Ordinarily. Although not at the moment. Do you come here often?" Christ! he was awful at this—whatever this was.

"Fairly," she said.

"I come here fairly often myself. I don't think I've seen you before, though." He smiled. "We'll have to synchronize our watches or something." Well, that wasn't too bad, he thought, not too bad at all, really.

"What do you do in the executive end?" she asked and moved, interestedly, resting her elbow on the backrest of her stool, pulling the silk of her blouse taut across her right breast; at its center there appeared the lovely, tiny bump of an unbra-ed nipple.

Love's first button, Press Here To Start. She probably wore bikini underpants, too (most girls did these days, certainly the ones who wore no bras), the delicately flowered ones he had seen in Saks Christmas-browsing a few days ago. Why wouldn't Miriam wear them? She had a *beautiful* body, she would look *wonderful* in them. But her underpants still covered her goddam navel.

"I'm in Standards and Practices," he answered her finally, hastily, reluctant to elaborate on that which he hoped he might soon be able to leave behind him forever.

But the phrase, he could see, was too cryptic to satisfy her and her eyes demanded elaboration. He explained the requirements of good taste and propriety in network television programming; offered a few brief, assuaging examples; defined his own high-echelon role; and denied her suggestion—with its implied overtone of accusation—that he was a "kind of a censor." He was prepared to expound a little on the distinctions between censorship and self-policing when she suddenly pivoted further toward him, swiveling on her thinly sheathed buttocks and for the first time looked directly at him gazing gravely over the rim of her glass.

For a time that seemed to him endless, he felt them to be enveloped in a suffocating, breathless silence, the voices of others gone, and he knew that the next voice he heard would be hers. He knew too, what it would say: Her eyes told him, like the blast of the impact from a distant explosion before the sound reaches the ear. Knowing, he panicked in advance for an answer.

"Do you want to take me home?" she asked quietly.

He lifted his glass like a shield and discovered it to be empty of everything but ice, a cold sliver of which slid through his teeth; he slid it back into the glass as unobtrusively as possible.

So soon! It hadn't been twenty minutes since . . . *Was it this simple now?* In his day it had usually been hours before such a definitive stage was reached. Even if one knew the girl was an eventual sure thing and the girl knew he knew it, there was nevertheless an unspoken understanding that there would be a reasonable period of enjoyable give and take, feint and parry, some pretense at least of maidenly reserve on the bedrock principle that the too easily had was not worth having.

But this! It was so . . . uncomplicated! Was this it, then? Was it, after all these faithful years, to be this glorious-looking, black-haired, bra-less, bikini-panted teacher of English?

Impossible.

She was waiting. She wanted an answer! "You're very high," he said finally, for his own desperate benefit, but managing to suggest his interest in hers, implying possible morning sorrow for her night's inebriated rashness: What would the school board think?

She stared at him for a long, inscrutable moment.

"I don't know your name," she said at last.

He was obviously dealing with a nonsequential mind here. *Or was she giving up on him already? So easily!*

"Walter," he said, with a worldly half-smile, preserving a cautious partial anonymity for the moment.

"How do you do, Walter?" she said gracefully.

He nodded. "And yours?"

"Celeste Starbright."

Oh, God.

"Call me Celeste."

Call me a cab.

"It isn't my real name," she added.

Relieved, but confused, he said, "Oh?"

"I change my name. From time to time. So many times. Looking for a name that rings a bell in the heart."

Oh, God.

"I like this one. Celeste Starbright?" He nodded. "Very imaginative."

"It serves," she said distractedly. "To distinguish me from the others."

"Ah. Other what?"

"The others," she replied, gesturing vaguely toward the world beyond the Mod Hatter's walls. "Them. Out there."

"Ah." Nodding, nodding. "Yes, I see what you mean, uh-huh." *Jesus Christ.*

"There's something I should tell you," she said, somber.

"Oh?"

"I despise false pretenses, you see. I don't think I should allow you to go any further in your commitment to me without declaring myself. Doesn't that seem fair?"

"Yes, well, I guess that's a . . ."

"I'm going to kill myself, you see."

Oh, well of course! Of course you are!

"One must never say a thing like that, you might say. But I must say it."

Must you?

"Because it's true. When a thing is true I have to say it. It's an emotional trait I have."

He nodded, wondering how soon he might be able to excuse himself to go to the men's room which lay close by the street door.

"You're angry," she said accusingly. "Aren't you."

"Angry? No. No, not at all, I . . ."

"I only told you, you know, because . . . well, I didn't want you to be hurt unexpectedly. I knew the moment you approached me, the moment you asked to take me home, that I shouldn't hurt you. Do you see?"

"Yes, well, I . . ."

"Of course, it might not happen."

"What might not?"

"My . . . final departure."

"Oh?"

"Why mightn't it, you might ask."

I might. On the other hand . . .

"Because something else might happen."

"Ah?"

"One can, after all, survive a lifetime living from one postponement to the next, is that not true? I'm an existentialist, you see."

"Ah!"

" 'Cast a cold eye on life, on death. Horseman, pass by!' W. B. Yeats."

"Ah. Uh, huh. Right."

"Perhaps you're right, Walter."

"Right? About what?"

"Perhaps *you*'re what might happen."

"I? Ah. Yes, well . . . I didn't quite . . ."

"All right, Walter," she nodded thoughtfully. "I'll let you come home with me."

An insane, alcoholic, suicidal, existentialist pseudonymous English teacher! *He'd have been better off with a hooker!*

She put her hand on his wrist, weightlessly, barely touching him. Her voice sweet, soft, uncertain, she said, "It'll only be fifty dollars. Is that all right?"

4 His knee hurt badly. He felt foolish being so high as to have slipped on the ice like that. But the cold air was clearing his head a little.

He had handled it all right, he felt, not badly at all. He was confident that he would not have gone through with it even had she been on the level and not a hooker. Not that there really could be any certainty of her professional status. After all, what kind of a cockamamie hooker asks if her price is all right, as if it were *negotiable?* She *had* to be an amateur.

Christ, it was getting harder and harder all the time to spot the kooks before it was too late.

Yet at the end he had been oddly touched by her insanity, and had spoken the necessary lie: some other time maybe. Even then, flight imminent, he was capable of a twinge of guilt at the strange creature's sad, disappointed smile of personal rejection.

Christ! he had been tempted, though. But, no, that wasn't the answer! *Would not, could not, would not, could not, could not join the dance.* And certainly not with a semipro hooker!

Whore's man, pass by.

He passed through the door held open by the new night doorman whose name he could not remember, muttered a friendly hello, and limped across the lobby to the elevator door. Would

Miriam be awake, had she waited up for him? And what would be the emotional climate? Fragile, handle with care, *this end up!*

The television was on in the living room, but Miriam was nowhere in sight. He triple-locked the door, hung his coat in the foyer closet, and went to the bar with one eye on the television screen, chagrined at his failure to remember that this was the night *Boom Town* was on. Gable, Tracy, Claudette Colbert. And, Christ, yes, Hedy Lamarr! He looked at his wristwatch and saw that the movie had been on for no more than ten or fifteen minutes, he hadn't missed much.

He took Cassie's broad-brimmed hat from the seat of his chair and sat with his feet propped on the edge of the coffee table. It was a hell of a good movie. And he hadn't seen it in two or three years.

"Hi," Miriam said.,

He turned to find her standing near the door to the bedroom hall, smiling cautiously. "Hi!" he answered pleasantly.

She moved toward him as though the expanse of carpet between them were a mine field that she was testing carefully, one step at a time.

"Where'd you go?" she asked, casually.

"Just for a walk, mostly."

She nodded. "How is it out?"

He leered, seizing opportunity. "I don't know, I haven't had it out today."

She mocked a willing grimace, loving victim, acquiescent butt of her irresistibly comic husband.

Encouraged, he watched as she moved around the sofa and sat, her legs tucked beneath her, her skirt dragged high across her thighs. She had removed her stockings, he noticed, and determined to turn off the television as soon as the present scene came to an end, it couldn't be more than a few minutes more, Gable and Tracy, toe to toe.

"You sound a little high," Miriam ventured, picking up a half-filled glass from the end table.

"Maybe a little," he admitted boyishly.

"Where were you, that Mad Hatter place?"

"Mod."

"Mod."

"For a while."

"Would you like some coffee? I just made some."

"That's a myth, Miriam," he said, too curtly, he knew. "It doesn't make a damned bit of difference. Coffee has absolutely no effect on——"

"That's right, you told me that," she replied, retreating fast with an amused but loving condescension.

"And even if it wasn't a myth," he added, "I mean, I'm not so far gone that I need someone pouring pots of coffee down my throat."

"I didn't imply that, don't bite my head off," she said softly, her back against the wall of the sofa arm.

"Sorry," he said. He was overreacting of course. He had grown rather sensitive of late, he noticed, to any suggestions that he might be drinking too much. He smiled at her, sheepishly, mollifying. "You may have noticed that I sometimes have this tendency toward exaggeration."

He knew he should turn off the television. But, Christ, here was Lamarr now. Was there ever such another face, before or since?

"I'm sorry if I was a little impatient with you before," she said abruptly, "but you have to admit, to hear you talk sometimes, anyone would think I wore hair curlers to bed and was *frigid* or something."

"I certainly never meant to imply that, Mimi," he responded reasonably, watching Hedy Lamarr's breasts that he was certain were unhaltered beneath that blouse. "You don't and you're not. I mean, that's really the point, I guess. It's what I find so encouraging."

There was a silence that forced his attention so that he was already turned to look at her the instant before she spoke. "What do you mean, encouraging?" she asked flatly.

"Well, you know," he shrugged.

"No, I don't know."

"What's the matter?"

"The matter is that I find 'encouraging' a singularly patronizing word to use, under the circumstances, Walter."

"Why?" he asked, sincerely puzzled.

"Well, if you don't know, I can't explain it to you, are you going to watch this?" she said, her eyes on his, her head jerking toward the television.

"No, I just wanted to see that scene, what's the matter?"

"Nothing." She rose so abruptly that a small splash of her drink left the glass and scattered on her skirt and the carpet.

"Where you going?"

"I guess I'll get ready for bed."

She was gone. Again. He sat quite still, more puzzled than contrite. What was patronizing about that? He had meant only that where there was smoke there was probably fire. What was wrong with that? But he had offended her, however unwittingly, and now repairs were necessary. Because an offended Miriam would not likely be a loving one. *And he was in need of a loving one.* Between the moon maid Celeste and his own wife, pleasure's pump was well-primed.

He switched off the television and watched Gable and Colbert disappear in an ever diminishing square of light. He decided on coffee. Myth or no myth, it was advisable to accept it for truth at the moment. Temporary belief in myths was sometimes unavoidable and often necessary.

By the time he entered the bedroom carrying an already half-emptied cup of coffee, he had begun to wonder if perhaps the trouble was himself. The bathroom door was closed. He sat in the armchair and put the cup to his lips. His knee still throbbed faintly.

It was a courageous thought, he thought. Was it possible? Because if the problem for Miriam was not herself, but him . . .

The bathroom door opened and she emerged wearing only her underpants. They covered her navel. She was momentarily and mildly startled by his presence in the room; but otherwise she evidently wasn't going to pay too much attention to it. She sat at her dressing table and began to brush her hair. Her nipples were hard, he had noted instantly. *Could she be hot, in spite of everything?* Or was it only a cold-tile chill from the bathroom floor, shot up her legs to tingle those points? He sipped from the cup and watched her full breasts swing gently, maddeningly, with each stroke of her slender arm.

"Maybe it's me," he said.

She turned her head to look at him askance from beneath the sideward fall of her hair, with no break in the rhythm of the brush in her hand, her visible eye cool. "I beg your pardon?"

"Maybe it's because you're married to me." This was perilous ground, he knew. Suppose she were to turn to him now and say— right between the eyes, so to speak—yes, that was exactly what the trouble was! What *then?* He was suddenly fearful. He went on quickly, almost blurting, "I mean, maybe if you were married to someone else, you'd be different."

The brush paused on her hair. "Different how?"

He didn't want to go on with this! He definitely didn't! "Less inhibited, I mean, more eager to explore the further possibilities. I mean, maybe it's me that's the problem. For you."

She gazed at him for a moment. "Can we get off it now, Walter?" she suggested with a deadly even tone. "Can we just get off it now? Okay?"

Yes, why couldn't he? Why couldn't he get off it? At least, for tonight. All he really wanted and needed now was to lay her, a conviction and desire that grew more strongly with every swing of her swaying breasts, with every pressured undulance of her buttocks and thighs on the dressing-table stool. Nor did he especially require complexity. No, he would be perfectly satisfied, *more* than content, with a simple, straightforward, unsophisticated hump!

At least, for tonight.

But why wasn't *she* bored? Why wasn't she as bored as he with the endlessly repeated and unvaried patterns of their sex. Because to be bored requires imagination? Might that explain her complaisance—her total inability to imagine other than what existed?

But, then, if that was indeed the case, she might be the fortunate one. Because imagination could be a terrible burden. How well he knew.

"Like if you'd married Tom Aptheker, for instance," he said reflectively. *Why couldn't he stop himself! What was this insane impulse to jump off the cliff from which so many others were content simply to admire the view?*

The brush stopped for an instant against her now shining hair; then resumed, stroking evenly. "I'm ignoring that," she said.

"No, I meant that in the best possible way," he assured her.

"Uh, huh," she doubted.

Yes, of course she had misunderstood. She thought that he might be about to begin harping on *that* again. Understandable, perhaps. Since he had harped on it jokingly a good deal over the years; more, perhaps, than was wise. But, what nagged so persistently was why—if what she claimed was true was really the truth—*why didn't he believe it?*

Because, considering Tom Aptheker, it was hard to believe that nothing had ever happened between them. They had "dated"—as Miriam had always so sedately put it—for nearly half a year, hadn't they? Was it so unreasonable then to doubt that in all that time nothing had transpired between them beyond the most elementary physical intimacies, those to which she had admitted in response to his natural early curiosity? (*Yes, he touched me there. Yes, I came sometimes.*)

Considering Tom Aptheker, it was hard to believe. He had known Tom practically all of his life and Tom had been more or less of a sex maniac since he was seven years old. Nevertheless, she persisted in her claim that until meeting Walter no one had gotten to first base with her. (*Got to it, hell, most of the boys I knew couldn't even find it!*)

Except Tom, of course. He found it, all right! *And having found it, failed to score? It was hard to believe.* Damned near impossible, in fact. So, could he be blamed for refusing to ignore the sound of his intuition scratching and snuffling so persistently at the door?

But why did it matter at all? What was the point anymore? It was years ago. At the time of her relationship with Tom she and Walter had not yet even met. So, what would it have mattered then, what would it matter *now*, if Tom *had* had her?

He thought he knew the reluctant answer. Did it matter simply because Miriam was the only virgin he had ever had? Was that why? *Because it was extremely important that every man have at least one virgin in his life and he would never have a crack at another?*

And Miriam was his virgin. Never mind the fact that there

had been none of the expected evidences of chastity at the time
of their first time; no twinge, no membranous delay, no slightest
trace of maiden's delicate gore. It was as she had said: Some
girls just didn't happen to have a maidenhead for one reason or
another (one girl she knew—she claimed—lost it horseback
riding), it was not all that unusual.

Yes! Miriam was his virgin!

Wasn't she?

Ah, but it was all so long ago and far away. Or should be.
Why was he squandering all this emotional energy that might
be put to so much better use at this very moment? But unfortunately, the damage, it seemed, had already been done and he
felt himself abruptly overcome, as was so often the case recently,
with a kind of ennui near to weariness, a Sisyphus of sex, his
slope the Mount of Venus, despairing of the summit.

He recalled the depressing findings of the most recent intimate
scientific investigations which had proved conclusively that
women had their best orgasms when they masturbated. Shit!
they probably all fell hopelessly in love with their middle fingers
at the age of twelve and never really got over it! Remained for
the rest of their clitoral lives the dreamers of hopeless dreams
of phallic impossibilities! *The Impossible Penis, A Manual for
Beginners,* by Walter A. Hartman.

It was an extremely depressing thought, reluctantly faced,
barely accepted, that this proud pendancy hanging heavy and
ever-ready between one's legs, whose blood's ebb and flood so
ruled and shaped one was no more to *them* than a necessary and
unavoidable (and probably never quite satisfactory) substitute
for their goddam *middle fingers.* Some so-called primitive tribes,
he remembered, performed clitorectomies on their women as a
matter of course—the real McCoy or nothing. Maybe they had
something there.

Her voice intruded on his hostile reflections. "Do you love
me, Walter?" she asked.

She sounded prepared for the worst. He was relieved to be
able to offer her the best. "Yes. I love you." It emerged, perhaps,
more aggressive than amorous, but—he hoped—unmistakably
sincere.

She glanced at him out of the corner of an eye, then looked

away again. She placed the hairbrush carefully on the dressing table with a small click against the glass top and stood and walked to'the bureau. With her back to him she removed her underpants, bending to pull them off. Walter gazed lovingly at the first part of her he had ever seen.

Thereby hangs a tail.

It was surely a unique distinction. How many men, after all, could say that the first part of his wife he had ever laid eyes on was her naked behind. Hands, maybe, yes. But, eyes? In the Deke house on the Dartmouth Homecoming Weekend, five years an alumnus, and accidentally stumbling into one of the rooms on the third floor that was traditionally reserved for the members' female guests and the first thing confronting his startled eyes, directly opposite the door, this beautiful ass. The girl on her hands and knees, groping under the bed for something (an earring, he knew much later) and stark naked. She turned at the sound of the opening door, looking across her shoulder, and gasped. After an instant of mutual immobility, she pushed herself backward onto her feet, swiveled on them to face him seizing a corner of the bedspread and, imperfectly covered, squatted there, wide-eyed and speechless. Shrugging, grinning, he backed out the door, closing it after him. Later that afternoon he was introduced to her by Tom Aptheker as Tom's date. He said she looked familiar and suggested that they might have met somewhere before. She blushed and said nothing. He had never in his life seen a girl actually blush and he fell in love with her on the spot.

He watched now as that part of her first known, perhaps first loved—fuller now, of course, and with the two gentle humps of over-thirty flesh high on the back of her hips, but still beautiful and desired—watched as it was obscured from sight by the short nightgown that lowered over it. She took up her underpants and went into the bathroom. He heard the lid of the metal laundry hamper squeal open and shut.

He grimaced, bitterly, remembering the fact that, beginning with the onset of Miriam's first menstruation and continuing throughout her adolescence, her mother, who he was sure must have been some kind of religious fanatic, strictly forbade the wearing of normally snug-fitting underpants on the theory that they had a tendency to abnormally arouse a girl "down there," as Miriam had characterized it when telling him the story years ago. Thus she had spent her teenage years in oversized, loosely fitting pants in which a tuck had been taken in the waist and wondering if she was truly less horny most of the time than her friends whose tight, pretty underpants were constantly rubbing and pressing. During those same years the fanatic mother had also discouraged the ingestion of pepper or mustard by her daughters on the grounds that these foods tended to overheat the naturally troubled blood of pubescent girls. (He had once had a vision of Miriam as a girl, in the locked privacy of her bedroom, wearing nothing but a pair of secretly bought under-pants a size too small and gorging herself on pepper and mustard sandwiches, her deprived quiff in incredible uproar.) Under such circumstances it was only fair to consider, he thought, what questionable effect that kind of thing might have had on her subsequent sexual development. It did not augur well for an adventurous and uninhibited future with the man of her dreams. Who was presumably he.

He wondered if Faith had been subjected to the same regula-tions when her time came. Presumably so; there was no reason to suppose that she might have escaped her older sister's ado-lescent fate. Yet he was inclined to think that Faith had managed to emerge sexually unscathed where her sister had not. It was not that Faith was necessarily a sexier woman than Miriam. She was not. Not exactly. No, it wasn't that, quite. But, she was dif-ferent. . . . Faith was . . .

Miriam emerged from the bathroom and sat on the edge of the bed and set the radio-alarm clock as always on WQXR for 7:30.

"We shall wake to music and live our days dancing," he smiled.

She turned to him with a distracted look. "Hm?"

He repeated the comment but failed to reproduce its original lightheated verve. She smiled vaguely.

"Are you coming to bed? It's late," she said, and stood to pull the bedspread to the foot of the bed.

"Yes," he said, temporarily, playing back her words to himself: Was it an invitation or merely a considerate suggestion?

She drew back the blanket, the lace hem of the nightgown delicately brushing the backs of her thighs.

He felt the thighs encircle his mind's waist. He was reluctant to stand, however. To stand would be to risk exposing his condition to her most cursory glance—barring a hand in the pocket to hold it down, and that shamefully far he would not go. And to reveal his condition could well put him at an awkward disadvantage. (*Was there anything so disconcerting and annoying and finally embarrassing to a man as his unresponded-to hard-on, after all?*)

He watched her climb into the bed and lie on her back. Stiff-lipped, she stifled a yawn.

It was his answer!

One had constantly to be on the alert for these subtle, sometimes almost imperceptible, but always significant signs and signals! If she was uninterested, she would not have tried to stifle that yawn! She would know that an open and undisguised yawn would be interpreted by him as a desire for sleep, a declaration of intent that would most certainly deflect him from any other more active bedtime plans he might have. But however sleepy she might truly be, she was obviously not disposed to let it stand in his way. Or hers. She was interested!

At the very least, amenable.

He stood, making no attempt to conceal his urgent and now encouraged condition. *Take a glans at this, baby!* And so she did, as he had suspicioned she would: Her look was fleeting, careful, but deliberate and searching. She knew what was coming her way! He moved to the bed and sat, leaning over her, one hand on the pillow beside her head. She gazed up at him with a half-grin of cautious neutrality that touched him. He smiled and lowered his head and kissed her softly. "You wanna get laid?" he asked, quietly lustful.

"I wouldn't mind," she said, and smiled.

He slid his hand beneath the blanket and downward, kissing her again, tongue in cheek, his in hers. His hand instantly discovered the lubricious condition that put the lie to all her neck-up camouflage. She accommodatingly parted her legs. "Are you ready?" he whispered.

"Can't you tell?"

"No, I mean do you have to get up first?"

"Oh. No."

So she had been prepared all along! Not only hot, but ready! Hot as a pistol and diaphragmed to go! And trying her best not to show it. All this time they had been playing hide and seek with each other! Christ! Fucking should be so simple! How had it gotten so complicated! When! Why!

Ready or not, here I come!

Quickly undressed, he soon discovered the extent of her preparedness. In less than five minutes she was on her back and pulling at his shoulders with her usual decorous urgency. He raised himself to his knees between hers.

"Ow! Oh, shit!" he said.

She stiffened, her fingers tightening their grip on his back, their message suddenly not passion but alarm. "What! What is it!" she cried in a breathless whisper.

"My knee, I hurt my goddam knee, I can't kneel on it!"

Unhesitatingly, without either curiosity or commiseration, she said, *"Here,"* and pushed hard at his chest. He rolled, or fell, onto his back, less in carnal cooperation than to ease his throbbing kneecap.

Instantly, she was astride his hips, moving hers, searching.

"Need a helping hand?" He grinned up at her, but distractedly, his twinging knee still making demands on his attention, as he reached under her, effecting necessary alignment.

"Oh, God," she breathed in assent, descending. "Oh, *God.*"

But he had a better idea. Before he could be deflected from it by her already deliciously accelerating motion, he placed his palms against the underside of her heaving thighs and applied a firm upward pressure that stilled her.

"What!" she gasped. It sounded impatient.

"I have a better idea!"

"This is *fine!*" she answered frantically, persisting against the pressure of his hands in a determined attempt to resume her interrupted rhythm.

But, despite the awkward leverage of his position, his resolve (strengthened by his utter faith in the superiority of his sexual imagination) prevailed and she uttered a soft, bereaved mew as connection was lost. He eased her from above himself and slid off the bed, pulling her gently toward the edge of the mattress, deftly rolling her onto her stomach in transit. Quickly, as she remembered, her body complied. She put her feet to the floor and raised herself. Her back to him, she parted her feet, fell forward from the waist, where his hands held her, and placed her palms on the bed. He moved on bent knees, fitting himself between her tense, trembling legs, Quarterback to her Center, third down and goal to go. He curled over her back, her breasts in his hands, and paused, poised precariously on the wet, slippery lip of bliss.

"You want it?" he whispered. She only breathed heavily through her gaping mouth, sucking air. *"Do you want it?"* he insisted.

"Yes! Yes!"

He feared that her reply was more impatience than passion; annoyance with his attempt at a bit of playful further incitement.

"Do it! Do it, Walter! *Christ!*"

Now you're talking, baby! Ready or not, here I . . .

"Go!"

. . . COME!

SHysteria again?

Too hopeful to entertain the thought before there was proof of the fact, he typed it quickly, his fingers, all four of them, pounding the keys with an authority he had not felt since the beginning months ago, in his days of innocence.

He hit the period with a triumphantly rigid middle finger and sat back hard, nearly breathless.

Was this it, finally? Could it be? Dare he hope, *again*, after so many false starts, wrong turns, dead ends on the Yellow Brick Road to his personal Oz?

Somewhere over the rainbow bluebirds fly, Walter!

Sing it again, Judy.

He lit a cigarette, his palms sweating slightly.

Four lines. Only four. What came, might come—*would* come—next, he didn't know. But that wasn't the point of course. No, the point was whether or not this was a real beginning this time, a beginning with the guarantee of a gratifying end, unlike the television play and the seven short stories and the screenplay and the novel and the stage play, all such serious efforts, begun with hope; and all, *all* hopeless finally.

Hope is the thing with feathers, Walter.

A bluebird?

Or perhaps he was getting hysterical again, perhaps it was only that. Again. He wondered, checking the checklist of hysteria's necessary factors. He was tired, true. Necessary Factor One: weariness. On the other hand, he had had only one drink so far this afternoon. No. Two . . . Three? Nevertheless, he was perfectly sober. Finally, it was broad daylight. All in all, then, hysteria was not indicated. Prognosis good.

But the review of hysteria's concomitants brought with it the memory of its occasions, the mad inventions of the dark nights of recent weeks.

In daylight's sober shame he remembered. Remembered the Jewish Eskimo songwriter who comes to New York to make it in the Bigtime. Nanook Feldman. Begotten during World War II on (in the cultural custom) a friendly Eskimo's culturally accustomed and eager wife by a U.S. Air Force corporal stationed in Reykjavik. Not that Nanook wasn't doing musically all right right there in Reykjavik, but New York is where the action is, songwriting-wise. There was the short story, Do Me Dirty, Daddy, Like You Done Last Night, the Touching, Heartwarming Story of a Young Girl and Her Affectionate Father. There was the musical comedy based on the life of Christ, A Pocketful of Miracles or, perhaps more in keeping with the current trend on Broadway of short, punchy titles, simply Oh, Jesus! with an exclamation point. There had been the novel about the Chinese cook who accompanies his knight-master (the first-person narrator) on one of the Crusades, later taking his master's place on the battlefield following his, the knight's, wounding. Title: The Chink in My Armor. Then there had been . . .

But these attacks of literary dementia, all, had come upon him late at night, he had been, in every instance, exhausted, depressed, at least mildly smashed, and with time running out! And, of course, increasingly more apprehensive about Miriam's increasingly less veiled references to the possible imminence of some tangible results. Under such conditions, he told himself, a certain degree of panic was justified. Perhaps even inevitable. Even professional writers must surely experience some such fearful hours; so, certainly in the case of one such as he . . .

And besides, no one of those insane, desperate inventions of his weary, boozed brain had ever been put to paper, it was not as though he had ever, for an instant, entertained the possibility of their being committed to type.

Finally, warily, as though in the face of uncertain danger, he reached for the typewriter and rolled up the paper before him, clear of the bar, exposing the small block of black print to unobstructed view. With cautious eyes, he read:

> On the eve of her fourteenth birthday April Holliday, wearing a smile and a diaphragm, stepped into the bedroom and threw herself, in celebration, upon the pale, quivering body of her fifth and last lover.

Through the study's open door at his back he heard the apartment door close with a loud thump of unwelcome interruption. Cassie or Miriam? He listened to the wooden rattle of coat hangers in the foyer closet, then the closet door closed on its cheap, imitation brass-plated hinges with the usual flimsy-wooded crack against the jamb. It was a sound that often depressed him and caused him to remember with some longing the solid thump of his boyhood doors on Central Park West. There was no question about it: If he could feel the weight of a good door in his fist he felt sure he would be able to accept on its own spurious terms the remainder of this angular, architecturally graceless cheesebox of a Luxury Apartment in this insanely expensive orangecrate of a Luxury Building.

On the eve of her fourteenth birthday, April Holliday . . . It was Cassie, he heard, her spurs jingling gently with each light-stepping, heavily-padded blow of her heels as she crossed the thick living room carpet toward the study door. . . . *Wearing a smile and a diaphragm . . .*

It could be hysteria. Again.

He crossed his arms on the typewriter, rested his head upon them, and permitted his eyes to close; he found it very restful; perhaps the imminent intrusion might not be quite so unwelcome after all. At the door, the tinkle of steel ceased. There was a brief silence.

"You asleep?" she asked softly, with enough voice to be heard but not so much as to wake him if he were.

"Yes," he mumbled into his forearm.

Tinkle, tinkle as she moved. "What's happening?"

"I'm working." *Daddy's working,* he thought, a private irony, remembering.

"Oh . . ." She hesitated. "I didn't hear the typewriter so I didn't think you were writing."

At the beginning, at the time of his decision, in the course of all the congratulations offered and procedural advice rendered by several of his writer friends (all of whom—with one exception—worked their craft in their homes), he discovered the one factor shared by all was that the words "Daddy's working," spoken by the wives to the children, carried much the same weight as In God We Trust or You Can Be Sure If It's Westinghouse. The closed door to the professional writer's room of work was a fact never violated.

But he was not a professional and his door was open.

And, after all, excepting the last seven months, Cassie's experience of his "work," for all the days of her ten years, had been watching him leave home in the morning and return again at evening. "Work" was something he did elsewhere. And got money for. A lot of money. "Writing" was something he did right here in the apartment. And it wasn't bringing in a nickel. He couldn't fairly hold her responsible for failing to grasp significance that even he had begun to suspect might not exist at all.

It might not! Face it!

"How's it going?"

"The outcome is still in doubt." His head remained in the comforting cradle of his arms, his eyes fluttered shut again.

"Not so good, huh?" she said gently, seriously.

He lifted his head, turned to look at her, and smiled. "How's it going with you?"

"Fair to middling," she nodded, lips pursed.

"Did you get the *TV Guide?*"

She pulled the small, folded magazine from her hip pocket, handed it to him, and dropped herself onto the tweed sofa, swinging her boots up.

"Watch the spurs," he said, opening the magazine to the week's Movie Guide and watching her out of the corner of his eye with secret pleasure. She moved her feet, dangling her spurred heels harmlessly over the cushion's edge and pushed her wide-brimmed, high-crowned, mauve-colored hat to the back of her head. She pulled one of the tooled-leather holsters from its place on her hip, rested it more comfortably between her thighs and pulled the toy six-shooter from it. Her middle finger thrust through the trigger guard, she proceeded to execute a warming-up maneuver. In her hand the gun was absurdly large and cumbersome, with a heavy authenticity, but she handled it adroitly and with the usual utter concentration she brought to everything she did.

The half-smile of love lingering on his lips, he slid his eyes to the open *TV Guide*. *It's a Wonderful Life* jumped up and hit him almost instantly. Wednesday on the Late Show. James Stewart, Donna Reed. 1946. Directed by Frank Capra, if memory served. He hadn't seen that one in years! He took up a red ballpoint pen and carefully circled the entry. Then he saw with some chagrin that at 11:35 that same night *Wing and a Prayer* was on Channel 11. 1944, Don Ameche, Dana Andrews, aircraft carrier in the Pacific, World War II. A good one, he remembered. It would be a hard choice to make. He circled it, deciding he would wait until Wednesday and see which way his mind blew.

He started at the sound of Cassie's pistol thumping to the floor and turned to watch as she leaned over to retrieve it, the two long, auburn pigtails dangling from beneath the hat. This cowboy phase wasn't a sexual thing, he was sure. There could be no girl child more feminine than Cassie. Then, gazing at her, she unaware of his rueful attention, he wondered again as he had so often lately: How much longer a child? Her breasts had already begun to bud, faintly, faintly. They would have to get her a training bra one of these days soon, he had said to Miriam, a joke that emerged with a soft edge of regret that surprised him. Christ, in all likelihood she would begin to menstruate one of these days. Months. He had read not long ago that girls were maturing much sooner than ever before, menstruating at an earlier and earlier age with each succeeding generation. Ten years old? It seemed too soon, so early! But times were changing. *Everything* was changing. And, menses commenced, *then* what?

With kids these days, who knew? Anything. Everything. You had only to look at the kids these days to know that. You could figure maybe six out of every ten kids you passed on the street these days were balling each other's brains out every chance they got! And there were so many of them! Millions! All that post-war frenzy of fucking had caught up with us at last. At thirty-eight years of age it was very depressing to feel as though most of the people in the world were seventeen, and most of them girls, sweet young snatch, stunning creatures (why were they all so beautiful, girls weren't that good looking when he was a kid) with long, straight, shining hair and soft, round rumps and eyes that knew everything.

And balling constantly! Without giving it a second thought!

He could remember, with morose regret at having been born too soon, his own youth, his coming of carnal age, when the most to be hoped for was the furtive clutching of a fifteen-year-old breast with, maybe, *on a very special occasion*, the rewarding pressure of a hardening nipple under the sweating palm (Oh, heaven!), testimony that the usually terrified, trembling girl was amenable in spirit if in no other, longed-for, sense. In *his* youth the consummation most devoutly dared wished were thighs that would part to the groping stealth of an adolescent male hand on the silk between them; not clamp shut, hot, damp, immobilizing.

And here were these kids today boffing each other's brains out every chance they got! . . . *wearing a smile and a diaphragm, stepped into the bedroom and threw herself . . . on the eve of her fourteenth . . .* Maybe he wasn't getting hysterical again. April Holliday was possible.

"When are we going to get the tree?"

"What?"

"When are we going to get the tree?" Cassie repeated, standing, settling the holster comfortably at her hip.

"What tree?" he asked, vaguely, his mind on April, wondering where she might take him, after throwing herself upon that pale, quivering body.

"The Christmas tree."

"Soon," he nodded, listening to April whisper possibilities in his ear. Suppose that pale, quivering body was . . . a female! . . . No. That was out. Definitely. The waiting flesh on April's busy bed must be pale, quivering, and *definitely male*. But . . . try this. Perhaps . . . *perhaps . . . lacking an erection?* . . . It was a thought. . . . He thought . . . Yes, he liked it, April was falling upon a body at the moment unprepared, in the desired sense, to respond to her obvious intentions.

He turned abruptly from the terrace door and hurried back to the desk. Ignoring the typewriter—the thought was too form-less and undeveloped for that yet—he seized a pencil and scrib-bled on the notepad: *No erection!!*

"If we wait till the last minute," Cassie said, whipping the pistol from the holster, "there won't be a decent one left."

"Decent what?" Fifth and *last* lover. Why *last?* What did *that* mean?

"A decent tree."

"Cas, don't bug me about the tree right now, okay, hon?" He took up his glass, cracked an ice cube against his teeth in drain-ing it of what little watery gin remained in it, and left the study, pondering the seeming indifference of April's last, lamentably limp lover.

He felt almost feverish. *This could really be it.* Soon, soon now, he might be able to look Miriam directly in the eye, no more evasions in response to her polite inquiries about his progress, no more frantic typing of the goddam alphabet, feigned industry at her approach, *How's it going?* He might soon be able at last to offer her some part of the results that she had every reason to expect after so long a time. How many reams of mis-used, crumpled paper had rattled down the incinerator chute in seven months? Five to go. Five more months and his year of long-dreamed freedom would be at an end. . . .

But, enough of that, enough.

How old was he, this pale character on the bed? Older than April, certainly. That felt right, he didn't quite see April messing around with someone her own tender age. Not that it wasn't a possibility, of course, where April was concerned, nothing might prove to be beyond the realm of possibility. But at the moment her companion felt older. *Much* older? No. No good, old Vladi-mir had fenced off that literary preserve for all time. But defi-nitely older.

The telephone rang.

"Walter?"

"Yeh?"

"It's Faith."

"Faith!"

"How are you, hon?"

"I'm fine! Where are you?"

"Here."

"In New York?"

"Yes."

"Wonderful. Wenjigemin?"

"What?"

"Sorry, I was lighting a cigarette, I said when did you get in?"

"This morning."

"Well, when do we see you?"

"When do you want to?"

"Well, I'd say right now, but I promised Cas we'd get a tree today which usually turns into an expedition till we find one that suits her discriminating tastes, and Miriam isn't here. So, how about, oh, about five, you can stay for dinner."

"Fine. How is Cassie?"

"Just fine."

"And Miriam?"

"Oh, fine, she's fine. Listen, we saw your latest picture just last week."

"Ugh."

"Nevertheless, *you* were wonderful. As usual. Where are you staying, by the way?"

"I borrowed a friend's apartment, she's out of town. Well, I'll see you around five, then."

"Perfect. It's good to hear your voice. Why don't you ever write?"

"Would you believe I broke both my hands?"

"I'll believe anything once."

"That's going to be your downfall one day."

"I don't doubt it. Will you be in town for Christmas?"

"Looks like it."

"Wonderful."

"See you later, Walter."

" 'Bye, Faith."

As he stepped again into the study, his glass full again, Cassie, without taking her eyes from the twirling pistol, said, "What does 'Eros, who was a god for the ancients, is a problem for the moderns' mean?"

She flung the pistol end over end in the air, pirouetted on one heel in a full circle and caught the glinting butt an instant before it hit the floor.

Dazzled, he said, "What?"

" 'Eros, who was a god for the ancients, is a problem for the moderns'," she repeated. "What does that mean?"

"You've been snooping around my desk again, Cassie. I told you about that."

"No, it was on a piece of paper I found on the floor, right there," she protested simply, genuinely innocent, pointing the gun barrel at a spot on the carpet next to the desk. "I just was putting it back on the desk and I couldn't help but see what was written on it."

He wondered whether his required privacy about his "work" was a little overdone, as Miriam had suggested. But, if nothing else, it saved him from having to answer impossible questions from Cassie, who asked unhesitatingly about anything she didn't understand. He smiled, remembering the night at the dinner table when she had taken her first sip of milk and asked what does cunt mean? Where—after the expected silence—had she heard that? her mother wanted to know. It was on a piece of paper on Daddy's desk, Cassie told her. Casually. Of course, the word in question had been contained in a perfectly legitimate line of dialogue (or "snatch of dialogue" as he had actually put it to Miriam later; but she didn't catch it, or pretended not to: He sometimes suspected that she was not too crazy about his puns and occasionally pretended ignorance of them—possibly in an attempt to discourage them). But Cassie had plucked it out of its context as the sentence's only uncomprehended word and dropped it—hot and steaming, so to speak, disconcertingly exposed—in the middle of the dining table. There was nothing to do but deliver a brief and circumspect explanation of the uses of anatomical slang following which Miriam, as casually as possible, suggested that it might be best for Cassie to abide by her father's rule about his desk and what he was writing on it.

Cassie spoke.

"Hm?" he murmured, turning his gaze from the window.

"I said, did you write it?"

"Write what?"

"Eros who was a——"

"Oh. No." Would that I had, my girl, would that I——

"What does it mean?"

"It's a little difficult to explain."

"I gather it's some sort of clue."

He smiled vaguely. "Yes, something like that. Eros was the name of a sort of god that people worshiped once, you see. He represented love, you see? So——"

"Like God is Love? That?"

"Well, no, this was physical love. Purely physical." *None of that* spiritual *shit, kid!* "This wasn't God. This was *a* god."

"*A* god," she agreed.

The good old ancient days when there was a god for all occasions, occasionally Eros, and all those nubile virgins screaming prayers at the tops of their sweet voices and humping themselves practically to death on those carved stone phalli. They were shaped from marble, weren't they? They must have been. What other kind of stone would have, could have been acceptable? Texturally.

He sipped, grinning: Were there sadomasochists in that day and age who took their pleasure in, say, granite phalli? *The Rough Raunchers: The Psychosexual Lunatic Fringe in Pre-Christian Theology,* by Walter A. Hartman, 1127 pp. (Illustrated.)

He was getting hysterical again. Or stoned. Stone, stoned. He sipped. Waldo. That's it. The kid in the bed is named Waldo Stone, he's twenty-six years old, a virgin but not a fag. And limp as an empty sock.

Jesus Christ! *Gunga Din!* The Late, Late, Late Show, Thursday. Well, Friday morning, actually, 4:15. He hadn't seen *Gunga Din* in at least three years, maybe four. Cary Grant, Doug Fairbanks, Jr., Victor McLaglen, MGM, 1938, '39?

He circled and asterisked the entry in the *TV Guide.*

He could go to bed a little early Thursday night and set the alarm.

"So, what's the problem?" asked tenacious Cassie.

When Faith failed to appear on promised time, they waited a while longer then went ahead and decorated the tree. Cassie was anxious to get on with it and it was unfair to keep her waiting indefinitely when it began to look as though Faith was not going to arrive at all.

Miriam was disappointed that her sister was not there to help with the tree trimming, it would have meant a lot to Faith, she told Walter—just like old times. Walter wondered if trimming the tree would have been Faith's most exciting event of the week, but did not voice his doubt. He was far less puzzled than his wife at Faith's defection and shared her alarm (which soon developed) not at all. He reminded her of the last occasion on which Faith had been in New York, nearly a year before, when she was to have met them in a theater lobby fifteen minutes before curtain time; she never appeared and they next heard from her a week later via a picture postcard, Air Mail Special Delivery, from Acapulco (*Apologies. How was the play? Love. F.*).

Miriam conceded his point but wished Walter had gotten Faith's telephone number or a more accurate idea of her whereabouts beyond her vague friend's vague borrowed apartment. They might at least be able to reach her, to know if something had happened to her.

Walter was unable to think of Faith as someone to whom "things happened." Faith, Walter thought, was at no one's mercy.

When finally the tree was trimmed, he returned to the study where April Holliday and her last lover awaited him in the typewriter. (Why *last?* he wondered again. Was it to be an early Juliet death for April, would his readers never see an adult result of her sexually insane childhood and adolescence?) He worked enthusiastically for an hour or so and was reluctant to call a halt that evening when finally it came time to dress for the Finleys' party. He would readily have canceled out on it, but

Miriam was eager to go. And, although it was ostensibly no more than an ordinary Christmas season party, he knew that there would be an element of special celebration for Jack's recent promotion at the network to vice president and he was friendship-bound to put in a congratulatory appearance.

He pushed himself away from the desk and delayed yet a few moments more to consider the book which, since the day before, had lain secreted in the bottom desk drawer in its cheery wrapping.

Timing was important. As always, in all things. Earlier in the afternoon he had thought to present it that very night, on their return from the party, confident that Miriam would be in her usual gay and receptive post-party mood. (The time last summer in the deck chair on the terrace had been after a party.) But he had decided finally that its introduction must be matter-of-fact, almost clinical in its detachment. (Time enough later to put passion where the scientist's cool-headed mouth was.)

Tomorrow morning, then. Cassie would almost certainly be off somewhere on one of her usual Saturday morning expeditions. (If not, he would *send* her off somewhere.) There would not even be the otherwise distracting presence of a maid since the latest of what began to seem like an endless parade of them had not been heard from since leaving work on Wednesday evening, would almost certainly never be heard from again, and her replacement had yet to be found.

Yes, it would be perfect. Undisturbed privacy in the cool-headed light of morning.

At the party he stood in a quiet corner listening with commiseration to Sam Fleming who was relating the latest disastrous situation at the network involving the last script with which Walter had been involved before beginning his sabbatical leave. Sam was the producer, and regretting it. Walter admitted to his share of culpability inasmuch as it had been he who had suggested the casting of Barbara Finch in the lead role—despite the problems the network had had with her on a production the year before—and it was Barbara who was now the cause of the serious difficulties. Sam graciously demurred, reminding Walter that it had been, finally, he and he alone, Sam Fleming ("sometimes referred to as Fleming the Brilliant," he accused himself) who had approved the hiring of Barbara Finch ("sometimes referred to as Barbara the Beast"), knowing full well her alarming reputation for terrifyingly erratic behavior.

"But this time she's outdoing herself, Walter," Sam said, mournfully. "It's madness, madness."

Jack Finley's voice intruded behind Walter's ear. "Listen, you fuck, when are you going to stop that jerking off and come back to work?" he demanded affectionately.

Walter smiled. "From the sound of things, you need me."

"I've been telling him about *All or Nothing*," Sam said to Jack, sadly.

"That cunt," Jack said. "Did he tell you what she's doing to that play?"

"What kind of way is that to talk about one of your favorite people?" Walter asked.

"It's easy for you to joke about it, you prick," Jack said fondly, then, with an accusatory jerk of his head at Walter, turned to Sam Fleming: "First he tells us to hire her, then he walks out and leaves us holding the bag. On second thoughts," he added, turning again to beaming Walter, "*don't* come back—you've fucked us up enough as it is."

"She sends her regards, by the way," Sam said to Walter with the parenthetical irrelevance of despair.

"If it was up to me," said Jack, "that cunt'd be out on her ass tomorrow."

"It's too late for that," Sam said, regretting it.

Patty Finley joined them and asked whose ass they were discussing and would it be of any interest to her.

"Not unless you have some interests I don't know about," Jack told his wife. "I'm telling you, Walter, there isn't an actor alive, male, female, or undecided who doesn't belong in a cage or a playpen, one or the other. Have you heard the one about the little Dutch boy and the dyke?"

Later, Walter spent quite some time with a tall, big-breasted volatile English novelist who drank a great deal, but well, and called him luv and darling with the distant intimacy of the English that he always found charming and, in women, sometimes provocative. She was in America, she told him, to research for a film she was to write on the alleged American sexual revolution and claimed that in the course of her observations to date she was coming to believe that the average American bedroom was a "disaster area," and, "to borrow a word or two from the economics chaps, underprivileged and undeveloped." Walter wondered to himself at the nature and extent of the research that might have led her to her U.S. bedroom crisis conclusions, and tried to change the subject. He assumed his attempt had been successful until a few moments later when, following a brief review of the current New York theater scene—hopeless in her estimate—and slyly chewing on her martini's lemon peel, she abruptly asked him if they might get together one day, lunch perhaps.

He tried to remember if he had said or done anything that could have planted and nurtured such a possibility in her mind. He found himself guiltless—beyond the occasional glancing blows his eyes had dealt her marvelous breasts, a harmless assault to which she must surely have been accustomed. He murmured a noncommittal possibility, pointedly failing to ask where she might be reached.

Still later that night he found himself again thinking about the superbly-knockered novelist, imagining hers the thighs that so tenderly vised his head, hers the . . .

Distressed and guilty, he concentrated on the identity of true flesh and guiltily moved up and over Miriam and guiltily covered her, and guiltily grinned into her gaping mouth: "I guess I nipped *that* in the bud!"

She seemed not to have heard.

He had recovered from the injury to his knee, allowing for a positional straightforwardness that was no less satisfying for all its traditional simplicity.

It was the end of a perfect day, he thought, drifting limp into sleep.

Bring on tomorrow!

Tomorrow the World, United Artists, 1944, Frederic March, Betty Field, Skippy Homeier, directed by . . .

6 In the study the next morning Walter saw the Apollo 8
astronauts safely off on man's first journey to the moon,
then switched off the television and went directly to the
desk drawer and lifted the package from it. By now fully prepared, confident, in sly, high spirits, he went without hesitation
to the door.

In the living room, Miriam was speaking on the telephone.
"Fine," she smiled, nodding. "That'll give us time to get out the
red carpet, we keep it stored in the basement. 'Bye, hon." She
hung up and said, "That was Faith, she's coming over later."

"Again? So soon? After that lovely visit we had with her only
yesterday?"

"She sounds very odd," Miriam said.

"Odder than usual?"

"What do you mean?" she asked, with a frown of defense for
her sister.

"Nothing," he shrugged. "You have an odd sister, you've said
so yourself occasionally. What happened to her yesterday?"

"She didn't say exactly, she said she'd explain later. But she
wants to stay for a few days." She frowned at the floor and toed
the carpet. "Those damn spurs are wrecking the rugs."

"Stay where?"

"Here," Miriam said vaguely, chewing her lip.

"Here?" He pointed at the floor, trying to clarify the geography.

"Yes," Miriam said.

"Why? I mean, fine, but it's a little unusual."

"Yes. She didn't say why, just if she could stay here for a few days. She sounded very strange."

He had devoted as much time as he cared to to Faith and her sounds of strangeness. His mission had been delayed long enough, he thought, and he was impatient now and anxious to proceed.

He hesitated a moment more, then placed the package in front of her on the coffee table and sat in a chair and looked at her.

"What's that?" she asked, preoccupied.

"A present."

She smiled, brightening somewhat. "So soon?"

"Well, it's not really a Christmas present. More of an all-year-round present, you might say."

"Oh!"

Pleased, curious, her attention fully attracted now, she took up the package and tore the brittle, crackling gift wrapping from it. Then she frowned, and gazed for what seemed to Walter to be a rather long time at the cover of the book. He saw, not with her, but in retinal memory, the bright distinctive cover design, above the title the male and female symbols limned thickly in blood red, the male arrow perpendicularly penetrating the female circle, and experienced a moment of suspicious uncertainty and hesitation: Was there something unnecessarily suggestive and vaguely pornographic about that design? *Had he been taken in by a piece of cleverly disguised smut?*

"What's this?" Miriam finally asked, warily.

"Well, it's a book," he pointed out, and cleared his throat.

Clearly puzzled, she looked at him for an instant before she spoke again. "It's a sex book," she said.

"Well, yes, I guess you could call it that, something like that."

"What do you mean, you guess? That's what it is, Walter. *The Amorous Arts in Marriage*," she said, reading the cover. "It's a sex book." Frowning, she riffled quickly through the pages, an act not so much of curiosity at their content as unseeing confusion at the fact of their presence in her hands. "What am I supposed to do with this?"

"Well, books are to read, darling," he answered pleasantly.

"Is this some kind of cruel joke, Walter? Are you putting me on or something?"

"Of course not," he protested.

She looked at him in silence as though waiting for him to go on; but he already sensed that his best procedure for the moment would be response, not initiation: He would take his cues from her.

"Well, I don't understand, Walter," she said finally, fretful. "I mean, would you mind explaining to me what this is all about?"

"Well, if you read the book, you'll see," he said encouragingly, maintaining his equanimity against the pressure of an already gathering tension.

"Why should I read the book? It's a *sex* book," she repeated, thrusting it at him face up as though the repugnant nature of the book had merely escaped his attention until now.

"Why do you make it sound so distasteful?" he asked. It was the gentlest of rebukes.

"Is there supposed to be something in this book I don't already know or something?" she demanded. "It that the idea?"

He hesitated for an instant. "Well, *is* it?"

The gauntlet was thrown down; he eyed it warily for a moment before he risked picking it up. "Well, yes." Her face became dangerously inscrutable. "You can't tell until you read it," he went on quickly. She opened her mouth to speak, then hesitated and closed it again: As intended, his assertion was difficult to deny. In her hesitation she had lost valuable ground: He occupied it quickly, rising, gesturing for the book. "How about this?" he suggested, taking it from her hand. "Do you know anything about this, for instance?" He thumbed hurriedly through the pages, searching for one of the chapters that he had found especially promising. He found the page he sought and opened the book forcefully with determined hands, cracking the cheap spine's hard glue. He returned the book to her, nodding with conviction and encouragement. "How about this, do you know anything about this? Just as an example."

She took the book from him reluctantly but refused to look at it. She averted her face and with pursed lips clenched and un-clenched her teeth, rippling the flesh of her checks.

"Will you at least look at it?" he asked patiently.

She turned to glance briefly at him, then moved her dark eyes to the opened book. He read with her in his mind. *Chapter Seven. Ceremonial Lovemaking for Special Occasions.* Too soon, he knew, to have read much beyond the chapter heading, she looked up from the page and directly at him.

"You've got to be kidding, Walter," she said, quietly.

He pounced. "Miriam, that book was written by a very repu-table man who obviously knows what he's talking about. *I* didn't write it. Don't you see, that's just the point, I mean, we aren't the only ones who have this problem. There's the proof right in your hand. We're not the only ones. If we were the only ones there wouldn't *be* books like that *around* these days. *Thousands* of them."

There was a pause. "What problem?" she asked, forcibly un-perturbed.

"Well, sex, Mimi! Sex! Haven't you been listening!" As angered with his loss of control as with Miriam for provoking it, he strode to the bar. He had already mixed a drink and taken a first impatient sip before it occurred to him to wonder what time it was. Too early for a drink, certainly. Under ordinary circumstances. But these weren't! He took a second, defiant swallow and said: "You realize of course how most men solve this problem for themselves."

"No, how?" she said levelly.

Head atilt, with a sigh that regretted the inescapable truth for which he personally was of course not responsible, he said, "They seek solace elsewhere, Mim."

She gazed at him for a moment; but he refused to flinch. "Is that some kind of a threat?"

"Have I ever threatened you?"

"Is it a threat?"

He withstood the deadly assault of her eyes for a moment more before he turned away slightly daunted. "No."

"Okay," she said.

He wheeled on her. "Well, don't be so goddam *smug*, Miriam! The situation could change anytime!"

"It *is* a threat," she said threateningly.

"Oh, for Christ's sake." His weary shoulders collapsed. "Miriam, would it kill you to look through it a little? Would it kill you?"

"No, it wouldn't kill me. I'd just feel pretty silly."

"Why?"

"I don't know why. I just would, that's all," she said reasonably.

Too reasonably, he thought. This was something new. Always in the past during confrontations like these she had exhibited a demure reserve that was occasionally touching but which he most often found exasperating—there was something absurd about a thirty-two-year-old, married, much-laid woman coming on like the Reluctant Virgin. This time, however, her conviction seemed too assured to permit of the possibility of that usual shyness and he wondered nervously what might be the implications of its absence. "Well, try to tell me why you'd feel silly," he coaxed.

She breathed a vexed sigh and snapped her tongue against the roof of her mouth and waved the book at him. "Well, for God's sake, Walter, I mean, just for an example, *what special occasions?* It's ridiculous!"

"Well, obviously those are for us to decide, Mim," he said grinning. "I mean, whoever reads the book. You can't expect doctor whatsisname to do *all* the work, a certain amount has to be left to the imagination and discretion of the reader. Or *lack* of discretion, possibly," he added, smiling more broadly.

But she was not amused. "I'm not reading any sex book, Walter, and that's that." She stood and moved to the terrace doors and stopped there as though she didn't know where else to go.

"We're never going to get anywhere," he began, a shade too didactic for even his own taste, "if you insist on having such a closed mind about it."

"Where does it end, Walter?" she asked abruptly, turning, and with a decidedly bull-by-the-horns demeanor.

"Where does what end?"

"All this," she said, gesturing vaguely. "I mean, how far exactly do you want to go? Suppose I do read the thing, and we . . . do something, and then we do something else . . . and something else? When will it be enough for you? I mean, where will it end? Have you thought about that?"

She had touched the single exposed nerve in the complex, sensitively balanced network of his erotic system. He had of course thought about it. He had thought about it a good deal, in fact, and was not unware of the implications, the possibilities. On the one hand, hopefully it would never end! There would always be something else, more, another, higher level of experience, of fulfillment, of . . . of bliss!

But (on the other hand) was that true? Was it *possible?* Could he believe that? More importantly, could she?

What happens when secret dreams aren't secret anymore?

"I don't know," he answered defensively. "I mean, I'm not programming some kind of computerized program, you know."

Christ! It was degenerating into some kind of goddam *debate!* It wasn't supposed to be an intellectual discussion! These matters were the stuff of the emotions! Intangible! Nebulous! They were to be felt, sensed! Not nailed to the wall like a goddam chart! And you either felt them or you didn't!

"Walter," she said, attracting his attention with her quiet hesitancy. She paused, evidently experiencing some difficulty in continuing. "After the last time we had one of these—discussions . . . well, I sat down and I counted. I made a careful count to the best of my memory."

She fell silent again.

"A count of what?" he urged, encouraged.

"Well . . ." She faltered again briefly, shyly, then seemed to gather the necessary force to speak and said quickly, "Well, at one time or another we've had sex seven different ways, Walter. Plus all the other stuff."

"I'll accept your count," he smiled, anxious to know what she was getting at. If anything.

"I'm serious, Walter," she said, with a trace of warning.

He straightened his cautioned mouth. "Sorry. Okay. Seven. So?" She hesitated again and he thought to use the time to make a quick mental count of his own and arrived at six. How did she remember better than he? As to what she called "the other stuff" he assumed she meant what little—and so pathetically limited!—variety he had so far been able to inject into . . .

"Well, what more do you want, Walter?" she asked, with a desperate impatience

He felt suddenly very depressed. He wasn't getting through to her at all! If this was the extent of her independent thought the future was hopeless! How do I love thee, let me count the ways, I love thee in the Basic Man Above Face-to-Face Position, I love thee in the Woman Astride Position, I love thee in the Standing Position, Approach from the Rear. . . .

Even the expression she used. Had sex. Why couldn't she say she had made a count and they'd *fucked* in seven different positions? (He still counted six.) Or, screwed? (No, wait. That was it: the time on the kitchen table. Was she counting that as a position? Which of course it was not, it had been more a matter of location than technique.) Or, *balled. You've balled me in seven different positions, Walter.* Impossible. It made him smile to think of it.

"What's so funny?"

"Nothing," he said, averting his face. *Nobody balled Miriam!* You balled that plump chick in the book store, you balled the hooker-schoolteacher in the Hatter's, you balled that secretary of Jack Finley's with the wild legs and the screaming eyes. But you definitely didn't ball Miriam!

"Well, what are you grinning about?"

"Nothing. Really," he protested, and moved away to escape her. He was afraid he might laugh aloud. The booze, probably, it was certainly too early in the day to be drinking, he was probably a little high, already! He had to stop thinking about it. *Ball me, Walter, ball me, darling, oh baby ball me* . . .

Oh, good God.

He clenched his teeth and his throat and tried desperately to hold it in; but the laugh swelled in his mouth like a filling balloon, there was no stopping it.

When it burst he watched helplessly, unable to speak, while her face passed through the beginnings of a variety of possible responses, surprise, bewilderment, consternation, pain, outrage. Outrage it was, finally, and her face went white.

"Well, all right, Walter, if you think I'm so goddam *funny*," she bellowed, "you can just go *fuck* yourself!"

He wailed, tried to speak to her furious back, "No, Mimi . . . wait . . . no, you don't . . . you don't . . . understand. . . . Listen . . . Mimi . . . ?

The bedroom door crashed shut.

She didn't understand!

7

"Am I still welcome?" Faith said.

"We're still trying to decide," Walter smiled, "but come in and wait in the foyer while we work it out."

He took the single piece of luggage from her hand as she stepped through the door and kissed her offered cheek awkwardly; he heard her lips kiss the air near his ear. She held his free hand in both of hers while he nudged the door shut with the suitcase and they exchanged extravagant admirations, each for the other's appearance of blooming health. Then she released his hand and before he could ask for her coat she moved and, mini-minked, brown-suede-booted, her lightly tinted sunglasses gazing eyeless at the ceiling from the top of her dark-red head, drifted into the living room in her familiarly vague, distracted way. (To Walter, Faith seemed quite often to be in the process of working out some troubling and impossibly complex problem whose solution required her almost total concentration, leaving only a fragment of her attention free to be applied to the natural demands of normal social intercourse.)

He watched her skin herself of the superb looking coat which she threw carelessly across the back of the sofa. She sighed deeply then turned, smiling abruptly, and directed the startling violet of her eyes at him.

"Is Mim here?"

"Oh, yes, sure!" he answered, after an instant's distraction of his own at the uncoated impact of her. Awkwardly, he remembered the suitcase in his hand, put it down, and faced in the direction Miriam had been moving when last seen over half an hour before. "Miriam! Faith's here!" he called, with what he knew might, under the circumstances, be a false gaiety. (The fact that Miriam had not emerged from the bedroom since she had disappeared so furiously into it might be merely coincidental, but he doubted it; in fact, he had allowed for what he thought to be a suitable cooling-off period and had been ready to make his cautious advance on the bedroom, with explanations and apologies, but Faith's arrival had interrupted that.)

"Before I forget," Faith said, "what's the picture with Jack Benny where he's an angel or something and uses an elevator to——"

"*The Horn Blows at Midnight*," Walter said unhesitatingly, "Jack Benny, Alexis Smith, Allyn Joslyn, directed by . . . Raoul Walsh, I think, around, oh, 1945. Why?"

Faith beamed. "You're too much, Walter."

At that moment, Miriam burst into the room, her arms spread wide, and cried out her sister's name. In the intensity of the subsequent excitement she generated it was several minutes before Walter realized that she was very clearly directing nothing his way, evidence enough that his earlier, misunderstood laughter was not forgotten and certainly unforgiven. Finally, when the mood began to shift to a calmer key, she appeared to be making some attempt to acknowledge and include him, providing (for Faith's benefit, he assumed) the sketchy outline, if not the color, of domestic harmony. Between his preoccuption with Miriam's mood and the natural confusion of the reunion's opening babble (who, what, when, where, why, how is? and have you seen? and did you hear?) the first clearly recordable question and answer was Miriam's demand to know what had brought Faith to New York and Faith's cryptic response that it was a long story, promising to tell it. Her elusive manner, however, implied (at best) perhaps and eventually. Then she turned to Walter abruptly and asked what he had to warm up a cold girl. He asked her to name her poison; she suggested he name it, that she would drink it. It was all somewhat absurdly Act One, Scene One stuff, Walter thought, banter, banter on the surface with a lot of tense subtext. Then the telephone rang. *On cue,* he said to himself, and almost smiled, wondering if perhaps they didn't really exist at all, had been imagined by Abe Burrows who would any moment now pop up from behind a chair and tell them to take it once more from the top.

He picked up the phone at the bar, listened for a moment, then spoke across the room to Miriam to tell her that it was the meat department at Gristede's answering her call, her order seemed to have been misplaced, would she care to give it to them again. Miriam made a sound of impatience, rolled her annoyed eyes at Faith, and said she would take the call in the kitchen. She spoke back across her departing shoulder.

"We saw your latest just last week."

"Let's not discuss it," Faith suggested.

"Well, it wasn't very good," Miriam agreed, regretfully, "but as Mama would have said, you stood out."

"All over," Walter smirked. In one of her scenes she had been, so far as one could tell, stark naked. He remembered her thighs, covered now (but not all that very much) by the short suede skirt; he remembered the tantalizingly brief glimpse of the gentle pale valley at the base of her spine which curved now invisibly against the arm of the sofa. And the even more tantalizing (because even briefer) flash of one magnificent breast (the left, he calculated). Faith smiled toward him, vaguely appreciative of his appreciative comment. Miriam was less amused and her glance grazed his eyes like sandpaper as she passed him.

Gone, Miriam left behind an inexplicably nervous (for him) silence which Walter felt an urgent impulse to end as quickly as possible.

At the bar, pouring, his back to his sister-in-law, he said, "You get better every picture." He half-turned to her and, mock oracle, added, "I predict stardom."

"I haven't decided yet," Faith replied.

"Whether you'll be a star?"

"Whether I want to be one."

Her reply suggested that it was a matter entirely at her disposal, a unilateral decision having nothing to do with the intercessions or influences of others, and Walter marveled a little at her self-confidence. He admired self-confident women. On the other hand, they sometimes made him a little nervous, too. "The critics seem to agree you're a very promising young actress," he said.

"Which is rather presumptuous of them," she replied vaguely, and added (charmingly, he thought), "I mean, I haven't promised anyone anything."

Walter smiled and turned from the bar and nearly stumbled, splashing a bit of liquid from each of the glasses, his hands instantly atremble at the sight before him. Faith sat gazing upon *The Amorous Arts in Marriage*, opened in her hands, her face concentrated but otherwise expressionless, revealing no attitude about what she read, offering no opinion. He cursed himself for having forgotten the book's presence on the coffee table and wondered how long she had been sitting there, just so, *reading*. He could see clearly even from where he stood that the book had quite naturally fallen open to the place at which the spine had been cracked earlier, by him. Hands shaking, face hot, with no other option open to him, he resumed his aborted approach; at which she glanced up briefly, closed the book, and replaced it carefully on the coffee table.

Then, as she took one of the trembling glasses from him, she looked up and, with the very gentlest and sweetest of obscene grins, asked, "What special occasions?"

He was beyond words. But even as he groped for them her smile altered, took on other dimensions and meanings. She raised her glass, bid him cheers, asked how things were in the TV racket, and sipped delicately.

Not only was she beautiful, mysterious, confident! She was wise and kind, he knew now! Still, he needed a moment more to recover, even to begin his recovery. He gulped at the glass seized tight in his fist while she waited, patient, understanding, inscrutable. "Well, fine," he said at last, nodding violently. "Wonderful. But without me at the moment." He smiled achingly, inanely, desperate to know what his course should be. The book was there! Ignore it, explain it, seize it?

She nodded upward. "Vacation?"

"Well, not exactly. In a way. But not really. I'm involved in other work, so you couldn't really call it a vacation." Ignore it! It was the only thing to do. "Of course, it *is* a vacation from television, if you look at it that way, just for a year, though, a kind of sabbatical, I've given myself a year," he said, forgetting instantly what it was he had just said.

"And he only has five months left," Miriam announced, coming through the door.

Left for what? Walter wondered, already pitying her, unprepared as she was for what awaited her on the coffee table, vulnerable, pathetically unaware of the fact that he and Faith had already agreed to pretend it was not there.

"For what?" Faith asked him. He looked dumbly at her, grateful for the postponement of discovery caused by Miriam's detour to the bar. "A year for what?" Faith asked.

"Oh. Yes, well . . . I'm writing, as a matter of fact," Walter nodded demurely into his glass. "A novel. I thought it might be a short story, a long short story, but it looks as though it'll be a novel. On the other hand, it could just possibly end up being a short story again, the issue is still in doubt at the moment." He grinned, shy, Henry Fonda.

"It seems to me," Miriam said, "after seven months you should know." Then, as though she realized the remark might have sounded excessively unkind, she looked at Faith, shrugged, and admitted, "But then, what do *I* know?"

"It's a kind of lifelong dream of mine," Walter said (stupidly, he thought), wondering how long it would be before Miriam saw what she could not fail, sooner or later, to see; and knowing that she would hold him solely responsible for the resulting ordeal of embarrassment she was about to endure. "Anyway, now that I can afford to, I've taken a year off to give it a try." Miriam left the bar, glass in hand.

Now?

"That's wonderful, Walter," Faith said with a quiet sincerity that warmed his pounding heart.

Then, steeled for the imminent discovery, he was abruptly discomposed as Miriam turned on her heel and started back toward the bar—another ice cube, a forgotten twist of lemon? *Why couldn't she sit down and get it over with, the suspense was killing him!* But she was asking Faith if it was true, as she had told Walter, that she would be here, in town, in New York, *home,* for Christmas. Faith was pleased to say that it was, and tallied the ghosts of her Christmases recently past, Rome last year, L.A. the year before, and the year before that, Lord, yes, Tucson, Arizona. He thought Tucson, Arizona, a bizarre place to be at Christmas, watching Miriam leaving the bar again, a touch of new yellow bobbing in her glass. Faith agreed.

Then Miriam was settling beside Faith on the sofa.

Now?

Expectant, almost conspiratorial, Miriam turned to her sister and said, "I can't wait any longer, is it true what we read about you and George Brady?"

Faith seemed vaguely startled. "About George and me?"

"Well, it was a blind item, naturally," Miriam conceded, "but I worked it out."

"What did it say?"

"Well, first of all, that he wants you to marry him."

"He's married," Faith pointed out.

"Mimi never has had too much patience with technicalities," Walter offered desperately, grinning.

When?

"Well, naturally, I was interested." Miriam smiled roguishly. "If he's anything like his movies. Is he?" she asked, and leaned forward toward the cigarette box on the coffee table.

Six inches from the cigarette box lay *The Amorous Arts in Marriage,* face shamelessly up.

Now!

"He *is* a movie," Faith said.

It was not necessary that Walter see Miriam's face: The sudden arrest of her cigarette-reaching hand, the abrupt rigidity of her forward-curving spine described her face's expression. Ignore it, Mimi! That's what *we're* doing! "Faith? How about a refill?" he shouted.

"No, hon, I'm fine, thanks," Faith said.

He rose nevertheless, in flight; but did not escape Miriam's darting look: If looks could kill, he thought, he estimated a fifty-fifty chance for his survival. But pitied his wife for all her unanswered, unspoken questions.

Behind him as he fled toward the temporarily safe cove of the bar, Miriam's voice cried out: "Of course, he might be a little old for you! How old is he, anyway! Forty-five?"

He wondered if she knew she was screaming.

"Fifty-one," he heard Faith answer.

"Fifty-one! Good Lord, you'd never think it!"

"Good living," Walter thought.

"Surgery," Faith corrected.

"Well, who are we to say?" Miriam asked, in her own panic forgiving George Brady his. "A movie star, his face is his fortune."

"That's very true," Walter said, embarrassed for his wife in her helpless banality, but helpfully joining her in it as ally as, with glass hastily brimful again, he floundered back toward the center of the storm. Where Miriam was wildly demanding (or so it sounded) to know the truth of the "nervous breakdown part of it." "It" being the column item in which George Brady's desire to marry Faith had been suspiciously coupled with the innuendo that he was on the near side of a mental collapse.

"*Is* he having a nervous breakdown?" she repeated.

He saw immediately that while his back was turned Miriam had somehow managed to turn the book face down, concealing its title, at least.

"He had it," Faith said.

She put a cigarette to her lips and leaned toward Walter for his hastily offered flame. He watched as Miriam took reckless advantage of the moment's distraction, snatched the book clumsily from the table and tried to bury it behind her in the sofa cushions. With the faintest flicker of an eye toward the tense activity beside her, Faith leaned back again with a sigh, exhaling smoke.

"He *had* it? *Really?*" Miriam said, managing a delayed, preoccupied shock.

"Yesterday," Faith nodded. She appeared to be elsewhere, deep in privacy.

"My God, are you sure? I mean, it was really a nervous breakdown?"

"I was with him at the time," Faith said, eyewitness to the certainty. "Flipped out completely."

"It was here in New York?" Miriam asked, momentarily startled, evidently having mentally placed George Brady in his more natural West Coast milieu.

"Mm," said Faith.

"That's why you didn't show up," Miriam guessed.

"More or less."

"No wonder. Well, how is he?"

"If Janine had her way I imagine he's under restraint at some discreet private hospital at the moment."

"How awful," Miriam said.

She was beginning to relax a little now, Walter saw, the desperate banalities were beginning to taper off. Although her hands were still trembling perceptibly and her face was a little flushed.

"Who's Janine?" she asked in afterthought.

Faith said, "His wife," and rose and drifted to the bar with her empty glass.

Intrigued now (provoked, as always, by the mystery of her), Walter prodded lightly: "Sounds like a complex situation," he smiled.

"Yes," Miriam offered, "what's it all about, anyway?"

"He wants me to marry him," said Faith.

"Lucky girl," Miriam said, but clearly with mixed feelings— Brady might very well be a desirable man, but he was a married one and there was a moral issue involved here, after all.

"No, I don't want to," Faith said.

"Oh," Miriam said with equal parts of disappointment and relief.

"So I decided to depart the scene for a while. I mean, this has been going on for a long time, you understand, and I finally decided to get away from it for a while. So I came here. But he had a private detective following me, of course."

"Good Lord," said Miriam.

"Who I didn't spot until after I arrived here, but I was able to get rid of him easily enough. In Bloomingdale's, yesterday morning."

"Bloomingdale's," Walter said.

"I had him arrested," Faith smiled.

"Really?" Miriam said.

"How did you do that?" Walter asked.

"Well, it wasn't really fair of me, I suppose, he was only doing his job, following me around, but he made me lose Greta Garbo and it made me mad, and——"

"Greta Garbo?"

"Yes, I was following Greta Garbo and I got so distracted at one point by the detective, I lost her in the crowd getting into an elevator. So, naturally I was angry and I took it out on the poor shlep of a detective. Anyway——"

"Why were you following Greta Garbo?" Miriam asked warily.

"Well, I thought it would be interesting," Faith replied, suddenly reflective. "I almost bumped into her coming out of a store on Fifty-seventh Street and I started following her and we wound up in Bloomingdale's." She paused to sip pensively at her glass. "And, do you know something fantastic?" she continued. "In all that way as far as I could tell not a single person recognized her. Garbo. Isn't that incredible? I mean, give them some tenth-rate television star and they'd all be stopping and turning and twittering and twitching, but the real thing—nothing." She shook her head and sighed, world-weary. "I think maybe the world is getting so full of crap no one can tell the real thing when they see it anymore." Walter restrained a warm smile. He became fascinated with the play of glittering lights reflecting off her hair as she paced back and forth before the terrace doors and was not aware that she had lapsed into another of her habitual and mysterious silences until he heard Miriam's voice, jarring him out of his reverie.

"Well, what about Brady?"

"Yes, well . . . where was I?" Faith said, concentrating.

"You lost Greta Garbo and had the detective arrested," Miriam prompted.

"How did you go about getting him arrested, by the way?" Walter asked, and took an annoyed glance from Miriam for having again deflected Faith from the pertinent facts.

"Oh, well, that wasn't so difficult. Actually I wasn't really sure he *had* been arrested finally, because I left before things got to that stage, but George told me later that he had been. Because, that's the point, you see, there really wasn't any point in my bothering about the detective at all since George had already followed me here, I mean he already knew from the detective, I guess, that I came to New York. Which I didn't know when I called you yesterday—that George was already here. But the detective probably called George in L.A. as soon as he realized I was going to stay on the bus all the way to New York, so——"

"What bus?" Miriam said.

"The bus I was on. Also the detective, of course, he was with me all the way, naturally."

"From Los Angeles?" Walter asked.

"Yes."

"You came all the way from L.A. in a bus?"

"Mm. So, once he was here, of course, George found out from my fink of an agent where I was staying, after I'd made him swear to promise not to tell anyone because of course I knew George would be looking for me. But he was also George's agent for years before George got into this new thing of his and, as George put it, when the chips were down, his ten percent of George had been a lot more than his ten percent of me so naturally he fessed up and told where I was."

"Agents are very realistic people," Walter grinned. "Who is this agent, by the way?"

"Harold Hall."

"Oh, Harold, yes, I know Harold well, he's——"

"Walter, would you let her tell the story?" Miriam suggested quietly.

"Sorry," Walter conceded.

"So, naturally, George called me—right after I talked to you, as a matter of fact," she said toward Walter, "yesterday, and said if I didn't come over to his hotel and talk to him he'd jump out the window."

"Good Lord," Miriam said.

"Of course, he didn't actually say it, he just intimated as much, which is what he always does, he knows when it comes to something like that a subtle innuendo is a lot more effective than an out-and-out threat. He also knows I always believe people when they say things like that, unfortunately—I mean that they're going to kill themselves. But yesterday I finally decided it was a pretty stupid weakness on my part, especially where George is concerned, and I told him no dice and goodbye. But then I got to thinking about it and getting worried again so I thought I should at least call him back. But there was no answer. So it was Faith Nightingale to the rescue again, of course, visions of George all over Central Park South, and when I got to the hotel he was in the bedroom sitting on the bed watching one of his old movies on TV and sort of redirecting it. That's something he does quite a lot. But the thing was, this time he was sitting there stark naked and the television wasn't turned on."

"Oh, boy," Miriam said.

"I'd call that a tip-off," Walter said.

"And to give you the whole picture, frankly, he had a pretty serious erection at the time."

"Good Lord," Miriam said.

Walter nearly laughed; but, in the face of Miriam's perhaps more appropriate concern, bit his lip and opted for gravity. He continued to experience the same ambiguity of response as Faith went on with her story, which was often amusing in its surface details but vaguely alarming in its implications considering George Brady's imminently official position in public life as a servant of the people.

With the vision of the naked and erectile Brady vivid in his mind (and, he presumed, certainly, perhaps even more so, in Miriam's) Faith explained her first crucial decision: not to confront Brady with the truth of the unoperating TV and the illusory movie, on the grounds that, first, anyone having a nervous breakdown was not likely to believe anyone who told him he was and, second, it might possibly be dangerous to do so; like waking a sleepwalker, Faith thought. Then, as with a sleepwalker, she decided on cautious observation, a waiting game, in the hope that Brady's condition might be only temporary, a passing response to his life's loosed demons. Having chosen her course, she settled down to respond on demand to Brady's occasional comments to her about what he imagined he was seeing on the television screen. Not to her as Faith, but as merely another presence in the room; so far as she could tell, he did not really know who she was. By staying alert (and with a good deal of sheer luck, she admitted), she was eventually able to identify the movie Brady was watching, *Thunder* in someplace, she could not remember where. *Thunder On the Yalu,* Walter told her, a Korean war movie. Yes, she told him, right. Fortunately she had seen the picture several years ago and, hazy as it was in her mind, she was able at least to inject some sense of legitimacy into her comments when Brady required them from her; then soon found herself sharing his intense concentration on the black TV screen as if perhaps the sheer force of his own conviction might cause her, too, to see something there. She laughed, admitting to the absurdity of the picture she was drawing for them; but then suggested in her own defense that it might have been nothing more than an extreme case of what everyone met with almost every day of their lives, when people needed you to believe in what they believed: Didn't Walter want everyone to think that one of his TV productions that he thought was good, was good? Of course he did, she told him before he could confess. In this case, with George, it was an extreme example, maybe, but no different, a matter of degree, mostly. People often needed you to believe in what they believed. If you couldn't, the least you could do was to pretend you did wherever possible. Besides, who knew? she asked them: You might just need it yourself from someone else one day, God forbid. Bread upon the waters. She smiled. *Is too soggy to eat, as George would say,* she said.

It was sometime later in the afternoon, evidently, that Brady's wife arrived on the scene. Not without warning for Faith however since, shortly before, she had finally conceded her inability to cope with the seriousness of the situation and called Harold Hall who told her he would be there as quickly as possible but to be prepared for Janine to get there first. Janine, Faith thought, was at home, in Los Angeles. She was not, Harold told her, Janine having just called him to say that she was to meet her husband here in New York and, stupidly, had forgotten at what hotel they were staying. A lie, Harold knew now and, together with Faith, quickly pieced together the probability: Faith had fled: George had come after her: Janine had come after him. Or both of them. Faith did not elaborate. Neither did she elaborate on the crucial opening moments of the confrontation between the two women. Crucial, inasmuch as what wife, at such a moment, could be expected to note her husband's emotional condition and react accordingly with some degree of compassionate restraint before seeing his physical one—and reacting accordingly? There was the physical Brady, after all, with a girl, in a hotel suite, stark naked and—was it possible? All things considered, yes—yet erect? So Faith excised Janine Brady's response and offered them Brady's.

Brady went berserk.

"Good Lord," Miriam said.

"What did he do?" Walter asked.

"He wrecked the joint is what he did," Faith said.

She briefly described Brady's demolition of the hotel suite, beginning with the bedroom naturally enough and gradually working his way into the living room at which point Harold Hall arrived. Screaming obscenities, Brady proceeded to make relatively short work of what remained of the suite's expensive decor. Appeals to reason and restraint failed early, Walter gathered, and physically subduing him was out of the question, naturally, without risk of serious bodily harm. There was little for the three of them to do but dodge the furniture and wait for Brady to wear himself out, Janine suggesting that he might at least have the decency to put some clothes on.

When Brady turned his attention to the window drapes and tried to set fire to them (*They must have been fireproof*, Faith said, *he couldn't get them lit*) the intent alone was apparently enough to convince Harold Hall that matters had reached the intolerable stage and—regretfully, Faith emphasized—he suggested the police be called.

"Agents are very realistic people," Walter grinned.

"Not for Janine," Faith said. "She was furious. But in her own quiet way, of course." She smiled, then drew herself up haughtily in mimicry of Janine Brady and turned her lofty head to speak to an imagined Harold Hall. In an impeccable upper-class British accent, she said, " 'No cops, you cunt!' she says to Harold."

Walter laughed and looked at Miriam who appeared less amused than dazed.

"Anyway, I guess the hotel manager didn't feel the same way about it," Faith continued, "because he showed up soon after with four cops. The neighbors must have filed a complaint about all the racket."

She commented especially, and with a kind of excited respect unusual in one of her age these days, Walter thought, on the cool professionalism with which the police quickly evaluated the situation and deployed themselves, three of them closing in on Brady while the other held himself in reserve, one of the main assault force crooning softly at their prey, assuring him that he was meant no harm, that it was time to calm down now, that the party was over, while Brady retreated carefully backward through the debris, a table leg clutched in his fist, murder in his eye.

(Walter recalled a snatch of graffiti scrawled across a subway poster pushing the Police Athletic League, a handsome, smiling cop, one affectionate, protective arm around the shoulders of a securely grinning young kid. Across what little available clear space there was, the dissenter had written in a tiny hand, *This is a policeman, See him smile, He is your Friend, Be nice to him, If you are not he will kill you.*)

"I think he would probably have put up a good fight," Faith suggested, "but he slipped on something and all three of them hit him at once and that was pretty much it. When I left— slipping away unobtrusively, as they say," she smiled, "the cops were sitting on George and tying him up with a lamp cord or something and Janine and Harold were haggling with the manager—who was pretty hysterical by this time—about his price to keep it all out of the newspapers. I guess they had to take care of the cops, too. Harold once told me George has spent a fortune over the years squashing bad publicity and he's constantly after his accountants to come up with some way to make it tax deductible as a business expense."

Walter laughed, but on reflection thought it a not entirely unreasonable idea.

"So, that's what *my* day was like," Faith said, affecting a comic boredom, "how are things with you? That's a fabulous tree," she finished abruptly.

Too abruptly, Walter thought afterward. It was like the television channel that had the frustrating habit of cutting in with its last commercial at the end of a movie just a moment too soon, sometimes perhaps only seconds before the true, originally filmed fadeout; one was left with a distressing feeling of incompletion, to have come so far, for two hours, and be cheated of THE END. Faith had faded out too soon, and gone to a plug for the Christmas tree.

Through lunch, Miriam—her sense of propriety struggling briefly with her curiosity and losing—continued to probe for more details. But unsuccessfully: Faith had all too obviously abandoned her earlier talkativeness and retreated into one of her mysterious possessor-of-private-information moods (not, Walter noted, her working-out-of-a-complex-problem mood which might have been more natural and far less provocative to Miriam). About the most that could be gotten from her was the explanation of her wish to stay with them for a few days: Having eluded Brady's private detective and, through the timely onset of his mental collapse, Brady himself, she wanted only to guarantee her unreachableness until she could be certain that Brady's wife had gotten him under control and hopefully, almost certainly, out of town. And, practicality aside, she was glad to be here, she told them, smiling, just to spend some time with them.

On that note, warmed, he watched Miriam lead her from the room (she had really incredible legs, Faith) to show her the guest room.

Alone, he took the opportunity to retrieve *The Amorous Arts in Marriage,* rummaging with hasty hands under the back edges of the sofa cushions. Already it looked a little the worse for wear, the wrong manner of wear, he thought with bitter, boozy disappointment, not the evidence of an avid reader's eager hands, merely the result of Miriam's panicked, careless attempt to conceal it. Better to have bought something more durable, in hard cover—if this was the kind of treatment it was going to get, the thing would be in shreds in no time!

Despondent at its initial reception, he carried his latest source of hope into the study and replaced it carefully in the desk drawer, wondering when and how he might contrive an occasion for its reintroduction.

When the door buzzer sounded he went to answer it himself, assuming that Miriam was still occupied with Faith. He was halfway to the door when they appeared emerging from the bedroom hall into the living room. He opened the door, interrupting a second, more insistent demand from the buzzer. A man stood in the hall. He was tall, about Walter's height. He wore a battered and soiled gray felt hat, dark glasses, a shabby, too long overcoat that reached to mid-calf, and unbuckled rubber galoshes. The coat collar was turned up and this, together with the dark glasses, almost totally obscured the man's face.

It was a startling sight.

Startled, Walter asked, "Yes?"

In the coat collar's shadows, the man's lips seemed to work silently for a moment before sound came: "Is Faith here?" he demanded.

Walter wondered briefly how such an apparition had managed to get by the doorman unannounced but was too amazed to pursue the thought and, in unconscious reflex said, "Faith? Uh, yes, she's . . ." He moved backward half a step, cautiously, to address Faith in the living room, keeping a wary eye on the figure at the door. "Faith, it's someone for . . ."

But the man strode by him quickly, and directly into the room. Walter raised a restraining hand, in reflex again and too late; then his eyes darted in search of whatever might be lying near at hand to be employed as a makeshift weapon—his golf clubs were stored at the back of the foyer closet, he seemed to recall. Faith and Miriam had turned toward the visitor and all four were frozen in tableau for a moment. Walter was about to make demands for explanations of the intruder, spotting a heavy crystal vase on the foyer table, more accessible than the golf clubs, thinking of *The Desperate Hours*, a family held captive and in terror by psychopathic escaped convicts, Frederic March, Bogart, but his confusion lasted an instant too long and the man spoke first.

"So where the hell were you when the chips were down?" he wanted to know.

Walter glanced at Miriam who, like himself, was clearly too astonished to speak. Faith, however, appeared composed and lowered herself softly onto the arm of a chair, watching the man intently. "How do you feel?" she finally asked.

"I'm on the verge of feeling just great," the man told her with a trace of threat in his voice.

Faith smiled. "That's unusual."

"Exactly. So don't say anything that might tend to upset me," he advised, a time bomb, set and knowing its potential.

Faith moved at last, breaking the pattern. "Miriam, Walter," she said, "this is George Brady, you may have already guessed. Of the Hollywood and Washington Bradys. George—my sister Miriam, and Walter Hartman."

Miriam nodded tentatively and murmured, "Hi."

Walter, still at the door, closed it and moved forward, fascinated, to take Brady's hand.

"How are you?" Brady said absently, ignoring Walter's hand and returning his attention immediately to Faith.

"How did you get out?" Faith asked.

"I *walked* out, how the hell do you think I got out?"

"Like that?"

"Certainly, like this!"

"One would think you'd have attracted some attention," Faith thought.

"In *this* town?" Brady asked. "Are you kidding?" It was an apparent reference to New York's collective indifference to the bizarre. "Get your coat," he ordered.

Faith ignored the demand. "Where are your clothes?"

"They took them away from me, naturally. Janine's idea, no doubt. They figured to box me in. But I foxed them."

"Evidently," Faith mused.

"Let's go," Brady said, jerking his head backward at the door.

Faith contemplated him with interest, almost fascination—or as near to it, Walter thought, as it was possible for her ever to appear to be. "Where did you get the clothes?" she asked.

Brady sighed fretfully. "From an attendant, a male nurse or something. I traded him my watch for them and five bucks cab fare. Will you get your coat and let's go, Faith?"

"Your watch?" Faith asked. "You don't drive a very hard bargain, do you, George?"

Brady fell suddenly still as though finally, if only momentarily, checked by Faith's persistent refusal to offer a direct response to his direct demand.

In the momentary impasse, Walter tried but could not guess what might happen next. Like a passerby stopped to watch a mild street altercation, he readied himself to piece together whatever fragments of information came to light until it might be determined who did what to whom and why.

"How did you know I was here?" Faith asked neutrally.

"How do you think?" Brady said. "I've had a tail on you, of course, that's how."

"I thought I got rid of him."

"That was another one," Brady said and, for the first time, turned to Walter and Miriam. "Do you know where she was yesterday? In Macy's following *Greta Garbo*, she says. Christ!"

Pleased at his sudden inclusion, Walter nodded eagerly. "Yes, well, she . . ."

"Bloomingdale's," Faith corrected.

Ignoring her, Brady said to Miriam, "She accused the private detective of *assaulting* her. Can you imagine that? In an *elevator*. Then she splits. But they arrested him, anyway. I had to have him bailed out."

"I didn't say he assaulted me," Faith said calmly. "I said he made an indecent advance."

"He says you rubbed up against him in the elevator," Brady accused.

"Yes, well, I feel sorry about that," Faith admitted, "but I was angry at the time, I wanted to make him suffer a little."

"Faith, you didn't," Miriam hoped.

Faith shrugged at her sister and turned again to Brady. "What's this about another detective, George?"

She seemed to Walter to be something near to annoyed, her first response of any appropriateness, he thought, since Brady's arrival.

"What do you mean what's this about another detective, George," Brady said. "You think I didn't have another tail on you yesterday the minute I found out where you were?"

Who followed her here, of course, Walter thought. Who Brady would have contacted on his escape from the hospital. Who would then have told Brady where . . . Yes, falling into place now, bit by bit.

"I didn't think of that," Faith said.

Walter had the impression that she might have been less angry with Brady for having placed her again under surveillance than with herself for having failed to realize he would.

"Greta Garbo," Brady said, shaking his head almost imperceptibly. "I'm telling you, Faith, you're getting more spooky every day."

"Glass houses, George," Faith said. "Coming from one who was so recently the subject of a discussion about straitjackets."

"I was excited, that's all!" Brady pointed out. "Excited, not nuts! Is it *my* fault if no one could tell the difference!"

Walter thought he might have an interesting point there, and wished there might be some truth to it.

"What about now?" Faith asked.

"What *about* now!"

"Well, look at yourself, George. Walking through the streets like that, barging in here—it's an irrational act on your part, wouldn't you say?"

"Impulsive, maybe. Impetuous," Brady conceded. *"Not irrational."* He turned again to Walter. "Right?"

Caught unawares again, Walter was still not yet prepared for the possibility that he might be included in the discussion and be expected to comment from time to time. Quickly, he offered,

"Well, yes, I could see that, it wouldn't necessarily be irrational, no."

Brady moved toward him. Walter realized that he had in that instant made himself an ally of Brady's and that now Brady was coming at him as though he intended to put the strength of the alliance to the test. He regretted his too hasty accord and set himself for its possible consequences: He sensed somehow that behind the opaque disks of Brady's dark glasses the eyes might be menacingly wild, in expectation of nothing less than utter compliance from whomever they were directed at. At the moment, they were directed at Walter.

"Whose fault was it, anyway!" Brady demanded, whipping off the dark glasses (Walter noted instantly that he had been right about the eyes), then seizing the battered fedora and ripping that from his head, close enough now for Walter to feel the draft from the hat as it slapped angrily against Brady's thigh. The famous face was completely revealed now, tanned, craggy, faintly lined. "Everything was fine until *she* busted in, right?"

Faith? Walter wondered desperately.

"We were having a fine time, perfectly peaceful, watching that picture, weren't we?"

No, his wife, Walter decided, what was her name? Jasmine? Janice?

"But that's what she does to me!" Brady accused. "She *upsets* me! Is that *my* fault?"

Walter groped hopelessly for an answer; it seemed to him that there was no telling what might happen if he failed to come up with one. But, abruptly, Brady turned from him and moved again toward Faith.

"Get your coat."

"Why?" Faith asked, lighting a cigarette, squinting at Brady through gray smoke.

"Because we're going."

"Where?"

Brady's advance on her had continued uninterrupted. She retreated and they began a generally circular movement around the room, the sofa roughly at its center, Miriam seated upon it.

"Someplace where she won't find us," Brady said doggedly.

"Then what?"

"Then we'll get married."

Faith was momentarily distracted as she backed into an unseen armchair. "You're already married," she pointed out.

"Well, I'm going to divorce her, naturally!" Brady shouted. "Eventually," he added hastily and with greatly diminished force.

Too unforcefully, Walter thought, enough so to cast at least some slight shadow of suspicion on the definiteness and clarity of his plans. Yes, he might certainly have made a tactical error there. Faith could not have failed to note such a gratuitous qualification, but of course her face held no trace of an opinion about it: Like electric clocks that keep perfect time without offering the reassurance of ticking, Faith was seldom inclined to offer too obvious indications of the perfect functioning of her inner works.

Brady took up the mink coat from the sofa and thrust it toward Faith. "This yours?"

Faith ignored the coat and its suggestion of departure and kept moving. "I don't want to marry you, George," she told him simply. "I think I may have mentioned that."

"Why not?" Brady asked, quite reasonably.

"I have other plans."

"Will you stand still goddammit!"

"I will if you will," Faith offered.

The balance of power teetered for a moment, then tipped in Faith's favor as Brady came to a halt and hurled the coat at the sofa. Faith fulfilled her part of the agreement. (Graciously, Walter thought, no show of victor's arrogance.) The coat slid to the floor and Miriam absently but respectfully retrieved it and arranged it carefully across the sofa-back as Brady, his face wet with perspiration, asked:

"What other plans could you possibly have?"

It might have been an unwisely supercilious question had he not sounded so sincerely perplexed.

"I haven't formulated them yet," Faith answered. She extended her empty glass to Walter. "Walter, would you, please?"

Walter moved away from her carrying her empty glass. At the bar he found the ice bucket empty and, with a haste born of reluctance to leave the room, carried it to the kitchen, leaving behind the silence of another impasse. Brady, he saw, was un-buttoning his coat—was he only too warm, or planning to stay? *Don't say anything important till I get back,* he pleaded without speaking.

Surely there was a history to all this, he reflected, prior in-formation as yet unknown, requiring the withholding of out-siders' too hasty judgment. (He remembered the young man arrested a few days ago for the murder of his mother, who said he did it because she had that morning put cream in his coffee and she knew he liked it black.)

Returning ice-laden to the living room he saw that Brady had removed his overcoat and stood, glass in casual hand, in a wrinkled blue cotton hospital gown, open at the back from the waist up and tied behind his neck in a neat little bow; the tanned, hard muscles of his back were visible through the open-ing; the calves of his legs were very tan, too, muscular and quite hairy.

Walter was more curious than surprised. And what little sur-prise he did experience passed rather quickly, he thought. *Too* quickly? Was he becoming so inured already to the bizarre, was there no grotesquerie that could any longer cause him more than momentary pause? Surely there must be a more appropriate re-action to the sight of one of the biggest motion picture stars in the world, now a United States congressman-elect, recent escapee from a psychiatric ward, standing in his, Walter Hartman's, living room wearing a hospital gown and a pair of too large galoshes with unbuckled metal clasps that rattled and clanked each time he moved.

". . . kept it out of the papers at least, I hope," Brady was saying.

"Well, almost," answered Faith. "It was played down and cleaned up. In case anyone should ask you, you slipped in the bathtub at the hotel and were rushed to the hospital for X-rays, but you got a clean bill of health and are now en route to Lon-don for story conferences on your forthcoming Anglo-American production of the Charles Dickens classic, *Dombey and Son,* in which you will appear in the title role."

"Well, that sounds okay," Walter said approvingly. But he

was vaguely puzzled by some indefinable flaw in the contrived newspaper story that he was unable to put his finger on.

"It certainly *was* played down," Miriam said comfortingly, and with a seeming eagerness to take hasty advantage of her first opportunity to contribute. "I didn't see anything about it at all."

"Two paragraphs on page five in the *Daily News*, George," Faith continued. "The *Times* didn't even bother."

"Well, at least she managed that much," Brady granted, reasonably satisfied it seemed, if grudgingly so, with his wife's press relations.

Walter handed her refilled glass to Faith. Her fingers touched his briefly in the exchange and his response—a warm, pleasurable tingle behind his ears—startled him. He found himself looking at her breasts again. His eyes fled guiltily to her face, in safer, less suspicious admiration; a face of pale, soft luminescence, apparently so devoid of makeup that there was visible the faint band of freckles across the fragile bridge of her nose and beneath her wondrous violet eyes. She looked like an ad for Coca-Cola, the old-fashioned glossy ones that once shone over the counters of soda fountains, The Pause That Refreshes. Except for the mouth. The mouth knew too much. He glanced quickly at Miriam to determine if she might perhaps have been aware of what had just happened to him. Whatever it was. But her attention was fixed on Brady as though she was trying hard to think of something to say.

"*Is* that your next picture, Mr. Brady?" Walter asked. He wondered if he sounded as absurd as he felt, addressing Brady with such formality under the circumstances. Brady eyed him, distracted, over the rim of his glass that was almost filled with un-iced Scotch and voiced an interrogatory grunt. Walter wanted not to pursue the ludicrous turn he might be causing the conversation to take. But he was committed now and Brady was attentive and waiting. "*Dombey and Son?*" he asked. "Is that your next picture?"

"I never heard of it," Brady said with, to Walter's relief, finality and dismissal, turning toward Faith. Then abruptly he swung again to Walter, alert, and asked, "Why? You think it would make a picture?"

"Well," Walter began, and faltered.

"Good properties are getting goddam hard to come by these days," Brady explained. "And Dickens might be public domain, a big plus going in if you've dropped enough bundles buying properties that never got shot like I have."

"Well," Walter said, ". . . it's been years since I read it, as a matter of fact, I don't really remember what——" He broke off as his eyes discovered Faith's and he knew in an instant what the flaw had been in the newspaper story as she had related it to them. Her expression was one of imposed, innocent attentiveness, the practical joker who has just lit an exploding cigar for an unsuspecting victim. Of course! She had invented the story! At least *that* part of it! How could Brady be on his way to England for a movie? *He wasn't in the picture business any more.* She'd been putting them on! No. Not *them.* Brady. *And he'd gone for it.* What was the matter with him? There was some excuse for himself and for Miriam: The idea of George Brady no longer in the movies, George Brady as a United States congressman, took some getting used to and could easily, understandably, slip the mind in the heat of this perplexing state of affairs. But what of Brady? How could *he* forget? Unless he was really——? It was not entirely unthinkable: Madness could sometimes be a condition of great subtlety, of course.

"What are you going to do, George?" Faith asked.

Brady looked vaguely at her. "What?"

"Has it occurred to you yet that Janine probably has an army of private detectives out looking for you at this very moment? And that right behind them there are probably at least three doctors ready to sign all the right papers to put you right back in the hospital?"

"Why would she want to do that?" Miriam asked. To Walter her voice suggested a hint of consternation. Lines were being drawn here, he suspected: slowly, subtly; but surely. And he was reasonably certain on which side of the line Miriam would come down when and if allegiances were called for. So far he could see no particular reason to object to her choice of alliance: He was growing rather fond of Brady himself. With reservations, perhaps; but fond.

Brady shrugged and offered Miriam what he clearly believed

to be the most natural explanation in the world. "She's vicious, she hates me," he explained simply.

"She wants you in a hospital, George, because you belong in a hospital," Faith said, and glanced at Miriam and Walter as if to assure herself of their understanding.

Brady's face clenched in outrage. From his slumped seat on the bar stool, he drew himself up, his back rigid, then slid to his feet, the smock billowing around his calves in the brief updraft, the buckles on his galoshes tinkling. "What do you *mean*, I belong in a hospital!" he demanded. "What is *that* shit?"

Faith sighed, sank deeper into the armchair, and gently placed the soles of her fawn-colored, leather boots against the edge of the coffee table. "You're in the middle of a nervous breakdown," she suggested, coolly, level-eyed.

"Goddammit, I'm as sane as anyone!"

Faith grinned sweetly. "Well, if we pursued that line of thought it would make it kind of a tricky argument, George. We'd have to get into matters of degree."

Brady whirled on Miriam. "Do I look crazy to you, Marian?"

"Miriam, George," Faith corrected quietly.

"Miriam," George said, accepting the correction without any suggestion of apology.

"Well . . . no," Miriam said.

But not too certainly, Walter thought, as though she were leaving herself an avenue of retreat should Faith prove to be right. But "crazy" was after all, a rather extreme word. Even nervous breakdown might be going a little too far. On the other hand, there was the fact of that imaginary movie on TV—that couldn't be entirely discounted. For the moment. But Brady withdrew from Miriam with a look of satisfaction, taking sustenance from the seed of her words and discarding the chaff of her manner.

Reinforced, he wheeled again on Faith. "I'm filled to the back teeth with something, maybe," he acknowledged, readily. "Thorazine, probably. That's what they gave me the last time. Otherwise I'm fine!"

The *last* time? Walter thought. There's a *history* of this?

"You're in the middle of a nervous breakdown, George," Faith persisted.

Brady laughed bitterly. "Who *isn't!*"

"You're begging the issue again."

"He may have a point, though," Walter offered, grinning. He was unquestionably establishing a real fondness for George Brady. His presence here, even the insane hospital gown and the galoshes, it *wasn't* necessarily irrational, it *could* easily be impetuosity, the impulsiveness of a desperate man. Couldn't it? After all, he was clearly a man of intense feeling and great emotional force, and how often in the history of mankind had the intensity of one's convictions been cruelly mistaken for madness? *Very* often, of course. *Madness: Its Uses and Abuses*, by Walter A. . . . And, as Brady had pointed out quite forcefully only moments ago, he had been angry, not crazy, and it was not *his* fault that no one had been able to tell the difference.

As now. He was certainly angry now. And perhaps very justifiably so: There *was* something maddening about Faith, her quiet, undefended, and unsupported insistence of her claim about Brady's mental condition. Nor was the gentleness of that insistence any mitigating factor: Water erodes stone. Gazing at her, the hem of her skirt pushed by the attitude of her dazzling legs far back along her thighs, he thought, Jesus, what would it be like to hump her?

He was stunned at the thought.

"Why are you doing this to me," Brady said, almost plaintive, a new and surprising note.

"What am I doing?" Faith asked as though suggesting he be more specific.

"I need you. What can I say that will——"

"Try goodbye," Faith said.

She mocked a wry breeziness that was clearly calculated to be not offensive but charming. (She *was* charming, Walter thought. He had never especially thought that of her in the past: Or was it something new in her? Or was it something he had never noticed before . . . ?)

Checked, and admitting it gracefully, Brady smiled broadly and dropped the level of his voice as though to find what sounded like just the right tone of warm intimacy: "Now, you *know* good-bye is the most terrible word in the language."

"I saw that picture, George," Faith nodded, "I didn't like that line then either. Shouldn't you be in Washington or someplace?"

"Why the hell should I be in Washington!" Brady cried, reversing his emotional field again.

"Performing the duties of public office?"

"I don't start performing the duties of public office till next month! Didn't you go to *school!*"

Faith had risen from the chair, hugging herself (Christ! she had something to hug there, too, Walter regretted thinking), and walked slowly across the room; then stopped and faced Brady again. "George," she began, hesitated, then continued almost reluctantly, "there was no movie on the TV yesterday."

Irritably perplexed, Brady grimaced and said, "What?"

Walter was apprehensive: Was she making the right move? This might not be the propitious moment to offer him that information. Remember the days of old when kings were sometimes known to inflict awful punishments on the bearers of bad news.

"No film, George," Faith repeated. "No movie. The TV wasn't even turned on."

The room was very still for a moment. Walter glanced at Miriam who returned his look, clearly aware of the significance to Brady of what had just been said, and its possible consequences. Brady was taking the news badly: It was a subtle reaction, in the eyes mostly, but it was definitely a bad one; he looked a little frightened. Walter's heart went out to him.

Then, surprisingly, startlingly, Brady laughed. But it was a nervous laugh, Walter thought, a giggle at the graveside.

"What do you mean the set wasn't . . . ?" Brady said. "Baby, we watched the picture *together,* remember. The *two* of us," he said, waving a hand to and fro between himself and the absurdly forgetful Faith. Then, without pause, as though he had irrefutably cleared up that minor point of misunderstanding, he said intensely, "Did you see what I was talking about, though? The way that schmuck of a director loused it up?" He whirled on Walter. "That was a great script when we started, it could've been a *great* picture!" He pivoted to Miriam. "But he *butchered* it!"

Miriam nodded, acquiescent on demand.

"He got an Academy Award for that picture," Faith pointed out quietly. It might have seemed merciless, Walter thought, but was not. No, someone had to do what had to be done, the dirty work, pitch right in without fear or favor. *It was for his own good!*

But Brady ignored his tormentor, fixed his attention on Miriam. "That's what I really want to do," he said.

"I beg your pardon?" Miriam said helpfully.

"Direct. What I really want to do is direct. Pictures. So you're Faith's sister. She's told me a lot about you."

"Oh?" Miriam said, nodding. "Yes. Well——"

"George, will you listen to me?" Faith suggested.

Yes, listen to her, George! Walter hoped silently. She has something to tell you: You can't direct pictures: *the voters wouldn't like it!*

"This is some sister you've got," Brady continued at Miriam, shaking his head, grinning, with a lover's condescension. "Did she tell you how she came to New York? In a *bus.*" He turned to gaze at Faith. "Now, what kind of a sweet, lovely nut would come all the way from L.A. in a *bus?*" He flicked his head sharply to Walter. "The private dick I had following her'll probably charge extra just for the discomfort," he exaggerated, and laughed.

Walter laughed with him, and nodded. And wondered why he was laughing and nodding. And wondered then: *Why not?* But the best Miriam could summon up, he saw, was a polite, glazed smile as Brady's eyes swept her face, the laugh (grown excessive now, perhaps desperate) still bursting through ten thousand dollars worth of perfect teeth.

No one heard Cassie come in. She had closed the door, removed her coat, and was well into the room before anyone saw her. Miriam was the first.

"Cassie, honey," she said desperately, "look who's here!" needlessly directing her daughter's attention to Faith who was already on her feet and approaching the child, smiling.

"Hi, Aunt Faith," Cassie said, as though she had last seen her aunt yesterday and not ten months before.

Faith stooped to embrace her, accidentally crushing Cassie's Western hat that swung on her back, suspended by the leather thong around her neck. "How are you, hon?" she asked warmly.

Cassie nodded. "Fair to middling. How are things on the Coast?"

"Beautiful," Faith said. "You've grown about a foot since the last time."

"Yes, I'm beginning to worry about that," Cassie said. "I don't want to be too tall. I'd like to end up about your height, I think that's just about the right height." Her eyes found Brady then; gazing at him, she continued distractedly to Faith, "I'm sorry you weren't here yesterday to help decorate the tree. We waited."

"I'm sorry, too, hon, it's a beauty of a tree."

There was a brief silence. It was clear that Cassie's attention was totally arrested by Brady and that, however unexplainable the apparition was, it had at least to be acknowledged.

"Cassie, this is Mr. Brady," Miriam said at last, with an apprehensive brightness. "This is our daughter, Cassie," she added.

Brady grinned, then crouched, his left hand extended tensely before him, his right hand slapping imaginary leather at his blue-cotton hip, getting the drop on her with a conjured Colt from a dreamed holster.

The question is, Walter thought, *is he only fooling around or does he really believe it?*

Miriam was smiling encouragingly, clearly with the hope that Cassie would respond in a reasonably suitable way. Walter watched, half-grinning, knowing well she wouldn't. *And who could blame the kid?*

There was a momentary but awkward pause before Brady finally surrendered to Cassie's enigmatic gaze, assumed a normal stance, and said to no one in particular, "I've always been lousy with kids."

Faith was loving it. "You can't have everything, George."

"You're right," he nodded philosophically.

Cassie turned to her mother. "Mama?" she said. "He's wearing galoshes and a nightgown."

That's my Cassie, Walter thought, the emperor was clothed, but inappropriately, unsuited to the occasion.

Faith gave full vent to her pleasure and laughed delightedly. *What a beautiful laugh she has,* Walter realized, smiling with her, at her. . . . *For* her?

"Well, he *is,*" Cassie insisted to Faith, misinterpreting the laughter.

"Yes, of course he is, darling," Faith answered, asking forgiveness. "I wasn't laughing at you."

"Yes, well, it's not exactly a nightgown, sweetheart," Miriam demurred. "And it's a long story. Walter, do you have anything that would fit Mr. Brady?" She smiled at Brady. "I would say you could use some clothes for a start."

Brady snapped his fingers at her, returning her smile. "Good thinking," he said. "You're obviously a woman who knows how to put things in proper perspective," he told her, charmingly.

Miriam smiled, charmed. "It just seemed like the logical thing to suggest first, considering."

"Of course," Brady said. Then turned to Walter. "But I won't have to trouble you, Wallace, thank you just the same."

Walter, having already made a tentative start in the direction of the bedroom, stopped, smiling. "Walter," he corrected courteously.

"Walter," Brady agreed.

"I'd be happy to let you borrow some——"

"No, no, it's no sweat, Walter, really. I'll give my lawyer a ring, or my agent, have him send someone over to the hotel, pack a bag for me, have it brought right over here. No problem."

"Oh. Well, yes, of course," Walter said. "If you'd rather."

Brady suspended his hand over the telephone on the bar: "May I?"

"By all means," Walter said expansively.

Brady had already taken up the receiver and begun to dial when Faith spoke. "George," she said, casually. Walter turned to find her unexpectedly in the foyer, squatting (Jesus! what a behind!) over her now open suitcase and removing from it a small, brightly wrapped package. She rose and returning to the living room said, "You *have* no bags, George. You have no clothes. You have no hotel. Remember?"

Brady stilled for a moment, then dropped the receiver into the cradle from an altitude of several inches.

Walter smiled encouragingly at him and winked. "I think I have something that'll fit you." Brady nodded, absently, and mumbled his acquiescence and thanks, but it was clear that his confused and distressed thoughts were elsewhere. Faith had already handed the package to Cassie.

"For Christmas?" Cassie asked.

"For now," Faith said. "For Christmas I'm giving you a Rolls convertible."

"She'll take it," Walter grinned from the bar, pouring what he thought might be his fourth but could be his fifth.

"I hope you still collect these things," Faith said, watching Cassie unwrap the package. Miriam looked on with a pleased smile. Cassie finally revealed a small pink and white doll, with what appeared to be human hair.

"Oh, it's a beauty!" Miriam exclaimed, then turned quickly toward Brady. "Cassie collects dolls," she assured him brightly, as though to allay any suspicions of mental retardation in a ten-year-old child who might still be playing with dolls. "She has every doll she ever had, she has about thirty-seven dolls," she added with mock dismay.

"Forty-two," Cassie said, reading the large tag that hung by a thin white cord from one of the buttons of the doll's dress.

"What does *this* one do?" Walter asked. "Have babies?"

" 'My name is Sweet Tears,' " Cassie read. " 'I am made of soft moulded plastic. I can be bathed. I drink my bottle. I wet my diaper. I cry real tears. I go to sleep. I have lovely clothes. If you want me to cry real tears, remove the pacifier from my mouth. Hold me in your arms and give me a bottle of water to drink. After I drink my bottle, put pacifier back in my mouth. Then if you squeeze my tummy I will cry real tears.' "

Leaning dispiritedly against the bar, Brady said, mournfully, "Except for the bottle being water, that is a frighteningly accurate description of my first wife."

Walter was convulsed. In his overwrought transport he was only vaguely aware of the not quite so appreciative reactions of the two women, of Cassie's going off toward the kitchen carrying the doll and the miniature replica of a baby's bottle. When, finally, his laughter subsided he was aware of what struck him as a rather odd and distracted silence in the room.

Then he heard, began to hear, truly, what he realized he had been subconsciously aware of for the past several seconds. He shot a quick glance at the ceiling then saw that the others, too, had already heard. Were hearing. Were listening. Brady was re-filling his glass and gazing upward, developing a slow grin of comprehension. Faith's head rested against the sofa-back, comfortably full-faced toward the ceiling. Miriam sat staring at the floor, her head supported by her hand, rhythmically stroking her forehead with the tips of her fingers.

From beyond the unmarred white expanse of plaster above them, the woman's moans declared her purpose.

"Someone's playing a matinee," Faith said, interested.

"Is it lunchtime already?" Walter asked, grinning crazily toward Miriam.

Ignoring him, Miriam said to the carpet, "God! these new buildings, they make them out of paper, or something."

Walter contemplated Faith, her face turned to the ceiling as to the sun, a half-grin of sweet salacity on her lips. For the first time that afternoon, with everyone's attention—even hers—safely elsewhere, he felt free to regard her fully, openly, without his earlier vaguely guilty restraint. Then, distressed and alarmed at what was happening and wondering at its cause, he felt the blood begin to pound in his loins. He tore his eyes from the inside of Faith's innocently exposed left thigh (*the thigh's the limit, baby!*) as, upstairs, there was another shift into a new and higher pitch of intensity.

Miriam shot to her feet. "Good God, this is *terrible!*" she cried, looking wildly around the room as though for a place to hide.

"I think," Faith said, impishly speculative, "it's going to be over any minute now."

She sounds as though she could go all day! Walter remarked to himself, shoving a desperately restraining hand into his trouser pocket.

"Day" was the key word, the clue that put him on the track of the answer to the vague, nagging sense of the aberrant that had been flicking at his mind for the past several minutes. Today was

Saturday! But she didn't do it on Saturdays! Never! Yet there she was! Doing it! And it was past lunchtime, too! The schedule was changed then. The pattern altered. What was happening? First, Faith with the Coca-Cola face and an ass that would make you weep with longing! Then Brady with his insane galoshes! Now this, and on a Saturday! *And I'm standing here like a goddam adolescent with my hand in my pocket holding down a hard-on!*

His head swam, the nape of his neck went cold.

What was happening?

By the time Cassie returned a moment later, carrying Sweet Tears by the back of the neck and holding the now water-filled bottle to its mouth, the woman in 11B was uttering short, sharp, high-pitched shrieks in the perfectly timed, repetitious rhythm of consummation.

"Whoopee," Faith murmured.

"Good God," said Miriam.

Through a lewd smile, his voice quiet, hoarse, Brady said, "Go, baby."

There was nothing to be done about Cassie now, Walter knew. He watched askance as she too turned her eyes to the ceiling. Presently she spoke, more intrigued than alarmed:

"Why is that lady screaming?" she asked.

11.
Sudden Defections

. . . something new . . .

8 Walter rose, endlessly it seemed, in the rattling, shuddering elevator cage until finally it stopped with a violent
lurch, buckling his knees, forcing him to touch the wall
for momentary support. He stepped out into the immense ball-
room of the dilapidated Upper West Side hotel.

It was a room that must once have been reasonably elegant
during the West Side's better days, but which was no longer
ever used for its originally intended purpose. As someone had
once characterized it to him, you come into this neighborhood
at night, you come well armed. He was inclined to agree. And
now the semiopulent hotel ballrooms had become dingy rehearsal halls for Broadway plays and television productions.

In the center of the room, and surrounded by vast expanses
of unoccupied space, the set for the play had been marked out on
the floor with broad white tape; a random assortment of available odds and ends of old wooden chairs and tables did temporary service for the real furniture which none of the actors would
see until the production moved into the studio where the show
would be taped. The rehearsal that should have been in progress
now had come to a standstill. Walter felt the despondency in
the hall wash over him, cold, chilling. It was familiar; he had
felt it before, had seen it happen to other productions in serious

trouble. Usually those involved would at least temporarily refuse to acknowledge disaster's presence in the hope that, ignored,
it might go away. But Walter sensed instantly that that insular
stage had already been passed. The actors and various others of
the production personnel were scattered around the hall in small
groups, talking quietly, no doubt acknowledging calamity. (Except for the male lead who was sleeping soundly on a battered,
sprung sofa, the playscript open on his chest.)

Everyone, it seemed, had turned to the sound of the elevator
door, and all watched him steadily now as he crossed the floor.
He assumed that his arrival had been expected, its reason already
explained, and that he was being looked upon as the last possible source of a solution to the dilemma—possible, but unlikely,
their faces said; the odds, the faces said, were that it was only a
matter of patient time before the rehearsal would be called off
and they would be dismissed for the day.

Walter greeted the several familiar faces among them, moving
steadily toward Jack Finley and Sam Fleming who were standing at the far end of the hall, near the unused stage. As he neared
he could clearly discern the defeat and resignation in Sam's eyes.
Jack, on the other hand, was breathing fire.

Calmly, without preamble, Walter asked, "Where is she?"

"That cunt is going to come out and finish this rehearsal," Jack
said, "if I have to drag her out by the heels."

Walter smiled. "You could have done that already and saved
me a trip." Jack Finley wasn't called Blackjack for nothing. But
everyone knew that his frequent rages were, if not exactly bogus,
not quite to be taken too seriously. His volatile fits of anger were
mostly the product of a personal sense of drama that he injected
into even relatively small and unimportant crises; his inherent
charm and gentleness defeated his purpose.

"Sorry to get you out like this, Walter," Sam said.

"Anything for the network," Walter replied, feeling sorry for
Sam who, as producer of the show, stood to hurt most if Barbara
Finch was not gotten back on her feet and working.

"She's been in there for an hour and a half. She won't come
out," Sam said. "We've all tried."

Walter was being led across the expanse of worn, splintered

floor toward a door at the side of the hall. "Where's Freddie?" he asked.

"He gave up and went for a walk around the block," Jack growled. "He says he's directed some insane actresses in his time but he agrees with me, this one should be in a cage."

Walter grinned as they passed through the opened door into a poorly lit hallway, moved on a few steps, and pushed through the door of the ladies' room. Tommy Cole, a thirty-three-year-old juvenile actor who was playing the part of Barbara's younger brother in the play, was sitting on one of the sinks, smoking a cigarette. Walter greeted him.

"Your turn?" Tommy asked, grinning.

Walter said it looked like it.

"Christ," Jack muttered, "it smells like a Chinese whorehouse in here."

"I've been keeping her company," Tommy said to Walter and slid from the sink to his feet.

"Stick around," Jack said, "we may need all the muscle we can get."

Walter moved to the only closed door of the three cubicles in the room. He poised himself there, listening for a moment, while the other three men stood by silently. "Barbara?" he said finally, speaking at an angle to the steel, paint-chipped green door.

"Go away." Her voice echoed metallically from within the cubicle, husky with despair.

"It's Walter, honey. Walter Hartman."

"Walter," she answered, with a trace of animation. "Hello, darling. How are you?"

"Well, I'm fine, honey. How are you?"

"I'm going to kill myself, Walter." She spoke quite casually, as though she were merely conveying to him an interesting bit of information that had recently come to her attention.

"Baby, will you cut the shit and come out of the goddam can!" Jack suggested.

"I won't talk to that man, Walter, he's a monster!"

"*I'm* a monster!" Jack roared. "You got a three-hundred-thousand-dollar production flat on its ass out here and *I'm* a monster?"

"Jack," Walter said.

Jack relented. There was a brief silence.

"What are *you* doing here, Walter?" Barbara asked in a tone suggesting not so much interest as a courteous attempt to keep the conversation flowing, the hostess at a failing party.

"Well," Walter prepared to lie, "I was just in the neighborhood and dropped in to see how things were going, hon." He smiled in gentle rebuke. "I gather they aren't going too terrifically well."

"I can't do this play, darling."

"Barbara, suppose you come on out and let's talk about it," he coaxed, carefully.

"I don't want to."

"Why not, honey?"

"I'm afraid."

"Of what?"

There was a brief silence.

"I don't know," she said vaguely.

Walter could see, without seeing, the glazed, haunted look in her eyes. He had known Barbara since he had first started at the network. Socially they were virtual strangers (Miriam loathed her) but because she worked so much in television he had come into professional contact with her often over the years. Because of her puzzling (not always reciprocated, and rarely encouraged) fondness for him and her resulting inexplicable dependence upon him (in addition, probably, to his unique ability to deal so successfully so often with her frequent attacks of hysterical emotionalism), their friendship took on, in the eyes of others, colors and depths it did not actually possess. Walter had had reason in the past to regret that spurious intimacy. As now, when it was the cause of his presence: When all else failed, they called upon her "dear friend" Walter Hartman.

"Walter, darling, how is the writing coming along?"

"Well, fine, Barbara. Listen——"

"When he sells the movie rights he's going to insist you star in the picture," Jack said.

"Prick," Barbara said.

"Jack, will you knock it off?" Walter asked patiently.

"I wish you were here, Walter," Barbara said, plaintive.

"I *am* here, honey."

"No, I mean, *really* here. On this show. I miss you. Everyone hates me."

"No one hates you, Barb. There's no reason for you to think a thing like that," Walter assured her, watching Jack Finley roll his eyes toward the ceiling. "Look, Sam will call off the rehearsal for the rest of the day. You come on out and we'll go have a quiet talk, just the two of us. What do you say, hon?"

There was no sound but for the slow drip into one of the sinks from a leaking faucet. Sam Fleming paced, his arms folded across his chest, his eyes on the floor. Tommy had resumed his interested perch on a sink, one knee locked in his hands, the foot swinging back and forth. They waited. Barbara might be considering the proposition. Encouraged, Walter blew on the possible spark of her interest: "You mean a great deal to all of us, Barb. And you certainly mean a hell of a lot to this play. You know that."

There was another silence. They waited. Clearly, Walter was reaching her now, Sam Fleming's hopeful expression said.

"Do you have a cigarette, darling?" Barbara asked presently.

Jack raised his eyes to the ceiling again, blowing air sharply, like steam, through his lips and strode away to the door, stopped there, turned, thrust his hands in his pockets, and fell back against the door with a thump. Walter squatted and passed a cigarette under the cubicle door. He felt it slipped slowly from his fingers. He handed his lighter under the door.

"Thank you, darling, I have a match," Barbara said.

He straightened, replacing the lighter in his pocket. A cloud of blue smoke drifted up out of the cubicle.

"I can't do this play, Walter, I hate it."

"I thought you loved it, Barb," Walter replied evenly. "You told me you loved it," he reminded her.

"I hate it. It stinks," she said, quietly. Then, in a sudden hysterical shriek, "*It's a piece of shit!*"

"You don't *have* to like it!" Jack raged, lurching forward. "Do it for the *money*, you crazy cunt!"

"Fuck off, monster!" she screamed.

"We're *paying* you enough!"

"Fuck off, monster!"

"Jack," Walter suggested.

"We have a room full of some of the best talent in the country sitting on their asses out there while you're in here jerking off over your fucking emotional problems!"

"*Fuck off, monster!*" Her foot struck viciously against the inside of the cubicle door.

"Let's everybody calm down," Sam proposed.

Walter placed his forearm against the cubicle door, rested his forehead upon it and sighed, waiting. The room was still again. After another moment, patiently, quietly, he said, "Barbara? Come on out, hon. You have to come out sooner or later, right?"

Silence again, this time while they waited to know the effect upon her of a perhaps too simple logic: Possibly, in her present condition, the successful approach to her might require a more subtle complexity in order to attract her neurotic attention. "If it's a question of the script, hon," Walter pursued, "we can talk about that, certainly. If it's only a matter of changes, changes can always be made." He glanced toward Sam Fleming, anticipating his alarm and finding it. He gestured serenely to calm the producer. His gesture said that he knew what he was doing: First get the star on her feet, worry about the playwright later; playwrights could be handled.

"Walter?" Barbara's voice rose plaintively, disembodied.

"Yes, honey," Walter responded quickly, attentive and hopeful. There was a brief tantalizing pause.

"I have to pee."

Tommy trapped a laugh and sent it snorting quietly through his nose. Sam Fuller grinned helplessly. Walter sighed and shook his head. Jack addressed himself to the door of the cubicle and pointed out to Barbara at the top of his voice that she could not have found herself in a better place when the urge came on her.

"*Fuuuuuuuck oooooooof, mooooonsteeeer!*"

They filed through the door, leaving Barbara temporarily in her required privacy.

"They should all be in cages," Jack said, "where they can't get at us."

He passed Miriam and Faith, walking, as his cab turned the corner into their block; he waved at them through the side window but they did not see him. He got out of the cab at the building entrance, waved again, was seen this time, and waited for them under the sidewalk canopy.

"Where have you been?" Miriam asked when they were within a few yards of him.

He had assured her earlier that he would be at home all afternoon, at work, while she went out, with Faith, for her last-minute Christmas shopping. (Or, what Miriam considered to be last-minute: There was yet another day before Christmas, but Miriam never shopped on Christmas Eve, seeing the atmosphere of the stores as woebegone, lonely, tattered—it depressed her, she always said.)

He threw up his hands and shook his head in mock despair and on the way upstairs explained only as much of the Barbara Finch situation as he thought necessary, too exhausted by it all to go too much into detail. He was already half stoned from the session he had had with Barbara in the hotel bar after they had finally been able to coax her out of the ladies' room. It was not possible to be with Barbara drinking and not drink oneself, matching her round for round: She interpreted any innocent, self-preserving nursing of a drink as nothing less than an accusation of alcoholism. What made it especially difficult was that she was able to drink almost anyone he knew under the table without so much as slurring an *s;* the only perceptible effect liquor seemed to have on her was the gradual quietening of her voice until she was speaking in a hoarse, barely heard whisper. But should he dare to suggest that a word or a fragment of a remark be repeated, he was fixed with a killing glare and asked why he was not listening, was she *boring* him?

Barbara was a difficult woman.

Walter unlocked the apartment door and stepped aside to allow Miriam and Faith to pass. Miriam, protesting his involvement in the Finch affair on the grounds that he was technically not now connected with the network and its problems, interrupted herself in mid-sentence. He closed the door and turned to find her standing motionless, her shopping bag yet in her hand, gazing at a huge carton leaning against the foyer wall.

"What's this?" she asked, frowning at the carton as though it might answer.

For an instant, Walter was himself puzzled; evidently something had been delivered in his absence (and Cassie had opened the door to it despite their strict instructions *never* to open the door to anyone not personally known to her when she was alone in the apartment; he would have to speak to her). Then he registered the significance of the red-bordered cautions pasted numerously all over the flat, oblong box: FRAGILE HANDLE WITH CARE.

The mirror had come.

It was bad timing, he thought. Bad.

Miriam had already moved closer to the carton, peering at the shipping label. (It had taken Walter several minutes' thought in the store before settling on the precisely appropriate designation of addressee, the two of them, Mr. and Mrs. Walter A. Hartman. *This was to be a shared experience.*)

"What is it?" Miriam asked again, glaring at him across her shoulder.

But her eyes told him that she knew what it was: How could she not? It was huge, it was flat, it had square corners, it was breakable. She *knew!*

And without any warning! her eyes said, condemning him.

Not true! his eyes answered in defense. *Not true! Last week! I mentioned it last week! Remember? More or less. That could be called a warning of a kind. Couldn't it? Let's be fair about this, Miriam!*

"It's about time!" a voice cried out gaily behind them.

Startled, Walter turned to discover George Brady emerging from the study, smiling broadly, mopping his face with an already wet handkerchief. Cassie trailed out behind him. Walter greeted the saving intervention of his presence with happy, grateful surprise. Then he noticed the holster strapped around George's waist, one of Cassie's with the gun in it. He felt suddenly apprehensive.

"Your charming daughter said it would be all right for me to wait," George said with a warm smile toward Cassie.

"We were having a contest," Cassie said somberly.

"Well . . ." George demurred.

"Gun twirling," Cassie explained, registering the adult perplexity confronting her.

"I haven't done a Western in seven years," George said, "I'm out of practice."

"Ah? Uh, huh," Walter nodded, trying to calculate the implications. Barring the gun and holster, Brady appeared normal enough, his eyes—although perhaps unnaturally bright—far less wild, certainly, than when, the day before yesterday, he had left in an aura of demented mystery, wearing Walter's borrowed clothes and bound for a destination he would not divulge where he would be safe, he assured them, from discovery and apprehension by his wife.

"What are you doing here?" Faith asked mildly, frowning, removing her coat.

"Returning Walter's clothes," said George breezily, gesturing toward a corner of the foyer where Walter discovered a brand-new Gucci two-suiter, gleaming dully in tasteful, restrained luxury.

His charming manner, Walter knew, was all too clearly an attempt to assure Faith of his innocence of ulterior motive. To Walter, there was something rather wonderful about Brady's elan: Surely he knew that no one in the room would really believe he had to be his own messenger, but that did not deter him from offering the explanation, confident that Walter and Miriam would not be so discourteous as to challenge it, knowing that, for Faith, it was too absurd a lie to warrant comment.

At the moment, Walter's feelings were ambivalent. He still experienced a fond fascination for George and his style; on the other hand, were they really (as it began to appear) going to play the whole scene again, hadn't they had enough the other day? If that was indeed the way it was going to be, Walter was afraid that they would have to hold Faith responsible—George had called repeatedly all day the day before and that morning but she would not go to the phone. Her refusal, anyone should have known, was a virtual guarantee of his eventual personal appearance.

Yes, it very much looked as though they had failed to understand Saturday's history and were doomed to repeat it.

The history had been footnoted and appendixed to some extent in the interim, new light had been cast with which the casual student might view its further unfolding with renewed interest. George, Faith told them, had indeed had an earlier nervous breakdown, hushed up completely, some three or four years before, she was not certain. And if some kind of mental collapse was what George had suffered a few days ago, it was number two. *Three strikes and you're out, George!* Interesting enough, Walter supposed. But, what was most startling to learn, this from Miriam who had it from Faith (more or less in confidence, he assumed, Girl Talk), was that, far from being in the position of spurned lover desperately pursuing love's resumption (a perfectly reasonable conclusion for anyone to have drawn), what George so madly sought was something that he had never had. It seemed it was Faith's contention that George wanted her now primarily, if not solely, because he couldn't have her; it was not so much his need to lie between Faith's splendorous legs that drove him wild with frustration, it was Faith's continued refusal to allow him that enviable position. Denial, not memory, nourished his desire. The Cocksman's Fate, Walter thought: Sooner or later and from time to time he was bound to come across (but not over) someone who would turn him down. Faith admitted to Miriam that, in retrospect, it would have been far simpler and less taxing in the long run to have gone to bed with George in the first place, at the first asking. She conceded that he would then have probably gone his sated way, another notch on his infamous gun, so to speak, and that would have been that, fadeout, the end. The irony was that she had been forced by his relentless persistence into a commitment that she hadn't really felt all that strongly to begin with. The truth of the matter was that the first time George had made his pitch she merely hadn't happened to be in the mood, it was simple as that. (Walter speculated privately on the incidence of that chaste mood.) If George had had the good fortune to have asked the night before or the night after, she would have in all likelihood, she thought to Miriam, indulged herself, certainly George. Done so for all the usual reasons as well as, she admitted, to satisfy her own portion of the curiosity that a man of George Brady's reputation engendered in women, to know if that reputation was all, perhaps, hopefully, even more, than it was cracked up to be. On being turned down, George's first mistake, it seemed, was his astonishment, amusing at first, perhaps even charming in a way, but which became very soon, in retrospect, not a little offensive to Faith; as though there must be something suspiciously wrong with a girl who rejects the privilege of being banged by George Brady. And although he had altered his approach considerably since then—the assurance of marriage, Faith said, had become more or less a constant—she yet knew that it was that astonishment that drove him to persist, not the true feeling for her that he claimed. It was only, she insisted, such arrogant amazement that could have maintained him in his determination over the past six months when he could have—and certainly had, in the meanwhile, Faith assured—any number of women. True, she granted, arrogance in George was more charming than offensive because he really wasn't aware of it and did not really intend it. Nevertheless, however unrealized and unintended, it had forced her into this irrevocable position. And, nervous breakdown or not, she couldn't give in now. Too late now to turn back, assume a less inflexible position and offer even a therapeutically humanitarian hump.

Walter became vaguely aware of George thanking him again for "the use of the threads" and asking how Miriam was today. He glanced at Miriam. She was clearly preoccupied, unable to concentrate fully on George's presence. He knew the cause: The words FRAGILE HANDLE WITH CARE were still lodged in her brain like a bit of stringy, maddening meat in the crevice of a back tooth.

"Where'd you get the coat," he heard George ask. Walter turned to find Faith standing before the open closet door, slipping a coat hanger into the shoulders of her mink; then registered the accusatory edge in George's voice. It was as though George were seeing the coat for the first time, the coat he had been throwing all over the room only the day before yesterday.

"It was a gift," Faith said evenly, staring him down.

"A gift," George said flatly.

"People give me things."

In return for what, George asked her (a little crudely, Walter thought). Faith told him in return for what they think they're going to get and don't, and Walter felt the tension stretched between the two like a taut wire that might snap and indiscriminately lash them all.

"You must have a lot of annoyed men friends," Walter said with a fast smile.

Faith glanced at him, amused. "Hardly any," she said mysteriously, and started toward the bar watched steadily by George with a frowning, slack-mouthed look of unfinished business on his face.

Yes, Walter thought, it was probably true. Hardly any. She would possess the secret, she would know how to say no with style, with class. She would have her style and be loved for many and varied reasons, many of which would have nothing at all to do with the old to and fro.

"Walter, could I see you for a moment, please?"

He shifted his attention hastily from Faith's hips to her sister's cool eyes. "Sure, hon," he said brightly and, turning to the others, excused Miriam and himself and followed her into the bedroom hall. Behind him, he heard Cassie say:

"Could I have my gun and holster back, please?"

Miriam turned into the bedroom and closed the door behind him. She turned to him, her back to the door, as though she were guarding the exit.

"What is it?"

"What's what?" Walter asked, affecting sly ignorance.

"The box."

"Oh." He grinned, looking at the floor. "A surprise."

"What's in the box, Walter?"

"Wait and see."

"I know what's in it."

He nodded, grinning. "I thought you might have guessed."

"This is very embarrassing, Walter."

"Why?"

"You know why. You had no right, Walter. Without even consulting me."

"Not so loud, they'll think we're having an argument."

"You can just send it right back!" she whispered.

"We'll discuss it later, darling," he said reassuringly.

"There's nothing to discuss."

"Well, I didn't think so, but you seem to want to discuss it."

"I *don't* want to discuss it, there's nothing to discuss."

"Good," he smiled, and taking her shoulders, kissed the side of her fragrant neck. "Shall we rejoin our guests? You smell good." His hand went to her breast.

"I'm really upset, Walter, I hope you realize that."

"Why do you wear a bra, you certainly don't have to, and no one does anymore, I mean no one seems to." He advanced his hips.

"I suppose you're thinking about that dumb mirror."

"Not entirely."

"Stop."

He had the lobe of her ear carefully between his teeth. "It's bigger than the Apthekers', you know. Bigger."

"Stop."

When they stepped into the living room a few minutes later, Faith was just emerging from the kitchen through the swinging door followed closely by George who was clearly under some tension.

"I'm telling you, Faith, I mean it this time," George was saying, "this is no shit this time!"

Faith had the small, ceramic plant-watering can in her hands. She went directly to the Christmas tree, leaned over from the waist, and tipped the spout into the container at the base of the tree.

"Haven't we imposed ourselves long enough on these lovely people?" George asked her reasonably.

"*We?*" she emphasized. Clearly she was giving George no room to maneuver. "Cassie said to tell you she was going to mosey on over to . . ." she hesitated, looking at Miriam, "Mary Alice Webber's?"

Miriam nodded. Walter quickly assured George that imposition was a word that did not apply here, watching Faith's buttocks, her white jersey slacks stretched tight, the outline of her underpants clearly defined as she stooped to readjust the cotton-wool matting around the trunk of the tree. He would not have minded very much at all were George to leave soon. With or without Faith. Although preferably without, of course. Then he wondered why preferably without. And why of course. Watching her move back toward the kitchen with the now empty watering can he reviewed his already fairly well-plotted-out afternoon and evening. Assuming Brady's imminent departure.

He would first get one of the handymen up to help him hang the mirror. Then the rest of the afternoon at the typewriter (when Jack Finley had called for help he had been well into Chapter 5, the virgin twelve-year-old April was on the point of succumbing to the seduction by her uncle, it was a scene he was looking forward to finishing). Then dinner. Then a little more work, perhaps. Then Faith off to bed. Then they would be alone. *Then* . . .

Then Miriam asked George if he would fix her a drink. George said good thinking and emptied his own glass.

"Now that you've watered all the plants," George suggested to Faith as she emerged again from the kitchen, "can we go soon?"

Faith appeared almost surprised at George's continued presence. She sighed. "George, will you please?" she asked him. "I'm not going anywhere with you."

"How do you know," George asked her, "until you know where we're going?" There was the hint of secret promise in his voice, the suggestion of extremely interesting revelations to be enjoyed by those who offered him their faith and trust in his power to shape his own destiny. Perhaps even theirs. He glanced first at Miriam, then at Walter, as though to be certain of their attention. Then he looked at Faith, timing his continuing pause with professional perfection and said, "We're going to see Janine."

George checked the room with a sweeping glance, half grinning, clearly pleased with himself, and knew he had hooked them all.

It was Faith's turn now to consult the others. "Did I miss a clue somewhere?"

"Did it ever occur to you that I might have finally have worked this thing out?" George asked.

Walter noted that George's grammar was slipping and wondered if that might be a clue to anything, speaking of clues.

Faith was silent but her expression indicated that the possibility George suggested seemed very remote to her.

"And that I now know now exactly what's to be done?" George added.

The grammar was definitely shaky, Walter told himself. It could be significant. These things were sometimes very subtle.

"But, you see, George," Faith explained patiently (and cautiously, it seemed to Walter: Was she too on the alert?) "you're being irrational again, I mean it's an irrational idea, don't you think?"

"Never mind that *irrational* shit!" George exploded. "You're in no position to be so goddam smug, kid, you're not exactly the most well-integrated personality to come down the pike in recent years!"

Miriam looked alarmed, Walter saw. Understandably. George's eruption (so quickly! so easily!) called to mind unavoidable images of that demolished hotel suite and suggested the possibility of something like that happening again, here, now, soon.

"So, what about Janine?" Faith asked George, settling herself receptively in an armchair.

George appeared to be pacified to some extent.

"Look," Walter intruded carefully, with a suggested move toward one of the doors, "would you rather be alone? Because Miriam and I can——"

"Oh, hell no, Walter!" George protested, abruptly amiable again, "this'll be over in about a minute!"

Walter judged it to be a too hopeful estimate, the unfounded but perhaps necessary optimism of desperation. He glanced at Miriam; she was sitting quite still, her eyes the only part of her in motion. The absence of animation in Miriam was usually the clue to tension. It was impossible at the moment to guess the shape and degree of her involvement, no less the direction of her sympathies. If any. As he was about to turn from her, she spoke.

"George, if your marriage has reached the state it evidently has, why don't you just get a divorce?"

Walter was startled. George was disconcerted. Faith appeared to be (not quite secretly) amused. Miriam's manner left little doubt that she had finally become impatient with George's indulgent peeling, leaf by complicated leaf, of this emotional artichoke of his and that she had serenely chosen the more direct, if less emotionally epicurian course to the heart of the matter.

"Good thinking," George finally nodded, uncertainly. "Exactly the point. Up to now it's been a little hairy," he added evasively.

"Tell them, George," Faith said, as though she were trying to be helpful. "You're among friends." Then she turned to Walter and Miriam. "I'll bet you didn't think there was anything that could embarrass George, right?"

"Who's embarrassed!" George protested.

"Look, it's really none of our business," Walter said, firing a look at Miriam that suggested she comply with that opinion.

But Miriam was not looking at him. "I'm just trying to be helpful," she said, her serenity and confidence unshaken.

"I haven't heard George asking for any help from us," Walter smiled, tried to.

"You go right ahead and be helpful, Mim," said Faith. "George can use all the help he can get."

"Well, why don't you stop needling him, then?" Miriam demanded.

Faith grinned, taking the jibe in good grace. "Whose side are you on?"

"Mimi's on the side of the angels," Walter smiled.

"Which is a big plus going in," George said.

Walter was intrigued. It was clear now what role Miriam had chosen for herself: that of neutral arbitrator, setting forth the rules of procedure to both parties with impartiality.

"The fact of the matter, Miriam," George said courteously, as though it were his gentlemanly duty to respond to her, a debt owed in payment for her defense of him, ". . . the fact of the matter is that by the time I'd decided I wanted a divorce I'd also already decided to run for office. And I couldn't risk what she threatened me with if I tried to divorce her which was that she'd turn it into a three-ring circus, that was a promise on her part."

"An exposé," Faith said by way of elaboration, "of his extramarital activities, with subpoenas, witnesses, the works. How many names did she have, George? About fifty-eight women, weren't there? All the sordid details," she added, to Miriam.

"There's nothing sordid about it!" George cried. "It's the most natural goddam thing in the world!"

Beautiful! Walter thought. He really believes that! And he wasn't defending his position, either; he was attacking anyone who didn't share the only position that any reasonable, rationally thinking individual could honestly hold! Beautiful! He glanced at Miriam to see how she had taken it. She was staring at George, perplexed.

"You know George," Faith said, "I read a marvelous thing in the paper the other day. You know you can be cured of infidelity with shock treatments now? Really. They show you pictures of your wife and say all kinds of nice things about her. Then they show you a picture of your girl friend or some other chick and give you a seventy-volt electric shock."

George nodded. "I can imagine where," he said gloomily.

"No, no, nothing like that," Faith said, grinning. "On the wrist or someplace. This goes on for a couple of weeks, evidently, and you're cured."

"Of *what?*" George suggested with heavy irony, his implication clear.

Walter laughed. "That's the question, all right! Of *what!*" He turned to Faith. "Somehow I don't think the idea is likely to catch on."

Faith turned to gaze at George with pursed lips and nodded speculatively. "Frankly," she said, "I think George may be a puritan at heart." Then, to Miriam, added, "Most philanderers are, you know."

George barked contemptuously and with an expansive gesture of his arm, presented Faith to the others. "Have you all met Faith Freud?"

Walter laughed, refilling his glass, and called back over his shoulder: "Get one with a license, George!"

"He's got one," Faith said.

"Listen," Miriam said, "what——"

"I'm telling you, Walter," George said, "marriage is, you know what marriage is? Marriage is Russian roulette with a fully loaded revolver."

"Hah!" Walter smiled, nodding appreciatively.

"And the wife," George added, tapping Walter as the only other male present and therefore presumably the sole ear within hearing sympathetic to his cry in the sexual wilderness, "the wife very sportingly offers you first turn at the trigger."

"I know what you mean," Walter grinned. And, sipping, wondered why he had said that. *Did* he know? *How?* What unknown sympathetic chord had George plucked with that tapping finger? He dared not look at Miriam. And at the sound of her voice he tensed himself for her offended reaction, her certain challenge: *What do you mean, you know what he means?* But it was George to whom she was speaking: How could someone who felt that way about marriage have been married four times, she was asking with a quietly mystified interest.

"It *is* four times, isn't it?" she assured herself.

"It'd make you wonder, wouldn't it," George admitted. He thought for a moment, nodding, biting his lower lip, his eyebrows raised high and crinkling the tight skin of his tanned, weathered forehead. He raked his fingers through his dark, graying hair. Finally he admitted that he did not really know, he just had this compulsion about being married, it was a serious flaw in his personality, he suspected. Not that he had anything against women (they must all understand), they were glorious creatures, the more the better. But marriage . . .

"I mean, a man can survive a lifetime of razor nicks, Walter, but he can only cut his throat once. You know what I mean?"

"I know what you mean." *Again?*

"The Gospel according to Saint George," Faith said. "Chapter two, verse twelve."

George ignored her and turned again to Miriam, swiveling with a marked grace on his narrow, well-exercised hips, across the front of which his trousers stretched perhaps too youthfully snug. "Do you know what Valhalla was?"

Miriam frowned, perplexed. "That place in *Lost Horizon?*"

No, Walter thought, that was Shangri La.

"No, that was Shangri La," George said. "No, Valhalla is from

Norse mythology, it was the Viking heaven where their dead
heroes could fight all day and at night their wounds would heal
so that next day they'd be fit again for more battle." He paused
as though to be certain she had grasped the salient facts, prelude
to the so far mysterious point; then smiled, his timing precise:
"Divorce is my Valhalla."

Beautiful, Walter thought.

"And adultery?" Miriam asked with a directness that surprised
and interested Walter.

"Well, to carry the analogy a little further," George conceded,
"I suppose you might say that the playing of an occasional outside gig is only temporary first-aid in the field. But, finally, you
see, one realizes that one can't keep taking aspirin when surgery
is indicated."

Beautiful! Walter thought.

"Chapter seven, verse four," Faith said.

George ignored her. "Are you against it?" he asked Miriam.

"Against what?"

"The playing of an occasional——"

"Yes, I'm against that," Miriam said categorically.

"It's very necessary for a man, you see," George said.

"Do you think so?" Miriam said, her dissent obvious.

"And for women, too, of course."

Miriam managed a condescending smile. "Women don't think
the same way as men."

"Of course you do," George said quietly. "The difference between men and women isn't to be found between their ears."

It was by now impossible for Walter not to take note of the
fact that George's attention had been for some moments centered
on Miriam, to the exclusion of the others. If Miriam was aware
of it, she gave no sign. Their exchange had begun to take on
what Walter thought might be an uncomfortably . . . well,
not intimate, but certainly private air. (It was familiar. Just
such a demeanor had he seen Brady assume, ten feet high, in
countless movies, usually just prior to the fadeout on the First
Kiss.) The tone of his voice had become fixed at a low, lulling
level of near intimacy that both softened and further emphasized
its naturally husky timber. (A voice, said a hostile TV news

commentator during George's recent campaign, a voice invented for the bedrooms of the mind and now bidding fair to be heard in the Halls of the nation's Congress.)

Walter glanced quickly at Faith and found on her lips that familiar enigmatic half-smile suggesting private knowledge while her eyes darted back and forth between her sister and George.

"You take a very fundamental approach toward things, don't you," Miriam told George, offering him a precarious smile and—at last—shifting her eyes from what a movie critic had once called the "blued-steel gun barrels" of his to her husband's, to her sister's, to the match which she then struck.

"A fundamental approach toward things is a big plus going in," George declared. "It's all only a question of culture, you see? A matter of what we're conditioned to think of as right and wrong. Look at the Eskimoes—they *give* their wives to friends as a courtesy." He shrugged and spread his large strong hands, palms up. "It's all a matter of culture, you see? That's what it all comes down to in the end. Culture."

"They also put their old out on the ice to die, George," Faith reminded him.

"Well, give a little, take a little," Walter said.

"You know," George went on dreamily, "there's someplace in the Middle East, if a man wants to dump his wife he just looks at her and says, I divorce thee, I divorce thee, I divorce thee, three times, like that, and that's it, baby, she gets lost *or else.*" He paused as though to permit the power and beauty of such a concept to have its full effect upon them. Then, with intense passion, he demanded to know: "*Isn't that the most beautiful thing you ever heard?*"

Faith laughed delightedly. Walter hazarded a careful smile, with a sidelong glance at Miriam who he saw was frowning.

Faith had risen and was moving toward the bar. George turned sharply as she drifted by, as if snared by some invisible hook, and followed closely behind her.

"So, I'm going over to see Janine right now," George said, "and tell her I'm getting a divorce and I want you with me when I do it."

"What about the three-ring circus?" Miriam asked.

"Right!" George declared, wheeling on her. "Too late!" he said, pointing a triumphantly quivering finger at her. "That's exactly the point! She can't hurt me now!"

"Oh," Miriam said.

"I'm elected!" George continued, his eyes shining, "and I won't be up for reelection for another two years! Whatever she does now'll be forgotten by then! The public has a short memory. You know what I mean, Walter?"

"I know what you mean." It seemed to Walter an unusually cynical observation from so freshman a public servant. It was very depressing. (He thought of *Mr. Smith Goes to Washington*, James Stewart, the idealistic young senator triumphing over the political cynicism and corruptions of Edward Arnold and Claude Rains, Jean Arthur dubious at first, "What a sap!" but soon won over, Columbia, 1939, directed by Frank Capra.)

"There's always impeachment, of course," Faith said speculatively. "They may be ready to try that by the time Janine gets through with you."

"It's a chance I'm willing to take, that's how serious I am this time, Faith. Do you see that? Besides, I don't think it'll come to that, I really doubt that, it may upset some people, but it won't come to anything like that. Shit, I don't even know if it's *possible* to impeach a congressman."

"Sure it is," Walter said.

"Is it?" George asked. Abruptly, he seemed apprehensive.

"I think so," said Walter, himself suddenly uncertain in the face of even so mild a challenge. He turned to Miriam. "Isn't it possible for a congressman to be impeached?"

Miriam looked at him oddly.

"I'd check it out if I were you, George," Faith suggested.

"I will," George nodded. "But it doesn't matter, anyway. I'll worry about that when it happens. If it happens. Which I doubt. Besides, I think there's a chance she won't make any noise at all."

"What makes you think that?" Faith asked, picking up a fallen ornament from the floor under the Christmas tree.

"There have been indications," George answered cryptically.

Faith glanced at him, doubtful, and rehung the glistening,

fragile ball on the tree. "The thing is, George, you've made your bed and I think Janine is really going to expect you to sleep in it from time to time for a while."

"Why are you doing this to me!" George cried, agonized.

"All right, George, all right," she said quickly, with a pacifying gesture and, without so much as a glance at the others, moved to the foyer and opened the closet door and was already putting on her coat before George was able to react.

"Where the hell are you going!" he demanded.

"To see Janine," Faith reminded him calmly, opening the door. "Are you coming?" Without waiting for an answer, she stepped through the door and was gone.

George turned to Walter and Miriam with a look of mingled confusion and triumph. He opened his mouth to speak and then, as though fearing the delay of speech, hurried to the door, seized his coat and, without farewell, raced after Faith, slamming the door behind him.

In the sudden stillness Walter gazed at the door, dismayed at the abrupt and unexpected turn of events; then experiencing the beginnings of something akin to the feeling of vague melancholy that usually came upon him at the end of a party when the last guest had gone.

He was enjoying this! Why the hell did they have to rush off like that!

". . . means?" he heard behind him.

He turned distractedly to discover Miriam slowly touching a match to the cigarette that protruded rigidly from her tight lips, gazing at him over the flame with a calm fixity, expectantly: He knew he had missed something important. She blew out the match with what he thought was a somewhat exaggerated deliberateness; it looked familiar; then he remembered the Nazi general in *Paris Underground* symbolically snuffing out the life of the captured leader of the French Resistance who refuses to talk. "Hm?" he asked finally.

She exhaled lengthily before she spoke again. "I said, what do you mean you know what he means?"

Confused, finding some difficulty in ordering his thoughts (between Barbara Finch and George Brady he had gone far too heavy on the sauce this afternoon, there was no question about that in his muddled mind), it took him a moment to understand her reference, and another to grasp her meaning.

He grinned weakly. The party was definitely over. Time to tidy up.

9 With the tips of his numb, stiffened fingers Walter held the glass at its rim and revolved it slowly, turning the cocktail napkin beneath it, full circle, in order to read the message printed angularly along its border, *I don't suppose there'll be a tree left standing, for ever so far around, by the time we've finished.*

The Mod Hatter's was crowded and noisy. The night before the night before Christmas. In numbers, the vacationing college crowd seemed to have a substantial edge over the regulars who suffered their interloping presence with patience, knowing that holidays had to end.

Like youth, Walter reminded himself, despondently. *Like youth.*

How had it happened? he asked himself again. *Why? No man should be denied his only virgin! It wasn't fair! To have at least one virgin was every man's birthright!*

He tried again to piece it all together. In his attempt to reconstruct the disordered events, the unfortunate revelations that had followed George and Faith's departure that afternoon he was being consistently thwarted because he was still unable to remember the precise words that were first spoken after the door slammed behind George. His memory of the afternoon was a confusion of unmatched fragments and gaps for which he was unable to account. It was like watching one of the very old pictures that were broken with age and with the repeated use throughout fifteen years of late-night television and carelessly spliced together again with segments missing: One was aware of the absence of certain crucial scenes, but could only guess at their probable content.

Not that he was entirely secure in his desire for total recall. There were fears. For surely things were said that he would probably prefer not to remember (weren't there always?), and which would only gradually, unwelcomed, come to light as memory did its dirtier work.

He did know that Miriam spoke first. And that he had answered her. Of course. Whatever was said, he did not recollect having been aware just then, so soon, of any intimations of disaster. That lack of awareness, he knew now, was probably his first mistake; but he tried not to blame himself for this, reminding himself that disaster, if it announced its approach at all, did so subtly; no man could be truly held to account for failing to realize its presence until it was well upon him. And it had been well upon him, he knew now, by the time Miriam demanded to know what had happened to The Book (she seemed to speak of it capitalized) and almost instantly following her demand (had he refused to tell her; or merely hesitated an instant too long?) was turning the apartment upside down in unaided search. Well, no. That might be an exaggeration. One couldn't honestly say that she had quite turned the apartment upside down. She had merely conducted her search in angry haste and great determination with not too much regard for the inevitable disorder that followed in her wake. And, in any event, it had not been too very long before she hit upon the most likely place and found The Book in the desk drawer in the study.

His next clear memory—and even now he could smile at this, at least—was of her standing at the terrace railing, tearing handfuls of pages from The Book and casting them with a kind of useless violence (she did not take the time to crumple them and anyone knew you couldn't effectively hurl an uncrumpled sheet of paper) over the railing while he watched them caught in the wind, fluttering out of sight toward the street.

Watching her, he caught himself wishing that he could be on

the sidewalk at that moment to see who might find those tanta-lizing fragments of amorous arts and what they might make of it all. (As it happened, on his way out of the building later, he glimpsed a fragment half in a puddle of water, lodged against the base of a tree. Picking it up, he found the print to be already nearly illegible but it seemed to be concerned with the emotional hazards to both marital partners of *coitus interruptus.* On a sly, drunken impulse he flattened out the fragment of the page and placed it under the windshield wiper of the nearest car parked at the curb, whose owner would first suspect a parking ticket, but to his relief and eventual edification, would find that it was not punitive, but educational.)

He was reasonably certain now that the girl two tables away was giving him the eye; and had been, off and on, for the past half hour (too long for coincidence), glancing at him carefully from time to time while making a show of listening to her com-panion who was seated a few feet to Walter's left on the ban-quette along the wall. The table between was unoccupied for the moment, affording Walter an unobstructed view of the girl. She was quite pretty. In a conventional sort of way. Why were they all so pretty? He couldn't recall having seen an ugly girl in weeks. Months!

But he did not like the girl giving him the eye like this, he had never really liked that, not when the girl was with someone else. If you were with a màn, be with him! That was all there was to it! On the other hand, he had sometimes unavoidably wondered what would happen if, in just such a situation, he were to confront the couple and say to the man, This girl has been giving me the eye and I think if truth be told and we're all perfectly honest and adult about this she'd rather be with me, and turn to the girl and ask, Do you want to be with me, and she would say, Yes, I do, and they would go off together and be together and it would be wonderful!

The girl looked at him again, sidelong, over the rim of the glass touched to her full, pinked lips, the direction of her eyes the only clue to her interest; not their expression which was inscrutable. He turned his eyes away carefully, not wanting to offend her with too blunt a rejection.

The mirror. That was really the cause of it all. If not for the mirror she would probably never have made her revelation about Tom Aptheker. Almost certainly not. Yes, the mirror and the truth about Tom were directly related. She had even kept referring to the mirror as an Aptheker Special. Which was amusing at first. Until she went for the broom.

Had that come before or after she told him about Tom? After. Yes, first she told him that it was Tom Aptheker who had gotten her cherry; it was later that she'd gone at the cardboard carton with the handle of the broom. She had been able to pierce the cardboard easily enough, with rage's strength, leaving perfect round, puckered wounds, but could not penetrate through the excelsior packing within; at least not effectively enough to smash the glass.

Tom Aptheker! Christ! Of all people! His suspicion of years not paranoia, after all, but intuition!

Oddly enough, his impression at the time (and he had found no reason to alter it since) was that not only had there been no malicious or hurtful intent in her confession; but that, initially at least, she seemed as distressed about it as he.

I didn't even know you yet when it happened!

Well, that's something, at least!

And it was, of course, some comfort. In fact, it might all even have ended right there if she hadn't then offered the dumb remark that was presumably intended somehow to cushion the blow she had just dealt him. As though it was not enough to know that his best friend of nearly lifelong duration had humped his wife (before she was his wife, of course!) and that they had later made a pact never to reveal the truth to him. As though that wasn't enough! Couldn't she have left it at that? No! Not Miriam!

Besides, it was only once!

What do you mean, only once! That's all it takes, Miriam!

There was no question about it, he had been more distressed (and still was!) at this absurdly illogical attempt to defend her action than he had been at her divulging of its happening. But, naturally, she would try to shift the responsibility for his new knowledge onto him!

Well, are you satisfied now? Now that you've hounded me about it for all these years?

(Unfair: an occasional mild curiosity, maybe: hardly "hounded.")

So now you know! Are you satisfied?

Was Tom?

It took her a moment to understand, but when she did she was quick enough to meet him on his own chosen, sarcastic ground.

I don't know, I didn't ask him! I sure wasn't!

That's a comfort!

And it was. It gave him great if perverse satisfaction to know that Tom, who had always been so self-assured, sometimes to the point of boastfulness, about his sexual prowess, had been unsuccessful in his only attempt to fulfill the mysteries and delights of sex for Miriam. But Miriam had misunderstood and it was then, he supposed, that matters had begun to get truly confused.

How can you be so insensitive about such an important thing!

What thing!

My goddam cherry, that's what thing!

Her cherry? It was disconcerting, of course, so coarse a word coming from Miriam. Naturally, her thin veneer of sophistication (sometimes all the more endearing for its thinness) did not always adhere tightly to her and in times of stress had a tendency to buckle and crack; whereupon she might rarely resort to the earthy vernacular of her girlhood's Yorkville streets. But rarely. Her *cherry?* Obviously, she was a good deal more overwrought than he had realized.

And how I felt when I lost it!

I didn't even know you at the time!

What's that got to do with it!

Well, it's what you just said to me a minute ago, I didn't even know you at the——!

I'm still your wife! You're supposed to care about something like that! And what about that I've been lying to you all these years! What about that! I suppose you don't care about that, either!

He signaled the waiter and pointed to his empty glass.

He did care, of course. And it was certainly a factor to be considered. If he had seemed indifferent to it, it was merely that until that moment he had not been prepared to deal with that aspect of the bewildering situation. But, yes, it was exactly as she said, she had been lying to him for all of their married life, eleven years, even before, twelve, it was a long time, a long lie! How could she have been capable of such a deception for so long a time? What was this disturbing, duplicitous facet of her nature that he had never before seen, had never before been aware even existed? "Deception," she claimed, was far too harsh a word under the circumstances, since what she had done she had done for *his* sake, out of concern for *his* feelings, to spare *him* any possible hurt.

You should have thought of that before you did it!

Thought of what! Did what!

Thought of my feelings before you screwed him!

Walter, I didn't even know you at the time!

Well, he had been pretty plastered by then, his confusion was understandable. . . .

He wondered what time it was, his watch had stopped at eleven minutes after ten, it would have to be much later than that, but he could not see the wall clock from where he was sitting.

So! She wasn't a virgin, his had not been the first eager hands to part her legs, his not the first . . . Did she speak the truth about her justification for the lie? That she would never have told him she was a virgin in the first place had it been anyone but Tom Aptheker, had it been someone unknown to Walter who would always have remained unknown, forever nameless, faceless? But, Tom, always known, who would always be present in their lives, a constant reminder to her husband . . .

Lifting the empty glass, the waiter placed a full one before him on a fresh napkin, *If everyone minded their own business, the world would go round a deal faster than it does.* . . .

She had a valid point, he supposed, hard to contest, assuming it was true. Had he known about Tom, Tom and Miriam, he would ever after have been able, whenever he liked (and often, unquestionably, when he did not like), to visualize Tom's as one of the backs of the beast with two that Miriam had made with him.

He pictured it now.

Quickly, commuting his sentence of torture, he directed his attention and applause to the singer who had at that moment stopped screaming in the corner. He thought of Mad Celeste and wondered if he would ever see her again. Maybe she really was a teacher, moonlighting, a little hustling on the side, who could blame her, teachers barely made a living wage, one of the most important and vital of society's professions, probably the sole support of her invalid mother, and the poor kid had to put it out a few evenings a week just to make ends meet.

Faith . . .

Why Faith then? . . . Ah. Yes. At some moment in the course of the afternoon Miriam had said that Faith lived a somewhat eccentric sex life. But had refused to elaborate on that provocative remark. What had caused her to make it in the first place? . . . Yes, of course, Faith had somehow become something of an issue, briefly, during the afternoon. He remembered vaguely admitting (but only finally under insistent, and perhaps masochistic pressure from Miriam) that he did indeed find Faith to be an unusually attractive girl. And why shouldn't he? She was, wasn't she? Could Miriam deny it? Could anyone? Yes, it was then that Miriam had suggested that Faith might be more the "mirror type" since she "seemed to lead a somewhat eccentric sex life."

And they were back to the mirror again, she seemed obsessed with it; but it was of course a perverse obsession, one of antagonism, utter opposition, total rejection. And if she was going to refuse to submit—no, not *submit*, Christ, he didn't want her to *submit* to *anything!* Accede. If she was going to refuse to accede to, and show some natural enthusiasm for, so simple and relatively unsophisticated an erotic device as that, what kind of hope could there be for the other pleasures and fancies that he had been mentally cataloguing to introduce at careful intervals in the weeks and months to come?

Tom Aptheker? . . . Incredible.

He thought of all the hundreds of shared experiences with

Tom and Joan over the years, all the dinner parties, cocktail parties, theater dates, the weekends and vacations, and through all of them Miriam and Tom sharing their intimate secret, privately. How many times in all those years had their eyes met and remembered! *And how remembered? With what fond recall, what secret lipsmacking pleasure? Because the first time was the one no woman ever forgot, everyone knew that, she could go to the well ten thousand times in her life but it would always be that first raising of the bucket that would remain vividly etched in her carnal memory.*

And what about Joan! Did *she* know? She must! Tom would surely have told her, she would always have known! *Don't ever tell Walter, but the fact is I got Miriam's cherry.*

Yes, of course, it had been the three of them, all along, *all knowing!* And he tripping merrily along, on the outside looking in, *ignorant in his questionable bliss!*

But no longer. Not after today. The Truth About Who Got Miriam Farrell's Cherry and Why Now It Can Be Revealed.

Shit! One virgin in his entire life and now he hadn't even had that!

God! but it was disappointing.

He raised his sagging head and emptied his glass; then searched for the nearest waiter. He was fascinated to discover that the girl at that moment crossing his line of uncertain vision was Mad Celeste, making her way through the crowd toward the door, a young kid in tow by the tips of his fingers, a college boy obviously. He watched them all the way to the door. *Way to go, kid! She understands the needs of men!* . . . Of course, she has her little eccentricities, but if you can . . .

Why did she say Faith led an eccentric sex life? Eccentric how, precisely? What did Miriam know that he did not? And how did she know it? Girl talk? Intimate sisterly confidences?

He sighed and was suddenly bored and wearied by the Mod Hatter, and maudlin at his lonely presence in the midst of so much holiday cheer. *He wanted very much to go home.* But he was torn between that desire and the fear of being faced on his return with anything like the atmosphere that had prevailed on his precipitous departure. It might be best to call first, he thought, see which way the wind blew and what intimations of ease, if any, were carried on it.

He made his way to the booth near the door and dialed the apartment.

"Hello?"

". . ."

"Hello?"

"Faith?"

"Yes, hi, Walter."

"You're back?"

"Yes."

". . ."

"Walter?"

"How are you?"

"I'm fine, how are you?"

"I'm fine."

"*Are* you?"

"Sure. Why?"

". . . No reason."

"Is Miriam there?"

"Yes, she's here."

"Well, would you put her on for a minute?"

"She's asleep."

"She's asleep?"

"Yes, she went to bed about twenty minutes ago."

"Oh, she did."

"Shall I wake her?"

"No, no, don't wake her."

"What's happening?"

"What's happening?"

"Yes."

"Nothing's happening."

"She seemed upset."

"Oh, she did?"

"Where are you?"

"Now?"

"Yes."

"Well, I'm just over in a place nearby."

"With music."

"I beg your pardon?"

"I hear music."

"Oh. Yes. Yes, there's music here."

" . . . "

"Faith?"

"If I came by would you buy me a drink?"

"Came by?"

"Yes."

"You mean here?"

"Yes."

"Now?"

"Yes."

" . . . "

"What's the name of this place and where is it?"

"Well, it's called the Mod Hatter, it's just——"

"Oh, yes."

"You know it?"

"I passed by it yesterday. Are you alone?"

"Alone? Yes. Yes, I'm alone, sure."

"About ten minutes."

As she lowered herself into the chair opposite him, he glanced at the girl with the faithless eyes and saw that she had been sizing up Faith and turned away now as he sat again; she gave the impression, in the way in which she turned her full attention to her companion that, if the speculative issue and its outcome had been in some doubt until now, it no longer was: Faith's presence brought balance, established sexual symmetry.

Faith swiveled sideways in her chair, crossed one leg over the other, and removed her shoe. "I have a pebble in my shoe." She groped inside it with her fingertips. She removed her hand and, with a mildly puzzled expression, turned the shoe upside down and shook it. Still puzzled, she grasped the toe of her stockinged foot. "No, it's in my stocking."

"In your stocking?"

She straightened her leg, presenting the foot as evidence. He took it in his hand, cool and dry, and felt the small, hard shape under the nylon, nestled in the joint beneath her big toe.

"How the hell could you get a pebble in your stocking?"

"Your guess is as good as mine, Walter."

He smiled. "I doubt that."

She withdrew the foot. He wondered if she was aware of his hand's restraining pressure. She replaced the shoe and resettled herself in the chair, turning to discover the waiter who had been watching Walter with her foot. The waiter's face offered no opinion. She ordered a vermouth cassis; then, looking around with the expression of a buyer in a buyer's market, she said: "Nice place." She smiled at Walter. "A little cute, maybe."

"I thought that at first, too," he admitted, "but it grows on you." He lit her cigarette with fragile fingers.

She looked distracted for an instant, then refocused on him and said, "I just remembered, I had the wildest dream last night."

Why was she here, why had she come, what was going on?

"What about?"

She didn't know exactly what it was about, she told him, but Sir Cedric Hardwick had been in it. He waited for several moments while, eyes askance and with a frown of intense concentration, she appeared to be carefully reconstructing her until now forgotten dream. Finally she looked again at him, seeing him again and in that soft, direct way she often had, asked him how he was. He told her he was fine and smiled and nodded. Apparently the remark about the dream was apropos of nothing at all. Or was that really the case? Faith usually gave one the impression that everything she said, however cryptic it might sometimes be, was apropos of something. "What happened with George? How did it go?"

"I bluffed him and he folded."

"Oh. You mean it's off?" he asked, vaguely sympathetic. "With you and him?"

"It was never on," she reminded him.

"Well, you know what I mean, he isn't going to divorce his wife and all that?"

"Did you think he would?"

"Well . . . I don't know what I thought. I don't know what

to think about George. Incidentally," he began, then stopped himself, unsure whether to pursue his thought. She waited, looking at him attentively. "Do you think he still has someone following you around?" He grinned and muttered hoarsely, Bogart, "One of his private dicks?"

"No."

"Are you sure?" She nodded; confidently, he thought. She could have no real assurance of it other than George's word which he had given her the other day; obviously, for reasons of her own, she chose to believe him. "You could get away from him then now, couldn't you." She nodded again. "Are you going to?" He held his breath and waited.

"I don't know yet."

He waited again.

She smiled. "As George says, let's not roll up our pants till we get to the river." (It sounded familiar: a line from one of his movies?) "Do you think Mimi would mind this?"

"Mind what?" he asked falsely, knowing what.

"My coming here."

"Oh, of course not," he assured her. He shrugged; with conviction, he hoped. "Why should she mind?"

Faith gazed at him, head-on, her mouth promising a grin, not yet quite making good on it. Had her question been a cue of some kind? Did she expect him now to ask her *why* she had come? No, that wasn't Faith. If she wanted to tell him why she was sitting across from him now, the light and his blurred vision causing what appeared to be a kind of golden-red aura around her head, reflecting off the softly-waved, shining hair, if she wanted to tell him why, she would tell him. And when she did? *If* she did? *What would the reason be?* "So what happened with you and George and . . . whatsername?"

"Janine," she said, glancing in the direction of the performer's platform. "The kid sings real bad, doesn't he."

"Yes," he was forced to agree, feeling responsible for having inflicted the boy's lack of talent on her.

"Yes, well, we went up to see Janine," she said. "And they screamed at each other a lot for a while. And she screamed at me occasionally . . ."

She went on to describe a scene of bellowing uproar between Janine and George in which Faith herself figured less and less as time went on. George was evidently no match for his wife face to face. Her primary goal, apparently, had been to convince him that he was not responsible for his actions, that he needed rest, and help, that he must place himself in the capable hands of someone qualified to offer him that help, that he must trust her, only her, to see to that.

"Anyway, things finally began to quiet down and you could see George was folding by the minute. By the end, he couldn't take his eyes off her. Like he was mesmerized, or something. You can see she has a very powerful hold over him. Lot of sex in it, of course."

"Sex?"

"In the way she handles him. It's hard to explain, but there's a lot of sex in the way she is with him. She *is* very sexy, of course, Janine. George says she's a teaser but apparently when he's able to last her out she pays off in a big way. You know, the harder the wooing, the sweeter the winning—that sort of thing. Which I happen to think is a lot of shit."

"You do?"

"Of course. Anyway, by that time, it looked as though they'd both forgotten I was even there. George, anyway. When I started to leave he looked at me like he couldn't quite place me. Poor George. He might have been on the verge of another breakdown," she said, true regret in her voice. "Or a continuation of the last one," she added with less feeling. "By now they're either watching an imaginary movie on television or they're in the midst of a series of mutual climaxes, which is a big thing with George. No pun intended."

"That's all right," he nodded, vaguely dazed, faintly despondent, "I'm rather fond of puns. Sometimes I suspect life itself may be a pun of some kind."

There was a silence. She sipped from her glass, contemplating him over its rim. When she lowered the glass again, he discovered the half-smile on her lips. "How do you stand on that?" she asked quietly.

"On what?"

"The mutual climax."

Usually behind her. "I beg your pardon?"

"The simultaneous attainment of bliss in the act of love."

"Yes, I know what it is," he admitted, grinning, "I was just collecting my thoughts."

"Are you a proponent?"

She was being deliberately arch, of course.

"Well, it's certainly something to shoot for. Of course, bliss is difficult enough, one may be ill-advised to impose the burden of simultaneity on it." He smiled broadly. Actually, he thought, he was inclined to think of bliss as something not so much attained as apprehended, but it was far too subtle a distinction and he was in no condition, he knew, to pursue it with her.

"Have you been drinking all day?" she asked presently.

"Off and on."

"Do you drink a lot?"

"No. That is, not ordinarily. I seem to have been more lately, though. Recently."

"Did you have dinner?"

"No, uh-uh. Have you? Would you care for something to eat?"

"No, I ate, thank you. Why don't you have something to eat?"

There's only one thing in this place I want to eat right now, baby! Oh, Christ. "No, I'm not very hungry, actually. Besides, the food here is pretty awful."

She smiled dazzlingly. "Bad food, bad talent? What is it you like?" she asked with a faint twitch of her head at the Mod Hatter and everything in it.

"The atmosphere," he replied. "Besides," he smiled, taking up one of the cocktail napkins and displaying it to her, then waving it at the walls dotted with the plaques of further excerpts from Lewis Carroll, "I'm gradually getting through Alice in Wonderland—in a fragmentary kind of way. I never did read that when I was a kid. Would you tell me something?" She made no observable response. "Why did you go there today?"

"Where?"

"With George. To see his wife. I can understand George wanting to do a thing like that, I think George may be a little crazy, but you."

"Maybe I am, too."

"A little crazy?"

She merely smiled and was silent, allowing him to draw his own conclusions from whatever subtle clues she might yet offer. *Was* she a little crazy? Did she *want* this kind of thing, this madness with Brady? *Need* it? Did she perhaps thrive on turmoil, *was she one of those?* The terrifying ones, who went through their lives judging its fullness by the amount of wreckage they left in their roiling wake?

"Do you know what I'd love to do right now?" she asked, softly, suggestively.

Something simultaneous? his mind leered before he could remind himself that this was the sister of his wife, was he insane?

"I'd love to go for a walk," she continued. "It's been years since I walked in New York this late at night." In response to his sudden (and to her, surely mysterious) grin, she asked guardedly, "What."

Suppose he were to tell her what he had wanted her to say, what he had wanted her to want to do? "It's just that I came out without my gun, but we can risk it if it's really important to you."

At the checkroom waiting for his coat he wondered if this might be nothing more than a condescending ploy on her part, fresh air to sober him up. His eyes swept the plaque on the wall over the checkroom as he struggled with some difficulty into his coat, *Will you, won't you, will you, won't you, will you join . . .?*

He held the door, inhaling her scent as she passed by him into the street. *We are but older children, dear, who fret to find our bedtime near,* read the plague on the inside of the door where no one exiting could fail to see it.

A few steps from the door two shabby young men approached, hunched coldly into short, too-thin jackets, their eyes darting and dark with yearning. As they passed, one of them made a sucking noise with his mouth, staring at Faith; the other took a frozen hand from his pocket to clutch at his groin by way of offering her its availability. Walter stopped and half-turned with the vague intention of accosting them—an action he realized, even as he moved, he would probably never make if he were sober. Faith caught his arm, however, and shook her head almost imperceptibly, her eyes blinking once in a semaphore of warning. It took him only an instant to accept her wisdom. They turned into each other again, side by side, and moved away.

Dreamily, cadenced, as though she might be reciting a poem, she said, "There are wild animals in the streets, Walter, they make vulgar sounds with their mouths and call after me, suggesting all manner of obscenities . . . poor starving creatures."

Walter smiled uncertainly down at her. He discovered her arm in his, was abruptly intensely conscious of it, and couldn't remember when and how it got there. Yes, after he had come so close to being pounded into the pavement by the two punks—when they moved on she had just naturally taken his arm. Was it a noncommittal link, merely? Did he only imagine the intimate pressure on the arm locked in the furred crook of her elbow? Furred. Furry. Furry places, her furry place, her . . . "Did you know that *Dark Journey* was being shown again tonight?" It was a motion picture made for prime-time television two years before, later sold to smaller, non-network television stations for late-night showings; in it, Faith had had her first prominent acting role. "I made a note to see it again."

He waited.

Finally, she said, "Would you like to go back and watch it?"

She spoke the words carefully, he thought, perfectly, leaving no doubt about their implications: On the one hand, she would understand completely should he choose to take this opportunity to end this right here, now, at this place, at this moment; perhaps she would even watch the movie with him, friendly, but distant; on the other hand, if he chose the flesh Faith Farrell in favor of her shadow image he must understand that it would imply a certain commitment on his part, however limited, a willingness to explore further possibilities. . . .

He heard all of this clearly; clearly discerned the perilous remainder of the iceberg submerged beneath the surface of her cautious words. He felt a moment of mild panic at the thought that so much might depend on the single necessary word of response. He knew without any doubt what the word should be: He should already have spoken it, they should already have been

on their way back to the apartment where he would switch on
the television with a reluctant but uncompromised hand. His
palms were moist in his gloves. He stood at the lip of the chasm
and judged the distance across; without knowing why, he
jumped; in air, he said, "No."

They walked in silence for a moment.

"Are you serious about this writing thing?" she asked.

He had to concentrate for a moment. "Oh, yes, very. I told
you, it's a lifelong dream of mine. Well, not that long, but a long
time, yes."

"What took you so long?"

"To do it?" She nodded. "I don't know." It was an inadaquate
answer, but the truth. She held his eyes for a moment and
seemed to accept the truth of it well enough; but he had the
impression that she was accepting its inadequacy only temporarily. "Of course, I can't honestly call myself a writer, you
understand. I mean," he shrugged, "I'm a television executive,
there's no getting around that, that's what I am, this writing
thing is only . . ."

"You shouldn't say that," she admonished softly. "No one's
just one thing. In TV you're an executive, when you're writing,
you're a writer, when you're loving you're a lover, you know?"

"Yes, well, of course, I tend to look on people as somewhat less
fragmented than that."

She smiled. There was another silence during which he became fully aware of the attention she attracted from passersby.
Cassie had been right: People stared. She had been taken ice
skating by Faith on Sunday afternoon and later, while Faith
was out of the room and earshot, Cassie had told them how
interesting it had been being with Aunt Faith, people stared at
her. All the way down to the Rockefeller Center rink and all
the time they were skating and in the restaurant having hot
chocolate later and all the way back home. People stared at her,
Cassie said, reflectively. And not only men. Even women. Cassie
suggested that a good many of the starers must have recognized
Aunt Faith from the movies. Walter ventured carefully, smiling,
with a sidelong glance at Miriam, that that might be partially,
but not entirely, the cause of public attention. Only ventured,

and carefully, because Miriam might well have been sensitive to Cassie's making so much of Faith's attention-getting looks when she, Cassie, need not have looked farther than (but, alas, had never remarked on) the effect her own mother's beauty had on passing strangers in the street. (She could still stop traffic in a summer dress.) Cassie went on to agree that since Aunt Faith, she knew, was not all that famous yet, that probably it was mostly just because she looked the way she did. She had then put the lid on the dark box into which she had unwittingly discarded her mother, face, shape, all, wondering aloud as she left the room what it was like to be so beautiful and be stared at all the time. *Ask your mother,* he had wanted to call after her, but did not.

He heard Faith's voice, but too late. "I beg your pardon?"

"I said, what kind of things are you writing?"

"Well . . . it's hard to say," he answered, lying. It wasn't at all hard to say. Dangerous, perhaps, but not hard. "I've never really articulated it, I guess," he added, *never dared,* continuing his evasive action, barely making it, thick-tongued, through the verb without mishap; not that it mattered, certainly she knew how stoned he was, that was what all the talk about something to eat had been about. . . . *Something to eat* . . .

"Articulate," she suggested encouragingly.

How much was the risk? Was it a risk at all? It was a delicate decision. He hardly knew her, really. Could she be trusted? Somehow he thought she could, perhaps was just drunk enough to think so. Nothing ventured, nothing . . . "I want to write pure and beautiful love stories with sad endings."

Never before had he spoken the words aloud, not even to himself. Were they as ridiculous as they sounded now? He sensed her head turned, her eyes on him.

"You're in trouble," she said, like gentle warning.

He became aware that he had been holding his breath and exhaled now, slowly and quietly in order not to betray what had just proved to have been unfounded fears: She had not laughed. So far, so good. Something ventured, something . . . "I was afraid you'd say that," he nodded.

"The world is definitely not in the mood, Walter."

"I know I can expect a hostile response. It's very discouraging." He smiled to himself, at himself, remembering discouragement's hysterias.

"What is it?"

She was so very aware, she didn't miss a trick! Was there no hiding from her? How much did she already know, intuit, that he had not yet told? She was peering at him, waiting to know the source of his entertainment: Another venture was being required of him. "No, it's just that sometimes . . . sometimes I get so discouraged I think I get a little hysterical, and then I begin to come up with these insane ideas, it's terrible." He tried to suppress the broadening smile that would surely only tantalize her more.

"Well, tell me," she demanded, already smiling at his smile, a sympathetic vibration.

So, venturing again, with misgivings, he told her. He told her about Do Me Dirty Daddy Like You Done Last Night, the Touching, Heartwarming Story of a Young Girl and Her Affectionate Father, suggesting his possible alternate title, Her Part Belongs to Daddy. She seemed to enjoy that. Encouraged, he described the Jesus musical, A Pocketful of Miracles. He told her about The Chink in My Armor and Nanook Feldman the songwriter from Reykjavik. He told her his latest, of only a few nights past, I'll Blow My Nose Tomorrow or, Get Away From Me With That Handkerchief, The Autobiography of a Nose Whistler, by Willard Fest, as told to Walter A. Hartman.

He fell silent finally and listened to her laughter echo and die in the cold air, listening to her tell him, Walter, you're insane. Quickly, lest she suspect that what she had just heard might be the level of his literary dreams, he assured her, "But that's only when I'm discouraged and boozed up, I get a little hysterical."

She took his arm again and looked at him levelly. "Like now," she said softly.

"Like now," he admitted, almost without hesitation, finally discarding all caution like an unnecessary coat on a steadily warming day. She held his eyes for several moments; he was determined not to look away; but did, finally.

They walked in silence for the length of a deserted crosstown block. He tried to interpret the silence: Did it mark the end of something? A beginning?

When she spoke he was almost startled.

"You and Mim had a fight?"

"A fight?" Stalling.

"Mm."

"What makes you think that?"

She only glanced sidelong at him for a moment, and did not even bother to answer. After another moment he relented somewhat and said, "It's a complex situation." It was a tangential observation, he knew, but perhaps she would detect its pertinence.

"Were you fighting about me?"

"About you?" he asked cautiously.

"Yes."

"No. Why would we be fighting about you?"

"You look at me."

"Look at you? What do you mean?"

"I mean you look at me."

"I do? I mean, yes I do, of course, but I mean . . ." He trailed off, then finished lamely, "I don't think I understand the question." *What* question? She hadn't asked a question!

"Mimi may be a little square, but she isn't stupid."

Knowing further evasion to be useless, pointless, he surrendered unconditionally. "I didn't know it showed," he said, grinning weakly. "I mean, that I look at you." Was it true? Had it been so obvious, so unguarded that even Miriam had been aware of it? "*You* certainly didn't seem to notice," he said. But of course not. She must by now be so accustomed to being lusted after by men that it was no longer a matter of "noticing." She simply knew: as she knew she had this face, and these breasts and those legs; as she knew she was Faith.

"Do you think I should leave?" she asked him.

"Leave? Leave where?" He hoped he was masking his alarm. "What do you mean? Leave New York?"

"No. I mean, do you think maybe I shouldn't stay with you and Mimi. At least, not as long as we planned. Just a couple of more days, through Christmas, then maybe I should leave."

"Why? There's absolutely no reason for you to do that, believe me." Trying desperately to keep the rising sense of threatened loss from surfacing in his voice, he feared he was not being successful. "We really weren't fighting about you, if that's what you think. Really. I mean, what possible reason could we have to fight about *you?*" It was true, of course. She had in no way been a subject of contention that afternoon. At least, he hadn't thought so. On the other hand, Faith was on to something, perhaps. Now that he thought about it it did seem that Miriam had brought her sister's name into the argument rather gratuitously—along with that mysterious reference to her erotic preferences. (*What does she know that I don't know?*) He would have to be more careful, eternal vigilance is the price of secret lust. "And if it'll make you feel more comfortable, I promise not to look at you," he smiled.

She turned to meet his eyes. "Oh, but I wouldn't like that," she said quietly.

His throat constricted, he felt suddenly too warm. Care must be taken! No precipitous assumptions! The signs, if any, must be read carefully, always. How many unearthed fragments of ancient clay have reconstructed an exquisite vase from what was once a chamberpot? Beware the enthusiasm of unfounded hopes! Let's not take off our pants till we get to the river! *And besides all that, she's your fucking sister-in-law! You're practically talking about incest here!*

But it was useless. Echoing her suggestive tone (*suggesting what?*), he asked, "You wouldn't?"

She maintained her provocatively enigmatic expression for a time that began to seem endless, not speaking. *But,* he wondered desperately, *saying what with her eyes? Were* they speaking words that he should understand, to which he was expected to respond? Respond how? She was maddening! Why didn't he simply drag her into the nearest doorway (Henderson's Home Appliances) and shove his tongue down her throat and fondle those magnificent knockers that could not be, refused to be concealed even by the thick fur of her coat, that gift from an admirer, *people give me things, In return for what?*

She was speaking again. "I beg your pardon?"

"What were you fighting about?"

Sex, he wanted to say. *What else?* They had digressed occasionally, there had been tangents, but sex was unquestionably the basic issue. It so often is. But in the uncertain circumstances of the moment, it was an admission he dared not make. "Romance," he said, as neutrally as possible.

"What about it?"

"Well . . . its possibility, I guess," he grinned, choosing his words carefully, like a child at a candy counter trying to find the best at least cost.

She smiled. "Under what circumstances?"

After nearly eleven years of marriage, under those circumstances! A marriage that took place (Had Faith forgotten? She was there.) on St. Valentine's Day. Which was probably the high-water mark in his personal history of romanticism.

"The fix is in, don't you know that?" Faith asked.

"What fix?"

"On what you call romance. The cards are marked, Walter, the dice are loaded, the wheel is rigged, it's a shell game for suckers who never win because Reality has palmed the pea."

Walter laughed—appreciatively, he hoped she realized. She *was* putting him on, wasn't she? "You certainly state your case colorfully!"

"I'm getting cold," she said. "Could we go in here and get a drink?"

It was a dim, anonymous little cocktail lounge that whispered Mob to him the moment they stepped inside. It was practically deserted. The house hooker was sitting at the end of the bar near the door having her cigarette lit by the bartender. She gave Walter a glance and Faith a thorough going over, then turned away.

Walter checked his coat; then, surveying the small sea of empty tables, smiled. "Decisions, decisions," he whispered.

They allowed themselves to be led to an arbitrary choice of a table and gave their order to the young, dark-faced waiter who Walter placed to be the mobster boss's wife's nephew, twice removed, and starting at the bottom in the organization. The bartender, he had already decided, was the boss's second cousin and moving up fast.

"You've been married what, now? Ten years?"

"Yes. Nearly eleven."

"How often are you unfaithful to her? On the average?"

He smiled hysterically, his first line of defense, while he tried to find his best possible stance: He had been prepared for a general survey of the situation, not a probing in depth. *There was only one kind of probing in depth he was interested in at the moment!* "Unfaithful to her?"

"Yes."

"What do you mean?"

"Why do you keep asking me what I mean?"

He detected the faintest trace of impatience in her voice. "Well, never," he said, not nearly decisive enough, he knew.

"What do you mean, never?" She was subtly dubious.

"Why do you keep asking me what I mean?" he grinned. Her answering smile admitted turnabout as fair play; he felt he had won a small victory. And some delay.

"Never *once?*" she persisted, almost incredulous now.

"Yes," he nodded. "No," he added, striving for absolute clarity, shaking his head, refusing to shift his eyes from hers. *Talk about private dicks!* There was a brief silence during which she was clearly absorbing this information. He wondered what probing response his constancy was going to elicit from her and tried to prepare himself for it. As the waiter placed the two glasses on the table, she spoke again.

"What do you do for sex?"

Walter laughed nervously and glanced up at the waiter who was interested and lingered unnecessarily to empty the ashtray. "The usual things," he leered. *But ask me again in a few weeks!*

Assuming Miriam can be brought around, of course.

He looked again at the unconscionably dawdling waiter and gave him a push with his eyes. The waiter stole away.

"You do like it, don't you?"

"Sex?"

"Mm," she nodded.

He merely grinned desperately. *Want to see how much?*

"And you haven't made love to anyone but Mimi in ten years?"

"No." *Almost eleven!* "What's wrong with that?" But even he could easily discern the defensiveness in his voice.

She grinned suddenly, her eyes squinting suspiciously. "Are you putting me on?"

"No, of course not. I suppose it is a little unusual."

"You must be bored to tears," she suggested simply.

Not to tears, no! To action, maybe, bored to action. Tears were the last resort. "What makes you think that?" he replied, knowing he must sound like a fool. But what was she getting at?

"Walter, no one is *that* good," she said softly.

"Well, I didn't say it had anything to do with my being good, it's a little more complex than that, I told you before, it's a complex situation."

"I don't mean you, I mean her."

"Her?" He was confused. What did the goodness have to do with Miriam? It was *his* fidelity that was at issue, not hers. Wasn't it? (*It was only once!*) What was she getting at? "I don't understand."

"Are you telling me that Mimi is so incredibly good in bed that you've never had the need to——"

"Oh!" he interrupted, enlightened at last. "Oh, you mean *that!* Good *that* way." He forced a laugh that he heard fairly resound with hollowness, and which attracted the bartender's sinister attention. "Well, no, I mean that isn't the issue. I didn't realize that's what you meant. No, that isn't the issue, exactly."

After a moment she asked, "Isn't it?"

He tried, testing it first in his mind, the single necessary negative; but could not bring himself to repeat the lie that she so clearly disbelieved. On the other hand, the truth was equally unthinkable: How could he discuss his wife's erotic shortcomings with her own sister? He was forced again to take temporary shelter in evasion. "What are you getting at?" he asked casually.

"Don't you know?" she said, softly, intimate.

"Should I?"

She gazed at him, disconcertingly speculative.

"Maybe it's my fault," she said cryptically.

"What."

"That you don't know what I'm getting at." She looked at him reflectively for a moment with a tentative grin. "Either you really are putting me on or you're . . ."

She had interrupted herself by choice, he thought, not because she lacked the words to finish. "Or I'm what?" he asked innocently. "I'm not putting you on. Why would I do that? So, *what* must I be? Dumb? Is that what you were going to say?" He smiled, assuring her of his forgiveness and understanding in advance if she were forced to admit the unhappy truth.

"Of course not."

It was too tenderly offered a protest to be doubted. "What then?" he insisted.

She hesitated a moment, then smiled. "Very drunk," she said.

He knew those were not the words she had originally intended. Nor did she appear to truly expect him to believe they were. What was she suddenly evading? And why?

"It's the same for her too?"

"Is what the same?"

"She's never been unfaithful to you?"

So much for evasions. Back to facing the issues squarely, head-on, no flinching allowed! "Of course not." *She didn't even know me at the time!*

"Who got the book for who?" she said.

"What book?" he asked, puzzled; then flinched, remembering on the instant what book.

"The Amorous Arts in Marriage," she answered. "Or, How To Do It Real Good on Tuesdays and Fridays," she added with a beguiling grin.

He might have known she wouldn't have forgotten about the book! And that she would divine the significance of its presence, embarrassingly brand new, in the apartment. Now he knew what this was all about! "I like your title better," he said, with fluttering heart. "You think it'll make a TV series? The network's considering it, I have to give my recommendation by the end of the week, of course it would have to be very carefully cast." He was confident that she would accept his heavy-handed levity for what it was, a complete admission: who had bought the book for whom and for what desperate cause and carnal purpose, a full confession, where do I sign, and remember—I expect leniency in return for my cooperation in this matter.

"Do you think you're going to find the answers there, Walter?" she asked gently, her own doubts perfectly obvious.

What answers? How could she be so goddam doubtful about the answers? She didn't even know the questions yet! . . . Or did she?

"You won't you know," she continued. "They're hopeless, you see?"

"The answers?"

"The books. Of course, I can see how you might have been driven to something like that."

"You can?"

"Ten years is a long time," she sympathized. "And Miriam is very beautiful, very sexy-looking but . . . well, she never was terribly imaginative, I know that."

Her candor was numbing.

His impulse was to stand mute: He was certainly not getting his bargained-for leniency, why should he incriminate himself even further? "I love her, Faith, I want you to know that." It was either a warning to her—cease and desist—or an urgent, necessary reminder to himself.

Perhaps both.

"Do you?" She sounded not at all dubious; on the contrary, was apparently maintaining an open mind until all the evidence was in.

"Very much," he insisted.

She parted her lips to speak; then closed them and expelled the unused breath audibly through delicately flaring nostrils. She had a superb nose, he thought. And rather full lips, fuller than Miriam's. He considered again that theory about the correlation between a woman's lips and that other desired, sought-after, yearned-for mouth, the reputed similarities of conformation. Was it true? It was a fascinating theory, who could deny its intrigue? But provable? How? *A wide-ranging, comprehensive, orificial investigation?* (He thought this theory of the female mouth to be far more viable then the corresponding sexual hypothesis regarding the male nose, its size and comformation said to hint at possible penile proportions. That surely was an old wives' tale. All the same . . . might she at this very moment be secretly, speculatively eyeing his nose?)

The tip of Faith's pink, tender tongue flicked, licking the fullness of her pale lips and he shivered to know of those other soft, pouty, moist . . .

"Are you all right?" she said.

"Yes. Sure. Fine." Quickly.

"I thought for a minute you'd left us," she said, sweetly smiling. *I'd never leave you, never.*

"Anyway, that's not really the point," she said, serious again.

He scrambled in his mind, trying to recall what had been the point that was being rejected as such now. . . . Yes: Miriam, love. Very much. He did. "I thought it was," he said, smiling with an easy and innocent charm that gave no clue to his lascivious speculations about her mouth. Mouths.

"I see where you're making your mistake."

"What mistake?"

"You still think," she said, a hint of regret and commiseration in her voice, "that love and marriage and sex and romance are all in some magical and mysterious way related to each other. Is that what you think?"

"What's so magical and mysterious about it?" he protested. But could not deny the possibility that he might perhaps be defending, mad and single-handed, a private fortress of his own that had already fallen to the enemy. And who was the enemy? What? Reality? He knew it, knew it in his heart. "Put me down for an incurable romantic," he shrugged, covering himself with sophisticated ridicule.

"Oh, no, you mustn't think that," she said earnestly.

"Think what?"

"That it's incurable. It's not incurable."

"It's beginning to sound like some kind of an affliction," he suggested.

There was a pause.

"What do you think romance is, darling?" she wanted to know.

He coped first, unavoidably, with the endearment: meaningful, significant? "Discovery," he said.

"Discovery?"

"Yes."

"Of what?"

He had a flash of déjà vu; then remembered having exchanged

these precise words with Miriam only days ago. "Of something new," he said, again, to these new, perhaps more receptive, ears.

She grinned and sipped. "You mean what George calls Man's Eternal Quest for a New Position?"

He smiled carefully. "Something like that. I myself," he continued playfully, "have recently been characterized as the Christopher Columbus of the bedroom."

"And who do you hope to be your New World?" she murmured, artfully suggesting the unlikelihood of the role's being filled by Miriam.

"There's a certain resistance to the idea," he grinned weakly, accepting her suggestion, "I have to admit that."

"Because it doesn't make sense."

She was so serene, confident, reasonable. He didn't trust himself to speak: He might agree. And forthwith throw her to the floor, tearing at her clothing, and his.

"Do you really believe there can be anything left to discover about a woman you've been sleeping with for ten years?"

"Nearly eleven."

She nodded, advisedly. "You can't get into the heart with a crowbar, Walter," she said softly. "Do you know what I mean?"

He knew. She meant you can't get into a wife of ten-years-nearly-eleven with a book like *The Amorous Arts in Marriage*, ceremonial tips for special occasions notwithstanding.

"Particularly a man like you."

She was speaking so quietly now that he was barely able to hear her. But the invitation contained in her last words was clear: RSVP. "What's a man like me?" he responded, not daring to hope.

"I've always thought you were a man who's got the music inside, Walter."

He found himself incapable of dealing head-on with an observation so bursting with erotic innuendo. "Is that the impression I give?" he asked, smiling wildly, taking one giant step backward. Simon says.

"And being like that," she went on in pursuit, closing the gap again, "don't you realize what a burden your fidelity puts on poor Mimi?"

"What burden?" he frowned.

"Of responsibility, you idiot," she whispered. And covered the knuckles of his cold hand with the warm palm of her own, like silk. "It's terribly important, you know, not to require responsibility of people who can't be responsible. Would you ask directions of a blind man on a dark night?"

He dared not look, but the tips of her fingers now were almost imperceptibly stroking the back of his hand.

"By looking only to a single person for gratification of an ever more increasing intensity . . ." She canted her head at a delicate angle and moved it slightly from side to side. "It doesn't make sense."

"It doesn't, does it," he relented at last, but careful to affect a world-weary twist of a grin (William Powell in *My Man Godfrey*), that in his admission he should in no way appear to her to be defeated or self-pitying. "But, then, what does?"

"You know what does, Walter. It's history."

He wanted desperately to put his hand on the hand that was on his; but was not able to yet. Not yet. That would complete the circuit, currents would surge, flowing, unstoppable.

Impossible.

"What George calls the playing of an occasional outside gig is absolutely essential for a married man's physical and spiritual well-being." (*Why did she keep quoting George Brady? Was he the primary source of her corruption?*) "It makes for a much more relaxed atmosphere in the home, Walter, believe me."

"There's something very corrupt about that," he said.

"Isn't it logical?"

"Yes. That's what worries me most. I mean, when the corrupt begins to sound logical."

"Not to worry," she whispered. "It's only a question of means and methods. You've been pursuing hopeless possibilities, the wrong means to your desired end." (*Stand up and turn around, I'll show you a desired end!*) "You've been making a serious error, Walter." She smiled, beautifully. "But then, what is life, after all," she declaimed quietly, mock-serious, "but a comedy of errors?"

"The question is, which of us is in error?" he countered—

cleverly, he thought. "I thought the verdict was in on that."

"It's being appealed."

Was she right? *Was* he in error? He had only to admit it to himself in order to be able to admit it to her. And, once admitted to her, they had only to rise and leave this place and go somewhere and begin: It was, of course, a natural progression. It was impossible to believe, but true: *He could have her! He,* Walter, could take *her,* Faith, to be his unlawfully . . . Yes, he might have the privilege of being the latest bit of battered flotsam bobbing in that tumultuous wake of hers . . . But, why him? On the other hand, why not? *He was not an undesirable man, there was evidence to support that, evidence!* And, yet . . . she was Miriam's sister! Did that mean nothing to her? Odd—she had always seemed so genuinely fond of Miriam. What long-buried, unknown, unacknowledged sibling rivalries might be suddenly surfacing obscenely here now!

"Virtue doesn't triumph, Walter," she murmured. "It only sneers self-righteously."

From the Collected Works of George Brady? No, it sounded more like Faith. Do it! He who hesitates is trampled in the rush of those right behind him who don't. He turned his hand over beneath hers and made a tentative fist around those warm, slender young fingers.

But *was* she right about his methods? *Were* they hopeless possibilities? *You want a fried egg, Walter, you don't light a fire under a chicken,* Jack Finley once said—in another context.

"What's funny?" she asked softly, squeezing his hand as though she might wring the answer from it.

"I was thinking of something a philosopher friend of mine once said."

"The philosophy portion of this program is over," she advised.

Yes, it would certainly have to be marked down as one of the more intellectual seductions by a woman of a man, tracing a circuitous route through the cerebral cortex on the way to the heart—and to that equally uncontrollable organ that now strained and ached for its natural connection with what must surely be beckoning to it from two feet away under the table. Too far for comfort. But at least it had been truly that, a seduction. And that in itself was refreshing and exciting: He had never been seduced before; he and Miriam had always had their sexually traditional roles pretty well defined.

"You won't find the amorous arts in a book, Walter. There's no need to be like those lovers, so-called, with synchronized hearts, making love to the rhythmic tick of a metronome, dreaming of Playboy bunnies and Paul Newman. Passion is no nervous tic, it's no science, it's no pornographic Punch and Judy show. . . ." (He felt himself going down under a hail of words like buckshot, not fatal, but stinging and drawing vital blood, sapping strength.) "Passion is . . . something else. . . ." Her lips curled, her gaze turned inward. "It's the country of blue dreams where they all come true," she concluded quietly.

She looked down at his hand enclosing hers, the pad of his thumb passing back and forth over the hills and valleys of her soft knuckles. "That feels nice," she whispered, hinting at private connections causing secret pleasures elsewhere on her person.

He stilled his carnal thumb instantly.

Her eyes moved quickly to his. "Wasn't it supposed to?"

His eyes (Coward's eyes? he wondered. Was he, when the chips were down, a theorist merely? *Coward!* he accused himself. *Have some Faith!*)—his eyes and wan half-smile spoke regret and apology, hoping for understanding, despairing of getting it.

But after a moment she smiled and squeezed his fingers briefly. "Idiot," she murmured, surrendering.

They walked to Madison, the nearest avenue, to get a taxi, she with her hands buried deep in her pockets, her handbag slung on her wrist and bouncing against her hip at each step. Her hips, her beautiful hips, the hip bone's connected to the thigh . . .

She told him casually that the friend's apartment at which she was staying, to which she would return after her stay with him and Miriam, was just around the corner from where they now stood. The remark seemed at first to be without special significance. Then she turned to look up at him and smiled; and the smile revealed that while, true, the fact was no longer of practical importance now, it had been so no more than ten minutes ago. Of course. She had led him here, had planned it all from the first, artfully subtle in her prurient purpose, had, with that arm linked in his, urged him imperceptibly around corners, down streets, and into that nameless little bar from which, finally, they would not have had far to go to begin what she had all along had every intention of beginning.

He smiled back at her and nodded faintly to tell her that he understood. And at that moment they became, somehow, friends. It gave him a warm feeling. . . . But only for a moment. *I want to bang you, goddammit, not hold your hand!* . . . But, even so, bewildering and confusing as the encounter had been, there was something, a great deal perhaps, to be said for having had this opportunity merely to talk to her. He had had occasion in the past to wonder if perhaps the basis for a good percentage of the world's infidelities might be no more than the need for someone to talk to—who hasn't already heard everything you have to say. Repetition could very well be an affliction of the vocal chords as well as the other pertinent organs.

Getting into the taxi, he wondered when she had decided, at what moment in the course of these past few days had she determined to have him if she could. He resolved to ask her. One of these days. It was something he wanted to know. He didn't know why.

She took his hand, entwining her fingers in his, and rested it between them on the cold plastic leather of the seat: It was a friendly connection, he knew, nothing more. He stared straight ahead through the small porthole in the supposedly assault-proof plastic shield between the front and rear seat of the taxi, intended protection for the driver against possible criminal elements in the passenger seat. Walter thought the shields pitiable (if not actually paranoid) in their uselessness, and depressing in their necessity.

There was silence for several minutes except for the ticking meter and the driver's intermittent hacking cough before Faith lifted his hand in hers and touched her lips to it. "Poor Walter," she murmured, and lowered his hand again. "The Last of the Romantics. You're the ones most tortured by temptation, you know," she went on with gentle fretfulness, "and only because you refuse to submit to it. It's so simple. You haven't realized yet that the poets are all liars." She fell silent for a moment, then sighed. "Oh, are they ever liars, Walter."

He was instantly very depressed.

Then he remembered that this was Monday and that there was something on the Late Late Show that he had made a note to see. What was it . . .? Yes. *The Philadelphia Story*, Hepburn, James Stewart, Cary Grant, MGM, 1940, it wasn't all that late yet, they would be back at the apartment in plenty of time.

He began to feel a little better.

10

Walter awoke before full light, with a hangover and
an erection, both painful, and with one hand between Miriam's slightly parted legs. *Even in my
sleep,* he thought, not without a certain vague despondency.

Miriam made a small sound and stirred. His hand clenched
softly on her, in reflex, as though it had a mind (and heart) of
its own, reluctant to surrender its warm, furry bed. But Miriam
moved and rolled over and away. His hand crept back, rejected
and sullen, and sought comfort by his side.

He rolled onto his back, wishing that he might sleep again,
reluctant to get up in the cold room for the necessary trip to
the bathroom. *One of their first mornings together, before they
were married, she woke and said is that for me or do you have
to go to the bathroom?*

He spent several minutes reflecting on the ambivalence of the
morning erection, then sighed and struggled from his sexless
morning bed and shuffled rigidly to the bathroom.

Two hours later, the additional sleep having done little to
relieve his throbbing head and uncertain stomach, he came down
the hall hearing Walter Cronkite in the living room. Cassie was
watching a report of the moon voyage on the television; the networks would be interrupting their regular programming through-

out the day, of course, for progress reports. The astronauts, he remembered now, were scheduled to have gone into orbit around the moon early that morning.

"How's it going?" he asked, lingering.

"So far, so good," Cassie said. "They're in orbit fine."

"Wonderful."

"Can I stay up tonight for when they start back?"

"That'll be pretty late," he said doubtfully.

"It's a very important thing."

"They'll replay it tomorrow," he shrugged.

"That's not the same."

"Mm. Well, you'd better ask your mother."

"I asked her. She said to ask you."

"I'll ask her." He paused, then seeking the morning's first crucial information, he said, casually, "Where is she by the way?"

"In the kitchen. Could you settle it fairly soon so I'll know one way or the other?"

"I'll get right on it," he said vaguely, knowing that it had been futile for him to have hoped for more time, a postponement of this morning-after confrontation, that she might have already, so early, left the apartment on some vital last-minute time-consuming day-before-Christmas errand. No. Of course she would be in the kitchen, waiting. Was she as apprehensive as he? It might have helped for him to know. There had been no sort of resolution arrived at yesterday; left unresolved yesterday, it was far too much with them today. All in all, a morning impossible to face; yet face it he must. At least the guest room door had been closed when he passed it a few moments ago, there were no voices to be heard in the kitchen. . . . It was possible. "Is your Aunt Faith up yet?" he asked Cassie. Casually again.

"No, she's still asleep."

"Ah. Well, don't play that too loud," he nodded at the television, "no point in waking her."

Speculating on how he might have comported himself had it been necessary to face them both simultaneously, he turned from the blinking light on the television screen which simulated the Apollo capsule's position in relation to the moon and started toward the closed kitchen door. At the door, he stopped, and wet his lips, before pushing it open.

"Good morning," he said.

"Hi."

She answered his pleasantly noncommittal smile with one of her own.

He sat at the table and took up a defensive position behind the *Times* which he unfolded to the market quotations: "Sleep well?"

"Fair," she replied. "You?"

He nodded, unseen, needlessly. "Fair," and moved the paper to permit her to pour his coffee. He sugared it heavily.

"I guess you were out fairly late." She gave him his juice and returned to the stove.

"Fairly."

They seemed to have hit upon a carefully neutral word, one lacking in any firm commitment; and, having hit upon it, were clinging to it, safe for the moment in treacherous currents.

"I hoisted a few," he confessed pleasantly from behind the *Times.*

"I noticed that," she replied.

He thought he heard a smile.

Throughout his breakfast their conversation was desultory, the atmosphere not so much tense as cautious. But no reference was made to the previous afternoon. When he had finished eating he refolded the newspaper and rose from the table, much eased by the promise of the initial encounter's neutrality.

"Are you going to write now?" she asked, then added quickly, "Work?" (It had not been many weeks before that he had pointed out to her, reasonably, he thought, her habit of always referring to what he did in the study as "writing" never "work." She was unable to see what difference the choice of words made but had tried to be careful ever since.)

He smiled weakly and rolled his eyes, a clear reference to his uncertain physical condition. "I'm going to try."

"I'll bring your coffee in."

He nodded and pushed through the swinging door and, passing through the living room, saw instantly what he had failed to see earlier: The mirror was gone, the huge carton was no longer leaning against the wall near the front door. It had been there when he and Faith returned last night, he remembered clearly. It was still there when he went to bed after *The Philadelphia Story*. (In fact, he had a vague memory now of giving the carton a maudlin goodnight slap on its cardboard shoulder and wishing it a merry Noël.)

But now it was gone.

He went directly to the study, closed the door, and in a confusion of uncertainty and speculation, immediately fell onto his hands and began his morning push-ups. When Miriam entered the room a few minutes later he was still rising and falling, his elbows locking and breaking in steady rhythm, his eyes on the floor. He waited until she had placed the coffee tray on the desk. "Where is it?" he asked, striving for a tone of calm curiosity into which there leaked only the mildest accidental trickle of accusation.

"Behind the door in the pantry," she said presently, behind him. "I mean, it's still here," she assured him, reading his mind, "I didn't throw it out or anything."

He nodded again. Reasonably well out of sight, if not out of mind. Her intent was clear: There could be no question of dealing with so controversial an issue while Faith was staying with them; he could see the sense of that.

She was waiting, he knew. Still, he could think of nothing to say.

"Are you still upset about yesterday?"

He lowered and raised himself twice more, stalling for time, then lay chest-down on the carpet, his face turned to one side, his arms straight out, palms down. He was breathing heavily. She was waiting. "Which part?" he said, grinning.

"Any part. All of it," she replied carefully.

"I hardly even remember what it was all about." He inhaled deeply and expelled breath noisily through his mouth; then hauled himself abruptly to his feet and began running in place: The activity might discourage her; his daily exercises, a recent determination, exhausted her just by watching them, she had said.

"You hardly remember?"

She was understandably perplexed: Yesterday's bout had lasted for about six hours, with a short break for dinner, much of it tensely and unnaturally hushed behind the closed study and bedroom doors, walled from Cassie's sometimes incredibly acute hearing. Six hours: How could he hardly remember? "Well, of course I *remember,*" he explained. "You know what I mean. But I mean, we've had arguments before, haven't we?"

"Not for six hours."

Again he broke the steady rhythm of inhale-through-the-nose-exhale-through-the-mouth and grinned wildly. "Well, duration isn't so important, it's the content that counts," he panted. He could see she didn't like it at all. His unexpected flippancy was unsettling her: Naturally she would require him to give some indication that he shared her anxiety about yesterday's possible repercussions. If only he hadn't asked about the mirror in the first place! But he had to know!

"Well, I guess I could make a point or two on content alone, forget duration," Miriam said, tensely.

He stopped running and began to deep-knee bend. "What point do you want to make?" he gasped. His legs were beginning to feel numb, he noted, and wondered how long he could keep this up.

She hesitated a moment. "Well, no point really," she shrugged, managing, amazingly, to mimic to some degree his own indifferent air. He thought gratefully that that might be the end of it for the time being, then saw that she was unable to resist his invitation entirely. "I *would* like to think you weren't serious about agreeing with George Brady's philosophy of life," she suggested.

What had Faith called it? The Gospel according to St. George? "In what way?"

"That maybe he had the right idea about marriage," she said, too casually.

"Did I say that?" He discovered that it was extremely difficult to smile effectively when one is out of breath. *Had* he said that? "Well, I was a little high, of course."

"*In vino veritas,* Walter."

"*Semper fidelis,* Miriam."

There was a pause. She seemed annoyed. "I forget what that means," she admitted finally, reluctantly.

"Always faithful," he gasped, smiling. "It's Latin."

"I know what language it is," she said stiffly, in partial defense of her education. "The question is, is it applicable."

Yes! he thought. *Christ, yes! That's the question! Ask Faith!* "As a matter of fact, now that you mention it," he parried, breathing hard, remembering, "didn't you say it works both ways: If a man can play an occasional outside gig, a woman shouldn't feel called upon to sit home knitting?"

The front door buzzer sounded.

"If a man what?"

"Well, those weren't your exact words . . ." Faith's, of course, not Miriam's, by Faith out of George Brady. "That was the general sense of it, though."

He lay on the floor on his back, breathed regularly for several moments in merciful ease, then began his sit-ups.

"Aren't you overdoing it a little?" Miriam suggested. "So soon after breakfast? I don't know how you don't throw up."

"My superb physical condition. Well, what about that?" he asked, far more interested in her answer now than he had been a moment before—before she had evaded it.

"Did you think I really meant that?"

Before he could answer, there was a knock at the door, it opened, and Cassie's head appeared.

"A lady's here about the maid's job, you were expecting her, she says."

Miriam nodded, distractedly. Cassie withdrew, leaving the door ajar. Miriam walked to it, then stopped and turned to him again.

"Anyway, I certainly hope you don't think I really meant that. I have to interview this woman."

Without waiting for response, she left the room, closing the door behind her. Before it closed, he caught a glimpse of Faith standing behind the sofa, looking over Cassie's head at the television, a coffee cup in one hand, the saucer balanced on the palm of the other. He bolted to his feet, rushed to the door, and

glued his ear to it, holding his painful breath the better to facili-
tate his hearing: This was it! *Would she give any hint of last
night's exploratory rendezvous? Could she be so unwise?*

" 'Morning," he heard Faith say, brightly.

"Hi," Miriam said. "You're up early."

"Busy day. I haven't done any Christmas shopping."

"You'll have the stores all to yourself, everyone's finished by
now. Except Walter, he's a last-minute Christmas shopper, too."

"Maybe we can go together, keep each other company," Faith
said.

Oh, Christ.

"Sure. Why don't you ask him?"

Oh, Christ.

"I will. Is he still sleeping?"

"No, he's up. He's in the study, writing. Working."

Miriam's voice came from farther away, then he heard her
again, evidently speaking to the possible new maid in the foyer,
offering her coffee; the sound of her voice was lost, moving toward the kitchen, he judged. There was a moment of silence but
for the drone of a TV reporter's voice. He began to relax: How
could he have doubted her wisdom? Of course, she would say
nothing about . . .

"Are you going into the study?" Cassie said.

"Yuh," Faith said, only feet from the study door.

He froze.

"Do not disturb when the door's closed, that's the house rule,"
Cassie said laconically.

Wonderful Cassie.

"No exceptions?"

He heard the smile in her voice.

"Emergencies only," Cassie said.

There was a pause again. He waited, tensed.

"How are they doing?" Faith asked.

Safely distant again. He placed her near the sofa somewhere,
roughly, and eased the pressure on his aching ear.

"So far so good," Cassie said. "They're in orbit okay."

"This is the end of something, baby," Faith said.

"I know what you mean," said Cassie.

The typewriter, he knew, was the only weapon with which to defend his vulnerable citadel: He made the most of it, flaunting it—cracking, thumping, ringing—rattling his surrogate saber, counting upon Miriam's respectful (if sometimes uncertain) regard for his writing, his Work, to avoid another confrontation for the time being, to deflect her from her morning's unsettling inclination to pick up where they had left off yesterday. Unfortunately, since he had bogged down on Chapter Five two days before, it became necessary to retype the greater part of the other four chapters in order to keep the machine of his defense in constant evidence. It was tedious work, but accomplished his purpose—it kept Miriam at bay.

And, thanks to Cassie (wonderful Cassie), Faith, too.

It was a morning of buzzers and bells, an insistent busyness he became increasingly aware of in spite of his insulation behind the rampart of his study door. The telephone seemed never to be silent for longer than it took someone to hang it up and move ten feet from it. Gifts, he knew from experience, were being delivered to the door in a steady stream, most of them having their basis purely in business, from people with whom he had been associated in the course of the year. But Miriam was yearly fearful of last-minute, Christmas Eve deliveries, knowing that among them there were bound to be at least a few from people who should have been on her list and had been forgotten; now, too late, they reminded her with a basket of fruit or an immense box of imported Danish biscuits that they were thinking, as always, of the Hartmans at this Happy Season and shaming her for her forgetfulness.

One of the telephone callers he was able to identify merely through Miriam's response to the call at the top of her voice, in rage: "Oh, for God's sweet sake! Will you please stop! Would you just find someone else to annoy! This is getting very *boring!*"

The receiver was crashed into the cradle. It was Miriam's obscene caller, he knew.

More or less on schedule, he thought, which had worked out to be roughly once every two months or so since shortly after her brief stay in the hospital in April for her appendectomy. On his first call he had identified himself as an employee of the hospital —although he had offered no name and no indication of the nature of his employment. He then told her that he had a terrible confession to make. Her first wild thought, she admitted later, was that he was calling to tell her that the operating surgeons had left a sponge in her or a pair of scissors. She waited while the caller verbally suffered further guilt and remorse until finally he was forced to demand, in panic by then, what exactly he was trying to tell her. He told her. Mrs. Hartman, I performed intimacy on you. An *intimacy*, Walter had asked her. No, not *an* intimacy, just intimacy, Miriam specified, Mrs. Hartman, I performed intimacy on you. He wanted her to know how terrible he felt about it, his shame, his sorrow; he wanted her to know that she could not have known it was happening because she was so heavily sedated at the time, immediately following the operation, unconscious in fact. He wanted her forgiveness for having performed this intimacy on her, he told her, repeating the maddeningly mysterious phrase so swollen with obscene implications. By which time Miriam had recovered from her · shock and was able to find her voice to screech and her power to hang up, in a rage at having been taken in so completely and for so long by one of the most craftily obscene telephone calls she had ever heard of; but appalled, too, at the possibility that there might have been some truth in the caller's claim. She *had* been unconscious, after all, for a time after the operation, she reminded Walter, until the anesthetic had worn off, something *could* have happened. If only she had taken the local anesthetic instead of insisting on being put under completely, she regretted. Something *could* have happened! she insisted. At odd moments for days afterward, Walter would come upon her in deep, frowning thought and knew that she was conjuring up spine-chilling speculations on the nature of the "intimacy" that might have been "performed" on her. But, after his third call she began to accept Walter's assurances that her caller was no more than another disturbed mind, albeit with a more imaginative and complex approach than most.

Now, as he was about to turn his attention away from the door and Miriam's raging, victimized frustration beyond it, Walter was stayed by the continuing sound of her voice, still unnaturally loud in lingering distress. She was explaining the nature of the call to someone, although not its details. He moved to the door in time to hear Faith say:

"I once went along with one, just to see what would happen."

There was an unnaturally long silence of several seconds.

"Went along how," Miriam asked presently.

"Well, you know, usually you hang up as soon as you get the drift. But I was curious once, you know, to see what would happen if you just went along with one of them, see how far it would go."

"You encouraged him?"

"Mm."

"What happened?"

"Nothing, really. Well, I mean, I think he finally came, you know. I asked him if he felt better but he just gasped a lot and hung up. It was interesting, though."

In early afternoon, at last facing the futility of trying to postpone the inevitable, and anyway feeling substantially more prepared (time alone had done its traditional healing work, some of it) to be in the same room with Faith and Miriam together, he removed the last sheet of paper from the typewriter and placed it on the others and weighted the stack with the old rock Miriam had found on the beach in Bermuda on their honeymoon. Lifting the rock, he discovered how aching his fingertips were as a result of the key-pounding morning.

He emerged from the study feeling like the debuting actor who wonders if he will remember his lines and not bump into the furniture, introduced himself to the new maid, and was told that Mrs. Hartman had gone out with their daughter. Even as he asked about Miss Farrell, even as she answered, he remembered: Gone, too, of course, off on her rounds of the deserted stores.

Having stepped from the wings to find that the performance had been canceled, he was almost disappointed.

He watched the maid—an extremely pretty, very dark-skinned girl who spoke uncertain English with an unidentifiable Caribbean accent—walk away toward the kitchen and, before he was aware that it was happening, was well into the opening stages of one of his periodic fantasies involving himself and a pretty, dark-skinned, hot-eyed housemaid from some steaming, sultry Carib island, alone together in the apartment, a quiet afternoon, she is homesick, lonely for the warm, sensual nights of her native isle, in need of comfort in a cold, alien land. . . .

Had it been a sleeping dream he might have been able to incorporate the ringing telephone into it for at least a moment or two, postponing the premature end; awake, the telephone intruded instantly.

Even as he lifted the receiver to his ear he could hear a kind of high-pitched, snuffled gasping sound, and even before he could speak a greeting, a voice of psychopathic desperation cried out, delivering a sharp pain to his eardrum:

"*I performed intimacy on you!*" the voice shrieked.

Click.

11 He took the familiar exit off the parkway, slowing on the ramp to be certain that Arthur had followed him off. It was a reluctant care: He would not have been particularly disappointed had Arthur missed the exit and sped on past into the night, with Faith, with no hope of ever finding his way alone—or, more to the point, with Faith—to the Apth- ekers'. In fact, so unreasonably irritated had he been earlier, that there was a moment when he had actually considered losing Arthur deliberately in the heavy traffic on the parkway.

"Are they still with us?" Miriam said, half turning to look through the rear window.

The headlights of Arthur's car appeared disappointingly in the rear-view mirror, the car slowing to stop behind him at the inter- section with the quiet country road.

"Yes," Walter grunted. He turned left and began the last lap of the journey to Sneden's Landing, wishing again that Miriam had not invited them to come along. No, not "them." Arthur. It was Arthur he did not want. *Whoever Arthur was!* With his peacock mod clothes and his goddam Rolls convertible. And, with Faith, that intimately easy air of the former lover. Or, worse, a present one. Was he? Was she putting-out for this Arthur whatsisname? Was she going to put out for him tonight?

Why couldn't Miriam have kept her mouth shut? It was Faith he had invited to join them tonight. Faith alone. Disappointing enough to learn that she had already "made arrangements" for the evening, "a date with an old friend"; but she might have gone her way with her goddam "old friend," he might at least have been spared the distressing ordeal of seeing her for an entire evening in the intimate company of another man. But Miriam couldn't leave bad enough alone. No, not Miriam. *Bring him along*, says Miriam. *Love to*, says Faith.

How could she have been so unfeeling as to have arranged to be with someone else this night, the night after a night like last night? Had she no sense of propriety? She had offered herself last night, had she not? Delivered herself into his hands like some rare, exquisite Christmas gift? Of course she had! Simply because he had not as yet unwrapped it, so to speak, was no justification for her offering it elsewhere!

"We won't stay too late, will we?" Miriam suggested.

"No, whenever you say," he said pleasantly.

Miriam had spoken little during the trip. And idly. He suspected she might be as tense and apprehensive as he and wondered if her reasons were at least partially the same. Surely, yes. Surely she was as alert as he to the fact that they were at that very moment speeding to their first meeting with the Apthekers since the revelation of The Great Lie.

He half regretted again that there had been no graceful way to cancel out on this evening at Sneden's Landing. *It was too soon.* He would have liked more time to firm up his planned attitude for the immediate future, an attitude not of indifference (God knew, too much to ask of himself, an impossible hope), but of something resembling a mature and realistic acceptance of the true identity of the man who had been his wife's deflowerer. The prospect of being in the same room, the same house, even a crowded one, with Miriam and Tom, so soon after. . . . But of course there was no way out of it. The Aptheker Christmas Eve party was almost a tradition now. It was like eggnog and taking Cassie to the Christmas tree lighting at Rockefeller Center and getting out the Christmas carol records of the Mormon Tabernacle Choir and the Sinatra Christmas album.

They hadn't missed the Christmas Eve party at Tom and Joan's in years. There was no graceful way out of it. *But it was too soon, he was not prepared!*

Still, there was some ease to be had in bearing in mind the crucial fact that his new knowledge was precisely that: his. He knew now what Tom had known for twelve years; but Tom didn't know he knew. It was an important factor, he thought, in a situation such as this: The truth unshared, the difficulty of dealing with it successfully was cut by half. He had only to be careful now not to betray his knowledge to Tom, no subtle hints, no sly innuendos, *Hey, there, you old son of a gun, what's this I hear about you putting it to my wife even though it was only once and I didn't even know her at the . . . So! popped her cherry, did you?*

Laugh, clown laugh.

"You missed the turn."

Her voice startled him again; he was less surprised by its information. "Did I?"

"That was it just now," she said, gesturing rearward.

He took the next available turn and circuitously made his way back to the proper route, driving slowly through the dark, wintry lanes, trailed closely by Arthur and Faith in the Rolls.

Arthur and Faith . . . Arthur . . . Was she perhaps deliberately taunting him, exacting retribution for last night's rejection? Was that possible? *Was there a streak of cruelty and vengeance in her that he had so far failed to discern?* Vengeance is mine, saith the Lord, Bullshit, saith Faith?

But at least he would be free of George Brady, free of his presence in her life for the next several days. For small favors, gratitude. For one of that endless series of telephone calls during the day had been George, he learned later, calling Faith, who took his call this time, to spare them all the probable consequences of her refusal to do so. As it happened, she need not have been concerned; he was calling only to tell her that he was leaving New York momentarily and would not return until the end of the week, warning her that her failure to hear from him for the next few days was not to be taken as a sign of his withdrawal from their predicament. Walter wondered privately if George had put a tail on her again in his absence, who might at this very moment be trailing the Rolls at a discreet distance.

To spend Christmas with his children, Faith said. Or some of them, the youngest, she said. It was difficult to think of George Brady as the father of children. Yet he had seven, Faith told them, "more or less evenly distributed throughout the continental United States with their various mothers." These were the two youngest, evidently, living in Vermont or someplace with the most recent of the three ex-wives, a former columnist on one of the L.A. newspapers who had withdrawn after the divorce to run a small-town weekly bought, according to Faith, with a part of the proceeds from the settlement. She had been unusually exacting, Faith said, in her application of the California community property laws that entitled her to at least half of everything, counting out their three hundred and seventy-seven phonograph records, taking one hundred and eighty-eight for herself and breaking the odd remaining one in half. The joke going around Hollywood at the time, Faith told them, was that she intended to have one of George's balls too, and had instituted legal action to that end, but was thwarted by the intervention of a restraining order issued by a compassionate judge.

Walter wondered what George would do were he to know what had transpired the night before between his desperately desired Faith and her brother-in-law; George Brady, presumably one of the world's most desirable men, who could have almost any woman he set his erotomaniacal mind to have. *Almost.* What would he think if he knew that Faith was already the as yet unclaimed property of Walter Hartman? Who would have thought it possible that, given her choice, she would deny herself to George Brady in favor of Walter Hartman?

What must it be like . . .?

Does Arthur know? Will he? Tonight?

When they arrived the house was already crowded and clamorous. The Apthekers had an immense and varied circle of friends that seemed constantly to be expanding: Walter never failed to discover new faces at every Aptheker party. He supposed it could be said that, in a way—not, however, in an unattractive way—Tom and Joan collected people; collected them with a catholicity that gathered together stockbrokers and writers, doctors and painters, lawyers (of course), actors, musicians, politicians. Walter could not help but wonder on occasion who among all these might be members of the group that Tom referred to as their "private friends" who attended those other parties. Perhaps none. Perhaps the two groups were kept carefully segregated. It would be interesting to know. But of course he never would: How could he know without accepting Tom's winking invitation to "join the fun and games?" So, of course, he would never know.

Only moments after they stepped through the door into the spacious entrance hall, itself crowded with an overflow of guests from the living room and library that flanked it, Arthur was greeted by someone he knew who quickly took him off, with Faith, into the huge, jammed, cathedral-ceilinged living room where tall windows overlooked the dark, shining Hudson (breathtakingly beautiful at night when the garbage in it could not be seen). Arthur took Faith's hand. Walter knew it was no more than a practical gesture, insuring against separation in the crush; nevertheless he watched the joining of their fingers with a hangdog envy. Behind him, from the direction of the library, he heard a voice cry out Miriam's name and turned in time to see her disappearing into the smoke and noise. He moved tentatively, apprehensively, to the wide archway leading to the living room and stood peering into the noisy crowd, already smiling the vacuous, undirected half-smile of anticipation and readiness, prepared to share the party's high spirits, to accept the first offered pleasure from whatever quarter it might come.

A heavy hand seized his shoulder from behind.

"Walter. It's about time," Tom Aptheker said, "I was beginning to think you weren't going to show."

Walter turned to gaze blinkingly upon the beaming, healthily ruddy face of the man who had taken his wife's virginity twelve years ago or yesterday and smiled hysterically.

"Where's Mimi?" Tom frowned. "She came, didn't she?"

She says she didn't! "Yes, she's around somewhere," Walter said, gesturing wildly.

"Boy, you look half in the bag already," Tom smiled. Then,

across Walter's shoulder toward the door, cried, "Charlie! . . . Don't slow down, you know where the bar is," he said, again to Walter, thumping his arm. Then he was gone, greeting.

Two hours later he had spoken to Tom Aptheker twice more and to Joan once; Miriam he had seen again only from a distance across a room or turning a corner into another. On no one of the encounters with the Apthekers were there more than a few words exchanged (they were hosts to one hundred and fifty guests and in almost constant host-and-hostessing motion). He knew by then that the evening's anticipated significance was not to materialize; that the true test of their altered relationship could only really come when the two couples were next alone with each other on a more private occasion. He reached this conclusion after six drinks; and without any apprehension whatsoever about that impending confrontation—whenever it was to happen. He began to suspect, in fact, that he had been quite wrong in imagining that the Truth About Miriam's Cherry could seriously alter his relationship with his old friend. After all, he reminded himself, it had been only once and he had not even known her at the time. Had he been insane to think that under such circumstances his life could be affected one way or the other? Such a fear could have been no more than a temporary aberration in the heat of the moment, of course. He lifted his seventh glass from a passing tray, wondered idly what might be in it, and granted that there might be some slight, very slight, modifications of interpersonal relationships to be expected; they were, after all, his wife and his best friend who had balled each other once and then entered into a conspiracy of silence of many years duration, who might even have shared from time to time during that time (her naive husband's eyes innocently elsewhere) an occasional secret glance of sly, amused complicity, possibly even of aroused remembrance, certainly Miriam could not be blamed for a now and again sentimental memory, after all, the first time was the time no woman ever forgot, no matter how many subsequent . . . Yes, there might well be some slight modifications to come in the relationship; but certainly he felt nothing about them beyond a kind of dispassionate curiosity to know their nature, what precise form they might take. It would

not be entirely unnatural, for example, for him to occasionally . . .

"Walter, darling! How good to see you! Have you ever seen
such a mad crush! . . . Walter?"

" . . ."

"Lili, Walter. Lili Stein."

"Of course. How've you been, Lili?"

"Just fine, darling. How are you?"

"Oh, wonnerful."

"What you are is bombed right out of your *mind*, honey. Is
Mimi here? . . . Walter?"

. . . It would not be entirely unnatural, for example, for him
to occasionally, on rare occasions, experience a very brief, *very*
fleeting picture of Miriam and Tom, the Miriam and Tom of
twelve years ago or so, of course, although he might be, say,
sitting across a present table from them, the very fleetingest of
visions of the two of them . . .

It was only once . . .

But, wait! How literally, exactly, was that to be interpreted?
Only one occasion, of course. Yes. But, did that also mean, had
she also meant, that there had been only one . . .? That is, did
they only . . .? Or had there been, within the span of that one
episode, multiple . . .? That's to say, *did he hump her repeatedly, again and again, over a period of many hours until finally
. . .? Once in the sack, yes, all right! But how many times in
Miriam?*

"Walter! how are you, man!"

"Wonnerful, howsigoin?"

At the baby grand in the corner of the living room, Jimmy
Long, the aging but boyish cabaret singer, was crooning "Moon-
light in Vermont." Walter wondered how things were going with
George, probably banging his ex-wife at this very moment,
they had just such a postmarital arrangement, Faith had hinted.
An incredible-looking chick, four-fifths legs and the rest long
blond hair, was sitting on the piano and sucking on a joint of
pot. The marijuana smell was spreading in the house now and,
in a number of tight little cul de sacs, prevailed.

He found himself in the den. He had once wondered why the

Apthekers had called the room the den. (For that matter, why anyone would call any room a den.) Maybe because after all the other rooms had been accounted for by use and nomenclature, there was nothing left to call this one.

What iniquities in this den on other Aptheker nights with their smaller circle of select friends?

The television was on and everyone in the room was watching it. It seemed to Walter a stupid thing to be doing at a party. He tried to focus his eyes on the screen and listened for a moment to Chet Huntley. . . .

Of course. Tonight was the night. He remembered now. "Wha's happening?" he asked the girl beside him.

"Hi, Walter, how are you, love? Any minute now."

Joan Aptheker's voice drifted back from somewhere up front near the television, saying something about their all having heard for the last time a tune being crooned in June by the light of moon and that she was very depressed about it. Coming from Joan, it seemed to him an oddly romantic sentiment. He moved, skirting the rear rank of the semicircled group, in order to get a better view of the screen.

He saw them then.

In a far corner, apart from the others, and seemingly oblivious to them, Faith stood with her back to the wall, leaned against a tall bookshelf. She was smiling her secret smile and gazing up at Arthur who leaned over her, talking quietly, supporting his weight on his outstretched arms, his lace-cuffed hands gripping the shelves on either side of her head, enclosing her. His face was close to hers, his lips in intimate, sibilant motion. Walter felt a chill at the nape of his neck; his forehead began to perspire. He knew it! He knew this would happen! There was no need to hear Arthur's words to know what he was saying. *Let's get out of here and go someplace and ball,* that's what he was saying! And she was smiling! Smiling her secret smile! That she had smiled at *him,* less than twenty-four hours ago, promising blue dreams coming true.

And promising what now? Say no, Faith! Tell him you're already up for consideration, an offer has been tendered, tender offer, and you're waiting for a decision before you go elsewhere with your gift. Tell him that!

Faith brought her glass to her lips; lowering it again, her eyes strayed idly from Arthur's face in Walter's direction. Quickly, he swiveled his head toward the television, praying that she had not seen him so desperately seeing her. Frantic to know what was happening behind him in the corner, he nevertheless dared not turn again. *Say no, baby, tell him you have a prior commitment.*

The room grew unusually quiet. He sensed that something crucial was happening on the television screen and tried to focus on it. There was a view of what seemed to be the mission control center in—where? Houston? It was very quiet there, too. Then he remembered what everyone was waiting for, the space capsule was due soon to appear from behind the moon; or, to be precise, the astronauts were due to be heard from, assuming that their rocket engine had fired successfully, jolting them out of their lunar orbit and starting them on their journey home. Behind him in the now otherwise absolutely silent room he could hear the murmur of Arthur's voice. *What was the matter with them! Didn't they realize history was being made here? Couldn't they knock off the goddam sex for five minutes and pay attention!*

Then there was the crackle of celestial transmission from the television and one of the astronauts was saying something about there being a Santa Claus. A collective shout went up in the den and a scattering of applause and sounds of pleasure and relief quickly hushed by those who wanted to hear more. In the gradual quietening, Joan's voice rose, singing softly, boozy, melancholic . . . *of the silvery moon, I want to spoon, to my honey I'll croon love's . . .*

A scattering of laughter. *She must be bombed out of her skull,* Walter thought.

Then, out of the watering corner of his eye, he caught the rustle and color of hurried movement and turned in time to see Arthur and Faith leaving the room, Faith in the lead. Walter's legs went weak, a droplet of perspiration ran like a cold bug from his armpit to his waist. Throat dry, ears pounding, he watched them disappear through an alcoholic mist, down the hall in the direction of the front door.

After a desperately prideful delay of perhaps a minute and

a half, he left the den in pursuit; in pursuit of what he could not have said, unless it was the terrible confirmation of his worst fears. Over the heads of the crowd in the living room he was able to glimpse Arthur, his coat thrown over his shoulder and helping Faith into hers. Then they passed from view, moving in the direction of the door and Walter knew they were gone.

Where? To do what? He laughed bitterly to himself in a jealous rage of despair and lost opportunity. *Everything,* that's what. To do everything!

I'll bet she does everything!

Less than twenty minutes later, with no more heart for party, he searched out Miriam. She protested their departure at first, then, looking more closely at him, asked him if he felt all right and told him that he did not look well.

In the car on the return to the city she was considerably more animated then on the trip up. He tried to listen to her bright alcoholic-ed chatter, but only closely enough to enable him to respond politely from time to time.

His mind was otherwise occupied.

He'd had his chance and blown it! Opportunity had knocked, those soft, golden knuckles under his thumb. *That feels nice,* she said.

Bitch!

Wasn't it supposed to?

Bitch!

Idiot.

Yes! you bitch! Right!

"Do you think I was right?"

"Hm?"

"Do you think I was right to say anything or should I just have kept my mouth shut about it, I mean?"

"No, I think you were right, yes."

"I don't know if she liked it, though."

"Who?"

"*Janet,* of course."

"Ah. Uh, huh. Right. Well . . ."

"I'd better call her tomorrow, by the way, did you happen to talk to Phil Lessing?"

"Uh . . . no, uh-uh."

"Wait'll you hear this."

She couldn't wait? Couldn't have given him a little time? Didn't she realize that that was all it was, a matter of time, that he hadn't finalized anything last night, only asked for a short postponement? Didn't she *realize* that? Was she *stupid* or something?

But, she couldn't wait! Hot-pantsed little . . . It was all perfectly clear now! Crystal! Why couldn't he have seen it last night! It was so obvious! *All she wanted was to get laid!* And it didn't matter to her one way or the other who did the job. He should have realized that, seen it in her eyes, in that secret smile that knew everything and told nothing. She couldn't have cared less *who* did the delicious deed! Or *what!* Any Tom's Dick or Harry's, *A Study in Compulsive Promiscuity, by* . . .

"Do you belive it?"

"It's possible, I guess, mm, hm."

"Sometimes I think he just makes up stories like that just for shock effect."

"Pretty wild, all right."

"I'd really like to know if it's really true."

"Mm."

Hot pants, that's all! It was as simple as that! That is, if she wore them at all! *And she probably didn't.* She was just the type! He could see them right now, stepping into her goddam Arthur's apartment, she was dragging him instantly to the floor, right there in his goddam living room, raving, *Quick, Arthur! Now! I have no pants on!*

"Would you like me to drive?"

"No. Why?"

"You're driving a little wild."

When they walked into the apartment Faith was curled on the living room sofa watching a movie on television.

Walter feared he was hallucinating, until she spoke in greeting. He strangled a drunken cry of joy and relief that died as a small, unidentifiable (to the others) sound high in the back of his throat.

How could he have misjudged her so!

While Miriam prepared coffee, he joined Faith distractedly at the television to watch the final ten minutes or so of the movie. His attentiveness to the TV screen was his best, perhaps only, certainly most available camouflage for the moment; at least until he could get his bearings again, get himself reoriented. Only then would any reasonably normal, face-to-face behavior with Faith be possible. In the meantime, desperately, he could hide from her in the light from *Knute Rockne, All American.*

He had recognized the movie at first glance and felt some mild regret that he had missed it tonight. Pat O'Brien, Ronald Reagan, Gale Page, early '40s. The plot was hazy in his mind. Ronald Reagan as George Gipp, of course, the Notre Dame football star. Gipper. The Gipper. Injured. Or was it crippled? But they would go on without him, of course. Go on to win. *Let's win this one for the Gipper,* says Pat O'Brien. Or, *This one's for the Gipper.* Something like that. He would remember of course if his mind wasn't so muddled. Maybe it was, *Let's* make *this one for the Gipper.* He would remember exactly as soon as his mind cleared a little. It was a famous line. . . .

Faith laughed toward the TV. It sounded faintly derisive. But he was still too limp with relief to hold her to account for any lack of feeling she might demonstrate for a slightly dated movie. She was young, after all, too young to have accumulated the years and experience necessary to know nostalgia. And she was here: For that he would forgive her anything!

For there could be no question about the significance of her presence. It was airtight evidence. She had left the party no more than half an hour before he and Miriam; there could be no doubt that Arthur had driven her directly here and left her. She had even had time to change her clothes since. The best her goddam Arthur could have gotten from her was a goodnight kiss. If that. Anything more time- and energy-consuming was utterly out of the question.

How could he have misjudged her so!

The screen went to black. THE END.

"Oh, boy," said Faith.

There could be no doubt about the derision this time. "Well, it's not one of the great ones," he said reasonably, going to the TV, "but it's not all that bad really. Of its kind."

He turned off the television as Miriam emerged from the kitchen with a laden serving tray.

"What do you see in old pictures like that?" Faith asked softly.

He smiled. "You're too young to understand."

"But pictures like that aren't true," she said, with a gentle persistence.

Her questions—indeed, challenges, he thought—had already begun to induce in him an unaccountable tension. But Miriam set the tray on the coffee table and, unaware of the subject, or perhaps indifferent to it, changed it, saying something bright and animated about an occurrence at the party. Grateful for the diversion (his gratitude, like his tension, unaccountable), he threw himself into the conversation with a distracted enthusiasm and spent the ensuing half hour in a wild confusion of residual relief and excitement and anticipation and—his shining eyes darting between the women, from mouth to mouth, breast to breast, thigh to thigh—guilt.

He had begun to despair of relief before finally Miriam yawned and announced her bedtime, and rose.

"Are you coming in soon?" she asked him, casually.

An idle inquiry it would seem to Faith. But he knew other meanings.

The exhilaration of a party and the attendant consumption of unaccustomed amounts of liquor very often, almost always, had a tangible effect on Miriam's libido. Ordinarily she could be quite quickly demonstrative about it on their return from a party; but tonight, here was her sister, at the other end of the sofa.

Voicelessly, he begged her forgiveness: *It was an impossible proposition.*

Aloud he said, "I'll be in in a little while, yeh," noncommittally, pretending ignorance of her disguised intentions: Perhaps she would put it down to her own too perfect camouflage and blame herself and not be offended. He hoped so, he did not want to offend her.

On the other hand, if she left now and left Faith behind, with him, alone . . .!

"It's my bedtime, too," Faith said (*Was she reading his mind?*) as Miriam moved away, and rose to her feet in a flowing, sinuously graceful motion that pushed his heart into his throat.

What motives here? Had she perceived the truth of Miriam's need and was she removing herself as an obstacle to its relief? Or did she share his apprehension about being left behind, alone with him? Or, was it possibly that . . .?

Before he was able to draw any conclusions and too late in any case for a conclusion to matter, goodnights and sleep-wells had been exchanged and Miriam had reminded him that they were to be up early tomorrow for Cassie's Christmas morning and had invited Faith to join them, assuring her that she was under no obligation to do so considering the early ungodly hour and Faith had said she wouldn't miss it, to be sure to wake her and . . .

And he was alone.

Forty-five minutes and two more drinks later, muttering incoherent despairs, he switched on the television seeking respite and distraction from the bewildering disorder of his thoughts.

At this time of night there would be nothing on but movies. Slumped on the sofa with the remote control channel selector gripped in his fist, he switched from one channel to another, through several, before he came up with Mickey Rooney and Lewis Stone. He dropped the channel selector and opened the *Times* to find out which Andy Hardy this was. *Andy Hardy Meets a Debutante,* 1940. Wasn't that the one with Garland in it? Yes, Judy Garland, the *Times* said. If the *Times* said so, she was in it. He hadn't seen an Andy Hardy in about a year.

He dropped the newspaper and propped his feet on the coffee table and gazed over their toes at the TV screen. . . .

What do you see in old pictures like this, she asked him.

What did he? he asked himself.

He tried to concentrate and made out Lewis Stone evidently delivering one of his moral dissertations to a somber, receptive Rooney.

Pictures like that aren't true . . .

Tell me what is.

What would she say if she knew that as a result of a childhood of Saturday afternoons spent in the Loews 83rd Street, he was seventeen years old before he found out that rich people who lived in big houses on Long Island didn't necessarily speak with British accents?

You still think that love and marriage and sex and romance are related in some mysterious . . .

What would she say if she knew that when it came time for him to choose a college of his choice, all other things being equal, he chose Dartmouth because that was where they made *Winter Carnival* with Ann Sheridan?

But it's not incurable, Walter, because you're a man who has the music inside . . .

What would she say if she knew that . . .?

Garland was singing, sixteen years old and fabulous, *Alone, alone on a night that was meant for love . . .*

You've been making a serious error, Walter . . .

There must be someone waiting, who feels the way I do . . .

You're right, Judy, there must be!

Virtue doesn't triumph, Walter, it only . . .

When he got back from the bar Judge Hardy was at it again, telling Andy in the careful wording of the day that under no conceivable circumstances except under pain of eternal damnation in this world and the next should a young man effect sexual connection with a female not his legally wedded wife. Andy was eating it up.

Was that it? Did we stand at the Crossroads of Life and watch Andy Hardy kiss Junior Miss and did all our troubles begin?

The philosophy portion of this program is over, she said.

It was. It was.

Here's looking at *you*, kid.

12 Walter fell from precarious grace less by calculated choice than because Miriam sank, unrecallable, into a drugged, sated sleep at a moment that was for him as unfortunate as it was untimely.

On Christmas morning Cassie had gotten her snakes, four of them, small and brownish-green, in a large glass tank. The gift (bizarre under the tree, the tank bound in a single wide strand of red ribbon, its inhabitants writhing within) was against Miriam's wishes and Walter's better judgment. But Cassie had had her heart set on snakes and they could find no real objection once they had been assured at the pet shop that small snakes were available that were not only harmless and easily cared for, but considered to be rather interesting "by certain types of people." He, the pet shop proprietor, could take them or leave them, but there were those who went for them: He assumed that Walter knew one such. Walter took the snakes, having been assured that escape from the tank was impossible, and that he could "rest easy on that score, at least."

Among the other gifts exchanged that morning were two from George Brady that had been delivered to the apartment by messenger the afternoon before. Walter unwrapped the one addressed to him and Miriam. It was a silver cigarette box from Tiffany's.

On the inside of the lid was engraved in small, elegant script: *For Walter and Miriam, two of my favorite people. A vote for George Brady is a vote for the future.* It was the first indication he had had, Walter said, of the nature of George's sense of humor.

"On the other hand, who knows," Faith said.

"What do you mean?" he asked her.

"It might not be a joke."

They laughed. Walter was ultimately perhaps less successful than Miriam in dismissing the idea: After a moment's reflection he was was unable to evade the disquieting possibility that, all things considered, Faith's thought might not be entirely unthinkable.

The second of the Tiffany boxes was for Faith. In it was an exquisite and rare Angel-skin coral necklace. Walter knew at a glance that it was a one of a kind thing that could not have gone for a nickel under five thousand. Although he was more tactful (and sophisticated, he hoped) than to specify its probable price, he did observe aloud, more subtly, that George would have to adjust habits like that on a congressman's salary.

"George is a multimillionaire," Faith said casually.

"Literally?" Miriam asked.

"Of course."

Now that she mentioned it, Walter thought, it was probable and to be expected.

"A famous, millionaire congressman with excellent taste," Miriam said, mock-serious. "What more could you want?"

"What more indeed," Faith said and carelessly replaced the necklace in its box on the coffee table.

"Of course, your, shall we say, ambiguous relationship with him will naturally require you to refuse such a gift," Walter said, smiling.

Faith smiled at him—intimately, it seemed to him.

"No relationship," Miriam said, "is *that* ambiguous. Isn't it *gorgeous?*" She rested her fingers on the necklace and consulted Faith. "May I?" Without waiting for the unnecessary permission she took up the necklace and walked to the wall mirror, and held the fasteners together at the nape of her neck. "It's really gorgeous," she said.

I wish I could buy her one of those, Walter thought; then knew that he could not be absolutely certain which one of them had been the object of his wish.

"Cassie," Miriam said, "if you're going to *handle* those things, darling, take them into your bedroom or something, for God's sake."

In the early afternoon Faith left the apartment for a round of Christmas visits with friends, promising to return in time for at least a part of the Hartman Christmas day open house. Walter, probing shamefully but cleverly, told her to say hello to Arthur for them if she were to see him. No, she wouldn't be seeing him, Faith said. Ah, Walter said casually, his relief (he hoped) no more evident than his jealous curiosity had been.

He had been aware since morning of a foreboding tension building gradually in him auguring he knew not what, specifically. The tension was relieved in a perverse way by Cassie's announcement that one of the snakes had escaped; he turned the search into a determinedly lighthearted interlude, temporary distraction from his nagging apprehensions.

The snake had not yet been found by the time the first guests began to arrive, making it necessary throughout the rest of the afternoon to alert each of the visitors as they came through the door, advising them to keep their eyes open and watch where they stepped.

"Some cute way to start a party," Miriam observed, not at all pleased.

Personally he thought it was pretty terrific, Walter told her. Certainly original.

His first words to Jack Finley were to ask how matters stood with Barbara Finch. Jack told him it was still touch and go all the way; that they were scheduled to begin taping the play that coming Friday, for four days, and that as of today (Wednesday) the production was a shambles.

"When it's in the can," Jack growled, "I'm gonna have that cunt locked up."

"On what charge?" Walter smiled.

"I'm working on it," Jack threatened. His eyes stilled on something over Walter's shoulder. His expression remained levelly neutral, but was betrayed by the quiet intensity of his voice: "Holy Christ, what's this?" he said, hoarsely.

Walter turned to see Faith removing her coat at the door.

"Miriam's sister," Walter said.

"Never mind the shit," Jack said, in a buoyant undertone. "Introduce me, you prick."

"No, she really is."

"That's Faith Farrell," Jack said, taking no nonsense.

"I knew I'd heard the name somewhere," Walter said.

Jack contemplated him for a moment. "She's really Miriam's sister?" Walter nodded. "You never told me Faith Farrell was Miriam's sister."

Walter grinned, already tensing at Jack's inordinate interest in Faith: Jack had an impressive reputation for a highly selective philandering; his appeal to women was powerful and unquestioned, if not entirely understood by his male friends. "I'm sorry, I should have gotten a memo out on it," Walter grinned.

The fact was that Faith's ascent to her present public visibility had been rapid, and had not even begun when Walter was still seeing Jack Finley daily at the office.

It was with mingled pleasure and regret that he watched Faith heading straight for him (and Jack), her eyes fixed on his, and smiling that tantalizing half-smile. Jack offered her the usual easy charm that Walter knew was reserved for beautiful girls who might be possible lays and within minutes had her laughing delightedly.

Walter smiled, hating Jack Finley, remembering Arthur, doubting Faith. Then, with a sociability as reluctant as his smile, he allowed himself to be dragged away to meet the dragger's husband.

Throughout the afternoon he put himself through the necessary motions of host, but his attention never strayed far or for long from Faith and Jack. Each time he heard her high, sweet laughter rise over the party's noise, he managed to divert his attention carefully from his companions of the moment in order to know the source of her pleasure. It was always Jack; the context in which they were to be found altered repeatedly, the faces and shapes around them changed, but Faith and Jack were a constant. What was additionally disturbing was that Jack was willing to display such an absence of caution in the presence of his wife: Patty was sure to notice. At least Jack would not be able to leave the party with Faith. Walter was able to take only a moment's comfort in the thought before he remembered that Patty, down with the flu, had not come to the party.

Sometime during the early evening (he had lost all consciousness of the time) he watched Tom Aptheker disappear into the kitchen with Miriam, his arm around her waist, his heavy hand resting on—or was it grasping, clutching, caressing?—the soft, gentle swell of her hip. Walter was very warm. The tips of his fingers tingled. He gripped hard on his wet, icy glass and emptied it and tried to return his attention to Marion Haislip whose dress he had been looking down for the past twenty minutes (she in an armchair, he seated on its arm) while she tried to make him with a determination that was growing less and less guarded. She was a sensational-looking woman. Walter had already idly counted four men in the room who had had her. Not counting her husband. But despite the word of mouth on her, Walter, in his sexually discerning way, had always had the suspicion that she might well be non-orgasmic.

"What is it, darling? Why don't I turn you on?" she asked him now, softly, evidently having decided that time was too short and precious to be further squandered. "I'm a hell of a fuck, Walter," she murmured.

He grinned inanely. *Ask anyone?* He gripped his glass and lifted it to empty it and remembered he already had, *we are but older children, dear, who fret to find our bedtime near.* . . .

Hours later he emerged from the bathroom where Miriam reclined in the tub, the back of her head resting against the cold porcelain, her eyes closed, soaking in warm, scented water that lapped at her nipples; she looked like a television commercial; except that her hair was not pinned up in quite such calculated abandon and she looked exhausted. Not too exhausted, he had hoped, and thinking of Faith, and loathing himself, he had reached down in passing, grasping one shining, soap-slippery breast, touching the nipple with his thumb and said, his voice heavy with import, "Don't fall asleep." Her eyes had fluttered partially open and she had uttered a neutral sound of response disconcertingly devoid of meaning.

In the bedroom he turned off all the lights but one and removed his robe. Naked, electrically conscious of the weight in his already thickening loins, trying to drive images of Faith from his rebellious brain, he climbed into bed. Lying on his back he drew the covers to his chest and waited.

And waited.

He wondered if she was asleep yet: She had gone to bed—or, at least, to her bedroom—half an hour or so before he and Miriam. Another day had passed without sign or hint from her that she had any memory at all of what had transpired between them two nights ago. But what did he expect? What *could* he expect from her? Secret, weighted glances of sexual complicity, promising her patience, assuring him that all offers were still standing and in full effect, awaiting only his acting upon them? Out of the question, of course! She had been what she had to be, the *way* she had to be! Noncommittal. The ball was in his court!

The balls.

Well, at least she had not left the party with Jack, had not . . .

The bathroom door opened and Miriam emerged, wrapped loosely in a violet towel. She took a long nightgown from the hook on the inside of the closet door and with one thumb lazily loosed the towel; he watched it slide clingingly the length of her still-damp and glowing body to pile in a dark moist heap at her feet. She put her hands through the armholes of the nightgown; he watched that too fall the length of her body, the hem halting with a little bounce at her ankles.

She yawned audibly and moved to the bed, her feet brushing the carpet with the weight of fatigue. She pulled back the corner of the blanket and slid into the bed and threw her head back heavily onto the pillow with a thump and a groan.

"God! I'm *exhausted!*"

Heart sinking, phallus rising, he lifted himself to prop his head on his hand, thinking fast. She was covered neck to ankle in thin, delicately flowered cotton: There was no suitably subtle, easy access to flesh. Playing for time, he placed the palm of his trembling hot hand on the fabric of her belly and caressed it in a slow, circular motion. She yawned again, clearly oblivious to him. "Would you like me to wake you up a little?" he asked, kissing her ear.

"Why?" she mumbled with a perplexed frown, eyes closed, slack-mouthed.

He kissed her ear again, flicking the tip of his tongue into it this time, an added attraction; then, removing his so far obviously useless hand from her belly, he took hers in it and moved it to provide her with necessary information. Her fingers curled, clenching, but lightly, noncommittally, in reflex merely, as an infant will make a fist on any rigidity offered it.

"Oh, honey," she said.

There was nothing but regret in the words, he knew, and worse to come unless he moved quickly. Moving quickly, he left her hand to its own devices—however little he suspected it might devise for the moment—and replaced his own on her belly, moving it downward into the warm, cotton-lined declivity below.

"I'm so tired, darling," she whispered, almost compassionately.

"I know, I know," he murmured, offering compassion in return, opening and closing his hand, a facile motion that cleverly and simultaneously raised the gown and stroked the flesh beneath it in double-dutied economy. But her legs remained closed, the hand on him lifeless. She yawned violently again. Hastily he moved to employ his other hand, artful facility surrendering to the exigencies of time, and raised the nightdress somewhat roughly to her waist. The wedge of his hand (edgewise: the extent of her accommodation for the moment) slid between her thighs. She murmured words that he could not identify, that might have been mild protest, might have been the promise of possible interest were he to make exactly the right moves.

"I beg your pardon?" he whispered, and began to pivot his restrained hand on its axis, suggesting to her its need for the freedom her parted legs would afford it, in which freedom it could do its best work.

"I took a sleeping pill," she repeated, laboredly articulate.

Near to despairing of her conscious cooperation, he again brought his other, issue-deciding hand into play and parted her thighs, vaguely curious to know what it might be like to screw a completely unconscious woman and wondering if he might be about to find out. Disregarding possible intimations of some kind of fringe necrophilia, he urgently worked the nightgown to her neck, exposing the usually unfailing and perhaps true seat of her passion (once, she had actually come this way, a weak, "tickly" —her word—but palpable little convulsion which she claimed had been very pleasurable nevertheless).

He closed his lips on the nearest nipple and had instant proof of her response in the stiffening under his plucking tongue.

"Mmmmmm," she said, and raised her hand to rest it softly on the back of his neck.

He was further encouraged by the tightening, however vague, of her other hand's grip, an action perhaps finally induced by the subtly suggesting (he would not call it pleading!) back and forth motion of his pelvis.

"We'll have to be quiet," she whispered, languid.

"Why?" he whispered.

"Faith. She might hear us."

"Well, just try not to scream out in the throes of your unbridled passion," he muttered, grinning, into her armpit. Then bit it.

"What?"

"Nothing."

Several minutes passed without further participation from her while his hands and mouth worked with feverish determination. Then her hand slipped from the back of his neck, as though dragged by its own deadening weight, and disappeared somewhere into the darkness: He knew he was losing her, and was certain when the fingers of her other hand relaxed completely and slid away, abandoning his throbbing rigidity to lonely tension.

Then he realized that she was breathing too evenly.

"Miriam?" There was no response. He closed his teeth gently on the springy, yielding flesh of her breast. "Miriam?" He shook her softly with the hand that was between her legs and the sudden, absurd conversion of the hand's role from the erotic to the functional caused him to utter a snort of frustrated laughter.

The motion startled her back into semiconsciousness with a low, guttural sound of protest. "Gahrrrr," she said. Then, after a moment, finding some semblance of voice, "Honey, I can't even move. I'm sorry. That pill . . . just . . . knocked me . . . right . . . ouuu . . ." In a perhaps final, futile attempt at cooperation her hand found his nearest flesh and her fingernails, as though fighting for purchase, dragged ineffectually, sexlessly across his back.

Placing his last faith in the abruptness of motion that had nearly worked a moment earlier, he handled her roughly, jarringly, as he rolled onto her, parting her legs, too desperate to feel shame at his desperation. Uttering another unintelligible sound, she dragged her feet backward along the mattress, elevating her knees. Encouraged, hopeful, he moved himself forward; but at the instant of first contact, of imminent connection, her legs straightened, the backs of her knees sank slowly and fell to the mattress with a quiet thump.

He shook her again, his importunate, yearning hips in motion, probing, soliciting attention. "*Miriam?*"

"I'm not ready," she gasped, as though the effort of speech had taken her last strength.

Determined to resist and vanquish his onrushing melancholy, he seized her hand and thrust it between her legs and, grinning into her ear, said, "*You call that not ready?*"

Withdrawing her hand (with some difficulty) from under his, relocating it, wet and restraining, on his hip, she muttered, "No, I mean I don't have . . ."

"Ohh, shit," he moaned, a groan of remembrance, *thirty million women in this fucking world popping their daily pill and this one still had to . . .*

"Wait," she whispered weakly, "it'll only take a minute," and moved to get up.

"No!" he answered, urgently, restraining her. "It's okay! I'll be careful!"

"No, I don't want you to, that's no good," she gasped, struggling.

Had she, he thought crazily, before destroying The Book, sneaked a look at the section on the psychological and physical drawbacks of *coitus interruptus?* Refusing her the opportunity for further argument, he insinuated himself slowly, easily into her; his pleasure was excruciating.

"Ohh, honey," she moaned, nervous perhaps, but not unpleased.

He more sensed than felt the supreme effort of her rising legs as her calves slid against the backs of his thighs on their slow but determined journey upward to his waist. Then she moved her hips, tiredly but with some suggestion of commitment at last, in a small, lustful arc, prepared it seemed, to entrust herself to his carefulness.

But the motion caused his eyes to tear and it was too late, too late for care: It was as though all the emotional pressures of months, perhaps years, had gathered, in conspiratorial concert, at the base of his helpless phallus and were clamoring for easement, demanding it; he was forced to withdraw himself urgently in order to avert the possible disaster of an unprecautioned and, for her, all too premature release. For he was required now— his pride and guilt required it, having brought (brought? *forced*) her to this point of response and acquiescence—he was required to give her her reward before he took his. The Tyranny of the Orgasm. Engorged, throbbing, pained, he lay on her, breathing heavily, clenching his sphincter muscles in a desperate effort to retain, against every natural impulse, what he so wanted to relinquish.

"Oh, honey," she whispered, understanding, hoarse with exhaustion and sympathy. "It's all right. Here, let me . . ."

"No, uh-uh, no," he gasped, restraining her compassionate hand. *I don't want a hand job, I want a fuuuuuuuck!*

She might have heard his unvoiced scream, so quickly did she move. Comparatively.

"I'll hurry," she said, and dragged herself ponderously from the bed.

He rolled onto his back, writhing, not daring yet to relax the restraining tension of the muscles behind his scrotum, trying to think of other things. . . . The other things he thought of were all Faith's. He loathed himself. It seemed as though an hour had passed before a shaft of light emerged through the again opening bathroom door. She touched the light switch and stumbled to the bed in the darkness, jarring the bedside table as she climbed in and reached for him.

He withstood the test of her seizing hand. He was again in control, in complete possession of his powers, staying and otherwise, and prepared to make it more than worth her while for having come around at last. He lifted himself and descended between her wearily accommodating legs.

Going in, he noticed a peculiar absence of sensation in his organ and attributed it to the recovery of his control, to the relaxed rigidity of potent power. Feeling would be restored soon enough, he knew, feeling to burn, as soon as he . . .

He began to move.

"Yes, darling, don't wait for me, go ahead, I'm too tired, this is for you."

That's what you think, baby!

He felt as though he could go forever and started slowly in long, languorous strokes until her breath began to quicken and he felt the self-seeking response of her hips. (Sexual altruism, he knew, could be very short-lived.) He quickened his pace, bringing her along fast.

He had yet to begin to feel anything himself when finally, gasping, she opened her mouth and squealed, then convulsed, as always, with a long, constricted, sigh, Ahhhhhhhhh, ending in a breathy, guttural grunt of culmination, Huh!

He stilled for a moment and felt her thighs relax their tension around his waist in the beginnings of her drift into sleep. Clearly she was unaware of what had not happened. He knew she would be sound asleep in seconds unless steps were taken. He began again.

She responded as though startled. "Oh!" she whispered, "I thought you . . . Oh. Yes. Now you?"

He was perplexed at his failure to join her in her second climax. He rested for only an instant this time, then resumed again. She uttered a surprised noise of interrogation, then lent herself breathily to his purpose.

He lost count, but it was immediately following what he thought was her fifth orgasm that he began to grow seriously alarmed. He felt nothing but a blood-gorged, throbbing, swollen ache that seemed to have spread—or was this his imagination?—all the way to his now chafed, raw knees. It was that consciousness of the condition of his knees that called his attention to the fact that in his determination there had so far been a total absence of positional variety.

It might be the answer.

He rolled over, careful to maintain his connection with her. She was groaning now, in a state of inarticulate sexual exhaustion. He placed his hands at the back of her perspiring thighs and pulled until she rested on her knees, straddling him, her torso heavily on his chest, too weak to move.

He began again, bumpily, teeth clenched, *ride a cock horse to Banbury Cross, see a fine lady get on a white* . . .

"Oh, honey, honey, hon, no more," she moaned, "that's enough, really! *You* now. *Please!"*

You bet your sweet beautiful ass me now! Let's make this one for the Gipper!

He drove upward, pounding, discovering all too soon that the altered position was ill-advised: She lay heavily on him, a dead weight, too spent to be able to be anything more than merely available to him. The added burden was too much, he began to weaken seriously. Then she began to squeal again and then again erupted into a paroxysm that seemed to last for minutes. She began to scream a little (In terror? Did she think he was trying to hump her to death? *And could she be right?*), short gasping screams which she buried, open-mouthed, sharp-toothed, in his neck. He thought she would never stop coming, *he would not have the strength to extricate himself from beneath her, they would be discovered like this in the morning, he long since unconscious, she screaming and coming, she would have to be dragged off by the neighbors and carried out, rigid, frozen in the Woman Astride Face-to-Face Position, still coming, begging, no more, no more, you now, you now* . . .

He thrust and pounded and lunged until he felt as though the base of his levering spine had been beaten with a baseball bat.

. . . Nothing! . . . Nothing! . . . Where was it? Why wouldn't it . . . .?

What was happening?

Had he accidentally discovered and unwittingly mastered the ancient, legendary art of semen retention said to have been the secret of that now-deceased, archetypal Latin American playboy-lover's welcome and success in the beds of three continents? *Karezza and Me,* by Walter . . .

His strength failed him at last. Drenched in sweat, immobilized, he waited, ruined, through the last of Miriam's diminishing ripples until finally she became still. Her legs straightened slowly and lay limp and damp against his.

"Good . . . God . . . Almighty," she breathed. And was instantly deep in sleep upon him, unconscious.

Painfully, achingly, and holding her carefully—although he knew that there was no power on earth that could wake her now—he rolled her away and drew the ruined bedclothes over her. He lay on his back, motionless, feeling as though he had been hit by a truck on a dark, lonely road.

His phallus gave no evidence of subsiding. It was hypersensitive to even the most tentative touch, he discovered. To go so long without release was unnatural, certainly. . . . Was it also harmful, perhaps, might he have done himself some injury? *He would never detumesce, in some fluke tragic accident of nature he had inflicted upon himself a permanent erection, he would go through the rest of his days like this, a medical curiosity studied by the world's most eminent scientific minds, an eight-page cover story in* Life *with full-color photos of his permanently rigid cock (Walter's condition has necessitated many adjustments in his daily life. Above, he demonstrates specially designed bathroom harness that supports him in an upside-down position in order to urinate effectively. Earlier attempts in a normal position failed). He would journey throughout the world (all expenses paid) to all the great centers of medical research, dropping his specially tailored trousers before lecture halls jammed to overflowing with medical students and curiosity seekers, he would of course be sought after by all of the world's most desirable women, requiring a careful and fairly applied schedule of ac-*

commodation. There would be an autobiography, of course,
Hartman's Hard-on, The Amazing Rise of Walter A. . . .

Hysteria again?

He forced his mind clear of priapic fantasy. His condition
unabated, he seized himself in desperation and was tempted for
a moment, but refused finally to succumb to the seductive call
of Onan.

At last, his hopeless and unrelievable frustration found its
natural and inevitable target: If she was any kind of woman
she would have realized what was happening! Correction! What
was *not* happening! She would have applied a little ingenuity
and imagination and had him going off like a goddam roman
candle in no time at all! If she was any kind of woman!

Like Faith! For example. Could anyone conceivably imagine
a woman like Faith leaving a man, abandoning him, in such a
condition? Would a woman like Faith, for example, be lying now
as Miriam was, sprawled on her back like a nearly drowned
swimmer, humped to within an inch of her life, sated, satisfied,
asleep, while the source of all her happiness . . .?

Like Faith . . .?

Guilt, shame, smothered his potent rage. Perhaps there was
justice here, after all. On whom, after all, had his thoughts truly
been at the start, who his heart's and cock's desire? *A prick of
conscience, Walter?* . . . He saw her, at that very moment, only
yards away down the hall, thrashing sleeplessly in lustful need
while he, the cleverly confessed object of her longing, lay here
fully prepared to put her to rest.

And himself! . . . And himself, *he would leave this room,
hurry to hers, kick open the door, listen, goddammit, just take
a look at this, will you, this was really for you in the first place,
it's practically got your name on it, you want it? Why, thank you,
Walter, I believe I do, just put it right here, thank goodness
you've dropped in. . . .*

He lay for several minutes staring at the ceiling, knowing that
sleep was impossible. Finally, he sat up and put his feet on the
floor, discovering as he did so the weight on his thigh of his
finally mercifully melting flesh. *Who killed Cock Throbbin?* With
a crushing ache still lingering in his testicles he stood, carefully,

and, moving softly and with his feet somewhat apart to avoid undue pressure and any unnecessarily painful jarring, he put on pajamas and a robe and slippers.

He turned on a single light in the living room, poured a drink, and went into the study. The study was moonlit through the window and the terrace door: Its effect was soothing. He stood at the desk and sipped from his glass, gazing out on the clear, bright night. When Faith appeared on the terrace, he at first suspected a hallucination. But it was indeed she. She moved across his line of sight, one hand in the pocket of her coat, a cigarette aglow in the other, and stopped at the terrace rail. He watched, entranced, as she leaned against the railing, almost an ethereal vision for all her reality, looking out into the darkness across the neighboring roofs.

A moment passed. Then he smiled ruefully and nodded and sighed. . . . *Date with Destiny*, by Walter A. Hartman.

When he slid open the terrace door she turned sharply at the sound, startled.

"Hi," he said softly.

"Oh . . . I didn't know anyone was awake."

"Neither did I."

"Come on out."

"It's cold."

"Get a coat. It's a beautiful night. Look how clear." She filled her lungs with a perilous draft of polluted air.

"I should remind you this is New York," he said, grinning. "A deep breath like that could kill you. We who live here have learned to take only short, shallow breaths. As seldom as possible."

She smiled. He closed the door quickly and went for a coat. He was standing in the foyer struggling into his overcoat before he knew that it was not the dress for an occasion whose significance should not be diminished by the ridiculous figure he would cut in pajamas and an overcoat. Then, too, there were disturbing echoes of George Brady that he felt it vital to avoid.

In the bedroom he dressed quickly in the dark, keeping his eyes averted from the shadowy mass that was the bed. On the way back through the living room he altered his course, stopped to pour two drinks, discovered that his palms were perspiring, and forced himself not to hurry to the terrace.

"Terrific," she said, taking her glass.

"I'm beginning to think you're some kind of a fresh-air fiend," he said. He knew by her look that she had not failed to understand his primary meaning, remembering the last time she had lured him out into the cold and her ultimate purpose on that occasion.

She turned away and directed her gaze at the apartment building opposite. "There's something interesting going on over there," she said.

"Where?"

She extended her arm and stabbed a finger in the air, counting: "One, two, three, four, five windows down. From the roof. Right there."

He sighted along her furry arm onto one of the large picture windows almost directly across from and at a slight lateral angle to where they were standing. It was a living room. In it a man, middle-aged, sat on a sofa talking to a young woman seated across from him in an armchair.

"The guy and the two girls," Faith said. "You see it?"

"Oh. No, there's only one——. Oh, yes," he said, nodding, as a second woman appeared, handed the man a glass and curled up next to him on the sofa. He watched the scene in silence for a moment. "What's so interesting?"

"I have a feeling," Faith replied. Another moment passed in silence. "Ah. Here we go."

Walter watched as the girl on the sofa leaned over and kissed the man, long and lingeringly. The man's hand instantly shot up her leg and disappeared beneath her skirt. The blatantly intimate act was alone startling to Walter in view of the other girl's presence; then the second girl rose and moved to the sofa. She carefully removed the glass from the man's other hand and set it on the end table; then sat beside him. Her hand went directly to his trousers, unzipped them, and disappeared from view.

"Whoopee," Faith said softly.

"You have pretty good instincts, haven't you," Walter said, excited, but vaguely uncomfortable at his interest in the scene across the street. Or, he wondered, was it only the sharing of it

SUDDEN DEFECTIONS 199

with Faith that was disturbing? Then the three people were on
their feet and moving from view. "Show's over," he said, attempt-
ing indifference, betraying disappointment.

"No, wait," Faith said patiently.

He waited, curious to know what she expected might happen
next: He had to trust her instincts, they were proven.

"Yes. There," she said.

Even as she spoke, his eye caught the movement in the ad-
joining window as the trio appeared in the apartment's bedroom;
it too was fully lit, the drapes open.

"Do you have a pair of binoculars by any chance?" Faith asked
casually.

Walter laughed, shortly, nervously. "Binoculars?"

"Mm. Do you?"

"Well, yes. There *is* a pair around, I think, as a matter of fact.
Somewhere." He paused uncertainly, knowing exactly where
the binoculars were. He had had them for over a year, one of
those pointless business gifts that he had never had occasion to
put to their intended purpose; they were serving as a bookend
on a shelf in the study.

"Well, will you get them?"

He laughed again, still stalling for time. "Do you think they'd
like it if they knew we were——"

"Walter," she said calmly, "if they minded being seen would
the drapes be open?"

He didn't think that was quite the point, necessarily; she was
being selectively logical again. He glanced across at the window.
One of the girls was already down to her underclothes; the other
had removed only her skirt so far, probably because she was
helping the man undress.

"Walter, what's the difference whether we watch like this or
with binoculars?" she asked reasonably. "So, will you get them?"

He would not be accused of a lack of adventurousness, not by
her, not tonight. He was back with the binoculars in a matter of
moments. As he emerged from the study she turned, extending a
hand.

"Hurry," she said calmly, "things are moving right along over
there."

Wetting his lips, he handed her the binoculars. She put them to her eyes, adjusting the lenses. He turned hesitantly toward the window. The man was sitting on the bed, naked, watching the two girls, naked now too, and busy with each other.

"Oh, perfect," Faith said, evidently having focused the binoculars. "They're hookers," she said incidentally.

"How do you know?" The man had moved to kiss the girl whose mouth was not otherwise occupied. He wondered if Faith was going to give him a turn at the binoculars; he hoped he wouldn't be forced to ask.

"They work like hookers," Faith explained. "It's practically choreographed."

She handed him the binoculars without looking at him, her eyes on the window. He hesitated, wondering whether he would have had the audacity to use the binoculars for this purpose were it not for Faith.

The binoculars brought the three people close enough to touch, he might have been in the room with them. He had hoped to participate as a cool and objective observer, but found himself unable to suppress his physical excitement as he watched the shifting patterns of invention formed by the trio, the girls moving smoothly and skillfully, the man evidently having to do little but adapt readily to each new possibility offered him. The possibilities seemed extensive.

He wondered what it would be like.

"Don't be a hog," Faith said, her hand on the binoculars.

He relinquished them to her with a small smile. Moments passed. Then she said, "They're coming into the stretch, I think." The man was on his back, the girls alternately mounting him, each rising and falling on him for a few seconds before giving way to be replaced by the other. Walter was inclined to agree that under such circumstances the end was indeed probably near. It seemed not to have lasted very long. The more the merrier, but also the sooner? . . . He wondered what it would be like . . . Then the man rolled over, one of the girls under him.

"Here's the finish," Faith said, proffering the glasses.

"No, you go ahead," he said politely, "I can see fine."

"No, you," she persisted.

"No, really, I can see perfectly. Go ahead." *You're the guest!*

With a grin, she put the glasses to her eyes, and he turned again to the window, noting that for some odd and unexpected reason his excitement had caused a lessening of the ache in his groin. The thought reminded him of Miriam and he tried to concentrate again on the window.

The man's concern was solely with the one girl now, but his other partner, rather than withdrawing from the field (her duty done), continued to take part, kneeling behind him, her hands erotically out of sight between his legs. Walter wondered if the man was even aware of the second girl's continued participation. He thought it unlikely; and thought it rather honest and honorable of the second girl (particularly if they were, as Faith claimed, professionals) not to retire from the action but to persist to the end.

Then the man collapsed and it was over.

Walter wondered what it would be like.

"It beats the movies," Faith said, smiling impishly.

His face and hands were cold; he was perspiring everywhere else. He licked his lips and forced a smile and told her that it was obviously a single feature, they might as well go in now.

Moving to the terrace door, she said, "You and Mimi must have a ball living here."

He nearly laughed aloud at the absurdity of the thought of Miriam ever sharing such a scene with him. Instead, he offered Faith what he thought was a slyly ambiguous smile, leaving her to draw what he hoped would be a favorable conclusion about the extent of his and Miriam's sophistication.

In the study she removed her coat and sat sweetly, girlishly spraddle-legged in the swivel chair at the desk; she pushed herself from side to side in a short arc, telling him that she liked this room, that it was a nice room. Moonlit, he moved to touch a lamp; she asked him not to.

"It's nice like this," she said softly and, proffering her empty glass, asked if she might have another.

When he returned from the living room she had kicked off her soft red leather shoes and was curled up in the armchair. She was wearing a sweater and white jeans. He had seen the jeans on her before tonight; there were two small rivets in the seam at the base of the zipper, placing them low in her groin; he had watched them as she moved, imagining them two tiny, brass teeth nibbling maddeningly, softly, at her soft parts. And had imagined his own there.

She sipped, and kissed the glass's lip, then tapped the rim with her teeth. "You ever do that?" she asked.

"Do what?" he said, suspecting he knew.

"That," she said, gesturing casually with her glass at the terrace and the window beyond it.

He grinned nervously, hesitated. "No, as a matter of fact." *Why? Do you have a friend?*

He wondered what it would be like.

"I meant before you were married, of course," she said, as though by way of reminding him that she had not forgotten his confession of fidelity of a few nights ago.

"I know what you meant," he replied, his smile prevailing, wondering where this line might take them, wondering how vulnerable he might be now as a result of those earlier confidences. "No, I never happened to make that scene," he went on casually, feeling false at his uncharacteristic use of the expression, "for some reason or other," he added.

Has she? *Does she have a friend she'd like me to meet?*

There was silence.

"Mimi's asleep?"

"Yes," he nodded, "she's asleep." Unconscious, if truth be told. *Will the truth be told tonight?*

"She looked tired."

"Yes, she was."

"Christmas is exhausting."

"Yes, it is, isn't it." He discovered himself still nodding, and stopped.

"It's still early."

"Is it? I've lost track of the time, what time is it anyway?"

"About eleven thirty, I think," she said.

"Early," he said, nodding.

Silence again. Her face was turned to the window, in profile to him, delicately moonlit. Without looking at him, she said,

"You've been uncomfortable with me the past couple of days, haven't you."

He sipped too hastily from his glass, soaking his upper lip. "I guess you could say there's been a certain lack of ease, yes," he admitted.

And what of her, he wondered? Did the facts hold any significance at all for her, that she was guest in this very apartment, that Miriam was her sister? Vague intimations of incest arose again in his mind. But, of course not: She was *her* sister, not his! No, this act that he so desired, if not entirely moral, was at least not a felony.

"Did it excite you at all?" she asked, her face still toward the window, moon-glowed.

Her meaning was unclear: Was she suggesting some extremely subtle sexual effect his recent days' discomfort might have caused him; or had her mind doubled back to their most recent shared experience, the trinal revels across the street? Opting for caution, he said, "Did what excite me?"

She turned to him, obscuring her face in shadow, two tiny glints of light where her eyes would be. "The party over there."

"Yes," he said presently. "A little. In a . . . different kind of way." He paused, uncertain whether or not to proceed to what was almost the mandatory enquiry of his own. "What about you?" He asked finally. She was silent. He waited to know. She withheld her revelation yet a moment longer.

"Of course."

"I didn't think it had."

"Why not?"

"It didn't seem to." He wanted desperately to clear his throat.

"How would I have shown it?"

He considered this for a moment, then grinned. "You have a point there," he conceded, his mind searching wildly for possible hidden meanings in her question. "What *is* that perfume you use?" Her scent had finally, almost imperceptibly, permeated the closed room that smelled now like some impossible garden in a dream.

"Like it?"

"It's incredible."

She rose abruptly and moved in the direction of the terrace door, her arms folded under her breasts. He was almost certain now that she was wearing nothing under her sweater, to judge by the languorous way her breasts rested on her forearms. He pictured the tiny brass teeth nibbling at her, nibbling. Did they have unobstructed access to her or was she wearing underpants? They would be bikini pants, certainly; they would be very sheer, diaphanous, embracing her warm, tender flesh like humid air.

"Walter?"

He cleared his throat, too loudly. "Yes?"

Her back was to him. There was a moment of suffocating silence.

Still faced away from him, she said, "You do want me, don't you, Walter? Because I'm beginning to get the impression maybe you don't, really. Is that the impression I should have?"

He remembered the words in the book he had been reading, to the effect that constant cheating was less dangerous than the sudden defection of an honest man. Their full significance had been obscure to him; he felt himself closer to understanding them now. He remembered Mad Celeste in the Hatter's that night, saying that it was possible to live one's entire life from one postponement to the next. . . . *Maybe there are some things you should buy with your heart, not your head,* Melvyn Douglas in *Mr. Blandings Builds His Dream House.*

Not daring to think further, beyond the instant of the act, he released his now stinging lower lip from his teeth and rose quickly and turned her and kissed her.

When finally she withdrew her lips, smiling, she whispered tenderly, "What the hell, Walter, everyone's going for the good times—even the priests are getting restless."

He buried his answering smile in her wonderfully new mouth. This time she opened it to the penetration of his tongue and moved her hips heavily against him and discovered his condition.

"Have you been sitting there with that all along?" she whispered, almost accused, mingling lust with sympathy with reprimand.

He kissed her again, fearing words, his own as well as hers. *I've been sitting there with that for years, baby!*

"Now," she whispered.
"Yes."
"Not here."
"No."

In her borrowed apartment the bedroom was yellow and white
and soft. No Hollywood designer, he thought, could have fash-
ioned a more perfect setting in which to begin what he had
begun. She put a record on the phonograph. He remembered
that he and Miriam had once often had music with sex, but that
had ended years ago. Now, a girl with a guitar (and long straight
shining hair, surely) began to sing, sweetly mournful. He would
have preferred Sinatra, something along the lines of *Angel Eyes*,
but it was no more than a fleeting regret.

They stood on opposite sides of the bed, watching each other,
and undressed in a silence that was more exciting than any
words could have been.

When they were naked she grinned playfully and said, "What
happened to your knees, they're all chafed."

He almost laughed, hysteria hovering. "It's a long story," he
said.

But her attention, he saw, was already elsewhere on him. "So
is that," she murmured, and presently raised her eyes again to
his.

He gazed at her, his eyes moving slowly, luxuriously, while
she stood motionless. "Jesus, you're magnificent," he said finally,
his voice hoarse and cracking.

She smiled and raised her arms slowly, balletically, from her
sides, her hands drooping delicately, and turned, in voluptuous
pirouette, until she again faced him. "Am I?"

"You must know it."

"Some things we can never hear enough."

"I believe this has your name on it," he grinned.

"Has it?" she asked, peering through comically squinted eyes.
"I can't quite make it out."

"You need a closer look," he suggested and placed one chafed
knee on the mattress and extended a hand to her, hoping it was

not too ridiculously romantic a gesture. (*The question is, Walter, is that her husband up there or isn't it and is it romance?*) She walked across the bed to him on her knees. He waited for her, one kneecap stinging on the starched, rose-colored sheet. Her hands slid, cool and smooth, across his shoulders and clasped at the back of his neck.

"Noël, baby," she murmured, and kissed him. Her hands traveled down his back and over his hips. "Oh, boy," she whispered, seizing one hand's prize; the other, fondling, told him that his testicles were still mildly sensitive to even so loving a touch. "Oh, boy," she whispered again, squeezing.

He winced, "It's a projection of things to come," he murmured helplessly. She was evidently too aroused and preoccupied to be amused. His starving hands were voracious; he filled them with her, then emptied them, and filled them again elsewhere on her.

Then her mouth left his and she dragged her lips down the length of his body, her eyes closed, and, like a birth-blind kitten went to the source of life, her lips closing softly on it.

He nearly fainted. And held her head with both hands as much to support himself as to encourage her. Finally, she rose from him, upright on her knees again, lips glistening.

"How do you like it so far," she said, and pulled him down.

"This one's definitely for the Gipper," he said with a shuddery sigh, falling.

III.
Special Occasions

. . . something borrowed . . .

13 Walter bounced on his toes on the curb at the corner of Broadway and 45th Street waiting for the light to change and gazed upon the vast expanse of asphalt that covered the ground where once, until so recently, the Hotel Astor had stood. His high school class had held its graduation dance at the Astor Roof. Tex Beneke and the Glenn Miller Orchestra. Once, sitting at the horseshoe counter in the Astor Drugstore, he had met and fallen in love with a girl within the space of half an hour and, after two days of virtually uninter-rupted sex, was told by her that she was going back to Cleve-land and the husband he hadn't known she had. It was at the Astor Bar at the age of seventeen that he had first heard the words, You want a girl, kid? (*Go to Birdland, ask for Julio.*)

It was all gone. The ground was lying fallow now, in asphalt, a temporary parking lot, coming soon, On This Site, another skyscraper.

Two blocks south he passed the Paramount Theatre, in the balcony of which, his fifteen-year-old hand had first attained the forbidden country of a girl's upper thigh while Bing Crosby sang Too-ra Loo-ra Loo-ra to Barry Fitzgerald in *Going My Way*. The Paramount was closed now and being gutted for offices and a bank.

Any other day, he knew, it might all have depressed him a little. But not today.

He had been walking for hours, a spring of satisfaction and fulfillment in his step that he could not remember having felt for years. He tingled in every fiber and nerve. There was no other word for it, he thought: He *tingled*. He was indestructible. He was alive!

A little tired, but *alive*.

It was very puzzling.

Not that his physical state came as any surprise. After so many years, and with a woman like Faith to share his defection, what man would not feel a physical well-being that was near to euphoric? It was to be expected. What was puzzling was the failure of his other expectation to materialize.

The morning after always came: He knew that, everyone knew that. Yet this morning after had come and gone, he saw by the clock on the *Times* Tower (No, Chemical Tower now), *and he felt no guilt!* Or was what he felt now only a first early, lulling stage in the evolution of aftermath? Perhaps it came later, creeping in (like fog) on little cat feet, then, when you least expected it, belting you a stunning blow on the back of your dreaming head with its righteous hammer.

Perhaps.

But there was no sign of it on the way home with her last night; no sign of it now; had been no sign of it all morning. Waking and dressing quietly, and waiting in the kitchen for Miriam to get up there had been none of the perturbed, tremulous fidgeting and fumbling that one might have expected on such a momentous morning. In fact, he had been far less apprehensive this morning than he had been a few days ago after the evening when he had shared nothing with Faith but *words!* Maybe she had been right, *it makes for a more relaxed atmosphere in the home, Walter.*

That he had removed himself from the apartment so relatively early, before Faith was up and around, was not fear, but caution. One test at a time, he thought. And he had passed the first test of Miriam with honors; had known he was going to pass it from the moment she walked through the kitchen door, on her face that soft-eyed languid look of the well-laid and, seeing him at the table, meeting his eyes, the little smile, like Vivien Leigh in *Gone With the Wind* the morning after Clark Gable kicked down the bedroom door. (*He: How are you? Miriam: Wonderful. He: Good. Miriam: I ache all over. He: Sorry. Miriam, shy eyes burning: It was worth it.*)

He only wished he might have been a fly on that wall at the sisters' first encounter that morning. How had Faith comported herself, he wondered. With ease, he was sure. He would soon know, would have to know, would ask her. He smiled. Had there been some reflection on her face of what he had seen on Miriam's. He hoped so, there was every reason to think so, after all. He saw them in his mind's eye, each the other's unknowing mirror, their morning-after memory mutual, but unshared.

It was wonderful to think about!

He became aware of the odd looks he was getting from passersby and realized that he was smiling. And moving east on 42nd Street. He passed under a skin-flick marquee that declared unbridled passions, traps in webs of lust, unnatural desires. He was tempted to go in and see what skin flicks were all about. Another day, maybe.

About one thing she had been uncontrovertibly right, he knew now: Love had nothing to do with it. All the claims that had been entered about that were false; they were myths designed to trap and ensnare. He knew that now, for the simplest and best of all possible reasons: He loved Miriam, loved his wife, at this very moment. Loved her. There was no question about that. In fact, it might not even be going too far to say that he loved her more than ever. Even now, with Faith's remembered sounds whispering like small winds in his ears, with the remembered taste of her in his mouth. She had been right, *the fix had been in all along.* Fortunately, he knew it now, that was the difference.

He looked at his watch. It was time. In fact, he might have left it a little late, he thought. He had planned on walking there, but it might be best to take a cab now. On the other hand, there was something to be said for keeping her waiting. Not too long, just a little. But it was a short-lived temptation.

Climbing into the cab he opened his mouth to give the driver the address; then froze with his hand on the door handle when he realized he had forgotten it. He told the driver to go uptown, he would remember in a minute, and sat back in a panic. He knew the street but not the house number and all brownstones looked alike, certainly had in last night's dark. He had a vision of running up and down the block and in and out of vestibules looking for something familiar. Not even checking letterboxes would help: He did not know the name of the girl whose apartment it was! How could he have been so *stupid* as to have forgotten the . . . Then he remembered and leaped forward, shouting at the driver. The driver jumped and looked wildly over his shoulder. Walter smiled and apologized for having startled him. He sat back and saw that the driver was eyeing him warily in the rear-view mirror. Walter grinned and nodded reassuringly at the careful eyes.

His pulse began to slow again and he settled himself comfortably, feeling powers he had never felt. The specialness of this occasion was much with him. This was no accidental encounter toward which he sped, like the one on the terrace last night. Last night might have been accident or fate; it might not, had chance decreed otherwise, have happened at all. But this— this was an arrangement, an assignation, preplanned, anticipated. Last night when she had suggested it, dressing, (*She: Afternoons can be wonderful. He: I don't remember. She: Then we should definitely have one.*), he had barely hesitated. He had begun to think now that decreasing durations of hesitation might be taken as a fair indication of a growing sense of reality. It was a corrupt thought, he knew. And so he felt, for the first time in his life: corrupt. To his continuing (but somewhat milder) surprise, it was not an entirely unpleasant feeling. Why had he always thought it would be?

"Look, darling, look," she breathed.
He cleared his throat. "I'm looking."
They were standing in front of the tall, oval cheval mirror, gilt-framed, tilted carefully at an angle that would afford them the best image of themselves, their feet buried in the thick white shag rug. On her toes, she moved against him in slow circles.

"You like it?"

"I love it," he breathed. He watched the reflection of her sink to its knees.

"Round and round the garden," she said, her tongue flicking, "like a teddy bear (flick), one step (flick), two steps (flick), tickle you under there (flickflickflickflickflickflick)."

He nearly collapsed.

Half an hour later, anxious for his first relief (and hers) and about to move toward that end, he felt her extricate herself from him. "Wait," she said and rolled off the bed. Puzzled, disconcerted, but reassured by her parting smile that suggested worthwhile purpose, he watched her cross the room toward the door. "You have a beautiful ass," he said, a sentiment to carry with her in her mysterious and hopefully brief absence. There was something almost eloquent about her behind. Was that possible, could a woman's ass be an eloquent thing? An eloquent, elegant ass, the ass with the delicate air, there's a divinity that shapes her end.

She stopped abruptly at the door and, without turning, bent her knees then straightened them, thereby sweetly rotating the admired part, a gesture of acknowledgment and thanks at once charming and inflammatory. He was entranced anew at her talent for delightful salacity.

She was back in moments carrying what appeared to be a large aerosol can. Room spray? he wondered. Exotic scents? "What have we here?" he asked, hoarse with desire and impatience, taking the can from her. It was cold to the touch, he discovered.

When he looked at her again with a puzzled grin, she licked her lips and said, "We're branching out a little," then stood gazing at him as though waiting for him to understand without further prompting.

"Okay, I'll bite," he said finally, admitting defeat.

She grinned and took the can back. He watched with delighted apprehension as she leaned forward and released onto him a blob of creamy-white whipped cream. He sucked air through his teeth at the delectable shock of cold on his heat, then laughed at the result that looked like some outrageously obscene, whipped-cream lollipop. Then she knelt over him and deliciously removed the topping.

"Get the idea?" she asked, the pink tip of her tongue licking a fleck of white from the corner of her mouth.

He did. He uttered a small, happy cry and, snatching the can from her hand, pushed her down.

"Whoopee," she breathed, bouncing, her legs in the air.

"Let's play doctor," he said, "open wide and say ah."

She opened wide and within seconds was saying ahhhhh. Just what the doctor ordered.

Within a quarter of an hour he had half-emptied the can. She warned him finally, squirming, giggling, that he mustn't overdo it, he might make himself ill. True enough, he was beginning to feel a little nauseated. "And besides," he said, "it must be fattening as hell."

She laughed. "And besides that, I don't know about you, but I'm ready for the main course."

A short time later as they lay side by side, face up, breathing quietly again, she toyed idly in his pubic hair with the soft tips of the fingers of one hand, holding, in the same fingers, a lighted cigarette; he felt on his thigh the small hot spot from the glowing tip and hoped that she would be careful about the ash. He was unable to resist his curiosity any longer. "Why me?" he said. She made a quiet, languid sound of uninterested interrogation. "Why did you want me?" he elaborated, with an almost imperceptible emphasis on the final word.

She rolled her head on the pillow to face him. "Why *not* you?"

"I mean," he smiled, "you could have anyone." George Brady, for one. *You could be better than you are,* his mind sang, *you could be swinging on a star, Going My Way,* Paramount, 1944, Bing Crosby, Barry Fitzgerald, Rise Stevens. . . .

"You don't think much of yourself, do you."

"Why do you say that?" He forced himself to meet her eyes. There was a silence. Her expression told him that so obvious a retreat warranted no reply.

Instead, she said, direct and soft, "In the first place I hadn't been laid in a while."

"Abstinence makes the heart grow fonder," he grinned.

"And I thought you'd be lovely," she continued. "And I was right." He felt an assured and sophisticated silence to be the best response to such flattery. He was surprised, however: He had expected something more complicated for motivation. Life might be simpler than he sometimes made it out to be. She turned her face to the ceiling again and made a contented sound. "I feel wonderful." Her fingers that yet held the cigarette resumed their pubic play, more tantalizing now, he suspected, than idle. They were beginning to have their effect and he felt the faint, renewed fluttering of anxious blood in his groin.

He jumped when the hot ash fell onto his belly.

"Oh, darling, I'm sorry!" she cried, sitting up quickly, brushing the afflicted place with her silken hand, then caressing it. "Is it all right?"

"Kiss it and make it better."

She smiled and obeyed. Then he felt her probing finger, felt the pattern it defined and knew she had finally discovered his scar, the thin white line that ran diagonally through his pubic hair two inches from the base of his penis.

"Good Lord, what's this?"

He explained his Korean war wound. She shuddered at the nearness of such a bloodcurdling disaster. He told her that she was looking at the only man in the world with a part in his pubic hair, that he had it shampooed and set once a month at Charles of the Ritz.

She kissed the scar tenderly, then turned her head and looked up at him. "What the hell," she said, "as long as I'm in the neighborhood."

"Good thinking," he said.

He put his hands in her thick, glowing hair. She was masterful, he thought. Masterful! Then he thought that he might perhaps only be mistaking the newness of her for unusual skill. Then he stopped thinking for what seemed a long while.

"It's very healthy," she said finally. "Lots of protein."

He smiled uncertainly, wondering if she was serious. He had never heard that before. "So few drink at my fountain," he said. Then added, honorably, lest she attribute unjustified authorship to him, "Said someone."

"Whose fault is that?" she said, reprimandingly.

Guilty, he thought.

In the movie theater that night he sat between them, a natural enough arrangement in normal circumstances but one whose symbolism now, heavy and obvious as it was, gave him nervous pleasure.

The picture was about a young woman, married, who progresses from fantasies of sex to the acting-out of them (Faith had chosen the picture; he could not help but reflect on her possible motives), to the extent of becoming an employee in a brothel on a part-time-afternoons basis. Throughout the latter part of the picture Faith caressed his thigh with hers, but he felt certain that she was not aware of what she was doing, so engrossed did she appear to be in the film. Terrified as he was that the movement might, even in the dark, attract Miriam's eye, he could not bring himself to remove his leg from the caress of hers. It felt too wonderful.

Leaving the theater, Miriam was the first to put forth an opinion.

"Well," she said with wry good humor, "it's certainly an original way to kill those occasional dull afternoons."

Faith was highly enthusiastic about the film, its concept and its philosophy. Over supper at a nearby restaurant she suggested casually that, of course, it was a fantasy common to most, if not all, women.

"What is?" Miriam asked in a voice already hinting at protest.

"To be a whore," Faith said.

Walter grinned: He didn't know which he enjoyed most, Faith's way of saying it or Miriam's reaction to it.

"Oh, Faith!" she said, despairing. "Are you *serious?*"

"Now, Mimi, you mean it's never once in your life crossed your mind to wonder what it would be like?"

"I think about it constantly."

"I'm serious."

"No," Miriam said seriously.

"Not ever?"

"Not ever, Faith."

"That's a relief," Walter said, grinning. He was vaguely disappointed: Mightn't she have permitted it to even cross her mind? Just *once?* Even briefly? One small, hazy, ill-defined *belle de jour* dream?

Of course, she might be lying.

As though she might have heard his thought, Miriam said, lightly, smiling, "Besides, would you expect me to admit it in front of my husband?"

Faith smiled, looking at him. "Walter wouldn't mind. Would you?"

"The fantasy or the act?" he asked, flippant, with the beginnings of apprehension tickling at his nerve ends: How far was she going to carry this?

"The fantasy, of course," Faith said.

"Well, I should hope so," Miriam laughed.

Faith turned to her sister again and Walter knew, could see before she spoke, that she was not yet finished with it. "What about when you were watching the picture?"

"What?" Miriam asked.

"Even while you were watching the picture, didn't you wonder what it might be like? I mean, I understand what you're saying now, but what about when you were actually watching the picture, watching her in the cat house?"

"Oh, well," Miriam said quickly, shrugging, and stopped herself. The inconclusiveness of the reply had been admission enough, but there were clearly qualifications to come. "I mean, that's a different thing altogether. I mean, naturally, when you're *watching* a picture you, you know—well, identify to *some* extent with the character. Naturally. But that's not the same thing at all. Are you saying that's the same thing?"

"Of course," Faith said.

"That's ridiculous," Miriam declared. Faith lit a cigarette and gave Miriam a look that said the lady might be protesting too much, methinks. "Well, it is!" Miriam insisted, and laughed uncertainly.

It was going too far, Walter feared. He nearly seized a passing waiter, and asked for the dessert menu. Faith instantly changed the subject. But he was not attending to the new matters at hand: He could only wonder whereof Faith spake.

Miriam might have been a collaborator in her own deception, he was to think later, so unwittingly did she cooperate that night in his third and most terrifying carnal encounter with her sister.

Going up in the elevator, listening distractedly to their chatter (she was incredible, he thought of Faith, the picture and sound of innocence), he was wondering which one he was going to have that night. It was an almost insupportably corrupt thought, he *knew* that. It was nevertheless intensely exciting. It might have been a curious, even irrational, choice to an objective observer, he conceded, but he opted for Miriam. And the more he thought of it, the more excited he became at the prospect of making love to his wife tonight.

And besides, he thought, fair was fair.

But they had been back in the apartment barely half an hour when, emerging from their bathroom, he was surprised to find Miriam (who only minutes before had been chattering with Faith in the living room) in the bedroom and already partially undressed. Yes, she was going to bed, she answered his startled look, admitting the absurdity of the early hour and apologizing for it, telling him that she had evidently not yet recovered from the exhaustion of Christmas. He told her it was perfectly all right, he understood, of course, and glanced at the closed door and, although it was far earlier than he had planned, eyed her suggestively and suggested that he might join her.

She smiled and dropped her eyes demurely. Well, the fact was, she confessed, she wasn't quite recovered *that* way either. What way? he wondered. Well, she was still very sore, actually. Sore? He didn't understand. Well, she meant sore, after last night, she said, unfastening her bra. Ahhhh, he realized. *Really?* Well, that shouldn't be so surprising, should it, she smiled. She stepped out of her underpants and started to pass him and ran into his barring hand.

"Really that sore, eh?"

"Unhand me, brute."

"Tender to the touch, you say?"

"Don't, you'll get me hot."

"The spirit is willing but the flesh is sore?"

"I'll give you a raincheck. Or you'll give me a raincheck. Whichever."

"How long is this condition expected to last, my dear?"

"Not long. It's already better . . . than it was . . . this morning. Don't, Walter, I really mean it, I couldn't, it really would be very uncomfortable."

"Let me tell you a little about the Marquis de Sade."

"I'm going to scream in a minute."

"You already *know* a little about the Marquis de Sade."

"Walter, now come on, I mean it, it's not fair!"

He capitulated but held her long enough to touch her with a light kiss of affection and forgiveness.

She returned it and said, "Hold your thought," and sidled away toward the bathroom.

He bade her a hesitant goodnight as the bathroom door closed behind her. He stood for a moment looking at the floor; the moment stretched into several before he finally moved and left the room. He closed the door softly behind him. The instant he did so, he was intensely aware of the closed door at his back and the open corridor that lay before him. *Symbolism: Its Uses and Abuses,* by Walter . . .

He stood, his mind moving forward in confusion and speculation, making mental adjustments which were vaguely uncomfortable, but necessary. He reminded himself that his heart, after all, had been in the right place, as the rest of him would have been if . . . No debater with Fate, he moved down the hall toward the living room and what he knew would be a delighted—and, by this time, perhaps even pleasantly surprised—Faith. She would not know her standing on tonight's priority list; what she didn't know would not hurt her.

Besides, he would make it up to her.

She was not in the living room. . . . He would find her on the terrace, of course; people from California were always afflicted with a sense of claustrophobia and overheatedness when in New York, constantly turning down thermostats and throwing open windows. Either that, he grinned, or she was out there, binoculars in hand, ready for the main feature across the street.

He rolled open the terrace door and stepped out, already smiling in anticipation of the figure she would be cutting at the railing.

His smile faded somewhat as he crossed the deserted terrace and entered the apartment again through the study door.

He paused for a moment in the study.

He traversed the living room again, moving fast. In the kitchen he supported himself against the refrigerator and tried to reconstruct the probable sequence of events since his leaving the living room to take a leak. But it did not matter in the final analysis which of them did what first: The end result was that Miriam had gone to her bed to sleep and Faith had gone to hers either out of an absence of other desire this night (an understandable absence, he conceded, as visions of afternoon flashed and popped pornographically in his brain); or, on the assumption of such an absence of desire in him (reasons: ditto); or—it had to be faced —on her assumption that he would be otherwise engaged.

For the next ten minutes, morose, brooding, thinking of Olivier as Heathcliffe a few weeks before on the Late Late Show (*Oh Cathy, Cathy, do come! Oh do, once more! Oh, my heart's darling!*), he aimlessly prowled the apartment. Finally, resigned, he forced himself into purposeful motion, placing some hope in the therapy of a hot shower. Passing Faith's closed door there was no way to tell whether or not the light was on in the room (it was the only well-fitted door in the apartment); he was tempted for only an instant before he saw the picture of himself pecking, sly and desperate, at her door; he passed on hurriedly.

The shower was relaxing but did not put him to rest; and, anyway, the hour was too early for sleep. He threw on a robe. There was not the slightest hesitation as he passed Faith's door again. He switched off the lights in the living room and went into the lighted study, closing the door behind him. He took a book from the shelf, his eye falling on the binoculars, restored to their original function as bookend, and wondered if there was any action across the street tonight. He read one page of the book four times, put the book down and went to the desk and sat. He read through the half page of heavily corrected type in the typewriter, finding that his recent lack of interest in April Holliday and her lovers continued; but he discovered a typographical error and corrected it perfunctorily.

He was startled when he heard the door open behind him.

As he turned, she was already closing the door again, calmly, a full glass of something in one hand. She had removed all of her makeup (what little she ever wore) and had braided her hair in two short pigtails that hung in front of her shoulders framing her slender, pale throat. She looked twelve years old. She was almost smiling and completely naked.

He nearly screamed.

His mind's first leap was to a calculation of the odds against Miriam's waking up: She had been *very* tired, and had even taken a Librium—she had the bottle in her hand as he left the bedroom at least forty-five minutes ago; a thousand to one against her waking. But, in a circumstance like this were even *those* safe odds? The words caught in his throat at first, gagging him; then he said in a croaking, breathless whisper: "You're insane."

"I'm hot as a firecracker is what I am," she said demurely and raised the glass to her lips, the fragile tinkle of ice on glass the only sound in the breathless silence.

Despite the queasy churning of his stomach at the implications of the scene (infidelity was one thing, but bad taste . . .) he felt himself quickly beginning to become aroused by the splendor of her nakedness, the sound of her voice and the words it spoke. And certainly, most of all, by the demand the words implied: *You'll have to put this roomer to rest, Walter!* But, "This isn't a good idea," he said weakly.

"Why not?" She smiled and moved to the sofa and sat, crossing one naked thigh over the other, resting the palm of her hand softly on the soft swell of her belly just below the navel. Watching her, he could hardly breathe. Things were beginning to happen too quickly, he thought, too much too soon, events coming upon him precipitately, leaving him no time to think. It began to alarm him. But he continued to stiffen beneath his robe: *Our cocks have no conscience!* he reminded himself.

"How's it coming?" she asked.

For an instant he thought it a reference to what lay hidden beneath the voluminous folds of his new brown velour robe, one of Miriam's Christmas gifts; then her glittering eyes slid toward the typewriter on the desk.

"Tell me what it's about."

He nearly laughed and stole a glance at the door: Had she had the presence of mind to close the door to the bedroom hall? That would be three: the bedroom, the hall, the study. Still, they would have to speak softly, safety first. Last. Always. But, of course, she knew that—she was speaking *very* softly. "Are you serious?" he said finally.

She nodded solemnly and sipped again from her glass. She transferred the glass to her other hand and insinuated the cold one into the warmth between her crossed thighs; if she was aware of the sensuality of the act at such a moment, she gave no indication of it.

"Yes, well . . ." he began eagerly, seizing the manuscript from the desk as much for anchor as reference. He spoke for several minutes in general and disjointed terms about his heroine and her many heroes, then, because he was unable to speak to her without looking at her—only to see nipples and thighs and belly and thick dark hair pigtailed and triangled—he took refuge in the manuscript itself, opening it to the first page and reading the entire first chapter which was devoted solely to April's toil and eventual triumph over her lover's recalcitrant manhood; while his own hidden tumescence beat a taunting counterpoint to the spirit of the words.

When he had finished, he replaced the manuscript on the desk and with a tentative grin dared to look at her again. She was smiling and nodding. But he sensed there to be a somewhat distracted air about her now.

"That's one of George's special ploys, you know," she said.

George who? . . . Oh, yes. Of course. George. "What is?" he asked, distracted in turn.

"He's been known to pretend he's impotent."

She then launched into a description of one of George Brady's special methods of seduction, employed rarely and only when he suspected that the more usual and familiar procedures would meet with failure. The plan was diabolically simple. With a finely balanced blend of self-pity and stoic resignation George would confess to a recent inability (usually of some months' duration) to achieve an erection. The lie was almost always believed (its

failure was rare, he had told Faith), primarily, he suspected, because in a man of his sexual reputation, in a jargonized age of
half-baked psychoanalytic knowledge, such an affliction was
fraught with suggestions of Justice and the Cocksman's Fate.
The lie believed, what remained was only a matter of the
woman's reaction to it. Initial surprise, naturally. Followed by a
lulling, false sense of security, of course. Succeeded by some degree of compassion—occasionally of an amused nature, but George
could bear it, he knew who was going to come out on top in the
end. The end was curiosity and challenge: His affliction was a call
to the unique powers of her femaleness, hers alone among all
the women who had failed to arouse him for so tragically long
a time. It was then simple enough for him to attribute his re-
vitalized manhood to her mere proximity, pointing out to her in
awe and gratitude what no woman in months had been able to
induce in him. Faced with what she could not help but feel
proudly—however unwittingly—responsible for, she was inclined
to feel at the very least obliged to relieve it; and more often
than not, eager to.

Walter was as awed as he was amused by so original and
beautifully wrought a concept, and wondered if Faith had been
one of its failed objects. He might have asked had he not been
distracted by what she was then doing. She had removed the
green wedge of lime from her glass and put it to her lips, sucking
on it lightly as she spoke. Now, with her eyes on his, she touched
the piece of fruit to her belly, squeezed a bit of juice from it, and
rubbed it gently into her skin. In the next moment she had un-
crossed her legs and stretched them straight out before her, the
soles of her feet flat on the floor. The legs parted slightly and
he watched, speechless with wonderment and desire, as she
caressed the inside of each thigh with the fruit's juicy pulp.

He lifted his eyes to hers again to find her watching him
steadily. The silence lengthened. Softly, smiling, as though she
might only be referring to his continued silence, she said: "What's
up?" He opened his robe to show her. "And I always thought
Old Faithful was in Yellowstone National Park," she said.

He stood, leaving the robe behind him in the chair, and took
a step toward her before he realized that the drapes were not

drawn, that they had been exposed to full view from dozens of windows across the street—how many pairs of trembling binoculars and straining, unaided eyes were trained upon them at this very moment! But the momentum of his lust had carried him to within touching distance of her before his mind was able to adjust to his new, necessary intention. As he stepped toward the window, she grasped his reaching hand, staying him. He turned his face back to her. "The windows," he explained.

"What about them?"

"The drapes."

"So what," she said quietly.

His hesitation was barely perceptible. *Branching out again.* He descended on her, imagining frantic fingers at the adjustment wheels of a dozen binoculars, some of them equipped with zoom lenses, zooming now, zooming. But, soon enough, he had forgotten the world outside and was savoring the delicious result of her latest show of inventiveness, the taste of woman's juices mingled with the tangy flavor and scent of lime.

She was an eroticist of the first order!

Then they were on the floor. He lifted her legs frantically and threw one over each of his shoulders like the ends of a scarf, suddenly conscious again of the scrape of the carpet on his knees: *At this rate they would* never *heal!*

Then he froze.

Her toes twinkling at the ceiling, she said urgently: "What?"

"You locked the door, didn't you?"

"I don't know!" she gasped distractedly and locked her ankles behind his shoulders.

"Oh, Christ," he moaned, struggling to break her grip on him.

"It doesn't matter, Walter!"

It was an insane concern at this point, he knew, but he was on his feet and leaping to the door, *better late than never.* He turned again from the now impassable barrier of the door to find her on her feet and coming at him almost at a run. He had only an instant to brace himself, setting his feet solidly, before she leaped, locking her arms around his neck, her legs around his waist, and dropped, impaling herself. He staggered backward on impact, then forward in compensation, his knees buckling.

Indifferent to his plight, she commenced to rise and plunge, whimpering. He knew the sofa was a hopeless goal: It might just as well have been across the street. Too soon, with one final spine-jarring plunge, she went, shuddering and whimpering.

"Jesus Christ," he said. He managed to stagger to a bookshelf, seizing it with both hands for support. Books tumbled from the upper shelves onto his head and shoulders, fluttering, thumping to the floor at his feet with a sound like thunder. She seemed oblivious to what was happening. He could restrain himself no longer; a shiver gathered at the base of his spine, built up force, exploded, shot up his back and blew the top of his head off. Or so it seemed. Instantly the bones disintegrated in his legs and he collapsed with her, still joined, to the floor. He heard her head thump lightly against the carpet; somewhere far away a dull pain shot through his elbow; and the hard edge of something sharp sawed into his hip with each gasping shudder they made against each other.

If we survive, it will have been wonderful! he told himself.

Finally she became still, curled quietly into him. Careful not to disturb her, he managed to move his hip away from the sharp edge which proved to have been the side of the bookshelf. He wondered if he was bleeding on the carpet.

There was a long, enervated silence filled with the slowing heartbeat of contentment.

"Oh-dear-me-love, that was a fuck and a half, wasn't it?" she whispered presently.

"Constantly branching out."

"You've never come standing up before?"

"Uh-uh." Certainly it had been his life's most gymnastic orgasm.

"I'm glad. I think I hit my head. What are all these books doing here?"

He became conscious again, abruptly, of the undrawn drapes and the shameless illumination of the room. His impulse was to cover the windows: If the act itself was a private one, its aftermath was doubly so. But he could not bring himself to disturb the pattern they made together, or interrupt the slow caressing motion of her hand on the small of his back.

"That's the only really important thing," she murmured.

"What is?"

"Coming."

"Do you think so?"

"Mm-hm."

It seemed a dangerously uncomplicated doctrine. He thought of Miriam asleep less than a hundred feet away, behind three closed doors, one locked.

"I once came on a roller coaster," she said, adjusting her position, but maintaining her contact.

"Must've been tricky," he smiled.

"No, I don't mean with someone. By myself. I was about fift"een, I guess. On the rollar coaster at Steeplechase Park."

He remembered it from his boyhood. That was gone now, too.

"There was a boy with me but he didn't have anything to do with it. I mean, I just suddenly began to get terribly excited on the roller coaster and all of a sudden I started to come. The boy thought I was just enjoying the ride and all the time I was coming like mad."

"Did you always come the way you do now?"

"Pretty much. Do you like the way I come?"

"I love it."

She was silent for a moment. "It's the only really important thing. Where's my drink?"

She rolled from his arms and spied the glass still miraculously upright on the floor near the sofa. She moved on her hands and knees, feline, across the room, presenting him with an incendiary view of undulating buttocks, glistening pudenda. She grasped the glass and sat on the floor facing him, her back against the sofa, her legs straight out, ankles crossed. He was afraid she was going to leak wet spots all over the carpet if she didn't stay in one place, and hoped they would dry by morning. He smiled. "Would you like a fresh piece of lime, I think that one's all used up."

"Did you like that?" she whispered.

"Incredible."

"There's more where that came from."

The words and their promise brought him face to face again

with time and the future. There was no escaping it, she was a transient presence in his life. Tomorrow was Friday. She had said she would be leaving the apartment on Saturday. He considered the possibilities for a moment before he spoke. "What about after tomorrow," he asked, averting his eyes, that she might not see his concern and accuse him of romanticism and unworldly innocence.

"It's up to you," she murmured softly. Then smiled. "Hasn't it always been?"

"No, I mean New York, how long are you going to stay in New York?"

"Oh. I don't know," she said, indifferent. "Another week or so, maybe. Why?"

There was no suggestion in her voice that the words caused her any of the sense of threatened loss they engendered in him. "What about George?"

She thought for a moment as she began idly to stroke one of her breasts. "I don't know what to do about George," she said ruminatively. "I suppose it'll just work itself out naturally." She transferred her glass to her left hand and went to work on the other breast. The nipple of the first one, he saw, was already well stiffened: they were evidently independently excitable. Miriam's nipples worked together. "He'll be in Washington most of the time, for one thing." She laughed abruptly, quietly. "Can you *imagine* it? *Congressman George Brady?*"

"It boggles the mind," he replied absently: He was already beginning to feel the first stirrings of the effect her caressing hand was having on him. She still appeared to be unaware of what she was doing.

"And do you realize," she went on, delighted, "that now that he's started, theoretically there's nothing in the world to stop him from some day being president? I mean, theoretically it's possible, right? If that doesn't kill anyone's romantic illusions," she said ruefully, "I don't know what will."

In some surrealistic way, he thought, the movie star as president could be a kind of culmination of our American Way of Life. *President Brady's on the Late Show tonight, I see.*

The fault is not in our stars but in ourselves that we . . .

She had fallen silent again, introspective, and her hand had resumed its briefly arrested motion. After a moment she came to herself again and discovered him watching her. She looked down at her moving hand; then moved her eyes to find its effect on him. "You like that?"

Is there anything you could do I wouldn't like?

He felt the roiling in his loins well enough, but wondered if its promise could come to fruition. He made a quick tabulation. Once already tonight. And there had been this afternoon, how many times had it been this afternoon? He had lost count. And last night . . . He glanced surreptitiously down; semi-tumescent, it bobbed and weaved, groggily, like a brave but battered fighter uncertain whether to stand again for another round or surrender pride and go down for the count. Would she think him inadequate, unequal to her dazzling demands?

"What about this?" she whispered. "Do you like this?" and drew her feet backward toward her thighs, parted her resultingly raised knees and, her splayed fingers safaris through the deep, delicate jungle, slid her hand between her legs. She watched him steadily as his astonished eyes danced between hers and her shameless hand.

He was reminded of the long-ago girl who had devised a game they came to call Hold Out for Special Rewards, in which, with both of them undressed, she would touch and caress herself while he sat some distance from her, watching, the object being to see how long he could resist before he had to jump her, there being special rewards for him then, based on the length of time he had been able to restrain himself. It was a wonderful game. (Once, years ago, he had suggested it to Miriam. She didn't go for it. He knew it was the "special rewards" aspect of it that worried her most.)

Had he happened to tell Faith about that game and was she suggesting that *they* play a round of it now? And, good sweet God, imagine what undreamed-of erotic possibility *this* one might devise as a special prize! . . . But no, he remembered he had not told Faith about that. So this was entirely her own idea. And it had achieved her probable purpose.

He lurched to his feet and moved to her.

She lifted her drowsy eyes and smiled and reached up and grasped him like the handle of a slot machine that was about to bring in a jackpot. They rolled once and she was under him in the middle of the room. He remembered the windows again. *They must be going right out of their skulls over there by now, I should have put my robe down, what if the rug doesn't dry by morning. . . .* "Once more into the breech," he said, and sank ecstatically, belly-deep into wet velvet.

Her kneecaps sweetly socketed in his armpits, the padded balls of her heels joyfully thumping his kidneys like drums, she said, "Don't fire till you see the whites of my eyes."

Walter knew he had no right to expect the continued comfort of Miriam's unwitting cooperation. So he was disconcerted but not surprised when, the following night, the first serious complication arose.

At dinner Miriam served chocolate pudding for dessert; it had always been Faith's favorite and Miriam wanted to make the dinner a special occasion since it was her sister's last night as their guest. Cassie asked her mother if there was any whipped cream for the pudding. Miriam told her there was, in the refrigerator. Cassie returned from the kitchen carrying a tall can of Reddi-Wip and topped her pudding with a generous hill of it.

"Anyone else?" she asked.

"None for me, thanks," Faith said, her gaze gliding past Walter's eyes and away.

Walter could not speak, merely pursed his lips and shook his head curtly and was careful not to meet Faith's eyes as Miriam took the can from Cassie and topped her own pudding, stingily, watching her weight.

"You can get that in low calorie, you know," Faith said. "Not so fattening."

Miriam did not retire to the bedroom at her usual hour that night. At first, Walter attributed no special significance to her lengthening presence.

Marking time late in the evening, he spent an hour or so in the study, making needless notes and desultorily perusing his manuscript. He was finding it more difficult each day to concentrate on the concupiscent April. From the living room he could hear Miriam's and Faith's voices in animated conversation, muffled through the closed door, the words unintelligible. His impatience grew.

When he finally joined them he discovered them in a heated discussion of a current bestseller about Wall Street and the Stock Market. He had not yet read the book. (Miriam had: She had come by her knowledge of the market some years before in a desire to share with him what was clearly an important "aspect of his life.") Listening to Faith he was surprised and pleased to discover how extremely knowledgeable and articulate she was on the subject. *There was so much more to her than met the eye!* It was unfortunate in a way that what met the eye was so overwhelming.

But his appreciation quelled his impatience only briefly. He sat, caring more about what met eye than ear, and participated vaguely in the conversation for several minutes before Miriam remarked that it was time for the News and that there would probably be a Special Report on the splashdown of the astronauts that had occurred that morning. He glanced at Faith but her eyes were on Miriam and the slowly focusing image on the television.

For the next half hour they watched scenes of the culmination of man's first voyage to the moon (it would be no time at all now, it was said, before they would actually be landing on it), Faith neutrally, Walter impatiently, Miriam with what appeared to Walter as a somewhat forced enthusiasm. By the time the program ended his anticipation was at high pitch. He endured restlessly the next five minutes of final reflection, mostly Miriam's, on what they had just seen, certain that she would soon make her longed-for exit. At the naked, undisguised deceitfulness of the thought he experienced his first seriously sharp stab of guilt since there had been occasion for him to feel any at all. But he refused to permit it victory over him, knowing that an occasional pang was inevitable, reminding himself that the amputated leg sometimes gave evidence of its continued presence: It was merely a matter of reluctant nerve ends refusing to accept reality.

Then—suddenly, unbelievably—he was watching Faith stretch languidly to her feet, listening to her declare her tiredness, hearing her say that she would see them in the morning, that she would be packed up and out by noon.

He nodded, smiling inanely, teeth clenched to trap the heart that pounded behind them. And watched her go.

For what seemed like minutes he heard Miriam's voice, coming from far away. It finally broke through the wall of loss and disappointment and he was able to distinguish the words when she asked if he would care for another drink.

Returning him his refilled glass, she sat cozily beside him on the sofa, and said, "To coin a phrase, I thought she'd never leave."

He looked at her uncomprehendingly for an instant until she smiled, intimately: It explained everything. He wondered how he could have been so stupid as to have failed to recognize the situation long before for what it had been.

Why couldn't it have been last night when she was his choice in the first place!

Well, then. He was being faced with his first test of responsibility to her; he met it honorably, pulling her to him, kissing her. She muttered something unintelligible into his honorable mouth. "What?" he murmured.

"I said," she said, her face buried out of sight under his chin, "will you do what you did the other night, I'll be wide awake this time."

14

When, some seventy-two hours later, on Monday night, Walter found himself lying in post-copulative collapse beside Barbara Finch in a bed in the best hotel in Boston, her somewhat too heavy leg across one of his, the short, slightly thick fingers of one of her hands curled on his belly, he recognized it as a scene swollen with implications.

Barbara sighed and moved, lazily caressing his hip with her heavy muff of dark brown hair, and murmured, "That was such stuff as dreams are made on, Walter. Shall we round out our little lives with a sleep?"

He smiled at the head tucked into his armpit. "Good idea," he said, wishing that he might be able to act upon it.

She collapsed slowly, like a cooling soufflé, and soon lay limp and weighty against him in a snuffling doze. He reached to look at his watch on the bedside table. Eleven thirty-eight. Incredible. It was barely twelve hours since he had picked up the telephone in the study.

He had been lying on the sofa at the time, inhaling the tantalizing scent of Faith that still lingered in the weave, and reading the publisher's official position on Homosexuality and the Law in *Playboy*. Cassie had already gotten to it, he saw: Here and there words had been delicately underlined in red (Cassie's mark always), their definitions to be looked up in the dictionary: *fel-*

latio, cunnilingus, buggery. Would she find buggery in the dictionary? Failing there, she would ask him, of course. As always. He wished that someone might define precisely for him the limits of the modern child's fleshly education. *How in Christ's name was he going to explain buggery to her, for the love of God!*

He sighed and threw the magazine aside and waited for the telephone to ring. Faith had not called the apartment since leaving it on Saturday morning; he had waited (in willed and difficult self-restraint, that he might not seem too unsophisticatedly overeager) until Monday to try to reach her. But there had been no answer at her apartment to any of his numerous calls and, as the hours passed, he had become increasingly less certain in his hopes for their brief future.

Nevertheless, he leaped for the phone when finally it rang and seized it with a hand trembling with cautious optimism.

But it was only Jack Finley and his cry for help. Barely twelve hours ago. And now he lay in bed in a Boston hotel suite next to Barbara Finch who twitched and mumbled in a troubled dream.

But, as the saying went around the office, *When you've done your best, give it a good hard look and do a little more.* So said, often, D. J. Cramm, President. And Jack Finley's "little more" was, of course, to call on Walter Hartman, the last resort when it came to Barbara Finch.

"In Boston!" Walter cried. "What in God's name is she doing in Boston?"

"It took a while to get that out of her," Jack said. "You ready for this? She says she got on the first plane that was going anywhere and it happened to be Boston."

Walter laughed. "It could have been Paris."

"Maybe we're getting lucky."

Barbara Finch had flown, like the goony-bird she was, as Jack put it; flown and refused to return unless she was able to deal personally with the only person in the entire network with whom she had "any rapport at all." It was typical of Barbara to consider questions of "rapport" at a time like this; to bring about disaster and then demand that it be dealt with in terms of her personal emotional comfort.

Walter noted that Jack seemed to be watching his language

and suspected that he might be speaking in the presence of D.J. himself, a suspicion confirmed a few moments later when Jack said, "Hold on, Walter, here's D.J."

"Walter, how are you?" D.J. said. "We miss you around here."

"Sounds like it, Duncan."

"I don't have to tell you what we're faced with here, Walter. The implications. As Jack's just told you, we've got three days taping in the can, one to go. We've gone too far to turn back, it's too late to replace her, and we can't just scrap a production we've already got three hundred thousand dollars in. We're deadlocked, Walter. By this rather pathetically disturbed woman." Walter imagined he could hear the gristly crunch of Jack Finley's bitten tongue in response to D.J.'s calm and unrealistically compassionate appraisal of Barbara Finch's emotional condition. "Of course, there's absolutely no obligation involved on your part in this thing, Walter, that goes without saying. You're on sabbatical and in the purest sense you aren't even a member of this organization at the moment. For all practical purposes. I want you to know I understand that and that you're perfectly free to tell us to go fly a Chinese kite on this thing." Walter stifled the laugh, but permitted himself the unseen smile: If he refused, it might well be Walter Hartman who would be flying kites for a living and D.J. knew he knew it. "But the fact is, we're in the soup, Walter, and yours appears to be the only magic hand that can pull us out."

He was on the shuttle flight to Boston within the hour.

Now, as Barbara moved, rolling away from him with a groan, he knew that from agreeing to bring her back to sleeping with her had been an entirely natural progression—though he had not yet traced the naturalness of it in detail.

Not that there had been any intimations at first of what was to come. He had arrived on a mission of urgent business, nothing more; and she had seemed to welcome his presence on that basis alone. It was many hours before any suggestion of other possibilities was hinted at. And then with mind-boggling haste, acted upon. Throughout most of those many hours they spoke of everything but the purpose of his presence. He was subjected to a drunkenly detailed account of the miseries of her life, commencing with a breech birth (*I didn't even* come out *the right goddam way, Walter!*) and continuing to more or less that present moment. Despite his repeated attempts to guide her subtly toward pertinence, she was capable of responding for no more than a useless moment or two before her mind would turn again to the past (a horrendous one, he conceded) and, like a poorly secured boat slipping its mooring, drift off again into dark waters.

Finally, he ordered dinner sent to the room and managed to get some food into her. It sobered her to some extent; that, and his by then desperate determination to settle the issue that had brought him there. He managed to get her agreement to return to New York for the single day's work that was required. He agreed that she was in no condition to travel that night; it would be in the morning, then. And would he wait and accompany her in the morning? He would, of course. In fact, he would even remain at the studio for the day if his presence there would be of any help to her. It would, it would mean everything to her, just to have him there, he was the only one at the entire fucking network who understood her, the only one with whom she had the slightest fucking rapport, and did he realize what a tremendously vital factor that was, how vital it was to the creative artist to feel that intangible but tremendously important aura of rapport in order to be able to truly realize and fulfill the fullest potential of her——? He did, he did, he realized that. Of course. Completely.

It was after he had arranged for a room for himself and called Miriam to apprise her of the situation that Barbara had recalled some particularly terrifying aspect of her second marriage and broke down again, weeping pitiably. Even up to the moment he put his arm around her shoulders there had been nothing in his mind beyond friendly solace. And her hand that fell naturally to his breast suggested nothing more than the need for a place to rest it upon. But, when she had finally begun to calm somewhat and, a moment later, her hand began to move in slow, soft circles against the by now wilted cotton of his shirt, he knew that something else was happening. Muttering the words into his collar that was damp with her neurotic tears, she told him that she had always liked him, that she had always been terribly fond of him, didn't he know that? He told her he did, he did know that, told her carefully, neutrally. She wondered if he did, did really know. Of course he did, he insisted.

She lifted her head then and looked at him for only a moment before she seized his head in both hands and kissed him frantically. The force of her assault and his unpreparedness for it felled them; they went over sideways on the sofa, her mouth sucking at his, her hand burrowing in his groin like a hungry animal.

"I've always wanted you, Walter! Always! Didn't you know that!"

"I didn't. No."

In the bedroom, while they undressed, he was briefly distracted at the curious realization that he was uncertain about who the truest victim of this imminent two-pronged infidelity was. Or was he being unfaithful to Faith at all, really? After all, on what grounds could she claim injury? She had had no feeling about his infidelity to Miriam, certainly no objection to his sleeping with Miriam while she, Faith, enjoyed her liaison with him. Could a mistress, particularly an acknowledgedly transitory one, justifiably claim damage in a circumstance like this? he wondered, stepping out of his shorts.

"Oh, Walter, look what you've got," Barbara murmured from the bed. "You're so big, oh, I'm glad."

"I'm glad you're glad," he grinned, moving toward her. (Faith had remarked on it, too. Was there some truth in it? Any? Or was it merely a female courtesy extended, an encouragement offered, knowing, as they all must, of the male concern with dimensions, a perfunctory stab at a little ego support that might redound to their benefit as a result of the male's enhanced male pride in his maleness?)

"Oh, darling, you could core apples with that," she said, seizing him with both hands.

"Hell, that's what I've been doing with it all day, can't we think of something else?"

He found her body still attractive despite the ill care she had taken of it for most of its thirty-five or so years. The preliminaries were brief, almost perfunctory by comparison to, for instance (he found himself thinking), Faith's sensual, languorous, preambular explorations. But he found Barbara no less pleasurable in her way, perhaps in the very fact of her difference. Variety was the spice of . . .

"Oh, Walter, Jesus, are you going to do me good? Are you? Oh, I want a really good one."

"I'll do my best, Barb." Anything for the network.

She seemed peaceful now, snoring slightly. He rose from the bed and went to the window and looked down across the Common. It had begun to snow. Twenty-four hours from now it would be a new year. He felt exceedingly relaxed from the neck down.

Miriam . . . Faith . . . Barbara . . .

He had reason to think now that what he had had (was having now, it was not over yet!) with Faith might not have been the true beginning he had thought it to be; suspected now that Faith, for all her significance in his life, might really have been no more than prelude, an overture to the main body of what was to come.

Faith: An Introduction, by W. A. Hartman.

Yes, this—standing naked in a Boston hotel room, behind him the latest satisfied recipient of his life's energies and juices, the third within a week, curled contentedly in sleep—this might be the true beginning.

Of what?

Not long ago, he recalled, in an attempt to determine the limits of his erotic imagination, Miriam had asked, Where does it end? . . . He had wondered then; and wondered again now and with greater cause for wonder. Would it be safe to say that, given imagination and the opportunity to exercise it, there was no end to experience? *I go to seek a great perhaps,* said Rabelais as he breathed his last. . . . Who knew, he might even come across a virgin one of these days, it was possible, anything was possible, and every man should have at least one . . .

"Walter?"

He turned. Limply awake, she gestured, lazily but with purpose, suggesting his return, Circe on her island bed.

Already?

He smiled and moved to her and sat. "Oink," he said.

"Hm?"

"Nothing."

She pulled him down, his neck gripped in the jackknifed crook of her elbow, her other hand carefully cupping his weary testicles like overripe grapes. "Oh, do me again, darling! Do me again!"

Constantly branching out, I go to seek a great . . .

15

"Hello?"

"Can you talk?"

". . . Yes."

"Are you alone?"

"Yes."

"How are you?"

"Fine. How are you?"

"Wonderful."

"I've missed you."

"Already?"

"It seems like a year."

"It does, doesn't it. Have you been thinking?"

"About what?"

"About whether you want to see me again."

"There's nothing to think about."

"That sounds like you do, then."

"That's how it was supposed to sound."

"When?"

"Very soon, if possible. For you, I mean."

"What about you?"

"Anything's possible."

"When, then?"

"Let me check my appointment book. . . . You have a wonderful laugh."

"Don't be romantic, all laughs are wonderful."

"Sorry."

"When?"

"You sound anxious."

"Anxious isn't all I am."

"What else are you?"

"Come and see."

"This afternoon?"

"We should have another afternoon, shouldn't we. Afternoons are wonderful."

"I remember. Have you decided yet when you're leaving?"

". . . No."

"Are you sure?"

". . ."

"You have decided."

"Yes."

"Aren't you going to tell me?"

"Do you like the way I do things so far?"

". . . Yes."

"Not just those things."

"Everything."

"Then trust me to do it right."

"All right."

"How soon, then?"

"About half an hour?"

"If you're late I'll have to start without you."

"I won't be late."

"You sound a little tired. Haven't you been sleeping?"

"I had a hard day yesterday, I just got back from Boston this morning."

"What were you doing in Boston?"

"Just business. Something unexpected came up."

"Have you ever done it over the telephone?"

"Business?"

"No, silly."

"Oh. No, not that I recall. Why?"

"Because about a minute ago I got the urge to start without you."

"You did?"

"Mm."

". . ."

"Are you there?"

"Yes. I was just wondering about staying on the phone."

". . . Would you like to?"

"If I do, do I still get to come over?"

"How else would I repay you?"

"I think I'll stay on the phone for a while."

"I'll bet it's something you've always wanted to do and never have, right?"

". . . Guilty."

"You're incorrigible."

"But, coming along."

"Beautifully."

". . ."

"You're supposed to do some of the work, you know."

"Yes, I know. Well, let me see . . ."

"Setting the scene is usually a good way to start."

"Setting the scene."

"Ask me where I am."

"Where are you?"

"In that white plastic chair in the living room."

"Ah. Uh, huh."

". . . Ask me what I'm wearing."

"What are you wearing?"

"A pair of pants. Underpants, I mean."

"That's all?"

"Mm."

"They must be very cumbersome."

"Very."

"I think you'd better take them off, don't you?"

"Mm."

". . . Are they off?"

"Mm."

"That was quick."

"But, slowly now. This is a special occasion."

". . . Yes. There's a phone in the bedroom there, isn't there?"

"Yes, why?"

"I may want to move you in there eventually."

"It comes as no surprise to me that you're probably going to be very good at this."

Less than two hours later he was at last on the brink of blissful reward for his earlier, nearly unbearable telephonic self-restraint. On her knees and elbows, she lurched and bucked under him, his cheek glued tightly to her down-sloping back as he tightened his slipping grip on her.

"Now!"

He misunderstood for an instant and nearly responded wrongly before he became aware of her hand reaching back over her shoulder, the fingers open and frantically tense. He gave her the capsule that he had held in his fist at her request. This would be her third popper, he had already had two himself and wondered if she might be overdoing it.

She seized the capsule and crushed it in her fingers; holding it in her palm she clamped her hand over her nose and mouth, inhaling deeply, filling her lungs with the essence of amyl nitrate.

An instant later she screeched and collapsed under him.

"Jesus," he said, and followed her down.

The intensity of her pleasure was a little alarming—she wasn't a screamer by nature.

A long time passed in recuperative silence.

"See what I mean?" she said finally, her lips dry and barely moving.

"Yes indeed."

"That last one's the best of all."

"Next time for sure."

Her one visible eye opened and gazed at him across the pillow's snowy hills. "Yes," she said at last.

There was something about the way in which she spoke the word that struck him as odd.

When the door chime sounded, he was lying alone on the

bed, listening to the gentle tinkling sound she made behind the only partially closed bathroom door and wondering how the taping was progressing and whether Barbara was behaving herself. He had been enormously relieved that morning at the airport when, following her into the network limousine, she had released him from his promise. It wouldn't be necessary, she told him, to provide her with the moral support of his presence at the studio, he had already given her all the moral support a girl could possibly want.

He smiled now, too pleasantly sated and fatigued to be more than mildly startled that there was someone at the apartment door. The chime sounded again. He asked Faith if she was expecting anyone. Emerging from the bathroom grinning she told him only the Vice Squad and, dropping a short, flowered shift carelessly over her head, left the room, sedately closing the bedroom door behind her.

He heard her call through the door in the living room to ask who was there and then the sound of the bolt as she unlocked the door.

"Happy New Year, baby! How are you?" George said. He sounded exuberant.

"I'm wonderful, George. How are you?" Faith replied, with a coolness and reserve that Walter thought admirable under the circumstances.

While he dressed he only half attended to the conversation in the next room, concerned more with the investigation of his own composure. By the time he had laced his shoes he was forced to admit that the unfortunate source of his self-possession was probably nothing more than a kind of puerile conceit: He had been enjoying to capacity that which George Brady so much desired but was denied and he was pleased and proud that George was soon to know it. He knew that in its broader sense it was a dangerous impulse—that suppressed wish that others know or, at the very least, suspect: Look at *me*, look what *I*'ve got, look what I'm *doing!* Whereupon rumor might be expected to ooze like the very sweat of sex itself—not entirely unpleasant, even, in a sense, perhaps aphrodisiacal.

Yes, a dangerous impulse, that, for discretion was vital. And, so far, he had felt no temptation toward a disregard of it. But the only alternative at the moment—to remain, in hiding, in the bedroom, like a ridiculous character in a French farce—was really no alternative at all. And, even if there did happen to be in his choice any of that perverse impulse of indiscreet pride, he felt certain that there was nothing unwisely indiscriminate about it: It was directed toward George Brady and *only* George Brady. Because George alone was the only known competition from whom he, Walter Hartman, had won the day and taken the prize; and before whom he, *Walter Hartman,* could justifiably claim his victory.

His fingers paused on his shirt buttons while he hoped he wasn't rationalizing.

Buttoning his cuffs and wondering whether the tight feeling in his chest was due to some residual effect of the amyl nitrate or to his sudden thought of the possibility of a physically violent reaction by George to what he was about to discover, Walter opened the door and stepped out of the bedroom.

Faith looked only momentarily—and mildly—surprised, then smiled a warm, loving welcome. George was in mid-sentence and stopped there.

"Hello, George," Walter said, "how are you?"

George gazed in silence for a moment, squinting and blinking. He looked briefly at Faith, then returned his eyes to Walter.

When George began to laugh, Walter found it extremely disconcerting. He glanced warily at Faith and found her smiling at George; she returned his look fleetingly, then turned again to George. Then she too began to laugh.

Walter's reluctance to join them was short-lived. There was no denying it—*it was a hell of a funny situation.* George laughed until he had no more strength to stand and fell into the air-inflated white plastic armchair which blew a leak and exploded with a great whooshing thump under the sudden impact of his weight. Faith threw back her head and wailed at the ceiling. Walter bellowed, clapped his hands, and doubled over pounding his thighs with his fists. George lay on the floor tangled in sticky white plastic, rolling and roaring. Faith went to Walter for support, eyes streaming. His knees too weak to sustain their combined weight, Walter stumbled, falling with her into a black leather pedestal chair which, too precariously balanced on its single spindly leg to withstand the collision, tumbled over backward, carrying them with it to the floor, propelling the three of them into a fresh paroxysm of near dementia.

Walter knew then what he knew he should have known all along: No matter what he might wish it to be, in spite of whatever he might try to make of it, it was only, could only be farce in the end. As well for George to have discovered him hiding under the bed! Oh yes, oh yes, farce was the truth and the truth was just, a fair judgment on, the rightful penalty exacted for a lifetime of romantic illusions illustrated by Norman Rockwell, background music by Dmitri Tiomkin.

And why not? he asked himself, his face wet with laughter's tears, his rib cage aching, his throat raw and rasping. Why not indeed! As the man said whose heart failed him in the middle of the last hump of his life: *Is there a better way to go?*

George was the first to rise from the floor, able to speak intelligibly at last, and hastily apologized for what he called his "untimely intrusion." Through their last sporadic sputters of laughter Walter and Faith forgave him, but made no attempt to enjoin him to stay (they had shared the most it was possible to share, they all knew) as he took up his overcoat and slid into it, shaking his head and smiling as though to himself and murmuring:

"Beautiful. . . . Just beautiful. . . ." He opened the door, then stopped and turned for one final look at them. Once more he snorted, beaming, and, looking at Walter, shook his head. "Beautiful," he said again, then left, closing the door softly after him.

Walter rose from the floor and helped Faith to her feet. "I certainly would never have expected that reaction from him," he said.

"George is unpredictable," she agreed.

Yes, Walter thought, following her into the kitchen, true enough, of course, and yet . . . On reflection, no longer in the scene and hysterical, but beyond it and looking back with a sharper eye, there had been something in it, about it, that did not lend itself to his earlier, so facile appraisal of it as farce. Something nagged. Something in George, he thought, something in the quality of his laughter, some element beyond the obvious irony of the situation that he had shared with them, something *not* shared, something . . . private?

No. He smiled and shook his head, reprimanding himself for trying to manufacture significance where there was none, for reading between the lines where nothing was written.

"Want a Coke?" Faith asked.

"Mm. . . . Do you think this might slow him up a little?"

"Hm?"

"George?"

"In what way?"

"In his passionate pursuit, I mean," he smiled. *Of the happiness between her legs.*

"Oh. Well, I doubt it." She shrugged. "Why should it?"

"Yes," he nodded. "I suppose not." He reflected for a moment while she broke an ice tray free from the refrigerator freezer. "I suppose he would know this is only temporary."

"Yes, he'd know that."

"Do you think you'll succumb eventually?"

"I don't know." She dropped ice cubes into two glasses; then became still and appeared to be giving the question serious thought. "Sometimes I feel myself weakening," she said with a faint hint of something like consternation.

"And virtue," he smiled, "won't triumph after all."

She looked at him for a moment as though (he was sure) she had heard his failure to achieve his intended casualness.

She put the two glasses on the sideboard and moved to him. One ice-cooled hand went to the back of his neck, the other slid under his belt at the small of his back. "How would you like to triumph over my virtue once more?" she murmured; then added, almost as an afterthought, "Before you go."

"I'll be late for supper." He smiled quickly. "However . . ." He took her hand and stepped toward the door.

"No," she said, restraining him. She drew him back toward the large oval black Formica-topped table. Before he knew what was happening she had lain back upon it, drawn her shift to her neck and pulled him down after her. "Supper's on the table," she whispered.

Her fingertips flickered at the front of his trousers; in the utter silence of their held breaths he heard the zipper's slowly unclenching teeth.

All this coming and going is wearing me out.

That night Walter stepped into the shower stall as into a ceremonial bath, a rite of purification as prelude to the new ritual which Miriam, stunningly, had prepared for him during his illicit afternoon's absence. The last sound he heard before the water's steaming force drowned his ears was the telephone ringing in the bedroom.

Ceremonially soaping himself and thinking of what awaited him in the bedroom, he was reminded of The Book's chapter, "Ceremonial Lovemaking for Special Occasions." What lay beyond the closed bathroom door was indeed a Special Occasion. He wondered if, in light of this sudden unexpected development, he might risk another copy of The Book. Might it, too, be acceptable to her now?

He wished he knew what was happening.

He again recalled that morning on his return from Boston, and wondered whether or not her manner then had had anything to do with what was to come later in the day. Although he had taken no special notice of it at the time there had been a certain oddness in her behavior, bright and pleasant as she was, in a tight, forced kind of way. So, perhaps she had indeed already known then, that morning, what she was going to do later; it could certainly account for that bright tension that he had been only vaguely aware of then (preoccupied as he had been with the implications of his Boston night), but that he remembered quite vividly now.

He smiled and bared his teeth at the shower head to let the spray needle his gums and reflected again on the fact that for more than a week now he had barely thought at all about the mirror that had stood, formidably boxed, behind the pantry door, its disposition postponed until the time when Faith would no longer be a guest in the apartment. That Miriam was the one ultimately to determine that disposition and that her decision was what it was and arrived at without further prompting from him *and so soon.* . . . It was unthinkable.

Yet at this very moment the mirror hung—perfectly angled he suspected, and would soon know—on the bedroom wall. (It looked much bigger now than it had in the store; he wondered if he might have overdone it a little.)

The mystery was what had caused it to be there? What had happened—and evidently so suddenly—to bring about this change of heart and mind? A change of mind it certainly was, undeniably: The evidence was screwed into the very wall. But her heart? *Was* that in it too? Alterations in the heart, he reminded himself, were rare and, when indicated, were to be looked upon with respect, of course, but approached with caution. Danger! Heart at Work! Hard at work. Heartily.

He was feeling giddy now, liquored and steamed, and was beginning to suspect that his drug-distended blood vessels might not yet have fully contracted again to normality since the nitritic afternoon, despite Faith's assurances that the drug's effects were transitory and that any symptoms he thought he was still feeling could be nothing more than his imagination. (And saying that she had put the half-full plastic vial of capsules into his hand and walked him to the door. Her inference was unmistakably clear: He might perhaps want to introduce Miriam to Popper Pleasures. However oblique it was, it had been her very first real reference to Miriam and his sexual dissatisfactions with her. Putting the vial into his hands, Faith was suggesting the possibility of solutions not necessarily extramarital: It was a noble gesture, he thought. She really was quite an extraordinary girl.)

He wiped the cabinet mirror imperfectly clear of steam and combed his hair, wondering if tonight was the night to try a popper on Miriam. Too soon? Probably. One step at a time. *But why,* he again asked himself in the mirror, thinking of that other one on the bedroom wall. *Why so suddenly?* On the other hand, what did it really matter? It was done and that was what was important. She didn't know why (she claimed), she had just changed her mind about it, that was all. Wasn't he happy about it? Yes, of course he was, delighted—surprised, but delighted. He smiled now, feeling an enormous tenderness and affection for her, remembering her averted eyes then, when she suggested that she did not especially want to make the usual rounds of New Year's Eve parties that night, she just wanted to stay home and celebrate quietly this year, just the two of them. *Or, the four of us?* he thought, thinking of reflections.

She could be no more eager than he, he thought; even though the thing itself as a device could no longer be an entirely unique experience for him: That very afternoon, in fact, he and Faith had . . . But, no, he was no less aroused and anticipatory for all that because, of course—*of course*—his own experience was more than compensated for by Miriam's lack of it. She was his wife, whom he loved, *and it would be her first time!*

Of course, much remained to be seen, he thought, rinsing his face clean of the remnants of shaving lather. When it came down to it, she might not like it. . . . It could be very disappointing.

He pushed the unwelcome possibility away and dried his face. He broke the seal on the large bottle of cologne that was the Finley's Christmas gift to him, its exaggeratedly elongated neck blatantly phallic. (*If you don't like the way it smells,* Jack had muttered in an aside, *you can always fuck yourself with the bottle.*) He scented himself, sparingly. Humming a tune from an old Jean Harlow movie, *The night is filled with sweet surrender,* he put on his robe. He breathed deeply, then opened the door to his waiting, wanton wife.

"Hi," she said timorously, almost immediately.

"Hi."

She was sitting as he had left her, in the armchair, her legs crossed and showing much thigh below the new, short, barely opaque nightgown, one of his Christmas gifts to her. It came with matching bikini pants; he wondered if she had them on now. "What's on the Late Show?" he murmured.

She smiled nervously, averted her eyes to concentrate intensely on stubbing out her cigarette, and said, "That was Faith on the phone."

It took him an instant to remember the ringing earlier. "Ah," he nodded. "Uh, huh. How is she?"

"She seems fine. She called to wish us a Happy New Year."

"Ah. Uh, huh." he nodded.

There was a silence. "Did you have a nice shower?"

"Fantastic. It was probably one of the greatest showers I've ever had, I didn't know how to tear myself away from it. Let me describe this shower to you. Now, this particular shower——"

"Smartass," she said, grinning shyly.

He smiled and walked slowly to the side of the bed nearest her and sat. "Speaking of ass," he said.

She grinned again, shyly again, and raised her eyes. "I guess *I* am," she said softly.

"Hm?"

"I guess *I'm* on the *Late Show*."

"Come here," he whispered.

She rose and walked slowly to him. He took her hand and drew her down, assured hands already moving to remove her nightgown. (She was not wearing the matching bikini pants.) "From now on," she murmured, lending assistance, "I'm going to be what you want me to be."

"Are you?" he asked, absently, drawing the nightgown over her face, and wondering idly if it could be that simple. It was a rather touchingly romantic and unrealistic declaration, he thought, and wondered what had caused her to declare it. Mystery again.

He centered her on the mattress, laterally across the bed, conforming to the mirror's horizontal shape. "No holds barred?" he teased, lovingly, challenging her mysterious guarantee. She groaned what he took to be assent as her face again came into view, flushed, from under the nightgown. "All restraint cast aside?" he said, casting aside the nightgown. She mewed and smiled, her hand tugging at the tie of his robe. It was then that he realized what it was that had been vaguely distracting him for the past several minutes. "What's that you have on?" he whispered casually.

But he knew.

"Hm?"

"The perfume."

She was too preoccupied to respond for another moment. "It's Faith's," she said presently. "She left it in the guest room." She pushed the robe off his shoulders. "Do you like it?"

"It's all right," he said. *Forgot* it? *Had* she? Had she really *forgotten* it? God! she was corrupt!

"It was just for a change," Miriam breathed.

"Hmmm?"

"The perfume—it was just for a change."

"Yes," he said, watching not her but the reflection of her, trying to remember which ancient people it had been who believed that mirror images were not merely illusions, but real other selves that existed on another plane of being.

Then her other self seized him, and the self whose lips were at his ear said, "Cock."

The word sounded odd if only on the basis of its having come, as it had, in no particular context, thereby suggesting something not so much sexual as anatomic. But that was not what startled him; what startled was the apparent ease, the relative absence of self-consciousness with which she spoke it. Never had she been comfortable with lust's slang, even in the hard-breathing intimacy of bed; she employed it rarely and only then at his subtle (and, for him—yes, and for her too, he supposed—often exasperating) promptings. He had always had to put the Words in her mouth, never found them already there waiting for him. (And even then, she seemed to speak them the way they might once have been written in certain particularly daring Privately Printed Victorian novels, *Do you like my c--t?* asked the sweet Lisette, lasciviously, *Give me your c--k, my lord, and f--k me heartily* . . . It was always disconcerting.)

Perplexed, but playfully amused, he said, "I beg you pardon?"

"I said *cock*," she said, even more forcefully this time, almost defiantly, and this time the impression of anatomy was gone and it seemed all sex as she tightened her grasp on him.

He wondered what was happening. First the mirror, now the words . . .

"Eat me," she whispered.

It was almost too much for him. He was thankful that she was unable to see the expression on his face. What had punched this hole in the secret reservoir of her carnal vocabulary? What was happening? True, they were only words. *But, in the beginning was the word.*

She repeated her plea, this time less suggestion than demand, insistent.

As much baffled as eager to comply, he complied. Presently, as was his habit, he raised his eyes to see her face and was astonished. Propped on her elbows, open-mouthed, wide-eyed, she was watching him. *She had never watched before.*

Words, observation? *What next?*

"A little higher," she gasped.

Guidance? The Genital Kiss, Its Theory and Technique, by Miriam Farrell Hartman. "How's this?"

"On the button."

PUNS?

She was ready for the final test. So far as he had been able to tell, she had kept her eyes averted from the wall at the head of the bed. It was no accident, he knew, but a deliberate evasion. He interrupted himself again to say, "Look."

Seconds passed. "We love each other, don't we," she said finally, her breath short, her eyes closed.

"Yes," he said. *That's a big plus going in,* as George Brady would say. "Look," he said again.

Finally, hesitantly, she turned her head. "Oh, God," she breathed in a tiny, shivery voice. "It really works, doesn't it."

Then he remembered the New Year greeting card in the book store the day he had bought *The Amorous Arts in Marriage.* "Try this," he said, altering the image.

"Oh, my God," she whimpered, watching. "Oh, my God, it really works."

"Happy New Year," he said.

IV.
Natural Progressions

... something blue ...

16

She wrote in a large, bold vertical script, with a wide-nibbed pen on a sheet of heavy paper of the palest blue, her name embossed at the top in delicately tiny block print:

Dearest Walter,
I know you'll understand this way of saying goodbye. (You will, won't you?!) The other day (oh-dear-me-love, I've never had such a nice time on a kitchen table) would have been such a sad time if we'd both known it was going to be the last. And "sad" is not to be tolerated under any circumstances! Right? Besides, I think there's something perfect about saying goodbye to you and introducing you to Bonnie at the same time. She was very anxious to meet you when I told her about you. Ask her to tell you her real Indian name, I can't even pronounce it much less spell it, but it means White Bird in the Hills and the opportunity to meet a girl with a name like that doesn't come along every day in the week you have to admit so I hope you'll take advantage of it. I assume you've heard of her and seen her dance so you know how terrific she is. She really wants to be an actress but there isn't much call for Indian actresses these days and

besides the Hollywood boys would still rather darken down Natalie Wood and grease her hair for as long as they can get away with it. Why am I writing all this!!! I suppose because the truth is I'm a little sad about saying goodbye and don't really want to say it and at the thought that I probably won't see you again for some time. But as to that s–d sh–t, see above and repeat here. I'm off to London to see about a new picture. The Congressman is threatening to follow. Life is wonderful. As they say on the Coast (too often), Baby, what can I say? And as I often answer—try goodbye.

> *Keep the*
> *Faith*

He sat on the round, plump lip of the patched and reinflated plastic chair that had exploded under George Brady four days before on the day which she had known was to be their "last time." He smiled, thinking how like Faith it was to have caused that last time to happen on a kitchen table, a last special occasion to remember her by.

He refolded the letter and replaced it in its envelope. He was not sad, he realized; a little rueful, perhaps, but certainly nothing like sad. (*So long, baby—you're still tops with me,* George Raft to Joan Bennett, *The House Across the Bay.*) Nor—and he thought that this might be even more intriguing—nor did he feel any particular discomfort at the situation with which he was confronted at the moment. He supposed that there might be the vaguely disturbing sense in it of being procured for; but that, of course, would be looking at it in too puritanically harsh a light. No, in more sophisticated soft-focus, it was nothing so unattractive as that: He was being passed on, that was all, as one might pass on to a friend a book that one had especially enjoyed, or suggest a movie that one had found particularly worthy of attention, or the performance of an actor in a play that was not to be missed. And besides, there was no fait accompli here, after all.

The obvious question now was to what extent Little Miss Bird in the Bush or whatever·her name was had participated in the arrangement. Far enough, certainly, to have been here when he arrived, to identify herself at the door, handing him the sealed envelope and the package and excuse herself to withdraw discreetly to the kitchen. He had to admire Faith's elaborate and delicately involved plan for their parting, arranging to meet him here, knowing that she would be on her way to London by the time he arrived to be greeted by the girl whose apartment this was. Unknown to him personally, although of course he recognized her from the several appearances she had made on television variety specials. She was certainly one heap wild-looking piece of ass, there was no question about that. The publicity on her claimed her to be nine-tenths Sioux Indian. Presumably, the other tenth accounted for her (Anglo-Saxon) name, Bonnie Quinn; and her blue eyes.

He remembered the package in his lap. He smiled again. He had known instantly, by its shape, what Faith had left him as a going-away present. He tore the wrapping paper and unrolled it from the can. It was indeed an aerosol container of whipped cream, but the label read D'Zerta Low Calorie Whipped Topping.

The telephone rang. Still smiling, he rewrapped the can of whipped cream as the girl emerged hurrying from the kitchen and bounded across the room toward the bedroom door. He watched her go by. A brace of beauties bouncing buoyantly in her buckskin blouse, he alliterated secretly, grinning.

"Help yourself to a drink if you like," she said, smiling, and disappeared into the relative privacy of the bedroom as the telephone rang again.

One heap wild-looking piece of ass, he thought again, no question at all about that.

Was it possible? *It?* That ass? Her?

No more than a few weeks ago such a prospect would have been beyond his ability to seriously imagine. So much seemed possible now. . . . His mind turned naturally and unavoidably to Miriam, the suddenly and mysteriously new partner in the realization of his erotic dreams. In all justice, he knew, he should unhesitatingly reject any thought of spending the afternoon (even assuming it was possible) with the smoky-skinned Bonnie Quinn who now murmured quietly into the bedroom telephone, whose long slender legs in dance tights, he recalled, might be one of the three or four best pairs he had ever seen in his . . . But, in all justice and fairness to Miriam, who was so suddenly and startlingly *trying*. . . . No, it wouldn't be fair, it would be unjust. It had been only four days, after all! Three nights. Three nights reflected in their wonderland's looking glass. And it was only last night that he had tried the poppers on her for the first time. And she had been willing. Perfectly willing. Nervous, of course, hesitant, but *willing*. She was *trying*. Unfortunately the popper had only made her badly nauseated and given her a crashing headache that left her writhing, unable to think about sex much less to achieve what he had assured her were (as rumor had it, he was careful to specify) the soaring heights of an amyl-nitrate-aided orgasm.

But, she was *trying*. That was what mattered most. The bad reaction was disturbing, of course: He wondered why the popper had caused it. More importantly, perhaps, he wondered if as a result of her unpleasant experience she would refuse to chance it again. Yes, in all likelihood that was *it* for the poppers as far as Miriam was concerned. It was just his luck, he might have known. *They certainly didn't give Faith a headache! Faith they bounced right off the goddam walls!*

But then, poppers were not all, after all. His plans for the future went far beyond the sniffing of amyl nitrate. He had hardly begun to scratch this suddenly, amazingly resilient surface of the until now tough membrane of Miriam's pudency. There was this, for instance, he smiled, weighing the can of D'Zerta Low Calorie whipped cream in his hand before he put it down on the marble-topped antique chest that served as Bonnie's bar. Of course. It was perfect, another completed circuit (like the poppers, but hopefully more successful): from Faith to Walter to Miriam. Tonight?

And it wasn't fattening.

Yes. Fair was fair. *Thank you, Faith my sweet, but no thanks.* In the brief meantime, he would have a no more than sociable drink with the beautiful Bird on the Mountain, a courteous half hour with her in unspoken acknowledgment of and thanks for the pleasurable use to which, with Faith, he had put her apartment. Only that. Nothing more. He would pass up the passed-on pursuit of this particular happiness. It was only fair to Miriam, he owed her that now, she was *trying*.

"So you're Walter."

He turned to find her emerging from the bedroom, the fringe of the buckskin blouse dancing at her slender hips. "That's me," he said, and smiled. "Can I fix you something?" he asked, gesturing at the bottles.

"Never touch the stuff," she answered. "Haven't you heard what it does to us?" He didn't understand and must have conveyed the fact in his expression. She smiled. "Firewater," she explained. "Make injun crazy loco." He laughed. "Faith's told me all about you."

Not all, he didn't say.

"She thinks you're some groovy guy."

"Well, she's some groovy girl," he said, spuriously hip, but managing by his manner somehow to admit the spuriousness. She seemed, he thought, instantly charmed by his integrity. He waited for her to sit (with all the expected grace of a dancer) in the tan suede sofa; then sat himself. He hoped she would not be offended when the time came for him to leave, so soon— sooner, he wanted to think, then she would like.

She was surely one of the most beautiful girls he had ever seen, he thought. Certainly the most beautiful Indian. "Your family is Sioux Indian?" he asked, breaking the ice.

An hour and a half later he had been furnished a detailed and harrowing history of the Sioux Nation, from its first contact with the white man to the Battle of the Little Big Horn, in which her great-great-grandfather had participated. He learned that General George Armstrong Custer had not been quite the lovable and charming rogue portrayed by Errol Flynn in *They Died with Their Boots On* (Flynn and Olivia de Havilland, Charley Grapewin, Warner Brothers, 1941, directed by Raoul Walsh). He was on his third drink and the information, though distressing, like so much of the rest of her tale came as no particular surprise. He was at the bar again when she said:

"My great grandfather was killed at the Battle of Wounded Knee, that's a place in South Dakota, it was the last Indian battle in American history, listen—you mind if I turn on?"

He turned to her and smiled and cocked his head and shrugged, "Please do." He watched while a small spice jar appeared from a cabinet beside the sofa, and a package of flimsy cigarette papers from a cigarette box on the coffee table.

Expertly rolling a joint, she asked him if he would care to join her. The hesitation before his nod was almost too brief to be perceived. She smiled happily and, rolling a second delicately slender tube, she said, "Let me tell you about the Battle of Wounded Knee," and introduced him to the first marijuana of his ever-expanding life.

He watched her first for clues to its correct and effective use and within half an hour wondered why in the world he had ever bothered with the so transitory entertainments of amyl nitrate. "Though nothing can bring back the hour of splendor in the grass, of glory in the flower . . ." he intoned dreamily, nodding at his fuming hand, fully aware now that he was watching his resolve go up in that sweet smoke.

She giggled. "Oh, splendor in the grass," she agreed, head bobbing heavily. "May you live in interesting times. That's an ancient Chinese curse."

He asked her to speak for him her Indian name. She mouthed it voluptuously and, later, standing in the bathtub, in a drugged dream, he found himself able to reproduce it flawlessly, repeatedly, over and over again, like an incantation while she knelt before him, gripping the backs of his legs, her wet, gleaming body flapping and jumping like a caught fish, hanging by the mouth on a tender hook; he clinging for support with both hands to the gushing shower head that drenched them both. Then she was seated, dripping and slippery, on the edge of the tub while it became his turn to do homage on his knees, on the cold tile floor, his head moving in what was probably his favorite of sex's supplementary comments between the dark gold of her parenthetical thighs.

"Wahwoo!" she screeched. "*Oh,* you do that *good!*"
White man eat with forked tongue!

When he arrived home, Miriam told him that Faith had called to say goodbye. He expressed casual surprise and asked when she had called. Miriam offered an estimate. He calculated it to be just about the time he was arriving at the apartment for their never-to-happen rendezvous, Faith knowing that he would not be at home when she called to say goodbye to Miriam, having already prepared her goodbye to him.

"She was sorry she didn't get a chance to say goodbye to you," Miriam said, "but I gather she had to leave in a hurry, something about a new picture."

He nodded vaguely, hanging his overcoat in the foyer closet, removing the cylindrical package from the pocket, wondering who might be able to get hold of some grass for him or who might be able to put him in touch with someone who could.

"Would you?" Miriam said.

"Hm?"

"I said, *I* wouldn't mind being on my way to London right now, would you?"

"Way to where?"

"London. Do you feel all right?"

"Fine. Why?"

"You look a little feverish," she said, taking up the package from the foyer table. "What's this?"

May you live in interesting times, he thought, grinning feverishly at her.

17 When he finally realized her desperation Walter tried not to blame himself for having failed for so long to recognize it for what it was—for having mistaken hopeless desperation for passionate (and honest) intensity.

It really works, she had said. He remembered that, remembered the enormous initial encouragement he had taken from her endorsement of their writhing image on the wall over the bed. Her willingness was incontestable; what didn't bear scrutiny was the extent and degree of her conviction. His not to reason why had been his motto and standard; he was looking no gift horses in the mouth. (Or, as George Brady had once said in perverse variation, never kick a gift horse in the teeth.) No, his need for the successful pursuit of carnal adventure with his wife stayed his metaphorically prying hands and Miriam's gift of acquiescence was accepted without internal investigation.

So he was content for what he allowed himself was a fair and reasonable period of time, fencing his erotic pursuits within the confines of the increasingly generous boundaries marked out by Miriam's amenability. He felt only the faintest—and easily enough suppressed—desire to take advantage of the now known possibilities that lay beyond the now self-imposed confines of Married Love. Yes, of course there had been Bonnie Quinn of marijuana memory. (And plastic priapus: With the redolence of pot still in the bedroom air that afternoon, she had introduced him to his first experience, in practice, of the phallic vibrator seen in drugstore windows everywhere in recent months, sold and thinly disguised as a battery-operated facial massager but unmistakably, to anyone with the barest trace of erotic imagination, designed for more exotic employ in a choice of tasteful pastels. It had been high on his list of intentions for Miriam; but Miriam was late in coming around and Bonnie Quinn got there first, pink vibrating dildo in trembling hand.) But he forgave himself for Bonnie, having been at the time under the then unfamiliar and helpless influence of an (then!) unfamiliar drug.

So, but for that single—and, he assured himself, justified—lapse, he clove to Miriam, his wife, forsaking all others as he had once so long ago (eleven years!) promised to do. And he was content.

For a time.

Careful that the newly shared varieties would not become in their turn habit, he wisely spaced and apportioned exoticisms. Sometimes several days would pass without the use of the vibrator—or Pulsating Peter, as he soon came to refer to it (or Rhythmic Richard or Dancing Dick). Low-caloric whipped cream delights were no more than occasional ones. The Polaroid camera was put to wide-eyed, breathless use only once during the first month, two-figure photographs cleverly and gigglingly contrived with the aid of the mirror (and destroyed after one subsequent use in preliminary love play; plenty more where those came from when the spirit and the flesh moved them).

They mutually agreed upon once a week for the pot, its effect too gratifyingly extraordinary to be indulged in with more frequency—particular folly to hazard too much of that too-good thing. (Following her first use—he was amazed and pleased at how quickly she picked up the special method of smoking it required—she had had to agree with him that its erotogenic properties were unequaled, that it had indeed been an Acapulco-golden screw.)

He had had to surprise her, after the fact, with the tape recorder: Prior knowledge of it would of course have been inhibitory, he knew, which would of course have defeated its purpose. So he had tucked it secretly under the bed beforehand, the microphone peeping out barely but enough, a private ear to hear all. Afterward, its presence revealed (Portions of the Preceding Program Were Recorded, he said), she blushed and giggled and pummeled him with soft fists and refused at first to listen to the playback. Having listened, she told him it was very weird, it sounded like he was doing it with someone else because she had never heard her voice recorded and it didn't sound like her voice as she knew it, so it was like listening to him doing it with some other woman. She wanted to know if it was the same for him. He admitted that it was, although to a lesser extent since he was more accustomed to his recorded voice on the office dictaphone. She asked him if he wanted to play it back again, asked casually, too casually. Did *she?* he teased. Only if he did, she wouldn't mind, still casual, refusing to submit. He rewound the tape and began the second playback, but long before it was over they were no longer listening.

Nor was adventure solely dependent upon his desire alone. After the first two weeks she began occasionally to reveal her own sense of invention. It was a revelation that proved to him that which he had known in his heart all along: Even she had her fantasies. (Although what had caused her to be finally free enough to expose them he was unable to say.) Beginning one evening, mildly, with a guarded invitation to join her in the bathtub, she progressed quickly and it was only a few nights later, while watching the Late Late Show in the living room, that he looked up to find her standing before him wearing a skin-tight, one-piece garment of black lace that might easily have served as the opening costume for a blue movie. *Good Lord, what's this?* he wanted to know. It was a black lace jump suit, she explained, revolving slowly before him. He told her it certainly fit well. She told him one size fit all, the rest was up to the individual. He was stunned when she sat beside him and told him she wanted him to go right on watching *The Pride of the Yankees* and ignore her. *This is for you,* she told him, and commenced to confer voluntarily and with an apparent ease that gratification which had always been both infrequent and uneasy (privately, he had always felt that in her mind the act was one not so much performed as committed) while he watched Gary Cooper assure his movie mother that whatever the romantic involvements he might encounter in his manhood, she, his mother, would always be his best girl.

And he means it! Walter thought in an instant of revelation as a light burst behind his clenched eyes and he granted Miriam her wish (and later asked her if she knew that it was very healthy, full of protein).

But certainly the high water mark in the flooding tide of her erotic imagination was reached on the evening of the dinner party at the Sobels' when the discussion progressed from the new permissiveness in motion pictures to pornographic films and Miriam confessed that she had never seen such a film, actually. Cynthia Sobel laughed and asked her where she had *been* and asked Walter where he had been *keeping* her? He could only laugh, falsely, certain that in the eyes of the others he was guilty by association of his wife's incredible innocence and lack of worldly experience. In his distraction, he lost the thread of the conversation for several moments; when he again picked it up, Paul Sobel was saying with a sly grin, why didn't they leave it up to Miriam, then, under the circumstances.

It seemed that there was at that very moment in the Sobel apartment an especially fine example of the art of the pornographic film and that what was being left to Miriam's decision was whether or not there should be a screening of it right then and there. Walter found it interesting that none of the other guests, three other couples, made any comment whatsoever about the film—rented, he soon learned—being in the Sobels' possession; it seemed to be accepted as a matter of course. Then Miriam was saying, looking at everyone but him, well, if it was all right with everyone else, she wouldn't mind seeing it.

It was all right with everyone else and Walter was soon impressed with the sophisticated technical advancements that had been made in the field since the gray, grainy stag movies of his college-boy youth. For one thing, it was in color; he had never seen one in color before. Although the performances left something to be desired artistically, they were otherwise superlative. Titled *A Visit to the Dentist*, it was watched to the accompani-

ment of a running commentary of nervous jokes from the audi-
ence, *What a big drill you have, doctor, The plot thickens, That's
not all that's thickening, They used a yardstick to cast this guy.
Oh, that poor girl, Oh, I wouldn't say that, As You Like It, girls,
That thing's going to come out her left ear if he doesn't stop,
Well, it'll clear her sinuses* . . .

In the cab on the way home he asked, slyly, how she had liked
the show. Well, it was pretty good, she told him, not smiling. He
was unable to tell whether her reticence merely damned with
faint praise (a fair enough reaction, artistically speaking) or was
a sudden resurgence of her sense of propriety. He pressed for
clarity, speaking softly, aware of the cab driver's probably straining ears, *did it turn you on at all? Well,* she hesitated, *well, no,
not really.*

He was disappointed and unsurprised.

"I mean, it was, well, they seemed to be so . . . uninvolved,"
she said. "Didn't they to you? I mean, did it excite *you?*"

He was reluctant to admit to unshared arousal, but was even
more unwilling to feign indifference he had not felt, so confessed
to his erectile reaction in the Sobels' dark living room.

"Really?" she said, with a faint, superior loftiness.

The word plopped like the last one-drop-too-many in his already brimful, carefully held cup of impatience.

"Well, for Christ's sake, Mimi, that's what they're *for,* you
know, the idea is they're *supposed* to turn you on, you know!
He remembered the driver and lowered his voice. "It isn't *Love
Finds Andy Hardy,* you know!" he hissed.

After a moment she moved perceptibly away from him along
the seat. "I guess there must be something wrong with *me,*
then."

She was hurt, he knew. But, in annoyance and disappointment,
his silence condemned her, declaring the accuracy of her self-
judgment. Fortunately, tension began to ease after their arrival
home and later in the bathroom he found her cautious, unspoken
truce: her blue plastic diaphragm purse lying openly and obviously on the shelf over the sink, unzipped and empty. They
made love quickly, simply, while he found himself thinking of
the pubicly black blond girl in the Sobels' movie and wondering

if there was any chance at all that Miriam might be having thoughts about the Spanish-looking stud with the absurdly enormous cock.

But he was content, knowing that he could not have everything. He reminded himself that she had not merely agreed to but had actually prompted the showing of the film in the first place. That in itself was remarkable: It was one thing for her to expose the possibilities of her sexuality with him in the privacy of their bedroom (or the study, kitchen, bathroom—their recent geography had been extensive); it was quite another to reveal an interest in pornography to friends. It was nothing short of remarkable. And he couldn't have everything: He should be content, he told himself.

And was, again, the very next night, when she offered him what he took to be, and was, compensation for her poor response to *A Visit to the Dentist;* he came into the bedroom to find her silver fox coat spread across the bed, fur up, and she naked upon it, waiting and grinning. He considered it to be inspiration of a high order. Moments later, himself naked, and rolling with her in voluptuous luxuriance, he asked, "Where did you ever get an idea like this?" The question was more rhetorical than curious, but she answered nevertheless, tumbling.

"From Faith, as a matter of fact," she gasped. "I gather mink is the ideal, though," she added, and sank her teeth bluntly into his neck.

For a moment he experienced a faint, peripheral annoyance with Faith, that she had carried knowledge of such a fancy and had failed to share it with him. "That must have been an interesting conversation," he suggested. *Girl talk?*

"She just asked me once if I'd ever made it on a mink coat, ah, more, *don't stop.*"

"I have no intention of stopping, what did you tell her?"

"I told her I didn't have a mink. . . . She said this would do . . . Oh! . . . But I gather mink is the ideal."

"Does she . . . have a special mink for that . . . or is the one she has . . . a general all-purpose mink?"

Miriam giggled, her teeth climbing his thigh in jumping bites to their destination, and he was content.

Content enough, and secure enough in her certain amenability, to enable him two nights later to rise from the bed, apologizing for the interruption (*I hate to eat and run like this*), and go, weaklegged, to the bureau. He opened the top drawer and took from its week's hiding place a small package which he ·unwrapped quickly, enclosing its contents easily in his fist. It had been hard to come by; until the week before it had been years since he had seen one. Technically, they were against the law, of course—a sad commentary.

He returned to the bed where she waited, watchfully, clearly too intrigued by the purpose of the interruption to be distressed at having been abandoned so precipitately. He stood by the side of the bed in teasing delay for a moment, grinning down at her; she coyly played his game and made no demands.

Finally, he thrust his fist forward and opened it, palm up.

She stared. "*What in God's name is that?*"

"*That*, baby," he said, "is a *French Tickler!*"

And he was content.

He was still content several days later when he nearly collided with Barbara Finch emerging from a shop on East 57th Street, looking thinner and somewhat less haunted than on the morning of their return from Boston. (The rest of that day at the studio had been a great success Walter had learned when D.J. called to thank and commend him. Barbara had never been so cooperative, he was told. Jack Finley had called too, to ask what he had done to calm her down so, *And if you did what I think you did, all I want to know is how was it?* For reply, Walter had laughed noncommittally.)

Standing on the sidewalk, smiling, Barbara was effusive and warm, regretted not having heard from him in so long (it had been only a matter of weeks) and asked him if he had time to buy an old friend a drink.

He had time and world enough and later in her apartment, rising from the bed to dress, he wondered if he might have cause to investigate more deeply the true nature and extent of his contentment.

"Do you really have to go?" she asked listlessly.

"I really do, hon, it's getting late."

"God, Walter, you're wonderful," she said, stretching, then delicately drying herself between her legs with a corner of the sheet.

"I guess you just bring out the best in me, Barb."

She returned his smile and lit a cigarette and propped her head on her hand to watch him dress. "Are all your shorts blue or do you have other colors too?"

"I beg your pardon?"

"Your shorts were blue in Boston, too."

"Oh. Well, no, I have some blue, some white, a few pale green . . ."

"I'm getting married again, you know."

He managed a smile. "Really! That's wonderful, Barb! Who's the lucky man, do I know him?" He felt a twinge of concern for whoever it was.

"I don't think so. His name's Richard Humber, he's my doctor, my psychiatrist."

"Really," he nodded finally, and resisted the impulse to comment even in jest on the appropriateness of such an alliance. He asked instead when the happy day was to be.

"Oh, in about a month or so," Barbara guessed. "I have to go down to Florida for a few weeks first to try out a new play. I'm leaving next week."

"Ah," he nodded, and smiled. "Well, I'm very happy for you, Barb, I wish you the best."

She smiled vaguely and nodded and exhaled smoke. "Do you really, or are you just saying that?"

He caught the tone of challenge in her voice and looked at her and found it reinforced in the cautious fixity of her blue eyes. "No, I really hope that," he said finally, realizing he did.

There was another very brief silence. She seemed to be weighing the evidence. "I believe you," she said at last.

"Good," he smiled.

"Will I see you again before I leave?"

His fingers stilled for a moment on the buttons of his shirt. The intimacy and hope of her words filled the room. Did she mean . . .? "See me?" he said, carefully. "You mean . . .?"

"Yes."

He thought again of Richard Humber, this time with a certain alarm for the doctor's future. Then he grinned and said, "I'd like that, Barb, I'd like that a lot," knowing now, without question, that he had cause to investigate his content.

That night he sat carefully at the desk in his study and took up the one hundred and three pages of his uncompleted manuscript (plus seven pages of outline for three more chapters), knowing that he was finally prepared to read it through with a necessarily cold eye.

He lit a cigarette and smoked it to the end, then opened the bright red stiff fiber binder and read.

When he had finished, he replaced the manuscript carefully on the desk. He lit another cigarette and smoked it through, one hand resting lightly on the binder. Then he removed the pages from the binder, tore them in half, and dropped the fragments into the waste-paper basket.

The next morning he telephoned D. J. Cramm. D.J. was surprised but delighted to hear that Walter wished to cut short his sabbatical and return to the office as soon as possible. He asked if "that book" had been finished sooner than Walter had planned and hoped. Walter said it had. D.J. reminded him that he expected a copy, suitably inscribed, the moment the book was published. Walter told him that he was at the top of the list. They settled on the following Monday morning for Walter to resume work, D.J. saying that it would be good to have him back aboard.

"Now that you've got that out of your system," D.J. added jocularly.

"Yes," Walter said.

On the eleven o'clock news, George Brady was being interviewed in a corridor of the House of Representatives following the opening session of the new Congress.

The television reporter was asking George how he felt after his first day as a legislator. George said he felt wonderful. And did he expect to comply with the unofficial expectation that a freshman congressman should be seen and not heard during his first term in office? George, smiling wickedly, didn't think that the voters back home had sent him there to Washington merely to warm a Congressional seat and go to all the right parties. Any particular issues on which he might be expected to be heard, then, in the near future?

George smiled the famous smile again. "I have no particular axes to grind at the moment, no," he said. "But I'll have my eyes open for any targets of opportunity that come along."

Walter laughed. "George and his targets of opportunity."

"What?" Miriam asked.

"That's what he calls women."

"What's what he calls women?"

"Well, some women. The ones he wants to make. Faith told me. It's a military phrase."

"What is?"

"Target of opportunity. It means, well—say a bomber can't drop its bombs on the place it was supposed to, for one reason or another, they drop them on whatever likely target they happen to come across. Target of opportunity. So, that's what George calls women he thinks are likely prospects."

"Oh?"

Her response amused him. But, naturally, such an attitude—indeed, in George's case it might be called a life style—would be offensive to any woman. He conceded as much to her.

"Why offensive just to women?" Miriam demanded. "It's a pretty damned offensive idea, it should be offensive to anyone."

"You're right," he nodded. "It's a pretty damned offensive idea." But he made no attempt to suppress the grin that betrayed his reply for what it really was, not agreement but gentle assuagement, and hoped it did not seem too condescending. She gazed at him for a moment—oddly, he thought; inscrutably—then turned her attention again to the television.

Later, when he switched off the bedside lamp and slid in beside her, he said: "I'm going back to work on Monday."

She stirred in the darkness. "What work?"

"The office."

"*What?*" her amazed voice cried quietly. He felt her roll onto her stomach and raise herself on her elbows to peer down at him. "You still have three or four months left of your leave!"

He explained. She protested his decision; then accepted it, finally, with a reluctance and commiseration that touched him. He smiled up at her in the dark, the outline of her head and shoulders a blurred shadow. "You can't have everything," he said.

It was that night, sleepless and alone, slumped in an armchair in the dimly lit living room, he recapitulated the recent weeks' sexual high points and finishing his third drink, was convinced that her heart wasn't in it.

What he had taken, been taking for weeks, as honest, passionate intensity had not been that at all! She had not been so much participating as submitting. She had only—for whatever reason he would probably never know because he would never ask—capitulated to his carnal imagination, her enthusiasm contrived, feigned!

Her heart wasn't really in it!

Her cunt, yes, of course, her cunt was in it, certainly, who could deny it? Her breasts, and mouth, her legs, her marvelous ass, all, all were in it. Yes. *But not her heart!* Certainly she required an occasional orgasm! She wasn't frigid, after all! That secret mouth could be expected to salivate occasionally in conditioned reflex to his bell-ringing dong! (Ding dong.) (Laugh, clown, laugh.) Yes, right, her physical and emotional well-being called for a once-in-a-while hump. But nothing more! Not for her the gourmet indulgences, she required no more than a subsistence diet!

No, her heart wasn't really in it. Not like Faith (for instance)! And Barbara! And insane Bonnie Bird in the goddam Mountain! Their *hearts* were in it! Their hearts were in their mouths and their cunts, good God almighty, *their* hearts were in their very . . .

On the other hand . . .

He refilled his glass and drunkenly determined to consider the possibility of more sober alternatives to his outright and undefended condemnation of her.

On the other hand, for instance, there was the question of time. It had been no more than a matter of weeks, after all, since she had taken her first trembling step into a world she never made and for years had refused even to imagine. How quickly, after all (and in all fairness), could he expect her to alter the heart of a lifetime?

Yes, patience was required here. Demanded. Fair was fair, after all. Time was the prescription for this malady of the absent heart. Her debt to him had been assent; his to her was time. Time for this shy and reserved, this tardy heart of hers to introduce itself to love's other recently more amicable organs and join the dance. *Will you, won't you, will you, won't you, will you join . . .*

Time?

But, how long, oh Lord? Was there a forseeable end to this final reluctance? For that matter, where was the guarantee that inhibition's last bastion would *ever* fall? *You can't get into the heart with a crowbar,* Faith said. Shit, you can't necessarily get into it with a cock, either! And there was *definitely* no guarantee that any Pulsating Peter was going to quiver its way in there to deliver a response-prompting electrocardiac shock.

No! No forseeable ends in sight, then! No guarantees!

Time, then. It wouldn't be easy, but fair was fair. Time was his debt. I.O.U. Payment on Demand. And certainly he possessed those necessary assets, the resources of patience enough to keep him out of *that* debtor's prison.

He poured another drink, making a mental note to break his date with Barbara Finch for the following week. *Fair was fair.* He sipped.

On the other hand . . .

He made a tentative decision about his new secretary (his former one had left to be married some months before, he learned) on his very first day back at the office, but waited till midweek to confirm for himself Monday's and Tuesday's indicated probabilities. Rowena was about twenty, he guessed, small-breasted but compensatingly fully developed in the hips, with a delicately pretty face that was not at all marred by the dramatic eyeglasses she wore, of heavy black tortoise-shell. (He knew that when she took them off she would turn out to be, in reality, Loretta Young.) So, operating on the strength of her Monday warmth and Tuesday's cautious, demure but unquestionable attraction for him, on Wednesday morning he asked her (hesitant, ingenuous, Henry Fonda in *Young Mr. Lincoln*) if it would be at all possible for her to stay an extra hour or so that evening to help him clear away some small part of the avalanche of work that had descended upon him on his return. She wouldn't mind in the least, she told him.

He called Miriam in the afternoon to tell her not to expect him for dinner, he was up to his neck in work, they seemed to have been saving it up for him all the time he was away. The very banality of it afforded him a kind of nervous excitement of its own: hardly a newly minted cliché, but the first time he had found himself in possession of it, free to make use of it as legal tender in a transaction of some delicacy.

He reserved a room for that evening at the new hotel directly across town from the office (perhaps overconfident, he thought, but there was no harm in being prepared). The choice of hotel was not uncalculated: He had heard about and was intrigued by one of the special features of its accommodations. It also possessed the hugeness that assured anonymity. The price of freedom was eternal caution.

The latter part of the afternoon was spent in a preliminarily informal meeting in his office on how the network might handle the advertising spots for a certain new product. If, indeed, the network would handle them at all: Opinion was strongly divided on the propriety of carrying advertising for such a product on network television. Each of the four men directly concerned held mimeoed sheets of the ad agency's copy on a feminine hygiene deodorant spray due to be released on the market soon. Jack Finley sat on a corner of Walter's desk—empty-handed, having wandered into Walter's office with nothing better to do elsewhere.

"Frankly, Walter, I don't see how we can handle it," Sol Stein said.

"Let's face it," Freddy Wales said, "there isn't really any subtle way it *can* be handled. This copy is very subtle, okay, but there it is—they're hustling something for women to spray between their legs. A lot of women aren't going to like it."

"The spray or the sell?" Jack Finley asked.

"The sell."

"Why not?" Jack shrugged, a glint in his eye. "That broads have cunts isn't exactly an unconfirmed rumor."

"We'll get letters," someone said.

"It's a touchy thing, Walter," Sol said. "No pun intended."

"So were armpits once," Jack Finley said.

"An armpit isn't a cunt, Jack," Freddy said.

"No matter how you look at it," Walter grinned.

"Or slice it," Jack offered.

"This is serious," Sol said.

"What are the other networks doing about it?" Bill Prentice asked.

"No one knows yet," Walter told him. "But you can be sure they're as nervous as we are."

"I mean, shit, how can you possibly do a sixty-second spot on something for a woman to spray on her snatch! It's impossible!"

"We'll get letters," someone said. "We'll get letters up to our ass."

"Personally," Jack said, "when it comes to snatch I don't think you can beat Chanel Five."

Fresh lime is wonderful, too, Walter remembered.

He kept Rowena for an hour after the office emptied, even though he suspected that it might be a squandering of precious and better-spent time. He was sure he had detected in her a slight and quickly-masked surprise when she realized that it actually was his intention to do some paper work. When he asked her to join him for dinner she appeared immediately more relaxed, secure, as though on firmer, more recognizable ground.

Waiting for the elevator in the quiet office corridor, he noted that his name had been relisted on the floor directory: Hartman, W. A., Standards and Practices Room 908.

Dinner was intimately (and predictably: in for one cliché, in for two, he thought, he was new at this game and entitled to at least one of each cliché around) French. Over the first cocktail he expressed his pleasure at having returned to find a new secretary assigned to him, and that it should be one such as she. Over the chocolate mousse he found her, intimately, an extremely attractive young woman. She accepted it (as it was intended) as his declaration of intent and met it with a satisfactory—and, by that time, virtually guaranteed—response. The thought uppermost in his mind as he tipped the maître d' on the way out, was how easy it was. He didn't remember it being so easy in his youth. Women had changed. Or . . .

In the hotel room, she turned as he closed the door and they came together with an impetuous, long-delayed thump that nearly knocked the breath out of him. After one kiss she began to undress, stripping herself hastily with a delicate violence.

"Jesus Jeepers, let's hurry!"

Jesus Jeepers? he asked himself, tearing off the bottom button of his shirt in his haste.

She removed everything but her eyeglasses. He inquired about them as he joined her on the bed.

"In a minute," she said breathlessly. "I'm blind as a bat without them and I want to see!" So saying, she slid to her knees between his and fell on him, open-mouthed, her vision clear, and growled, shaking her head like a playful puppy with a bone. She took a brief hiatus to ask, "Did you sleep with your old secretary?"

"She wasn't old."

She bit him. "You know what I mean."

"No, I never did, do that again."

Somewhat later he asked her, as casually as possible in the circumstances (and, he thought, pretty goddam late in the game), if she was precautioned.

"I'm pilled up to my eyeballs!" she said.

He smiled. "Good. It isn't necessary to be safe that far up, of course."

She laughed again. "You're crazy. . . . You heard the definition of Catholic birth control, Rhythm and Blues?"

It was then that he remembered the reason for his choice of this particular hotel and, reaching for the electronic console by the bedside, muttered, "This bed turns on."

"No, not now," she said impatiently, drawing him back. "You can turn on later!"

"Not *me,* the *bed!*" he explained and, finding the button, pushed it. The entire considerable surface of the big double bed began to vibrate gently; it was a contrivance devised for the weary traveler in need of a lulling easement, a mechanical undulation into sleep, but one which Walter had thought might serve other, more exotic purposes for those whose dreams were waking ones.

"Oh, I *love* it!" Rowena said, quivering in sympathetic vibration, and whipped off her eyeglasses. She pulled at his shoulders and, deftly, in agile panic, insinuated herself squarely beneath him. "Oh, Jesus Jeepers! Quick!" Then, "Oh! Jesus!"

"Jeepers," he grinned into her ear.

The bed throbbing under them in robot collaboration, its vibrations most felt in the points of bony contact at his knees and elbows, his brained hummed, in a kind of psychotic syncopation, in upbeat rhythm with his downbeating hips, *Jeepers Creepers, where'd ya get those peepers* . . .

"Oh!"

Jeepers Creepers, where'd ya get those eyes . . .

"Go!"

Golly gee, when ya turn those heaters on . . .

On the morning of the day he was to have lunch with Barbara Finch she telephoned him at the office, weeping and hysterical: Lunch was impossible, she was in no condition to be seen in public, but could she see him anyway, at her apartment, *she had to see him.* By the time he arrived two hours later she seemed to have calmed considerably although her face bore weeping's ravages and she looked—as she herself accused—"ghastly."

Without preamble, she said, "He knows."

"Hm?"

"Ralph. He found out about you."

He gazed at her reflectively for a moment. "How did he find out?"

"I told him."

He waited until she had lit a cigarette, hands flying about

her face erratically, mouth blasting a jet of acrid smoke at the ceiling. He thought of Bette Davis in *In This Our Life* (Warner Brothers, 1942, Davis, George Brent, Dennis . . .) "Well, why the hell did you do that, Barb?" The gentleness in her voice barely survived his evaluation of her intelligence.

"Well, I had to! Sooner or later! I mean, he's my analyst! I have to tell him things like that, I can't keep things like that back from him!"

He felt impaled on the delicately sharp point of a terrifying logic. "So the wedding's off, huh?"

She looked up, perplexed for a moment. "No, of course not." She seemed to be annoyed with his assumption. "Why should the wedding be off? He understands that, Christ, he's been my doctor for three years," she shrugged in explanation. "No, it isn't that."

"Ah," he nodded. "What is it then, Barb?"

She began to weep, wailing. "Oh, Walter, you're not going to believe this!"

I am, he thought. *I'm going to believe it:* This was Barbara Finch; he, Walter, would believe it.

"He's a faaaaag!" she wailed.

"He's a *what?*"

"Yes!"

"*Ralph?*"

"Yeeeees!"

"Are you sure? I mean, how do you know?" A *psychiatrist?*

"He told me!"

He pictured the scene between Barbara and her betrothed, analysand and table-turning analyst in an exchange of compulsive and distressing revelations. He might have laughed had he not been so utterly fascinated. *Because this was Life!* And he was part of it now, touching it, had been touching it ever since Faith . . . He was a committed participant at last, involved in, and fascinated with Life, a great *pousse café* into which he had plunged prepared to consume level by level all its startling and exotic flavors, bottomless, endless!

Or, at least, he thought, trying to calm himself, *no end in sight.*

"Well, I can understand why you're so upset, Barb." He sat

beside her on the sofa and comfortingly took her hand. "You never suspected?"

"Well, shit, Walter, of course not! I mean, who expects a psychiatrist to have a problem like that!"

He considered it for a moment. "No, I guess not."

Weeping, her cigarette sodden with her tears, she wailed: "For three fucking years! I put my *life* in his hands! And he turns out to be a fag! Wouldn't you know it? I'd end up marrying a fag psychiatrist?"

He was pensive for a moment, staring at the pattern in the rug, her self-absorption covering his silence. "You are going to marry him, then? Anyway?"

"Well, shit, Walter, of course! I love him!"

"Ah." He nodded, his lips pursed, his mind humming, *Three little words, that's all I ask for, just three little* . . .

"Oh, you mean the sex," Barbara said. "Well, of course he sleeps with women. He's slept with me dozens of times, he sleeps with women. All the time." (Walter pictured therapeutic couplings on the analyst's couch, his Hippocratic oath in shreds on the floor.) She sucked on her dead cigarette then dropped it into the ashtray. "But not only." She added, "It's a very complex situation."

"What isn't?"

"Good point," she said, drying her eyes.

She blew her nose and sighed pathetically. She turned to him, put her arms around his neck and her clammy cheek on his shoulder. "Oh, Walter, I don't even want to think about it anymore right now. Let's fuck, do you have time?"

Fascinating . . . And there was no end in sight . . .

He had forgotten about the Woman in 11B. She and her mysterious companion(s) of the afternoons had passed from his consciousness until the evening he drew up in front of the building in a cab and caught a glimpse of the husband, deeply tanned, emerging from the building and hurrying away up the street. The sight of him reminded Walter of the silence above in recent weeks and the tan explained it. Southern climes in winter. Florida? Puerto Rico?

So, on Saturday afternoon in the drugstore on the corner of their block to buy cigarettes for Miriam, he knew her, even before she spoke, by her tan. Not that winter tans were all that uncommon in the neighborhood. Call it intuition. The voice had a face at last. And a not unattractive one at that.

They stood side by side at the drug counter waiting their turn behind the customer being served, a young man who had already ordered a small assortment of various items and who then quietly (but not quietly enough) asked for a tube of contraceptive jelly. The kid must have a very shy wife, Walter thought. Or girl friend. Or a serious problem. He happened to glance toward the nearby display window and discovered a young girl standing on the sidewalk, half turned to face into the store as though she might be studying the window display. He registered her attitude of rigid, lingering casualness and thought, *The shy wife.* That he recognized the scene for what it probably was was no special intuitiveness, but mere sweet memory: It was he who had bought his marriage's first tube of Ortho-Jel while tense Miriam hunched modestly over a Coke at the drugstore soda fountain.

While the druggist wrapped the young man's order, Walter heard the voice beside him. He was Mr. Hartman, wasn't he? He was, he said turning, wondering to himself how she knew. She was Mrs. Phillips, she told him, they lived in the same building. Ah, yes, he knew her husband, that is, knew him to speak to in the elevator. Oh, really? Yes. He could see they'd been away. In southern climes. Yes, they had, Jamaica, actually. He expressed polite, false envy as a matter of form. Yes, she supposed (reluctantly) it was all right, but frankly, she went only because her husband wanted her to go, she personally preferring winter, and certainly Christmas, in New York. It wasn't Christmas without snow, in her opinion. Walter agreed. And how was Mr. Brady these days? *George* Brady? Walter wanted to know. Well, as a matter of fact he hadn't seen George lately, but judging by the newspapers he was doing well, did she know George? No, not exactly, she had run into him in the elevator one day some time ago and couldn't resist saying hello, she had always been a great admirer of his work in films. He had happened to mention that he was on the way to the Hartmans' that day, that was how she knew who Walter was and that Walter knew George.

By the time she interrupted herself to place her order with the druggist, Walter was no longer hearing her voice clearly. He could only hear her screaming in the afternoon and reflect on the possible contours of what lay beneath the heavy, loose-fitting camouflage of her bulky coat.

When her order had been wrapped she stepped away from the counter. He smiled, preparatory to saying goodbye; then saw that she was not going anywhere. She was waiting for him. She was waiting.

They started back to the building discussing George Brady and the phenomenon of his apparent success as a politician.

He was barely attending to the conversation. She grew more attractive and desirable with every step they took bringing them closer to the building and the mysteries of Apartment 11B. By the time they reached the sidewalk canopy his armpits were wet. This was madness! Attractive and desirable she might well be; but *possible?* Surely not! Was he losing his reason? Had his erotic fantasies and the recent ease of realizing some of them finally begun to deprive him of all sense of proportion and reality? Were there no limits to his mad dreams? Enough was enough! *Would he never stop?*

He pushed the elevator button in the lobby and turned to find her staring at him. There was no other word for it: She was *staring* at him.

"Listen," she said abruptly, stepping into the elevator, pivoting quickly to maintain the connection her eyes had established, "do you happen to know anything about fuses?"

Fuses?

Ascending, she explained several unworking lights in her apartment; her husband's absence (Chicago, was it? He was hardly listening); her own total lack of comprehension of things mechanical; she had extra fuses in the apartment but, helplessly, knew nothing about where they went, perhaps he . . .

But he hardly listened; there was no need; her words were no more than temporary necessity. He knew that; she knew he knew it. Because, of course, husbands' absences notwithstanding, there were superintendents, there were handymen, there were, in desperation, doormen—all, all capable, for a small consideration, of replacing a dead fuse.

There were no limits, then? Anything was possible?

Half an hour later, undressing in the living room in front of one of the most enormous sofas he had ever seen, he inquired about, tentatively suggested, the bedroom. She gasped a no without looking at him, dropping her bra on the coffee table where it knocked over a small canister of cigarettes that scattered on the carpet. He remembered Miriam again, she was waiting for her cigarettes.

There was no further explanation of the geography of her lust. He could only, tearing off his socks, conjecture. Some last moral reserve, was it? Concupiscence, yes; in her husband's bed, no?

He would never know.

At the end, screams and wails sang him to his rest.

The rest was silence.

That night Miriam confessed to him that, while she could not be absolutely certain, there was a very strong possibility that she had slept with George Brady on the night that Walter had had to be in Boston to see about Barbara Finch. Her confession went a long way toward explaining a great deal (if not, indeed, everything), but Walter thought the information was an unfairly high price to pay for understanding. In ignorance, he had been enjoying an unknown bliss, he knew then. Perhaps, even unknown, the best bliss of all.

18

It was Walter's birthday, his thirty-ninth. Throughout that Saturday (except for the interlude in 11B) he had teetered, depressed, on the brink of the twilit chasm that was forty and beyond. One more year and he could deny no man who called him middle-aged. Forty, everyone knew, was official.

But, when he finally got back to the apartment with her cigarettes (she was smoking far too much lately, he thought), Miriam sprung her surprise on him and raised his spirits somewhat. In addition to the already planned dinner out and the theater, she had arranged for Cassie to spend the night at a friend's and made a reservation for the two of them at one of the best, if not most expensive, hotels in town where they would spend the night and a leisurely Sunday morning being waited upon hand and foot. It was by way of a special celebration for the occasion.

Walter thought it was a wonderful idea; a little romantic maybe, but sweet and touching. He questioned her choice of hotel, however. She spoke of quality and service and reputation. True, he agreed, but how would she feel about one of the newer hotels? But they were awful, she thought. He agreed, true for the most part, but there were compensations for the lack of the grace of aged tradition, one in particular he thought might interest her. She doubted it. He asked her to trust him, she would see, one good surprise deserved another. They canceled the standing reservation and made another.

In the course of the discussion she seemed to have forgotten her original interest in his whereabouts for so long that afternoon. He had prepared what he thought was a first-rate story, but was not disappointed that he did not have to use it.

That night he returned from the hotel suite's living room carrying two fresh drinks and humming the hit song from the musical they had seen, to find her just as he had left her, face-down on the bed, asprawl, one arm flung aside on the mattress, the other dangling over the side, her legs wide apart. He stopped at the door to gaze upon the sight a moment.

He continued toward the bed, singing quietly, his tune contrapuntal to that of the orchestral strings issuing softly from the Muzak speakers which flanked the bed, the background theme from *Spellbound.*

She rolled over and languidly took the glass from him and raised her heavy head to sip from it. He went around the bed and sat propped against the headboard, aware now of how very much the marijuana odor pervaded the bedroom. He wondered if Miriam might have had a point, she had been nervous about the grass here, fearful of discovery. Yet, surely the odor would be dissipated by morning. And if not? No matter: The physical evidence gone, what could anyone prove? He opened the small filagreed silver cigarette box on the bedside table; only two joints left.

All at once the bed began to vibrate; startled, he turned his head to discover her smiling slyly up at him, one hand on the bedside console button. The bed became still again.

"You *did* like that, didn't you," he smiled.

"Terrific. . . . Weird, but terrific. How much pot is left?" she asked lazily, thick-tongued.

"Two. Want one?"

"Not now. By the way, they're back, upstairs."

"Hm?"

"Our neighbors. Haven't you noticed how quiet its been up there lately?"

"Ah. Mm. Well, now that you mention it," he nodded.

"They were probably away."

"Right. They probably were."

"Anyway, they're back. At least, *she* is."

"Oh?"

"Mm."

"How do you know?"

"How else? She was at it again up there this afternoon."

"Oh? She was?"

"She certainly was. It's weird. But why all the time in the living room, that's what I'd love to know."

"It's a mystery," he nodded.

"It's very weird. Do you think she's just a hooker, or something? You know, in her spare time? Like that movie we saw?"

"I don't think so."

"It's very weird."

"That reminds me," he said abruptly, "did you read about that woman who wants to make it with a propoise?"

"Make what with a porpoise?"

"She wants to ball a porpoise. It was in the paper this morning. They're doing these experiments with porpoises or dolphins, whatever, in Florida someplace. So this girl heard about it evidently and said she'd be glad to have sexual intercourse with a porpoise if it'd be any help to them. Wild?"

"That's pretty weird. I trust they've declined."

"It said so, yeh. But you never can tell with these scientists, they'll try anything. Wild idea. I wonder if it's possible."

Miriam giggled. "I wonder how the porpoise would feel about it?"

"It would probably depend on the girl," he said, grinning, "they're supposed to be very intelligent."

"Girls?"

"Porpoises. Assuming it was intelligent enough to appreciate it, it'd probably feel fine about it. I wonder how they'd go about it, though, getting the porpoise to ball her."

"It'd have to be a very weird porpoise. I think I will have that joint."

"Are you sure? You're pretty high now, my love."

"How many have I had?"

"Two. And all the booze."

"I think I'll have it now."

"Your wish is my command," he said. He handed her one of the joints, retained one, and lit both.

"Turnabout is fair play," she replied.

It was a moment before the true cryptic nature of the remark registered on him.

For several minutes there was a sucking, sniffing, breathless hiatus.

"It turned me on," Miriam said presently, lazily.

"I should hope so," he nodded heavily.

"Not this," she said. "This afternoon."

"Hm? What this afternoon?"

"Upstairs. The woman upstairs."

"Upstairs?"

"Listening to her. Them. It turned me on."

"Turned you on?"

"I got very excited. Listening."

"You did?"

"That's never happened to me before."

"Just listening, you got . . . ?"

"It's never happened to me before."

"Well. That's very unusual then, isn't it."

"Mm."

He was to remember later, distinctly, that this was her first confession.

He put his hand at the nape of her neck, beneath her hair, and with the tips of his fingers stroked upward at the fine, slightly damp silkiness there; her shoulders trembled in a delicate shudder. "There isn't much that doesn't," he smiled.

"Hm?"

"There isn't much that doesn't turn you on anymore."

She giggled. "Popular Mechanics," she mumbled thickly.

"Hm?"

"It's a magazine daddy used to read all the time when we were kids. *Popular Mechanics.*"

"Ah, yes."

"That's what we have," she muttered.

"Hm?"

"Popular Mechanics." She giggled. "Vibrators and mirrors and cameras and tape recorders and poppers and pot and whipped cream . . . and vibrating beds. Popular Mechanics."

Her voice was too toneless to betray an opinion. "Are you rapping or boosting?" he smiled carefully.

She was silent for a moment, trying (he assumed) to decide. "I knew about the whipped cream, you know."

"Hm?"

"The whipped cream, I knew about using that."

"Oh? You did? You'd heard about that?"

"Faith."

"Faith? . . . Faith what?"

"Faith told me about that."

"Faith did? . . . Did she really? . . . What did she tell you?"

"She told me about using whipped cream."

"Ah. Uh,huh. . . . But, I mean, how did the subject happen to come up, a subject like that?"

She shrugged lazily. "Girl talk, just."

"Ah. Uh, huh," he nodded, and breathed again.

"And poppers, she told me about those, too."

"She did. . . . Well. You never said."

"I love it."

"The whipped cream?" he presumed; she couldn't mean the poppers, they had never worked out for her in spite of several tries.

"All of it," she said. "I love all of it. I really love it."

"You do? Well, I mean, I know you enjoy . . . What I mean is, I didn't know you really . . . Frankly, well, I never thought your heart was really in it. . . ."

"I never would have thought it," she muttered, her head rolling from side to side against the padded headboard of the bed. "That I would really love it. It's unnatural."

"Why do you say that? There's nothing at all unnatural about your liking it so——"

"Loving it."

"Loving it so much. I mean, natural, unnatural—those are just words that——"

"I didn't mean me loving it was unnatural. I meant the stuff, all that stuff is unnatural."

"Miriam, some people think it's unnatural to screw with the lights on, and God forbid the woman should enjoy it. I mean, it's all relative, of course." He inhaled deeply, hissing, sniffing.

"But where does it end, though, then?"

He couldn't respond for another moment. Finally, he exhaled. "Yes, well, that's up to the individual, of course."

"At least," she said, "you can't say you aren't satisfied now."

"No."

The room was silent for a moment but for the muffled sounds of traffic from the street far below to which his attention had been drawn by the scream of a distant fire engine.

"Are you going to get another vibrator or not?" Miriam asked.

"Oh, yes," he said, remembering. "Yes, sure. It just slipped my mind. I thought I might be able to fix that one. I didn't realize you were that anxious to . . . Yes, I'll get another one. Tomorrow."

Miriam giggled. "She didn't tell me about that."

"Hm?"

"Faith. She didn't tell me about Rhythmic Richard. I wonder if she knows about them."

"Well . . . I wouldn't be surprised."

"Do you think she's a hooker?"

"*Faith?*"

"No . . . the woman upstairs."

"Oh . . . no, I wouldn't think so."

"Mm . . . but why always in the *living room*, I wonder?"

"It's a mystery."

"You know what else I liked?"

"No, what?" he asked, hesitantly, uncertain whether he wanted to know more just yet. She was confusing him.

"That movie," she said.

His mind made the natural progression from the woman in 11B and her mysterious afternoons to the movie which they had all three seen that night, he and Miriam and Faith. Was she about to confess to the fantasy to which she would not admit at the time? *Secret visions of putting out professionally on spare afternoons?*

"I've always wanted to see a movie like that."

"Like what?"

"You know . . . a dirty movie, I mean," she said.

"Well, I wouldn't call it dirty, certainly. I mean, there wasn't anything . . ."

"Well, pornographic, blue, whatever you want to call it."

"*Belle de Jour?*" he asked, astonished. *Pornographic?*

"No, no, Walter," she said, lazily impatient. "Not that. The movie at the Sobels'. Don't you remember?"

A Visit to the Dentist!

"Don't you remember?"

"Yes. Yes, I remember, I . . . What do you mean you've always wanted to see one?"

"Well, I did. I just never realized I did. You know what I mean?"

"Not exactly . . ."

"Well . . . I can't explain it . . . I mean, I just knew while I was watching it . . . that I always wanted to see one but I never realized I did . . . I mean, I got very excited watching that movie."

"You said you didn't, Miriam."

"I know. I couldn't admit it. At the time."

"I see. Well." *Why was she admitting it now?*

She giggled. "It was probably just as well."

"What was?"

"That I couldn't admit it at the time."

"Why was it just as well?" She giggled again. He wished very much that she would stop with the goddam giggling, it was beginning to get to him! "Why was it just as well?"

"*Because,*" she drawled, playfully emphatic, "because if I had told you that much I'd have had to tell you the rest, I guess."

"The rest?"

"Mm."

"Well, what do you mean, the rest, Mim?"

"Well, actually, Paul was fooling around a little with me."

"He was what? When?"

"Yes."

"Paul was fooling around a little with you."

"You know—in the dark."

"In the dark."

"Just a little."

"What do you mean just a little, Mim, how little?"

"It was during the last half of the picture, the last part, toward the end. When the girls were going down on each other, around in there, that was about when he started."

"You seem to have a pretty clear memory of it."

"Yes, well . . ."

"But what exactly did he start, Mimi?"

He waited.

"It was very weird watching that part, you know? The two girls." She giggled. "I wonder if many women ever wonder what that would be like, to do it with . . . The same as with a man I guess, but smoother," she laughed suddenly, softly, "I mean, no whiskers scratching."

"Miriam?"

"Did you know that in these wife-swapping cults nothing ever goes on between the men but between the women it's pretty much taken for granted?"

"Really? How do you know?"

"I read it in a book."

"What book, Mim?"

"It was just a book I happened to be glancing through in a book store." She giggled. "Good Lord, do you remember that thing on the dentist?"

"Mim. About Paul Sobel."

"Yes, well, he was just touching me a little. You know."

"Touching you a little."

"Yes, just sort of . . . I mean, it was nothing serious, just sort of rubbing my leg, stroking my leg."

"Stroking your leg where, Mim?"

"Just here," she said, and reposed her hand carelessly on the top of her naked white thigh.

He saw Paul's hand on the nakedness that was now beneath her own; but of course she had been dressed. Unless . . .

"Well, was this under your dress, or what, Mim?"

"No, of course not. On top of my dress. What do you think I am?"

"On top of your dress."

"Mm."

"Stroking your thigh."

"Mm."

"Well, what did you do about it, did you do anything about it?"

"I didn't do *anything* about it. What could I do about it? I mean, it would have been pretty prudish under the circumstances—the movie was more or less my idea in the first place."

"Well, that didn't exactly obligate you to let Paul Sobel feel you up in the dark, Mim. I mean, shit."

"He wasn't feeling me up. Did I say he was feeling me up? I said he was rubbing my leg a little. Considering what we were all watching, it would have been a little prudish to . . . And besides, don't tell me that Paul and I were the only ones with something like that going on at the time. I mean, I doubt that, don't you?"

He remembered the sharp nail of Vivian Ames's middle finger tickling his palm. "That's not quite the point, Mim."

She sighed. "Well, actually, I know you're probably right, I should have stopped him I guess. I mean, he called me the next day. I guess that had something to do with it, that he called the next day."

"Paul called you the next day."

"He wanted me to have lunch with him, of course."

"What do you mean 'of course,' Mimi?"

"Well, I just told you, when I didn't do anything about what he was doing during the movie, he must have thought that meant something, and he called me the next day. I brought it on myself, I admit that."

"So, what happened, you had lunch with Paul Sobel, is that what you're trying to . . .?"

"No, darling, I didn't, of course not. I said no, naturally."

Naturally? Was it so natural? Did she really believe that? *No woman was so guileless! Not even Miriam!* And why such easy acceptance of that possibility-exploring hand? More important why was he suddenly hearing about it now? "Why am I suddenly hearing about this now," he asked, smiling casually.

He waited for what he thought must have been a full minute.

"I don't know," she said finally.

She seemed honestly perplexed, such honesty could not be challenged; he was irritated at having no choice other than to join her in the shadowy caverns of unknown, unknowable motives. Even more disconcerting was his suspicion that by her confession she might be evidencing something like a compulsion: Miriam was not the compulsive type, never had been, Miriam looked before she leaped!

"Walter?"

"Mm."

"Are we really all the same in the dark?"

"Hmm?" Puzzled.

"Women."

"Women? . . . Oh! Women! . . . Oh." *Why? . . . Did she suspect something?* Worse—*know?* About to turn another page in her book of revelations? What next, what else? How many cats were *in* this bag?

"Are we?" she persisted. "Are we really all the same?"

"Aren't *we?*" smiling hysterically.

Her head rolled on the pillow and she gazed up at him: He saw his error in her eyes; she was in no mood for dissembling, flippant or otherwise. Besides, it was hardly a realistic question to ask *her,* even in jest: How would *she* know? Two men in her entire life. And with one of them only once. Good Lord, was that the trouble, could that be the reason for her somber look, had she misinterpreted his remark, thought he had been cruelly needling her about Tom Aptheker? Well, he could certainly put her mind to rest on that score, at least. He altered his smile to one of warm intimate complicity. "Well, of course," he murmured, "I know you don't have all that much basis for comparison."

The bleakest of bleak, tight-lipped smiles informed him that she didn't think that was terribly funny, but it was a nice try. Her eyes slid away from his, but the flat curve of her smile did not alter.

"Let's watch a movie," she said.

This would have to go down as one of the most nonsequential conversations of his life. "A movie," he said.

"On TV."

"You want to watch a movie? Now?"

"We haven't watched a movie in bed for ages, it'd be fun."

"Well . . ." He tried to find some objection, but could not— the idea was odd but not really objectionable.

"There's an old one of George's on."

"George who?"

"Brady, George Brady. It was in *TV Guide*. The something Violence or Violence something . . ."

"*The Violent Day*," he said vaguely, gazing at her. One of Brady's first pictures, an American intelligence agent dropped into France. With Laura Forster. Laura Forster hadn't made a picture in years, the last anyone had heard of her she was making spaghetti Westerns in Italy. She used to be wonderful in movies.

"It's one I never saw," she said, "let's watch it."

"Well, if you really want to," he replied. He moved to roll off the bed then stopped and turned back to her and grinned. "What'll we do during the commercials?"

"We'll think of something," she said, languid, stubbing out the end of her joint.

She was as stoned as he'd ever seen her. She was going to have a mother of a head in the morning. So was he, for that matter.

He found the channel quickly enough. The picture was well started, it seemed, they had probably missed a good part of it. He told her he would be right back and went into the living room to bring back the liquor tray. Returning to the bedroom with it, he realized that the Muzak was still on. Miriam didn't appear to be aware of it. He switched it off.

"Look how young he looks," she said.

He looked at the TV and agreed and freshened the two drinks and settled down on the bed with her. Of its kind, the picture wasn't at all bad, he soon thought. And Brady was actually very good, better than Walter had remembered him to have been in his early career. During the commercials they turned their attention to each other.

They were interludes of a peculiarly unique excitement, a series of beginnings with the end deferred, the interruptions by the movie leaving them voluptuously anticipating the next commercial.

There was an hour or so of these provocative two- or three-minute intermissions before George finally flew off into a French night sky, under Nazi guns blazing, escaping by the skin of his teeth and with Laura Forster. Walter hopped eagerly from the bed and turned off the television. He turned back to the bed fully prepared to write a quick finish to all their beginnings, fully expecting to find Miriam waiting with open arms.

"Fernless," she muttered.

She was lying on her side in a semi-fetal curl; her eyes were open, but dulled, staring vacantly at a spot on the pillow a few inches away from them. Nothing about her said anything of sex. *So suddenly?* he thought. These unnatural progressions were driving him mad! On the other hand, he had been quite engrossed in the final fifteen minutes of the movie: For all he knew she might well have been lying just so for some time. All right, then, not necessarily so sudden, but bewildering just the same! His incipient erection, bewildered too, hesitated for an instant, and collapsed.

"What did you say?" he asked softly, continuing with less purpose toward the bed, head cocked.

"*Friendless,*" she said, enunciating laboredly.

"Friendless?" he said, sitting on the bed.

"I feel friendless," she said. "It's like feeling depressed—I feel friendless. That's the way I'm thinking of it right now." She was evidently finding it necessary to speak very slowly and carefully in order to make her heavy tongue work.

"What is it, Mim, what's the matter?"

"I once saw this place downtown, it was called Saint Zita's Home for Friendless Women. Isn't that sad? Saint Zita's Home for Friendless Women? It's the saddest thing I ever heard, Walter. I wonder who Saint Zita was and if she was friendless. Or maybe

she just had this thing for friendless women. You ever heard of
Saint Zita, Walter?"

"No, I never have, darling, listen . . ."

"She must have been one of those obscure saints, not well
known."

"Yes," he agreed, "probably, listen . . ."

"It's a very sad concept, though, I mean. Isn't it? A Friendless
Woman? Isn't that a very sad concept?"

"Let's not be sad," he suggested with a wheedling grin and
lay down on his side facing her and noted that his body's attitude, curled, fetal-like, had automatically duplicated hers.

"You're right," she nodded heavily, with a bleak smile. "Meet
Miss Smile of 1969."

He chuckled lovingly, his face six inches from hers. "You
know the trouble with you, don't you?" he whispered. "You've
had too much grass. Or too much booze. Or both." He touched
her nose with the tip of an admonishing finger: "You're stoned
right out of your mind." She made a sound that seemed respon-
sive but noncommittal, and her gaze flickered to his and away
again. He put his hand on the swell of her hip, stroking. "What
you need is to have your spirits raised a little. I'll tell you what:
We'll raise my spirits first, it won't take much, then I'll raise your
spirits."

"You wanna fuck me," she mumbled.

"That's another way of putting it, yes," he murmured, and
kissed the corner of her disconsolate mouth and caressed her
belly with the back of his hand. "We'll turn the bed on. You liked
that."

"George porgie, puddin' 'n' pie, kissed the girls and made them
cry, when the girls came out to play . . . Georgie porgie ran
away . . . At least you can't say you're not satisfied anymore."

"No," he said again. "Listen, hon, maybe what you really need
is some sleep, would you like to go to sleep?"

"No."

"No. Uh, huh . . . How about some coffee, then, I'll have
some sent up. Maybe something to eat, a sandwich."

"No."

Sex, sleep, food—what else could he offer, what else *was* there?

She was being impossible! . . . "How about a nice hot shower, hon? Or better yet, maybe, a cool one. That might pick you up a little," *If she felt better before it was over, he could join her in it.*

"No."

He nodded resignedly and sighed and sat up, dangling at the end of his rope.

"I was just trying to make it up to you," Miriam said.

"Hm?"

"But it didn't work out right."

"What didn't, darling? Make what up?" Maybe there was another movie on TV. He spied the *TV Guide* on top of the television.

"I think I slept with George," Miriam said.

He frowned for an instant, then smiled at the way her words, half-muffled in the pillow, had arranged themselves and reached his ears. Not that it really mattered what it was she had actually said—she had hardly said two consecutively logical things all evening. But she was in bad shape, the least he could do was help in whatever way he was able. "Hm?" he asked, turning to face her.

"Yes," she said.

"Yes, what, darling?"

"I think I did."

"Did what, Mim?"

"Slept with George."

No, you're confused, Mim, he thought. That's what I *thought* you said. You didn't actually say that, what I want to know is what you actually . . . But it was hopeless, he knew. It was the last cat, he knew that, it came out of the bag roaring, a rabid tiger it turned out to be, and went right for his throat. He was vaguely grateful for the anesthesia of the three joints and the booze, he needed every possible shred of apathy. How many legions of men, he thought, had listened to their wives confess to having done the deed with another? *Yes, darling, I did it with Dan.* He envied them such definitive knowledge, so easily dealt with. How many men had *suspected* their wives of doing the deed with another? He envied them the privacy of their suspicion which might in the end prove to have been mistaken. But, oh good God, how many husbands, *how many,* had ever heard a wife confess that she *thinks* she played an outside gig? One! It was his distinction, his, it could only happen to Walter Hartman, he knew that! It wasn't fair! No man should be put in the position of having to help his wife establish the certainty before he would be able to proceed to some normal, human, male response! It was an outrage!

"*Jesus Christ, Mimi, what are you saying!*"

"Oh, God."

"What are you talking about! You *think?* What do you mean, you *think?*" It could be a hallucination. The grass. Bonnie Quinn said she hallucinated all the time on nothing more than grass, she said it was not all that unusual for some under just the right conditions. These might be Miriam's right conditions, it was possible. The movie, with George, might have triggered it, it was possible. *It was possible.* "What? What did you say?"

"I said," she said, trying to articulate, "the night you were in Boston."

His mind tripped and stumbled, backward in time. Boston, what did she mean Boston, he hadn't been in Boston in, oh, Christ, of course, of course, of course, *I've always wanted you, Walter, didn't you know that . . .?*

"He was looking for Faith," Miriam said.

"Miriam, what do you mean, you think?" he said, clenched in calm like a vise.

"I'm telling you," she murmured.

Why, he wondered suddenly. *Why is she telling me?* It was an odd thought, he supposed. Normally, he supposed, it must fall low on the list of priorities for a husband's desired information, Who, When, Where, How, Why did you do it, would be the usual chronology, and *then,* if there was still energy and interest, one might ask why one had been presented with the answers to all the others in the first place. Perhaps the last had come first to him because he could imagine no reason on God's earth why *he* would divulge to *her* his own . . . He felt almost sorry then that he was unable to let her know in what safety she lay at that moment: Whatever else might come of this, no first stone would be cast by *his* hand.

Good Christ, she was speaking again, he had missed it. *He*

had to pay attention, at least! "What? Say that again. I didn't
. . ."

She said it again, that it was the night he was in Boston on
that Barbara Finch business and George came to the apartment
to see Faith, he had just gotten back from New Hampshire or
wherever it was, did he remember that night, did he know which
night she was talking about?

He did.

But Faith was gone, of course, had left the apartment a few
days before that (he remembered vividly). Whereupon Miriam
knew (she said) that it would be only a moment or so before
George would adjust to the unexpected circumstance, gather his
forces, and be on his desperate way to track down her sister.
She knew that. She knew she had only to stand by the door and
bid him goodnight and that would be that. She knew that. But
she asked him if, as long as he was there, he would care for a
drink or something. She didn't know why. He accepted and presently asked if Walter, who was nowhere in sight, was asleep.
She told him no, that Walter was in Boston. Then they talked for
a while, she could not remember for how long. They talked about
George and Faith and George and Janine and George and the
movies and George and Congress and eventually he told her that
he thought she was very charming, that he felt comfortable with
her, that beautiful women always made him feel comfortable, and
Walter knew that they had finally gotten around to George and
Miriam. Had Miriam too known? Surely, he thought.

Then George turned on.

"What do you mean, he turned on?"

"He had some grass, he turned on," Miriam explained.

"You mean to say he was walking around with grass on him,
a congressman?"

"*I* mentioned that, too, it didn't seem to bother him."

"He's out of his mind," Walter said.

"It didn't seem to bother him."

"All right," Walter said, vexed with himself for having spent
even a fleeting moment on George Brady's risk-taking propen-
sities. "So what happened then?"

He asked her if she cared for some, some pot. (*Oh, Christ, naturally,* Walter thought.) She refused. He told her it was very relaxing, that she looked as though she could use some relaxing. She denied this, she was perfectly relaxed, she told him. (*Lying?* Walter wondered. And had to know.)

"Were you? Relaxed?"

"No, I was very nervous."

"Because he was smoking pot?"

"No, because of him."

"But you didn't turn on."

"Not right then, no."

Oh, Christ. He swallowed hard. "What do you mean, not right then?"

"But later I did."

"You did?"

"Yes."

"So I mean, with me wasn't the first time you had pot?"

"Well . . . no."

"Ah," Walter nodded. "Uh, huh."

So, eventually she accepted the first marijuana of her life (*From George Brady, not from . . .!*) and eventually (all sense of time's duration was lost, then as now) George confessed to her the true source of his recent emotional distress, his impotency, a condition with which he had had to live and suffer for the past more than two months. She described her response, bewilderment, confusion, at such a startlingly intimate disclosure; but supposed, looking back on it, that she was less shocked and embarrassed than she might have been had she not by then been so high.

(Walter sighed. He might well tell her the truth, but to what end? If this was the maneuver that would ultimately prove to have done the trick—Faith had said it almost always worked— would there be any point in making her feel a fool as well as faithless? No. And yet, he could not help thinking it would be a small deposit of vengeance held in reserve for the time being on which he would be able to draw if he felt the need of that sweetness in the near future. *But, of course, nothing had yet been proved!* She still only *thinks.* She had yet to offer any conclusive . . .)

Then George told her that so far he had been doing all the talking, what about her? (Indeed, Walter thought, what about her? And wondered if the issue of the impotence had been resolved. Or just left dangling? Laugh, clown, laugh.) And she began to talk, and once started, couldn't seem to stop. She hadn't talked so much about herself to anyone in longer than she could remember. She supposed it was the grass. She didn't know how long her talking jag lasted, a long time. And then George told her that something incredible and wonderful had happened, he didn't understand it. It appeared that merely being with her, near her, had done for him what no other woman had been able to do for months. She couldn't imagine what. But it was no more than a moment before she knew what he was telling her. She giggled, remembering now. It was outrageous, Walter would have to admit that, wouldn't he? Who had ever heard of a man *telling* you he had an erection, *announcing* it. It was ridiculous! She told George it must be the grass. He denied this. Still, she refused to take credit where she was certain it could not be due: It couldn't have been her, she told him; she hadn't done anything. (She hadn't, she reiterated now, she was not even sitting close to him.) Then it occurred to her that perhaps he had been lying all along. About the impotence. Maybe, she thought then, he really was insane and went around making up things like that just to confuse people. Either that or it was no more than coincidence. He just had happened to be with her and not someone else when his ability returned, and he happened to be high on pot, and she was sitting there in her nightgown, after all. What was he trying to do, make her *responsible* for his condition? What was he . . . ?

"Miriam, wait a minute, what's this about your nightgown, when did you get into your nightgown, for God's sake?"

"I was already in it. I just had gone to bed when he arrived."

"You were in your nightgown all along?"

"Well, yes."

"You didn't say that before, Miriam."

"Well, yes, I had my nightgown on. A robe, too, though."

Walter sighed. "All right, go on."

George told her she had a beautiful name. She told him it

was from the Bible. He told her he had always been fond of Biblical names. (She fell abruptly silent. As the silence lengthened, Walter divined its significance: This must be it, they were down to the wire. Suddenly all impatience left him, he had no desire to urge her on. She had rolled onto her right side, her back was to him; she seemed to be chewing on the cuticle of one of her thumbs. Then he watched one hand idly stretch forth and switch on the Muzak. The sound of Mantovani-like strings filled the room softly; he tried to place the tune, it was very familiar, the background music for a movie, he was fairly sure. It at least eased the strain of the awful silence. Perhaps that had been her intention.

He was still concentrating on the music, trying to remember what movie it was from when he realized that she was speaking again) . . . so she didn't understand why she was letting him do it.

"Do what, Mim?" he said, craning his neck to see her face.

"Kiss me."

This was it.

That's what she couldn't understand, why she was letting him. In all the years they'd been married, she had never . . . Oh, maybe a kiss now and then at a party, late and loaded, from a friend of long standing, sometimes maybe a quick feel of her behind, maybe, on rare occasions, *very* rare, maybe even the barest little bit of tongue in her mouth if it was a very close friend and New Year's Eve or something special like that, a particular celebration, or special occasion, but there was certainly nothing in it and certainly never, *never under any circumstances whatsoever* encouraged further. Certainly the *furthest* she had ever gone, ever, was the time she touched Jimmy Tripler's erection through his pants at his birthday party last summer (*Oh, Christ*) when he locked her in the bedroom with him, but they were both very drunk and she only touched it because she felt sorry for him and because he dared her to and anyway it was all in fun (*Oh, Christ*) until he took it out, he was *very* drunk, and . . .

"He what? What do you mean, he took it out? What the hell did he take it out for? You never told me any of this, Miriam."

"Well, of course I didn't."

"All right, so what happened then, he took it out, what happened then?"

Nothing happened, Jimmy was just completely smashed and she herself was very high and anyway it was all in fun and besides he passed right out eventually. What did she mean *eventually?* Well, naturally, he was fooling around, but nothing happened, she just held him off, what else could she do, scream or something? Wouldn't that have been ridiculous? What did she mean, he was fooling around? It wasn't important. Maybe not, but Walter just wanted to get some idea of what exactly happened, how far it went. All right, then, Jimmy had gotten her down on the bed and got her pants off (*Oh, Christ*) but that was the end of it, he passed out right after that, *that was all there was to it.*

Walter sighed and nodded.

Anyway, it was different with George, she was admitting that, and that was what she couldn't understand, because she didn't fight him off, she was admitting that. She just didn't know what was happening or what to do about it. She just didn't know. Which she must have said to George because she remembered his asking her what kind of life it would be if we only did what we were sure was going to turn out right in the end. (*Beautiful.*) She told him he had a twisted mind and then she remembered Walter once saying that a lot of people were beginning to do something about their secret dreams. The trouble was she didn't *have* secret dreams. Unless a dream could be so secret that you didn't even *know* you had it, like waking up in the morning and feeling like you'd had a dream but not being able to remember what it was. Then George told her that the key to happiness is, when you itch, scratch. (*Beautiful.*) He knew she was excited, that was what he meant by that. And she was, she was excited, she was admitting that even now. Of course she was. Why shouldn't she have been? She was thirty-two years old and had been with only two men in her entire life and her husband was bored with her in bed and she had probably been having secret dreams all along without knowing it and she was drunk and high as a kite on marijuana and he was George Brady. Of course she was excited. Who wouldn't be? Could Walter understand that?

She didn't want to tell him the next part, it was the worst part in a way, but it was very important so she didn't suppose she had any choice. He would see how important it was and understand why she had to tell him this next part. (*Tell me, tell me for Christ's sake!*) It was about the diaphragm. (*Oh, Christ.*) It was funny, in movies nobody ever stopped to think about putting in diaphragms, they just . . . Well, anyway, the thing was, the thing was, the thing was she lost her diaphragm, she accidentally flushed it down the toilet, oh God, she hated telling him this part but he'd see how important it was in a minute, it was the only chance she didn't . . . Anyway, she had the diaphragm in her hand and she had to go to the bathroom and just as she flushed the toilet she dropped it, the diaphragm and . . . well, it was gone. And it must have been just about then that she blacked out, because the next thing she knew she woke up on the couch in the study and it was just getting light. She simply had no idea at all what happened in between.

"What do you mean, you have no idea, Miriam? You can't remember *anything?*"

"I remember being in the bathroom and I remember waking up on the couch. But . . . well, I didn't have anything on except I had a blanket over me, he must have gotten it from the bedroom."

"Well, Jesus, Mimi, what about George, didn't he . . . ?"

"Well, he was gone."

"Maybe you passed out. In the bathroom," he suggested, nodding.

"How did I get to the couch in the study without any clothes on?"

"But, you didn't . . . I mean, you weren't . . . well, the diaphragm . . ."

"It doesn't prove anything. He could have . . . we could have . . ."

"Yes, yes, right, I know, okay, Christ."

"Oh, God," she sighed.

"George knows," Walter said.

"Well, good God, Walter, are *you* going to ask him?"

"Yes, right, of course, I'm sorry." *Hello, George? This is Walter, Walter Hartman, listen I wonder if you could clear a little something up for us* . . . He remembered then, remembered George's laughter that day in Faith's apartment, that would be the next day, the day after Miriam . . . *But it was not conclusive!* It proved nothing about the *extent* of what had happened. Had George only gotten her as far as naked on the couch before she passed out, that alone would have held irony enough for George Brady when he found Walter with Faith. *It was not conclusive.*

"You could have passed out *after* . . ."

"After what?"

"After you were on the couch, but before you . . ."

"It's possible."

Christ, why did she have to sound so doubtful about it! He needed help! Odd: He had always thought she lacked not merely the impulse for infidelity, but the imagination for it. Now he knew she possessed both and did not know which was the more dangerous. "You really can't remember anything?"

"No."

"Well, try to remember, Miriam."

"I have tried."

"It's very important."

"I know it's important, don't you think I know it's important? But it's not the most important part, you know that."

He did, of course. The issue here was fact versus conjecture, not what she thought she *might* have done but what she knew she *did* do. Intent and act. Was the man whose gun jammed when he pulled the trigger any less a killer, was the woman who accidentally flushed her diaphragm down the toilet any less a . . . ? *Philosophy in the Bedroom, An Enquiry,* by Walter Hartman with Notes and Comment by Miriam Farrell Hartman. . . .

"I don't think you did it, Mim," he declared suddenly.

"You don't?"

"No."

"Why not?"

"I just don't think you would, that's all, no matter what it might look like, I just don't think you'd do that when it came right down to it. I don't think you did it."

"I think so, Walter."

Her conviction seemed so much more secure than his own. And obliterated it. He was very depressed. "Do you? You really do?"

"Yes."

"Well, but what makes you think that?"

"I don't know."

"I don't think so, Mim, I really don't."

"Maybe not," she murmured, without hope. "At least there are a couple of things in my favor, Walter."

"Oh?" he said, interested; almost anything would help now. "Yes?"

Well, for one thing . . . this was hard to say, she didn't want to think she was giving him unnecessary clinical details, she wasn't saying anything that she didn't feel she absolutely ought to say . . . but the fact was that after all, even if it did happen she certainly hadn't gotten anything out of it. Did he understand what she was saying? It wasn't as though she had enjoyed it, did he see? She meant, she didn't even remember it, so even if she actually had, well, enjoyed it at the time, it still didn't mean anything because she couldn't remember it and could you really enjoy something if you can't even remember it happened? Did he see what she meant? It was something to consider. She meant, he certainly would never be able to imagine her actually *thinking* about it, it was as if it never really happened at all. If that was any comfort to him. Comfort wasn't quite the word, but surely he saw what she was getting at. And he must remember, too, that she wasn't really herself, she was right out of her head on the pot, he knew well enough now himself what that did to her.

Yes, he admitted, he knew that, true. Also, the couch, she said. He mustn't forget the fact of the couch. (He had in fact fixed it well in his mind at its first mention: However unconscious she might have been of what she was doing, she had at least had the decency not to do it, *if, if she did it,* in his own bed. He probably wouldn't know about that, but the fact was that in the eyes of the Church a couch was definitely, well . . . a mitigating factor in a thing like this. (*The Church?*) All right, granted, she hadn't been inside a church in years now, the fact remained that the Church's more or less unofficial position was that if you did it on a couch it wasn't as bad as if you did it in a bed. The reasons, she thought, were very fair: A bed clearly implied premeditation, but a couch, a couch was someplace that something could happen on suddenly before you were even aware it was happening. (*After you've gone to put your diaphragm in? Oh, Christ.*) True, these things probably meant nothing to him, she wished they could, would, but they did mean something to her. But, when all was said and done, the most important fact, the *most* important, was that it was over. It had happened, at least *something* had happened, there was no getting around that, she was admitting that much. But it was over and it could never, never happen again, never in a thousand years. (Was the assurance as unrealistic as the duration? He would have wished for fewer years and more certainty.) There was no point in brooding about it, what was past was past, could he look at it like that? What mattered most now was that she had gone a long way toward making it up to him, she thought. Hadn't she? She had started the very next day, if he remembered. New Year's Eve. That was the very next day and she had had the mirror put up. And everything else since. Not, God forbid, that she had ever intended him to know it was a matter of making something up to him. (Then why did he know now?) And certainly not *what* it was she was making up to him, God knew. (Then why did he know now?) It was just . . . she didn't know why, it was just that finally she wasn't able to live like that anymore, live with that, she just had to tell him. . . . Did he understand? Could he? Could he at least try?

"Yes, well, of course, Mim, I . . . yes, sure."

"I suppose this has all been very depressing."

"Well, a little, yes."

"God, oh God, I'm stoned right out of my mind, Walter, I don't think I've ever been so stoned. Are you, too? You must be, too."

"Yes, well, I'm pretty high, yeah."

"But I feel so . . . so jumpy."

"I know what you mean."

She moved, slid to him across the mattress and put her head on his chest. "It'll work out all right, Walter. Won't it?"

All at once he knew why he knew now, remembered something

she had said earlier and knew now why she had confessed. Of course, of course! Her program of repentance and restitution had backfired on her! She had *enjoyed* her penance, had come to love it, need it! So her lustful acts of contrition would have to be confessed for what they were, pleasure, and once confessed as such their source would naturally have to be divulged because . . .

He gave out a huge sigh that ruffled her hair. "Meet Walter A. Freud, world."

"What?"

"Nothing. Listen, why don't we try this bed for what it was intended for? It's supposed to be very relaxing, you know. I mean," he smiled wanly at her, "that's what it was designed for."

He extricated himself from her and climbed across her body in order to reach the electronic console beside the bed. He pushed the starter button and the bed began to vibrate gently. He turned back to her to find her looking at him carefully, a wary half-smile on her dry lips. He was faintly annoyed: *Did she think he thought of nothing but sex? And in any case did she think that he would even be capable at a time like this of . . . ?*

"Just lie back, relax," he reassured her. "It'll probably feel very good."

She lay back with her face toward the ceiling. He arranged himself on his back beside her and relaxed his arms and legs, surrendering himself to the therapeutic rhythms of the faintly humming mattress. Presently he said, "It feels good."

"Mm," she said, neutrally.

Several minutes passed. The Muzak was playing the theme from *How Green Was My Valley.*

"I don't think you did it."

She did not respond for a moment. "Maybe not."

"I really don't think so."

"It's funny, though. In a way. If it hadn't been for him I would never have known about my . . . well, my secret dreams. I would never have tried to do all the things you wanted me to do. I would never have found out what it could really be like. . . . I guess it's what you always call a natural progression."

She sighed. The bed hummed.

"I really don't think you did it."

19 Tom Aptheker was delighted. Genuinely so, Walter
thought. There was none of the roguish, eye-winking,
lip-smacking sort of leering response which Walter
had feared and half expected. At least, he could detect none
over the telephone. No, on the contrary: Tom sounded quite
seriously pleased, as though he had just been given news of
some particularly wonderful development in Walter's life. These
people apparently took this quite seriously. (But, not too seriously
he hoped: It was supposed to be fun, wasn't it?) Tom told him
that his timing had happened to be perfect; there just happened
to be something on for that coming Friday night.

The office door opened and Rowena came in carrying a sheaf
of papers and wearing her unfailingly maintained expression of
easy, businesslike neutrality. Walter had been pleased and relieved to find that she was fully aware of the importance and
necessity of such a demeanor in the office despite the fact of
their intimacy outside of it, firmly established after three (so far)
quickly succeeding assignations. On the other hand, she was also
playfully and dangerously capable—when he happened to be on
the telephone and thus helpless—of positioning herself behind
the desk, beside him, where she might offer his free hand irresistible opportunities, keeping her eyes on the door, feigning paper-

work industry at the desk. She stationed herself so now, but somewhat to his discomposure inasmuch as at that moment Tom Aptheker asked the inevitable question that required his fullest concentration.

"What about Mimi, Walter?" Tom asked, almost casually.

"Yes, well . . ." Distractedly, loath to reject her offering and hurt her feelings, he absently placed his left hand on Rowena's silk-clad buttock and caressed it.

"I mean, will she be coming along?" Tom added, still casual.

"Well, not this time, Tom," he said, as Rowena took up a pencil and scrawled something on his memo pad.

Tom said, "I gather she's being a little reluctant?"

Walter leaned forward and read on his memo pad: *Guess what?* Cradling the telephone receiver on his shoulder and dropping his left hand affectionately to the inside of Rowena's knee, he began, "Well, as a matter of fact, Tom . . ." and wrote with his free hand on the pad: *What?*

"It's understandable," Tom said. "They almost always are at first, most of them."

"No, the fact is I haven't . . . well, I haven't brought the subject up." Rowena was writing again. His hand slid upward several inches to the inside of her lower thigh.

"Ah," Tom said.

"At least, not yet," he added quickly, reading: *I don't have any pants on.*

"Well, it goes without saying," Tom replied, "we'd certainly love to have her."

Glancing quickly upward out of the corner of his eye at Rowena he heard the possible double meaning but restrained himself since there was no sound of its intention in Tom's voice. He wrote, *You're kidding,* while Tom went on for several moments about the resistance Walter was likely to encounter when he did finally broach the subject to Miriam; even Joan had been less than delighted about the idea initially, but Walter might be amazed at how many of them (wives) came around sooner or later. In fact . . . Leaning forward, he watched Rowena write: *Am I?*

He glanced up again, sidelong, at his secretary. "Well, I think we'd better not count on it this time, Tommy," he said, almost apologetic, as his left hand, the dreamer, ascended, seeking Truth. Rowena leaned forward over the desk and altered the attitude of her legs as though the better to assist in his quest while she enigmatically conducted her own mock search for a nonexistent appointment among the pages of his desk calendar.

Tom suggested that, under the circumstances, Walter might care to bring someone else along; in which case, he would of course be perfectly welcome to do so, he was to feel free. New faces were always welcome, Tom told him, as Walter discovered the truth and eased a finger gently into his secretary who hissed quietly through her tight teeth and became very still. Walter considered for a moment the possibility of her Friday night company, then dismissed the idea as discretion and caution made their usual and wise demands for attention. "I think I'll just be along myself, Tommy. This time."

"Whatever you say, Walter, we just like to know in advance so we can keep things fairly evenly divided. Not that we're all that rigid about it, just so things aren't especially unbalanced."

"Yes, of course, I understand," Walter nodded, while Rowena's hips moved, circularly, once, her Spartan resolve momentarily shaken. She made a low guttural sound in her throat; then, rising on her toes, disengaged herself with slow—and seemingly reluctant—determination. With a quick steamy glance over her shoulder, she walked to the door where she stopped and turned momentarily, just long enough for Walter to raise one hand in temporary farewell. "I beg your pardon, Tom?" he asked as the office door closed.

"I say, needless to say, Joan will be delighted to hear."

"Will she?"

"Delighted. Need I say more?"

Walter beamed nervously. "I don't think so." Were Tom's implications as clear as they seemed? Could he expect an especially pleased welcome to the club from Joan? And with Tom's blessing? Was turnabout, in Tom's opinion, going to be fair play, even twelve years delayed? He wondered if he might one day let Tom know, subtly, that he knew the truth.

"Listen, I could have her talk to Mimi if you'd like," Tom suggested, like an afterthought. "That's very often a deciding factor, *the* deciding factor. You know: woman to woman."

"No, I don't think so, Tom. Not just yet, anyway."

"Fine, Walter, however you want it. Friday, then, old friend. Say nine thirty, ten?"

"Perfect."

"Looking forward to it, Walter."

"Bye, Tom." He hung up the phone. He barely had time to dry his palm before it rang again. "Yes."

"There's a Miss Quinn on Two," Rowena said from the outer office she shared with two other secretaries.

"Can you spare an hour at five?"

"Of course, Mr. Hartman," Rowena said.

"There's some unfinished business I'd like to finish up."

"Yes, Mr. Hartman."

"I think we'll be able to take care of it right here in the office."

"That will be fine, sir."

"Incidentally, isn't that a little chilly for this time of year?"

"I'll have it on your desk just as soon as possible, sir."

He punched Two. "Bonnie?"

"Long time no see," Bonnie Quinn said.

The flattery was undisguised: It had been less than a week since they had last seen each other. "If you'll forgive me, I'll try to make it up to you."

"How soon?"

"Would tomorrow be soon enough?"

On Friday evening he sat at the bar in the Mod Hatter, killing time and his nerves, his pretext for absence (a new play by a playwright in whom the network was interested) having carried him from the apartment too early for an immediate departure for Sneden's Landing.

The time had not been wasted. All through the day he had found apprehension threatening to smother his resolve and now, as the bartender placed his third stinger before him, he put his hand to it confidently, anticipation and excitement fully restored. He consulted the clock over the door and the condition of his

reflexes and determined that this would be one for the road to
Sneden's Landing.

He sipped sweetly. *The Road to Sneden's Landing or, How
I Fulfilled the American Dream and Became on Orgiast,* by
Walter A. . . . Sneden's Landing, he thought, frowning concen-
tratedly. Hadn't that been the place in *All the King's Men,* the
magical, boyhood homeplace of the cynical and world-weary
John Ireland? No, not Sneden's Landing . . . Burden's! That
was it, *Burden's Landing.* All the king's horses and all the king's
men couldn't put Walter Hartman . . .

He watched her walk the length of the bar from the door and
seat herself two stools away and, although she had changed the
color of her hair and its style, he recognized her instantly.

Was it still Celeste Starbright or had she changed her name
again as she had claimed was her habit and need, found one
that rang a bell in her mad heart?

He waited for her to be settled comfortably enough to permit
her semiprofessional eyes to wander, evaluating prospects. When
they met his he smiled and said across the unoccupied stool
separating them, "We never did synchronize those watches, did
we."

She smiled carefully, perplexed, "I beg your pardon?"

He moved and occupied the empty stool. "You don't remember me, do you?" He watched her thinking fast: Was he someone she had balled or was he a cop leading her on for a bust?
Perhaps both? All the while maintaining a careful, tentative smile
that would lend itself easily to adjustment, one way or another,
depending upon her decision. But her decision depended upon
clues, he knew. "Richard," he said, feeling sly and wicked.

Her face brightened somewhat. "Of course," she said. "Richard.
You're in—the theater," with a counterfeit self-assurance.

"Publishing."

"Of course," she regretted her error. "I'm sorry. Yes, of course,
I remember now," she lied.

"How's the teaching racket?"

"Oh," she smiled, "the same old grind."

He nodded, smiling intimately, dropping his voice: "Which

reminds me, I don't know if I ever told you that night, but you were wonderful."

She gazed at him for a moment. "Thank you," she said softly. "So were you."

"I'd very much like to be with you again tonight," he murmured, wondering why he was playing this game with her.

"I'd like that, too," she said quietly. She sipped at her Bloody Mary.

It might be interesting, he thought. To pay for it. Particularly so much. A high-class hooker couldn't be entirely without redeeming social value. Especially one who taught English on the side. Or taught English and hooked on the side. Whichever. He hadn't paid for it, he reminded himself, since Korea, in Tokyo on R and R. The Japanese girls giggled constantly while you banged away at them, giggle, giggle, it was very disconcerting, until you finally brought them to the right pitch, when they became more familiarly Occidental.

"What's the matter?" she asked, concerned, laying a weightless hand on his.

"Hm? Oh. Nothing. It's just that, much as I'd like to, I'm tied up tonight," he said with courteous regret. "I was just on my way out when you came in, as a matter of fact."

"Oh," she said, and pouted charmingly.

"I'm going to an orgy, as a matter of fact."

She laughed. "Oh! Well, in *that* case . . ." she said, going along with the joke.

"In Sneden's Landing. Isn't that a wonderful place for an orgy? Sneden's Landing."

"I'll bet it is."

"In Sneden's Landing did Tom Aptheker a stately pleasure dome decree."

"You bet," she said.

"Perhaps you'd like to come along, new faces are always welcome."

"Some other time, maybe."

Of course she didn't believe him, he could see that. He grinned: It didn't matter. He raised his glass to her. "Well. Here's to Sneden's Landing and the American Dream." She joined him in his toast, humoring him. He placed his empty glass carefully on the bar and slid from the stool. He took a step, then turned to her again. She was still watching him. "Do you know what the *real* American Dream is?"

"No," she said, smiling. "What."

"The Real American Dream," he murmured conspiratorially, "is to take the virginity of the Sweetheart of Sigma Chi. Unfortunately, one learns, through discreet inquiry, that she's already gone down on the entire chapter and is saving her cherry for her Wedding Night."

Her smile faded; whether the expression that replaced it was one of concern or hostility he was unable to tell. "You're either drunk or crazy," she said.

He considered the options for a moment; then nodded. "Yes," he said.

Sitting beside him on one of the sofas in the darkness of the huge, vaulted living room at Sneden's Landing, her hand absently caressing the inside of his thigh as they watched a film titled *The Siamese Twins' Wedding Night,* Joan Aptheker, for perhaps the fourth or fifth time since his arrival, quietly expressed regret and disappointment that Miriam had not come. Walter, at that moment retaining a fresh lungful of what was unquestionably the best grass he had ever had, nodded unseen, his grunt vaguely sharing Joan's regret.

The truth was that, on his arrival, he had been far more concerned with those present than with those not; until his eyes had become accustomed to the strange and appropriately erotic light that suffused the rooms, cast by the low-wattage red light bulbs with which all the lamps had been fitted (and which had since been turned out); he had recognized two familiar public faces among the twenty or so in the living room, but had been greatly relieved to find that there was no one present known to him personally. So his anxious imaginings during the drive up from the city had blessedly not been realized; there had been no sudden, unprepared-for shocks of recognition, no awkward confrontations: *Walter Hartman! you old sonofagun, imagine running into*

you here, I'd like you to meet my wife, Marie, run along upstairs
and get acquainted, I'll be along in a minute . . .

"It would have been nice," Joan whispered near the ear that
was cold now from the touch of the glass she clutched in one of
her hands, the left, inactive one.

She was one of the very few present who were drinking; the
dark air was heavy with marijuana fumes. "Hm?" he sounded,
distracted by a particularly complex physical arrangement by
the girl twins on the screen. He turned to find Joan's mouth near
his as her warm, exploring hand discovered his by now uncomfortably constrained condition.

"Mmmmmmmm," she said, squeezing.

"*What* would?" he insisted.

"Hm?" she murmured, short-memoried, the tips of two fingers
searching beneath his belt buckle, seeking the means of access.

"*What* would have been nice?"

There was a distracted pause, her attention fully concentrated
in her right hand. "For Mimi to be here," she said finally, bringing her other, colder hand into play.

His chest heaved in silent, narcotized laughter. *Miriam here?*
You bet! Together! Sharing Life's Experiences. In Sickness and
in Health. It was a little like one of those insane, hysterical plots
he used to invent in moments of drunken literary despair, *Booze,*
Sex, Dope and Abandon, the Shocking, Real-life Revelations of
a Housewife Forced into a World of Degradation and Perversion
by Her Satyr Mate . . .

"Move a little, darling," Joan whispered, "it's stuck."

He moved.

"Oh, *formidable*," she said, inexplicably French, success finally
in her grasp, and hissed her sibilant intention into his ear.

Christ, yes, he thought. "Mm," he murmured. A moment later,
as his eyes and a fragment of his attention drifted to the movie
screen, he experienced an instant of déjà vu; then remembered
the night he had watched *Pride of the Yankees* while Mimi . . .

It had been some weeks now, he realized, since he had last
watched a movie on television . . . except for *The Violent Day*
. . . and that had been Miriam's idea. . . .

A girl's laughter, soft and carnal, drifted like a dark cloud

from a corner of the room. There were other sounds in the darkness, susurrations, smothered moans, an occasional soft thump of
flesh on carpet; and there had been, all along, the intermittent,
rustling shadows of groping departures, presumably by those impatient for the relative privacy and further comforts of the upstairs rooms, from delights in the dark to dark passions in the
light. *Or maybe they've already seen this picture,* he thought,
wincing under the blissful sting of Joan's momentarily careless
teeth as her head floated upward again to his.

Tucking him in again with thoughtful care, her lips moist
against his ear, she said, huskily, "Let's go upstairs now."

Christ, yes. "Mm," he agreed.

"Shall we take a friend?"

Oh, good Christ, yes! "Good," he murmured, hoarsely, his
voice cracking.

"Male or female?"

His heart lurched. Yes, of course, there it was! There were no
foregone conclusions in *this* world! Connections were varied and
optional! They marched double-gaited to their different drummer!
If Mimi *were* here, it could be . . . it could be he and Mimi and
. . . and *Tom*. Or he and Mimi and . . . *Joan? . . . Imagine
my shock and horror, then, when my husband commanded me
to perform an unnatural act of female perversion, a felony crime
against nature punishable by a long prison term in our state, with
one of my dearest friends of many years standing who at that
very moment was waiting eagerly, her willing and receptive body
writhing and sweating upon the already rumpled and soiled
sheets! As I approached the bed of shame, disgust and horror
rising in my throat . . .*

"Do you have a preference, darling?"

He detected a note of politely lustful impatience in her voice.
"Female," he said quickly.

"How about Samantha?" she shot back without hesitation, as
though voicing a long-held intention finally ready to be divulged.

Oh, Jesus! "Fine," he said, calmly, his throat constricted.

"I'll get her," Joan whispered, and slipped away into the darkness in search of the stunning creature who had been one of the
last to arrive, with flesh the color and texture (*and taste? He*

would soon know!) of a bitter-sweet Hershey Bar; whose face he knew he had seen somewhere before—a fashion model, perhaps— and who had said to Tom, coolly surveying the room with an amused grin, *I feel like your token Negro tonight, darling.* Tom had laughed, but later privately assured Walter that Samantha's being the only Negro present was a matter of accident, not de- sign; that usually they could be counted upon to have any number of . . .

Two dark masses appeared, looming over him.

"Here she is, darling," Joan whispered. "Let's go."

He rose slowly in a weightless narcosis, and took the slender shadows that were their proffered hands. Ready to move, he felt himself restrained as Samantha's other hand touched the back of his neck.

"What's your name, love?"

"Walter."

"Hi, Walter. I'm Samantha," she said, thickly, and brought her lips to his while her hand relocated in his groin, clenching and unclenching rhythmically.

What was it, some kind of goddam audition?

"Down in front," a girl's voice muttered lazily.

"Come on Samantha, you idiot," Joan gasped, giggling.

Walter turned slowly to discover the silhouette of himself and Samantha, head and shoulders, fuzzily obscuring the movie screen where one of the twins was providing an incredibly com- plex combination of orificial and manual accommodation for her sister and the two men in what Walter supposed must have been a temporary solution to the dilemma of the bridegrooms' con- fusion of identities.

Joined at the hands to the two women, his brain flashing images of other possible varieties and combinations of connec- tions to come, he made his way with them to the door, stepping carefully in the dark. (The lights would not go on again this night in this room, Joan had told him earlier, explaining procedure. At which point a willowy young man wearing a ruffled shirt and a despairingly bitter smile had piped up, saying there were some here who knew what they were doing but preferred not to know with whom they were doing it, you see. Walter found it an extremely oppressive remark for such an occasion, hardly in the spirit of the thing at all.)

Joan drew apart the sliding doors and they passed into the dim, red-lit glow of the entrance hall. Samantha took Walter's face in her hands and bit and tongued it for a moment while they waited for Joan to close the doors again.

Then, clasping his consorts to him, alternately kissing each while they probed and caressed and grasped at him, his phallus raised and fluttering like a flag proclaiming his primary allegiance, he ascended the wide staircase as to his coronation, to take his rightful place on the throne of the country of blue dreams.

20

"You're insane," Miriam said finally.

He found himself wishing that she might have offered the remark more as a debatable possibility than a statement of probable fact. He felt as though he had been put on the defensive and thought it an unjustified position in which to be.

But, at least, she *was* calm. That would be the pot, of course. As he'd suspected, the pot had been a good idea for this occasion. And not only for her; he, too, felt beautifully relaxed, wonderfully controlled. Certainly, without it she would have been hysterical by now, outraged, screaming, accusing, threatening. Even Joan Aptheker admitted to just such a reaction when Tom had first broached the subject to her some years ago. And if Joan Aptheker could be affronted . . .

Her eyes drifted from his finally and she nodded her head as though in vague affirmation. "I always knew there was something funny about them."

"Who?"

"Tom and Joan."

"It's not at all the way you think, Mim," he assured her, and inhaled deeply with a sucking hiss.

She looked at him for a moment; then her glazed, half-lidded eyes discovered the long ash on her joint; she dropped it off carefully into the ashtray on the bedside table. She looked back at him again. "How do you know?"

"Hm?"

"How do you know how it is?" He held her eyes and let his silence speak. "You've already done it," she concluded.

"Yes, Mim, as a matter of fact, I have, yes."

"What, you went to one of these . . . get-togethers?"

He grinned: Not only one, he thought. But, one step at a time. "I guess you could call it that, yes."

"Well, that's what you called it, you said the Apthekers have these little get-togethers."

"Yes, right," he nodded.

She nodded, then put the joint to her lips and inhaled, swallowing, sniffing, her head tilted back. Finally, she released her breath slowly, her naked breasts falling again as the pressure behind them diminished.

"Did you do it with Joan?"

He exhaled. "Mimi, I think you're missing the point here. I mean, it's not a question of personalities."

"Is she better than me?"

"It's not a question of comparisons, Mim."

"I suppose you'll have an affair with her now."

"No, Mim, of course not! It doesn't work that way at all. You don't understand the philosophy behind this."

No more than had he when, alone with Joan that first time (Samantha having finally drifted from the room in search of further adventure) he had suggested—quite naturally, he thought —that he and Joan see each other again soon, perhaps she could meet him one day for lunch. But it was out of the question, and in no uncertain terms: She had absolutely no desire to have an affair with anyone, it would be terribly disloyal to Tom, it was an entirely different circumstance, this, didn't he see that? She hoped—and hoped that he believed it—that there would be many more times like this, he was wonderful, but anything that even *resembled* one of those sordid little Back Street *affaires* was absolutely out of the question. . . .

He exhaled and carefully clamped the tiny roach in the eyebrow tweezers (their supply of pot had run unexpectedly short tonight) and said, "No, Mim, you have to understand the philosophy behind this. There's a very fascinating kind of integrity involved. I mean . . ."

"Only with Joan?" she asked.

"Hm?"

"Did you do it just with Joan, or what? I mean, aren't there usually more than two people involved in that kind of a scene? Like in the movie at the Sobels' that time?"

"Ah, I see what you mean," he nodded. "Yes, uh-huh, right."

"You were able to do it with two women? I mean, you know, you were able . . . to . . . well . . . satisfy them both, I mean?"

He bit his cheek to keep from smiling. "Well, yes, uh-huh." Her face showed nothing. Did she doubt his ability? Was she secretly impressed? Not, of course, that his ability was unfailing, Supercock he wasn't. True, at the last party, the one on Central Park West, he had deemed it wise to make use of the anesthetic ointment, desensitizing the instrument of his companions' satisfaction in gallant sacrifice of some part of his own pleasure for the sake of theirs. There were tricks to this trade. Popular Mechanics.

"Just married couples, or what?"

"Well, no, not necessarily. Married, single. It varies. Depending."

"I'd be doing it with other men."

Her composure was beginning to disconcert him now; all pot aside, she was certainly not responding in any way remotely like his expectations. Not remotely. He hadn't anticipated such a *total* absence of emotion. And certainly not in regard to that particular aspect of this with which he himself had not yet entirely come to comfortable terms, the image of Mimi and other . . . Not that *she* was in any position to offer any very strong objections in her own behalf—there *had* been George Brady, after all. Hadn't there? Probably?

"Right?" she said.

"Not only," he replied, guiding the discussion into less difficult channels for the moment.

"Other women, too," she said, accepting his prod.

"Now, before you start throwing around unfounded charges of perversion, I want to . . ."

"Joan?"

"Hm?"

"Would I be doing it with Joan, for instance?"

"You're dealing in personalities again," he said lazily. Then he grinned. "But the fact is, Joan is very anxious for you to . . . join the little get-togethers."

"You mean me, particularly?"

"Yes."

"Did she say that?"

"She said that."

"What, is she a secret lesbian or something?"

"You see, that's what I mean, you don't understand this yet."

"I didn't say I did." She sighed. "I don't think I understand much of anything anymore, that's what worries me."

For the. first time, he thought her voice held some trace of feeling; unfortunately, it was forlornness, but at least it was a real emotion, something he could deal with in positive terms. "Listen, tell me the truth, now: You enjoyed that out there before, right?" He jerked his head at the bedroom wall, beyond which was the terrace, beyond which was the building across the street, in which was the apartment into the bedroom of which she had, only an hour earlier, been peering with binoculars. Had his discovery of tonight's action over there been one of those "planned accidents?" He didn't really know. Certainly he could say in all honesty that he had not been any more curious about the windows across the street than he had ever been, despite Faith. He had gone out onto the terrace tonight for a breath of fresh air, nothing more. That he should find the girls across the street in action again (with a different man, of course: Faith had been right, probably; hookers) was pure accident. . . . "Well, you did, didn't you? Enjoy it? I mean, it excited you, Mim, you can't deny you were excited." No. It was only moments after the climax and businesslike denouement of the scene across the street before he was able (and with no little encouragement from her) to search out the physical evidence of its effect on her. And found it. She couldn't deny it.

"So what's the point?" she asked.

The point . . . He was aware now of the inordinately long pauses in their conversation as though the sounds each of them made had to travel an infinitely long distance before falling on the other's ear. The pot, probably, he guessed. The point . . .

The point was that there was something veritably primeval about the scene they had witnessed tonight, its roots, its origins in myth! Which probably accounted for its attraction, its universal attraction! The Garden of Eden, after all! *At the First Fuck someone had looked on!* And that was Paradise! And *that* was the point! . . . No. No, the point . . . "The point is there isn't a hell of a lot of difference between, well, standing out there on the terrace and the get-togethers at Sneden's Landing." And not only Sneden's Landing! Already he had attended two other parties as a result of contacts made at the Apthekers' that evening. This thing was big! Bigger than anyone could imagine in their wildest dreams! But it wasn't time yet to tell her of the many-faceted aspects of this. One image at a time, in a natural progression of . . .

"Except I'd be a part of it," Miriam said.

"A part of life, Mim." A little pretentious, maybe, but true, goddammit.

"It's what's happening."

He grinned. "Exactly." Or was she being ironic, supercilious? It was impossible to tell; she was extremely unfathomable. Maybe the pot as a softening agent hadn't been such a good idea after all. "I admit the idea takes a little getting used to. But I hope you realize that I would never have asked you, Mim, if I didn't think that it would be, well . . . very fulfilling for you."

"You said that."

"Oh, I did? Uh, huh. Well."

"That was one of the first things you said. And that it saved the Apthekers' marriage."

"So she says, yes. Joan."

"And some others."

"Evidently." *Plenty of room in the Lifeboat.*

"Because their own private fucking was even better for it."

She had retained everything! Stoned as she was, she hadn't

missed a word! Although, if he remembered correctly, he had not been quite so blunt as she.

"Whips and stuff? What about that?"

"Hm?"

"Whips and leather and stuff like that, like in——"

"Good God Almighty, Mim, no!"

"——that weird play we saw downtown?"

"Mimi, believe me . . . Is *that* what you've been thinking?" The "delicate torment," as some poet had called it? "Good Lord, no, there's nothing even *remotely* like that involved. I mean, this is strictly straight sex, Mim, believe me. There's nothing, you know—freaky about it, believe me." On the other hand, he thought, there might be an aspect or two which she might be inclined to place in that category. *He* did not, of course; but she might very well be so inclined. Like the cat at the party in the Village, a big gray Persian that had followed him and his host and hostess and the little blond chick into the bedroom. *Guess what he wants, the nasty little thing,* the hostess said, grinning from ear to ear, and proceeded to show them. As the little blond had put it, *a real pussy cat, ain't it.* No. Miriam's sense of humor wasn't likely to embrace the concept of a cunnilingual cat.

"Do you want a decision tonight?"

He was sure he had misunderstood; he must have missed something. "I beg your pardon, hon?"

"I said, do you want a decision tonight?"

It was the pot! It had to be! She *couldn't* be this calm about it! She was probably totally anesthetized!

"Do you?" she persisted, languid.

"No, no. No, there's no hurry, take your . . ." He shook his head, shrugged. This wasn't Miriam speaking, he told himself. He might just as well face it. In the morning his true, un-narcotized wife would have exorcized her demon and would probably file suit for divorce! But, for the moment thankful that she was requiring no further argument from him, he rose from the chair and sat beside her on the bed. Cupping a breast, he kissed her. Her hand slid instantly, absently to his groin.

"It's insane," she said.

The verdict's being appealed on that, he thought, and went

eagerly to work. There was only the sound of her hoarse breathing for several minutes. Then she said, "Does Joan really want to do it with me?"

For the next three days, but for a strained look around her eyes and her vaguely preoccupied manner, it was as though the conversation had never taken place. (There was also a total sexual abstinence, in mutual but unspoken accord.) On the evening of the third day Miriam came into the study where he was idly ferreting out the double meanings in a subliminally pornographic beer commercial. She glanced at him briefly as she handed him one of the two drinks she carried, then turned off the television set, sat opposite him in the armchair, lit a cigarette, and raised her eyes to his.

"What's it like?" she said.

The invitation arrived in the mail several days later; she handed it to him, already opened, on his arrival home from the office. Its face was a grinning, gold-filagree cupid in rampant abandon on a background of red felt. Inside, a blue heart within which was printed in a florid script: Who Will Be Your Valentine? He stole a glance at her, wondering if she had even discerned the sly gaiety contained in the perversion of the familiar sentiment. She flashed a brief, nervous grin, said, Some sense of humor, and turned away. He looked again at the card. Beneath the heart, embossed in a darker shade of blue, were the words: February 14th/The Apthekers.

At the very bottom of the card, in Joan's spidery, delicate hand, he read: So looking forward to having you both. J.

On the evening of February 14, the Feast of St. Valentine, the day traditionally and ornithologically observed as the first of the mating season of birds, and their eleventh wedding anniversary, the Hartmans drove to Sneden's Landing, drinking martinis poured from a silver pint flask and discussing a movie they had seen the previous night. It had been an extremely funny movie and its recapitulation now, somewhat labored and artificial as it was, at least provided them with the necessary pretext for some semblance of gaiety. Near the end of the journey, a certain lightness of mood having been established, however nervously and in-securely, he thought to make use of it in more relevant and spe-cific terms. So he told her about the small silver bowls she could expect to see, in pairs, around the living room, filled with pills of assorted colors and shapes; in each bowl, embedded on end in its contents, a small, gilt-edged card bearing a single word em-bossed in Old English script: on some, the word Up; on others, Down. The pills carried no further identification (except perhaps for those who might be experienced enough to call a pill by its rightful name merely by looking at it); it was as if the direction of one's emotional trajectory was what mattered, the identity of the propellent was immaterial.

He thought that in her present reasonably receptive mood it might be safe to divulge some of the more baroque aspects of the Scene, assuring her beforehand that it was only by way of giving her a broader picture; he was not suggesting that she would be exposed to any of them tonight, perhaps never. Some of them were only hearsay even to him, although he didn't doubt for a minute that they were true. He personally found some of it rather amusing. He told her about the lecherous Persian cat in the Village. She laughed nervously and said that was weird whereupon he told her that as a matter of fact it was a rather tame example and hinted at the existence of what he personally considered some kind of lunatic fringe in which it was said that somewhat larger domestic animals figured prominently. He told her about the girl who had been described to him by Joan, a quite young girl whose specialty evidently was pretense of vir-ginity and who performed accordingly, with begging, tearful protest and physical combat, for men whose tastes ran to that sort of thing. Joan had told him the girl was quite expert at it, one could hardly tell her from the real thing. Miriam said that she thought for a man to go to those lengths was carrying the vir-ginity thing a little far. He agreed, it wouldn't be at all the same thing if one knew in advance that the girl . . .

He considered for a moment, then decided against, telling her of the auto-fellationist who would turn up at a party on rare occasions for an exhibition appearance. He had refused to believe the existence of such an individual when Joan told him about it, but she assured him it was God's truth, she had seen it with her own eyes, it was the wildest thing she had ever seen and she had seen some wild things. Walter thought it hysterically funny and told her that that was what was known as having your cock and eating it too.

"What about grass?" Miriam asked.

"I told you, by the bushel."

"Yes, that's right," she blinked vaguely, nodding.

They were quiet while he found a parking place among the many automobiles and was backing into it when Walter said that a blackmailer could set himself up for life just taking down license plate numbers on a night like this.

"Will they have a movie, do you think?" she asked quietly.

"Oh, absolutely."

She took his arm crossing the short stretch of driveway to the front door, touching her hair with the tips of her other fingers. As they climbed the steps to the door he remembered the matchbooks scattered everywhere around the house bearing on their covers the legend, *Mens sana in corpore sano* and told her about those.

She smiled tentatively. "Some sense of humor."

He pushed the bell button.

21 Walter had his nervous breakdown in the executive
dining room of the network offices on a beautiful
spring afternoon in mid-May, a week after St. Valentine had been dropped from the official liturgical calendar of the
Roman Catholic Church—the feast day of Love's Patron Saint
no longer to be officially observed—and three days following the
afternoon he came upon his wife and Joan Aptheker in bed
together in the Hartman apartment.

It was of these two disparate events that he thought in the
last moments of lucidity that preceded his collapse. The dying
man, he thought, might well see his entire life flash before his
eyes; evidently the man about to suffer a mental collapse experienced only selected highlights.

The morning he awoke with a stuffy head, a stiff neck, and the
ominously tight feeling in his stomach, he hoped it was only a
twenty-four-hour virus and not a full-blown spring cold which
he knew from experience would bring him at least a full week's
misery. He was inclined to stay home from the office for the day
and nip it in the bud, but Miriam suggested—rather forcefully,
he felt, and wondered why—that if he just carried on normally,

he would probably be feeling better in no time at all. He failed to see the logic in that reasoning. Probably, he thought, because there was none in it. Smiling (condescendingly, he felt) she suggested then that what he probably had was no more than a touch of spring fever.

But by lunchtime he was feeling too ill to remain at the office; ill enough by then, he thought, to justifiably expect a modicum of sympathy and tender loving care at home. Outside opinion confirmed his evaluation.

"You look like death warmed over, you fuck! Go home!" Jack Finley advised.

Marianne, his new secretary, said, "You look just *ghastly*, darling, I *wish* you'd go home and rest."

The apartment was mercifully quiet and peaceful: the new maid's day off, Cassie at school, Miriam out to lunch, then shopping, he remembered her saying that morning, with . . . he couldn't remember who with. Miserably, he headed directly for the bedroom. The bedroom door was closed, so he was not aware of the sounds until he was halfway along the hall; and did not hear them clearly until the very instant his hand turned the doorknob.

They moved instantly, in unison. Miriam's eyes appeared, rising, like two exploding stars, over the pale curved horizon of Joan's hip; Joan disengaged her head from the slack vise of Miriam's thighs and turned it sharply to look over her lightly freckled shoulder toward the door.

"Oh, my God," Miriam said.

"Good Christ," said Walter.

"Walter, for God's sake!" Joan said, annoyed. "What are *you* doing here?"

Lunch? You call this lunch, Miriam?

"Oh, God," Miriam said.

"Good Christ," Walter said. He was blurrily aware of a diplomatic rearrangement on the bed, Miriam sitting up and covering herself with a corner of the sheet, Joan swinging her legs over the edge of the mattress and lighting a cigarette.

It was a dream, he knew, a nightmare. He was not here, it was not happening, he had collapsed on the street somewhere between office and apartment and even now was being rushed by ambulance, unconscious, to the nearest hospital, dreaming this impossible dream.

"What in God's name is going on here?" he pleaded to know, knowing.

"Walter," Miriam began.

"Walter, before we say anything," Joan said calmly, "I just want to remind you that this isn't anything you haven't already seen on a *number* of occasions."

"*That was different!*"

"To some extent that's true," Joan admitted. "Nevertheless . . ."

"*I was there!*"

"Nevertheless . . ."

"Have you been doing this *all along?*" he cried.

"Oh, God," Miriam said.

Joan sighed. "I love her, Walter."

"You love *who*, for Christ's sake!" he shrieked, crazed.

"Miriam, of course," Joan said impatiently.

"Oh, shit," Miriam despaired.

"What are you, a couple of goddam *dykes* or something?" he screamed.

"I *beg* your pardon, Walter," Joan said, standing, affronted.

He was extremely annoyed with himself for allowing his attention to be even momentarily attracted by her beautiful full breasts, her nipples were still hard, didn't *anything* turn her off?

He was sweating profusely now, his stomach was painfully knotted, his legs were like water, the goddam flu. He desperately wanted to sit down, but he was damned if he would sit down in a situation like this!

"Walter, listen," Miriam began again; but then evidently had nothing for him to listen to. "Oh God," she said.

"Walter, darling," Joan said tenderly, "you look ill, I wish you'd sit down."

"He has the flu," Miriam said, gazing at him worriedly.

"What do you mean you *love* her, for the love of God!" he demanded, tearing his voice loose from the tight place at the back of his throat where it clung in bewildered terror.

"You're no more surprised than I was, Walter, believe me, darling," Joan said somberly. "This has never happened to me before, I would never have imagined in my wildest dreams . . ."

"This is impossible!" Walter screamed.

"Oh, Walter, God," Miriam said.

Joan grinned ruefully, and sighed again and picked up her bra from the foot of the bed.

She was the only woman he had ever known who took off and put on her underwear in reverse order. Every other woman, it was off bra, off underpants, on underpants, on bra. In that order. With Joan it was off pants, off bra, on bra, on underpants. *It was an unnatural progression!*

"If it's any consolation to you, Walter," Joan said, "Miriam doesn't love me."

"I love *you*, Walter," Miriam said.

"We'll work it out," Joan said, nodding softly.

"Jesus Christ!"

"In the meantime," Joan went on, "we might as well tell you now, we've decided," with a quick, sidelong glance at Miriam as though assuring confirmation, "we've decided we won't be going to any more of those parties. Miriam and I, I mean." Then, bra-ed but pantless, she moved toward Walter. "Will you excuse me, darling, I think you're sitting on my . . ."

Walter rocketed to his feet. Startled, Joan stopped and stepped backward half a pace. He tore off his jacket and was ripping at the buttons of his shirt.

"What are you doing?" Joan asked warily, eyes asquint.

"Walter?" Miriam wondered.

"What does it look like!" Walter cried, sitting again with a jolt, to remove his shoes. *It was the only way! Maybe something could still be salvaged out of this!* "Get back on that bed!"

"Walter, listen," Miriam said.

"Don't be disgusting, Walter."

"It's the only way! *Get back on that bed!*"

"You're sick, Walter," Joan said coldly. "You are really disturbed."

He leaped to his feet again and limped toward her, one shoe still on. "Why do you put your bra on first!" he cried and, hook-ing his trembling, clammy fingers behind a bit of fragile material, he ripped it from her. *"It's an unnatural progression!"* he screamed at the ceiling.

Then he fainted.

He passed the rest of the day, the next, and the weekend in bed, all but a few hours of that time asleep, in a kind of narcoleptic need, under heavy medication and (he was intermittently aware) the tender, watchful eye of Miriam. He knew (when he knew at all) with what foreboding she must have been awaiting his recovery.

Yet on Monday morning at breakfast, recovered not fully but enough, he surprised her by announcing his plan to organize a June Allyson Film Festival for the network, preempting two hours of prime time per night for, say, six consecutive nights. Sponsors would be no problem, they'd stand in line for it. And he was certain the network would go for it, he would speak to D.J. about it that very day. . . .

At a luncheon conference later that day in the executive dining room D. J. Cramm was detailing to Walter and four other executives his major points of reservation about a playscript scheduled to go into production several months hence when Walter, salting his steak, his eyes on his plate, chuckled and said: "Cocksucker."

D.J. fell silent and looked directly across the circular table at Walter with a tentatively friendly smile as though almost absolutely certain he had misunderstood. "Comment, Walter?"

"Motherfucker," Walter sighed, gathering a forkful of peas.

No one moved except Walter who carefully carried his fork to his mouth.

"What seems to be the trouble, Hartman?" D.J. asked heavily, finally.

"Shit, piss, fuck, cock, cunt," Walter grinned, slicing a sliver of steak.

"Hartman!" D. J. Cramm roared.

Walter leapt to his feet, sending his chair over backward with a thump, rattling the silverware on the table, tipping over tall, stemmed water goblets that shattered delicately on the edges of plates.

"Andy Hardy suuuuuuucks!" he screamed.

V.
The Last Dream

. . . something I've always wanted to do.

22 By the end of Walter's first month in the hospital the doctors were still unable to offer Miriam any especially encouraging news of his progress. They did assure her, however, that in such extreme cases of acute depression and withdrawal, recovery could be expected to be slow; the normal course of therapy was further retarded by a patient's inability or refusal to communicate verbally. By "communicate" they referred, of course, to normal speech in the accepted sense of normal social intercourse.

Now, as to this caprolaliac aspect of the case, this compulsion to utter obscenities. It appeared, so far as they had been able to ascertain, that this caprolalia bore some relation in Mr. Hartman's case to a rather rare psychosis called Tourette's disease. What was puzzling here was that Tourette's was a disease of childhood and adolescence; it rarely occurred in adults and when it did there almost always proved to have been a childhood incidence as well. So far as they had been able to discover, no such history existed in her husband's case. Nor had there as yet been any indications of the involuntary motor reactions of jerking and twitching usually associated with Tourette's. That it was not a true case of Tourette's probably accounted for the fact that, as yet, he was not responding to the normal course of treatment for that disease.

There was, however, one interesting—perhaps promising—development to report. They had discovered within the past ten days, quite accidentally, that watching old motion pictures on television seemed to have an unusually favorable therapeutic effect on the patient. Since this discovery they had been monitoring by means of a tape recorder in his room each and every one of these viewings and, so far, there had not been a single occasion on which he had uttered even the mildest of obscenities while watching an old movie. It was the wildest of chances, they admitted, and hardly standard procedure, but for the time being the nurses on duty had been instructed to keep a careful check of the TV schedule for all motion pictures dating backward from, say, 1945. (Movies of more recent vintage didn't appear to have any particular effect on him.) It might very well prove to be a promising line of inquiry.

In the meantime, Miriam was to try not to worry—they had every hope and expectation of a complete recovery. Eventually.

Nurse Mary Ellen Wilson glanced at the wall clock opposite the night duty desk. One fourteen. The Late Show would be over in a few minutes. Time to tuck him in for the night. She still wondered what he saw in those terrible old movies. Tonight it had been something called *Mrs. Miniver*. Mary had never heard of it. But, of course, according to *TV Guide* it was made in 1942, for God's sake. She hadn't even been born yet.

It was certainly an unusual kind of therapy. Just letting a patient stay awake so late was incredible, much less to watch old movies. But, supposedly, they knew what they were doing. Mary hoped so. Because she had grown very fond of Mr. Hartman, he was far and away her favorite patient on the floor. That particularly weird symptom of his had been a little difficult to get used to at first, of course; but otherwise he was an absolute dream of a patient, not at all like so many of the other males on the floor, with all the violence, and the mess, and trying to cop a feel every time she turned her back or wasn't careful.

She often wondered what Mr. Hartman was like before. He

had such a wonderful face. Sweet. Gentle. Except for the eyes. The poor eyes were so dead-looking. Except when he was watching one of those silly old movies, of course. Then his eyes came right alive.

And speaking of alive, she thought, if he had one tonight she would definitely make a note of her discovery on her report; or, at the very least, mention it to Dr. Landsman. Of course, it could be nothing more than coincidence, but in the week since she had first begun to notice it it had never failed, never, and he usually watched at least two movies a night during her tour of duty. It certainly seemed to be more than just coincidence. And it was the same with the day nurses. She'd checked with them and they had begun to notice it too. Not that it was anything you ordinarily took any notice of, certainly. Erections were certainly common enough. Poor men. Some of them had been here absolutely *forever*. (She had once had a terrible vision of all these erections just desperately throbbing away in the dark all over the ward..)

She didn't know why, just woman's intuition, maybe, but she would swear that Mr. Hartman wasn't relieving himself. There certainly were never any signs of it. Yet, there he was, every time, without fail, by the time one of those movies was over, with this lovely sad erection. Which just eventually had to go away all by itself. There was something very sad about that, Mary thought. She didn't know why they affected her that way, but they did, especially in Mr. Hartman's case.

The movie was over. The Late News was just starting.

"How was the movie?" Mary asked, turning off the tape recorder.

"Cuntlapper," Walter sighed.

Removing the tiny ear-microphone from his ear and coiling the long wire that led to the television, she said, "I've made a special note to the day nurse for one that's on at ten tomorrow morning. *Mr. Smith Goes to Washington*, it's called. 1939. Sounds perfect, right?"

"Prick," Walter said.

"James Stewart and Jean Arthur," she said, shaking down the thermometer. "James Stewart I know, who was Jean Arthur?"

"Horseshit," Walter said, as she placed the slender glass tube beneath his tongue.

She nodded absently and sat on the edge of the bed; keeping her eye on his expressionless face she let her hand descend in soft, scientific inquiry to the top of the sheet that covered him to his waist. Her expectation realized, she determined to bring it to Dr. Landsman's attention. It might be a perfectly screwy idea, but this case was already certainly screwy enough, one more screwy thing wouldn't surprise anyone. Certainly not Dr. Landsman, he was a little screwy himself, in Mary's considered opinion. Besides, she hoped that as a nurse she was more than just someone who took temperatures and administered injections, she hoped she was someone who cared enough about her patients to notice things about them that might be important.

She didn't realize that she had not yet removed her hand until she felt him—it—twitch rigidly beneath her fingers. She smiled, sadly. I'll bet *you'd* like to administer an injection right now, wouldn't you, she thought. It felt so nice under there. So *hard*. But so sad. And this certainly wasn't helping matters any for him, she reminded herself, and moved her hand to find his other pulse. She touched her gentle fingers to his wrist. Pulse very rapid. As usual, when that was going on down there. Well, why don't you *do* something about it, you poor man, do it yourself, there's nothing wrong with that!

She removed the thermometer from his mouth.

"Pussy," said Walter instantly.

"Oh, pussy yourself!" Mary said, stamping her foot. *Look* at you, your pulse going like mad and *that* standing up down there —and even your temperature is up a little—and to look at your face you could be sound asleep with your eyes open! . . . That sweet, lovely face . . . If you *did* have an orgasm, you wouldn't even feel it, would you, it wouldn't make a bit of difference . . .

Or would it . . .?

She reached down with tentative fingers. It was still there. Well, of course. Once he'd had one for about twenty minutes after a movie was over and he still had it when she left the room. As if it wasn't bad enough, they always seemed to last so awfully *long*. As if it was just waiting and waiting and waiting for someone to do something about it. . . . Then it always just gave up like out of sheer hopelessness or something and went away. . . .

It was too sad, that was all there was to it, in her considered opinion. . . .

She hesitated only a moment more; then went to the door. She opened the door and looked both ways along the corridor. It was deserted and silent. She closed the door and returned to the bed.

She sat gingerly on the edge of the mattress and clasped her hands in her starched, spotless lap and looked at him for a moment. "I hope you don't think I'd do this for just anyone," she said aloud finally, softly. "If you think anything at all, which I doubt," she added ruefully. She waited for the obscenity of his response. None came. He only gazed directly to his front as though at some spot on the far wall. She placed her hand on the hard mound in the sheet and this time applied a slight, motionless pressure. "And why for you, I don't know, except I'm extremely fond of you for some reason or other."

She folded the sheet back, saying, "This won't be as good as the real thing, I admit, but it's better than nothing, right?" She raised the hospital gown and stared. Yes, there was just no question about it, she told herself, something just had to be done about something like that. "But don't you go getting any ideas about this getting to be a habit or anything like that," she warned. At least, she hoped not, gently stroking his hip.

Her hand took flight and came to gentle rest, curling. Walter's eyes flickered closed as his mouth opened and he sucked in a swallow of air, sharply. Then a sound emerged from him that was like a long-trapped, shuddering sigh. Mary glanced shyly, sidelong, at his face, surprised and delighted to think that perhaps this might mean something to him after all—she certainly had never before heard him make so human a sound. Softly she altered her position to find balance in order to free her other hand to find its place. But very gently, for she knew there might very well be tenderness there; they might, indeed, be aching by now, after so long. Blue balls, boys called them. *How awful for them.* With compassion, tenderness for his possible tenderness, she weighed their weight and power, awed (as she always was), while one guileful finger departed from the others in search of the erotic perineal sensitivities to which she had first been directed by one of the three boys in her life for whom she had provided this merciful relief. Her experience had taught her at least one interesting and valuable lesson—boys might very well start out wanting desperately to put it in you, but pretty soon you found out that all they *really* wanted was just to shoot their stuff and when it came right down to it they didn't really care how.

Walter made a mewing sound in the back of his throat in response (she assumed and was delighted anew) to that experimentally exploring fingertip.

His breathing began to quicken perceptibly, she noted. Her pumping hand's pace accelerated in happy concord while on his face there began to appear traces of awareness and response.

She smiled suddenly with a sweet vulgarity at the realization of another significant aspect of what was happening. Had there, she wondered delightedly, ever, ever been a man of normal male impulses confined to a hospital bed who didn't entertain such a dream as this, with a partner such as she, a nineteen-year-old blond nurse? If only he could be aware of it! *Could* he be? Was it at all possible? Oh! how she wished it were!

Then, in a kind of uncontrollable, innocently carnal glee, she gave voice to her thoughts, whispering, "And I'm a virgin, too!"

She watched as his eyelids flickered and slowly opened and his lips began to move. She hoped with all her heart that he would not speak! No! she would be unable to bear a pointless obscenity at a wonderful moment like this. She watched, fearful, while his eyes appeared to be seeking out hers. That in itself was astonishing enough: Except for the movies on TV his eyes neither saw nor tried to see. Never. Then his moving lips defined the shape of the most beatific smile she had ever beheld and he spoke his first untainted word in forty-two days.

"Vir . . . gin?" he said.

She wanted to weep with joy. *It was not obscene!* His head fell back upon the pillow, his eyes closed again and, from beneath the clenched lids, two tears trickled to the corners of his open-mouthed smile. His gasps quickened, fervid, in near synchronization with the quickening pace of her determined, happily pounding fist.

She knew the end was near! Knew it! It was going to be heavenly! *Faster*, Mr. Hartman? *Faster?* Oh! it was going to be *heavenly!*

Although she felt only the faintest trace of sexual arousal, she realized now that in some wonderfully special, chaste way she was sharing his passion, and was joyful in the knowledge of how perfect—how *right*—that chasteness was.

Abruptly his breathing ceased.

"Yes! Yes!" said his angel of mercy, his virgin, Mary.

At that instant his startled heart betrayed him, lurched, drew back, clenched like a fist, and dealt him a mortal blow. He gasped and, for an instant of agony and bliss, life and death fused, were one.

"Oh! Wow! Wah!" said Mary.

And he was a fountain in a midsummer night's dream.

THIS BOOK WAS SET IN
CALEDONIA AND MISTRAL TYPES BY
H. WOLFF BOOK MANUFACTURING COMPANY.
IT WAS PRINTED BY
THE MURRAY PRINTING COMPANY.
DESIGNED BY LARRY KAMP.